A Kind of Hush

What readers are saying about
JoDee Neathery's *writing*...

*JoDee Neathery is a writer who understands how we should embrace
the wisdom of generations of those who have come before us.*
—**Joslyn Wolfe**, *Focus on Women Magazine*

*Ms. Neathery's detailed and vivid descriptions have the reader feeling
as if they're in the midst of every conversation and setting. Thrilling.*
—**Carole Fowkes**, *The Terrified Detective Mystery* series

Beautiful prose creates detailed images. I like her writing style.
—**Sarah Marlowe**, OnlineBookClub

*JoDee Neathery is a gifted storyteller who weaves her characters
like a fine linen and expertly tailors their relationships
into a tale you cannot put down. Clever dialogue adds spice
to her beautiful prose that makes it a joy to read.*
—**Connie Roan**, Dauphin Island Welcome Center and Library

A unique voice that resounds on every page...
—**Chick Lit Café**

*JoDee Neathery was a contributing columnist for our newspaper for
several years. Her ability to combine humor and keen observations
on ordinary things made her a favorite amongst our readers.
She weaves a story that is both delightful and insightful.*
—**Denise York**, Retired editor, *The Monitor* newspaper

Author's measured rich prose—tempered and subtle.
—**Writer's League of Texas** contest submission feedback

*JoDee Neathery can paint a family dynamic so vividly, you would
swear you were a member of the clan. I love reading books about
smart women written by even smarter ones!*
—**Joann Mancuso Pond**
Founder and President, Craig Ranch Women's Book Club
Chair, McKinney Public Library Advisory Board

A Kind of Hush

A Novel

JoDee Neathery

A Kind of Hush

Contact the author at
jodee@jodeeneathery.com

First Edition

ISBN: 978-1-7373920-0-2

Book Design:
Vivian Freeman Chaffin
Vivian.Freeman@yellowrosetype.com

Printed in the United States of America

Imagery Lit
315 St. Andrews Dr.
Mabank, Texas 75156

Family and friends—

I'm humbled by your love and support as my writing journey would not have taken this road if not for you.

Do one more thing for me and you…dream big, and if you leave a piece of yourself in whatever you do, your imprint will always be deeper than your footprint.

Acknowledgments

WRITING IS SELDOM a solo journey and I owe a debt of gratitude to my highly skilled, professional, trusted editor, Vivian Freeman Chaffin, whom I'm lucky to also call a friend. She played a vital role at the end of the process before my debut novel, *Life in a Box,* was published stepping into the fray as my editor succumbed to some serious health issues. I'm not sure Vivian knows how comforting it was that someone was adopting "my baby" as her own. She continued to assist whenever I panicked, calmly solving the problem, only asking for a chance to edit my next novel. Well, here we are, Ms. Chaffin, making my dreams come true again! It's your insight and honesty that stands above the crowd and I believe that comes from also being an author. You have a gift and I'm honored to be one of your clients.

My cheerleaders from Bookers—our community book club—dusted off their pom-poms, waving them feverishly as we crossed the finish line for *A Kind of Hush.* It's their enthusiasm that drives me and I strive not to disappoint them, although sometimes it's exhausting trying to keep up with all our energizer bunnies.

To the rest of our community, my cherished friends, colleagues, professional contacts, friends of friends, relatives of relatives, and of course my immediate and extended family members—each one plays an integral role fostering and encouraging my desire and passion for writing. Besides, how can one possibly fail when you have grandsons who frequently ask about word count? What a joy!

If your life ever takes off against the wind, I'll be there to lift you up if you fall...just like you have done for me.

A Kind of Hush

1

Slow Dancing in a Burning Room

BUFFALO, NEW YORK. Gabriel Mackie had just celebrated his fourth birthday the first time he visited the whisper room, a windowless enclave with lavender walls brimming with daydreams, obscured from reality. All he knew for certain was that his older brother, Griff, nicknamed Boo, was gone. His bedroom at the end of the long hallway had been transformed into a guest room with ecru lace duvets instead of the blue and white pinstriped spreads covering the twin beds. Vanished were his toy box and New York Yankee American League pennants that had plastered the walls, replaced by paintings of water lilies and wheat fields. A stray tear trickled down Gabe's cheek when he remembered Boo's curly blonde hair and how he snorted when he laughed. Silence is deafening and the Mackie household screamed heartbreak.

Tree branches dipped in the wind tossing shadows across the windows heralding a tempest gathering force. Matt sipped his coffee and thumbed through last night's restaurant receipts. Summer, lost in her on own thoughts, mindlessly poured herself a refill with one hand while twirling a strand of hair with the other. Gabe tiptoed to the kitchen doorway, jumping back when he heard his mother slam her fist on the counter.

"It's Willa's fault Griff is gone," her voice stringent and tight.

3

"Tickling him while he sucked on a gumball, for God's sake. I trusted her to take care of him for fifteen minutes—fifteen damn minutes—while I picked up Gabe from a birthday party. He couldn't find his shoes...I would have been home sooner and maybe...I love my daughter, but...She knew to call 911 in an emergency...Why the hell didn't she?"

Matt shook his head. "Summer come on...you've got to quit blaming her," his voice rising an octave in frustration. "You're as responsible as Willa."

Summer turned her back to her husband shielding the wounds caused by his words.

"I shouldn't have said that," regret echoed in his apology. "I'm so sorry...Please, we don't need to be playing this blame game...."

"I guess it's too much to ask for you to understand what I'm going through, Matt. What part of my daughter killing our son don't you get?"

"Honey, you're overreacting...."

They both turned as Gabe scampered into the room dragging a stuffed elephant by its trunk. "Mommy, did Willa find where Boo's hiding? Quackers and me wanna play next...you count to ten and say ready-or-not, here I come...okay?"

One heedless moment changed the Mackies forever as normalcy assumed a new persona for a family in crisis. Summer yielded to her debilitating grief and broken-heart syndrome, attending extensive counseling, struggling to coexist with what surely would be a lifetime of regret and guilt for her role in her child's death. Tina, Matt's college friend and partner in their restaurant/sports bar, shouldered more of the day-to-day operations while he concentrated on the needs of his preteen daughter, youngest son, and his wife, relegating his own suffering to the back-burner. Further complicating matters, the first global pandemic in forty years, dubbed the "swine flu," shuttered over nine-hundred schools in New York State for days including Willa's elementary school enabling their precocious ten-year-old to huddle nonstop with her best friends developing secret codes and unifying opinions of what they loved and hated from food to fashion to music and beyond. At night she played the *bed at nine o'clock is for babies . . . and give me some privacy . . . please* cards. She, too, was in therapy where her counselor reported a progression in her sketches softening her mom's devil-image and depicting herself and Gabe romping through fields of shamrocks. Young Gabe spent most days in the sanctuary of his own thoughts, languidly building marshmallow forts with toothpicks, doodling stick figures on gum wrappers, erecting statues with purple paradise and foam green Play-Doh and knowing with certainty the humming inside a seashell was for his ears only.

Neighbors and friends of the couple offered additional support—arranging play dates with the Mackie children, supplying an unlimited assortment of homemade cookies, picking up laundry, and hosting sleepovers allowing Matt and Summer some privacy. In the beginning, the family experienced progressions of despair and disillusionment like a bitter wind lacerating an empty heart. As hours turned into days and days into months, scars concealed the wounds and the most tormenting pleas—why and how could a loving God be so merciless—were placated with soothing testimonies sermonizing how He is too kind to do anything cruel, too wise to make a mistake, and too philosophical to explain Himself. Tears that uncontrollably sprung from some secret reservoir were replaced with shards of hope, sweet reflections, and moments of tenderness rather than grief.

Summer and Matt rekindled the relationship that began when she and a group of male coworkers walked into his establishment ten years ago. She appeared to have just stepped out of a refrigerated box while the others wilted in humidity and stifling heat. His future wife owned that "can't-take-your-eyes-off-of" look of a *femme fatale* wrapped in the wholesomeness of a Jennifer Aniston . . . a dangerous combination. His heart rate rivaled a thoroughbred on his way to the finish line of the Kentucky Derby. His bachelorhood was skating on thin ice.

The Mackies resumed the habits and routines that dictated daily life—both parents returned to their jobs, Willa traversed the halls of middle school and Gabe kept his first-grade teachers on their toes until a road trip once more toppled their lives into disarray.

2012 JUNE SOLSTICE. Albert Einstein's theory of relativity is easier to grasp than a teenage girl. Reportedly, a "typical" teen might exhibit all seven personalities associated with this age group with Willa Mackie's photograph at the top of the profile page. She changed gears faster than a race car driver, often a darling until spoken to then spewing the venom of a dragon spitting fire in response. Mornings before school introduced the drama queen of the day, as if the end of the world lurked nearby because it was Monday and she wanted it to be Tuesday. Spending time with family was seldom a priority in her teenage world.

The family's weekend outing was planned for departure around noon. While Matt and Gabe played tag football in the backyard, Summer, for the third time, climbed the stairs to Willa's bedroom. She jiggled the doorknob. It was locked. Praying for the ability to bury a groundswell of impatience amid the urge to take an ax to the door, Summer took a deep breath and knocked—the response from the other side, a razor-sharp, "Mom, if you keep bugging me, I'll never be ready."

"Is there anything wrong. Can I help?"

"Just leave me alone. All my jeans are dirty."

"It's warm today. Put on some shorts and let's go. Dad's getting antsy."

"No, my legs are all white and ugly and my hair—who did I get this bushy brown mess from? Have I told you how much I just hate it?"

"Yes, numerous times. Your curls are from my mother—your grandmother—Willa. It seemed to work for Emma Watson in Harry Potter—remember Hermione Granger?"

"She's a movie star. I'm *Brillo Pad Willa* at school."

"Honey, we can't fix that today, but I promise, we'll check with a beautician to see what we can do to relax your curls. I'm trying to give you space but...."

"Try harder, Mom...I'll be down when I'm ready."

Around four o'clock the family buckled their seatbelts and Matt shifted the Jeep Patriot into reverse, backing out of the driveway of their Lakeview home on Prospect Avenue. Willa nestled close to the window carping about a stomachache, arms folded across her lap at the sheer injustice of being hustled out of the house so fast she forgot her MP3 player loaded with her favorite Backstreet Boys' hits. Gabe's knees slapped together as he mouthed the words while reading one of his *Encyclopedia Brown* books. The catalyst of his imagination visible—he was the boy detective solving cases in the neighborhood. The whistling through the open windows brought to mind a wind instrument playing in harmony with Springsteen's "Dancing in the Dark" blaring from the radio. Matt side-glanced at his wife. Summer was blessed with almond-shaped eyes as vivid as a gentian sea under a cloudless sky, and a long raven-tinted mane that drifted in the breeze like a mermaid's weightless hair in a tide pool. The couple was finally doing something unencumbered and healthy. In an hour they would be soaking up the natural splendor of the Zoar Valley Gorge, absorbing the balmy weather, and, with a little luck, nestling back into symmetry, emulating the common place of Harper Lee's fictional house of Finch.

Following Point Peter Road for about a mile, they turned left on Valentine Flats at the paint-peeling farmhouse where the grommets on an American flag dinged against a tall metal pole in the front yard. The parking area dead-ended into the trailhead where the Mackies piled out of the car led by Matt and Summer holding hands while Gabe hop-scotched behind them. Willa followed, yawning and lamenting at the cruelty of spending time with her lame family in the middle of nowhere, when she could be hanging out with her friends. If her parents insisted on seeing waterfalls, they could at least have gone to Niagara for the real thing.

The path from the parking area led to where the trail down to the creek began. About halfway there, Gabe, jumping from one foot to the other, pulled on his mother's arm announcing he had to go to the bathroom.

"I asked you specifically if you had to go when we got here."

"But I didn't hafta then."

"Mom, like if it'll shut him up, I'll take him," said Willa.

Broody clouds darkened Summer's mood. "I can't lose another child. . . ." She gasped at how cruel her remark sounded, but she couldn't pull the words back. Willa walked away with a dismissive wave of her hand, showing Summer the dagger delivered to her daughter's heart was already leaking contempt.

Matt put his arm around Summer, his knuckle stroking her cheek. Her eyes cut over to meet his. "I'm sorry for what I said. I just panicked at the thought of Gabe...."

"I know but smothering him won't keep him safe. He doesn't need anyone to hold his hand. And, after all he's just going to the *forestroom*...instead of the bathroom...get it?" Matt snickered.

"Yes, clever but not funny."

"My customers think I'm a hoot."

"Owls hoot—don't give up your day job."

Gabe, unable to stick around until the potty issue was decided, wandered off to find the nearest tree, stopping on the way to pick up a flat rock. Examining it closely, he rubbed his fingers over the layers before putting it in his pocket.

"Gabriel...hurry up. We're waiting for you, son," hollered Matt.

Meanwhile, the rest of the family soaked in the spectacular views and fields of wildflowers dotted with kidney-leaf and golden swamp buttercups swaying alongside northern white violets. Time is a foggy notion to a child and for Gabe it was reminiscent of a feather in the wind charting its own path with every gust. He circled his tree twice while zipping his pants then gamboled back to where he had left his parents and sister, but before Gabe could call out to them, he was distracted by a clicking noise coming from a stranger running past. When he looked back, his family had vanished.

On that fateful day, the whisper room again shouted Gabriel Mackie's name. On this occasion the walls were moss-covered and painted quiet, the dirt floor moist with dewdrops, and the ceiling a canopy of nodding hemlock trees, sugar maples, and yellow birch shrouding a galaxy of stars flickering around an eyelash moon. Late night storms had cleansed the sky, and as the earth revolved, first light appeared hailing the onset of a new day.

Rescue teams rappelled two-hundred feet to the bottom of the Gorge to recover the body of Summer Mackie face-down in the shallow water, dead at the scene. Husband, Matt, was found disoriented with brain trauma. Willa resembled a hunted animal trapped in quicksand, her head whirling from side to side as if looking for an escape route. Dried tears streaked her face and blood dripped from the corner of her bruised lip.

"We're here to help, young lady. My name is Axl—yeah...my mom was a Guns N' Roses junkie. What's your name?"

"Willa. My arm hurts so bad and it's hard to breathe."

"Okay, Willa. We're going to get you out of here. A helicopter's waiting to take you to the hospital."

"What about my little brother. Did you find him?" her voice as wobbly as an inflatable balloon advertising a grandiose event.

Gabe sat motionless against a tree close to where his family vanished; knees pulled up under his chin while helicopter blades whirled shafts of light in a circular dance overhead. *Daddy always said if we were lost to stay put and someone would find us.* Muffled voices pierced the stillness as he withdrew deeper inside his safe zone instead of calling out. The small hairs on the back of his neck bristling until he heard a thick voice.

"Sheriff, we've got a little boy missing—the sister asked Axl if we found her brother. I've got this lone shoe—one of those fancy Converse All-Star Chuck Taylors. It's got to belong to a kid."

"I'm over here...can I have my shoe?"

Gabe, his face mucky with dried tears and grime, squinted at the man in a brightly colored safety vest. He reached for the shoe, slipping it on his socked foot, double knotting the laces. "I saw red balls in the sky last night," he said in a small voice.

"Awesome. My name is Conner and I'm here to help you. What's your name?"

"Gabe Mackie. My mom, dad, and sister left me...did you find them?"

"We're going to take you to them."

Sheriff Warren McAlister and Deputy Conner Boyle escorted Gabe out of the forest and into a waiting ambulance where paramedics evaluated his condition, determining he suffered from exhaustion, hunger, dehydration, and a few bug bites, but no serious injuries. Before the ambulance door closed, Conner patted

Gabe's arm saying, "I've never met anyone who has seen those red balls—it's called a red sprite. Astronauts are usually the only ones who get to see them because they form on top of thunderclouds and lightning triggers the burst of red light. You looked up just at the right time. They're gone in a split second. You rest now. These guys will take good care of you, and I'll see you at the hospital."

The Erie County Sheriff's Department—its storied past dating back to 1871 where United States President Grover Cleveland began his political career as sheriff—is the oldest law enforcement agency and the largest in New York State, maintained jurisdiction for the Zoar Valley Gorge tragedy.

A witness reported seeing Matt, Summer, and Willa standing on a narrow shale cliff leaning forward. Another stated either a man or woman described as slim-hipped wearing baggie jeans and sandals, approached the family, while a third observed someone wearing a navy hoodie over a Buffalo Bill's ball cap shouting at them before they disappeared. A final witness wearing coke-bottle glasses swore she saw all of them walk back down the path toward the parking lot.

Back in the Sheriff's Office, the response team assembled to evaluate the evidence and discuss the victims' backgrounds. Conner spoke first. "Here's what we've got so far. The family lost a young son three years ago in a tragic accident. Evidently, he was in the care of Willa, the mom's biological daughter, when he died. Summer Mackie took a leave of absence for over a year from her job at Buffalo General Hospital due to her grief. She also volunteered with the crime victims' assistance program as administrator of the Facebook group page which kept her presence at the forefront of her advocacy. She was back working full-time in the crime victims' treatment center at the hospital as a sexual assault forensic examiner until today."

"So, she's a doctor?" said Sheriff McAlister.

Conner pulled a notepad from his pocket. "According to the hospital, she's a PA who, and I quote, *conducts medical and forensic examinations on sexual assault victims, works as an advocate for patients and families, and testifies in court as an expert witness when necessary."*

"See if our Mrs. Mackie made any enemies while doing her job. We might just turn up our mystery man or woman. Also, Axl, check out that Facebook group. And while you're at it see if there's any dialogue on that other social media thing—the one with the bird. What do we know about the husband?"

"Matt's family is from Texas, but that's not a crime." Conner moistened his lips, slumping down in his chair as his attempt to lighten the moment produced raised eyebrows and feigned laughter. Returning to his notes, he cleared his throat, "Matt's dad played football for Texas Tech. Was an undrafted punter who joined the Bills in 1970—same timeframe as O.J. Simpson—remaining as a kicking coach after hanging up his pads. Opened Seasons LXX in 1995, the restaurant/sports bar named as a tribute to when he joined the football team in 1970. Matt was born in our little piece of heaven in 1977. He graduated from University at Buffalo and Dad turned the business over to Matt and his college friend when he moved back to Texas...It's still the place to be and to be seen. He's popular with his employees and customers...no red flags...no priors."

"I'm still stumped why the witnesses waited hours to report what they saw. Almost everybody these days has a cell phone," said the sheriff.

"Probably no coverage. It's pretty remote," stated Conner.

"Guess that makes sense. We need to chat with Willa Mackie when she's able. I want to know more about her relationship with her parents, especially the mom. The rest of you get to work. Conner, you and I will head to the hospital," said Sheriff McAlister.

The emergency room staff received the paramedics evaluation of Matt Mackie's overall condition including his vital signs, ability to follow simple instructions, movement of his eyes and limbs, and the coherence of his speech. The major concern was a traumatic brain injury signaling the necessity of a CT scan to rule out fractures, bleeding, blood clots, bruised brain tissue, and swelling. He was admitted to the Intensive Care Unit, hooked up to a monitor and intravenous drip loaded with diuretics and anti-seizure drugs. An additional issue was the degree of oxygen deprivation he may have incurred from landing in the creek. Since Willa Mackie's fall was cushioned by her mother's body, her injuries were less severe—broken ribs and left arm—but she was being treated under the concussion protocol after complaining of a severe headache, nausea, and sensitivity to light and noise. Gabe, after eating a peanut butter sandwich and two bowls of chocolate ice cream, let weariness win, curling into a ball, hugging a pillow, and falling into a fitful sleep. The doctor-ordered sedative hopefully postponing the difficult conversation of his mother's death until the next of kin arrived.

The sheriff and Conner visited the morgue to see if the medical examiner had anything to report since none of the victims were able to provide specifics, at least for now. He handed them Summer's Samsung Galaxy S cell phone found in her pants pocket and although the screen was cracked, they hoped the data might still be salvageable. The waters got muddier with the ME's words, "Summer Mackie was twelve weeks pregnant. The fact lingering is who knew?"

When the duo returned to the office, investigators met them with disturbing case histories resulting in families torn apart after Summer testified in court. One that caught their attention was that of an eight-year-old girl, sexually assaulted, and buried inside a concrete block. Her accused killer, Victor Kurtz, left messages, candy hearts and condoms on the handlebars of girl's bikes parked at a nearby school.

"Hard to believe but it ended in a hung jury. He's out until a new trial date is set. Mrs. Mackie had filed a noncontact protection order against him," said Conner.

"We need to talk to him. See if he'll come in for a little chat."

JUNE 22, 2012. Starla Jordan in her wildest imagination never expected she would be forced to identify the remains of a loved one, much less the body of her younger sister. Her knees buckled under the heaviness of sorrow when she turned her gaze to Summer's ashen face stained with magenta splotches, tiny lines framing her eyes, swollen, and closed to the trauma. Her sibling, as sweet as a honeysuckle vine and with a knowing demeanor, could launch into witty commentary on both familiar and remote topics. Summer the wonder girl, the best of the best at everything she undertook, especially being her sister. Starla scolded herself for being so jealous. *How ungrateful I was not to recognize this... and now, it's too late.* Summer had comforted Starla years ago when her husband died, the sentiment etched in her memory, "Death leaves a heartache no one can heal but love leaves a memory no one can steal." She would have to somehow make her nephew comprehend all that is left of his mommy are a few empty words.

Starla left the hospital to check on the Mackie's home, finding the front porch covered with tokens of sympathy...flowers, candles, stuffed animals, crosses, poems, and notes. Mrs. Brennan next door scurried to meet the next of kin, wringing her hands as she expressed her shock and sadness. "She was such a caring individual—but her job—how could she deal with all those sickos daily?" Opening the door with the spare key, they were greeted by a Goldendoodle puppy, Dude, enthusiastically chasing his tail, obviously delighted for company, while Hallelujah the cat—Halle for short—stoically observed from her perch on top of the refrigerator. Mrs. Brennan assured Starla the family would not go without food as she had organized a meal train to begin as soon as everyone returned home, except Summer, of course.

Starla unfastened the locks on her suitcase, hoisting it on top of the bedspread in the guest room. She was hanging up her clothes when the phone rang. It was the hospital. Gabe was awake.

— ∞ —

She peeked in through the open door to see her sister's child mesmerized by a rerun of the adventures of *Clifford the Big Red Dog* on television. "Gabe, sugar, can I come in?" He turned toward her, his tiny face incurably somber, his eyes misty and wounded.

"Aunt Starla. Did you bring Mommy?" he asked with a slight hitch in his voice.

13

"I bet you're not too big for a bear hug from your favorite aunt." She sat down on the corner of his hospital bed, using her fingers to brush his bangs off his forehead before wrapping him in her arms. "Boy have you grown. What are you—almost a teenager now?"

"No...just seven."

She gagged on the bitterness crawling into the back of her throat before delivering the grim news. "Gabe, I've got something very sad to tell you. Remember your mom, dad, and Willa were on that ledge and then they were gone. Well, doodlebug, they fell, and Mommy's body broke when she landed. I'm so sorry, but we won't ever see her again. Do you understand?"

He wiped his eyes with the back of his hand, choking down the lump in his throat before saying, "It means Boo's not alone. I wanna go where they are, Aunt Starla."

"It's okay to cry...it shows how much love you have to give. But your daddy and Willa need you here."

"On the cliff, I saw somebody else. I heard clicking. Then they...."

2

Confessions of a Dangerous Mind

THE MACKIE'S JEEP, towed from Zoar Valley to the Buffalo police impound lot, was examined for any evidence pertinent in the investigation of what happened at the Gorge and then released. Back at the office, Conner dialed the number for Brothers Towing Company arranging for the vehicle's delivery to their Prospect Avenue home. While waiting for everyone to return from lunch, he opened the folder containing Summer Mackie's work files to see if there were any others as disturbing as the Victor Kurtz case. Her bio, profile photo, and personal information stared back at him. He picked up her photograph, shaking his head in wonder at her choice of profession. He blushed reliving his sixteen-year-old boy crush on Long Island native, Carol Alt. Still tucked into his sock drawer was the 1982 *Sports Illustrated* magazine—she on the cover in a one-piece red swimsuit on the Kenya Coast...*Summer could be her twin. How did she get pulled into this line of work?*

He found his answer from her interview questionnaire included in the file. Summer, a ten-year-old Junior Miss contestant in an All-American Girl Pageant, was pinned against a wall by one of the organizers. She said, "I kneed him where it hurts the most," resulting in her disqualification and a ticket home verifying Summer Mackie was a defender of right and wrong from an early age. He flipped to her caseload files which included victims of a serial rapist who attacked ladies jogging around a bicycle path; a fourteen-year-old who, angry with her mother for watching a girlfriend's baby, sexually assaulted the child before drowning the two-month-old in the bathroom sink then called the Buffalo police and in a unrepentant, clinical, sterile tone confessed to her crime; a middle-aged woman raped with a foreign object and suffered blunt force trauma to the head from the same object—her killer then strangled her young daughter and posed her on top of her dead mother before leaving the scene.

His vision shifted to a photograph of his sister's boys playing ice hockey on a frozen pond, his young nieces bundled up in hooded wool parkas watching intently, arms intertwined with each other. As a single man with no commitments, his sibling's brood completed his world and he was Uncle Cool to them. Beads of sweat formed on Conner's forehead followed by a surge of clamminess. *I've seen a lot, but the late thirty-seven-year-old Mrs. Mackie witnessed the unimaginable up close and personal.* The knot in his stomach triggered a dash to the men's room.

Conner splashed cold water on his face, returning to his desk as other deputies filed in laughing at an inside joke.

"Hey, you look a little pale. Are you all right?" said the sheriff, a toothpick dangling from the corner of his mouth.

"Yeah, guess my Texas hots didn't set right."

"Stick to wings. They don't call wieners death tubes for nothing."

"Anything new on our Victor Kurtz coming in for an interview?" said Conner.

"He's due in later today...probably on the arm of his public defender. Not sure what we'll be able to get out of him, but who knows...he might get all blabby."

With the six o'clock hour nearing and still no sign of their guest felon, Sheriff McAlister told everyone to call it a day. Conner volunteered to stay as getting a first-hand look at Victor intrigued him more than sitting alone in his apartment in front of the television.

"Give him another half hour. If he's not here, we'll issue a warrant. What's his story?"

Conner thumbed through the file, touching on the highlights. "Born 1985 in Buffalo—father, Anthony, owner of a plumbing company; mother, Sophia, worked part-time as a senior page with the Buffalo & Erie County Public Library. Quit twelve years ago due to health issues. Victor is the youngest of three boys—the whereabouts of the elder two is unknown. Graduated Kenmore West High School 2003, member of the National Honor Society and Theatre West...says here he played the lead—the Stage Manager—in Thornton Wilder's *Our Town*. That same year his father went for a walk and never returned triggering the downfall of Victor as we know him today. Father's last known whereabouts he was employed by Beaver's Bend State Park handling cabin rentals in Broken Bow, Oklahoma. 2004—Victor worked maintenance at a middle school, ultimately fired—records indicate his behavior, although nonviolent, was creepy to some and cute to others. Seems he gave out candy hearts and valentines to the sixth-grade girls. 2008—he was arrested for possession of child pornography, charged with a class E felony, paid a $5,000 fine, and registered as a sex offender. With no priors he got probation instead of prison. He and his mother rent a small cottage on Stanley Street. Neighbors report the only noise coming from the residence is meowing from a parade of cats coming and going. Sophia, housebound with COPD, receives Social Security disability and Vic is the night custodian at the Movie Academy, clocking in after the theatre closes to the public."

"From the top of the heap to the bottom of the barrel...sad. What's in the trial transcript...there has to be more to this like what led the jury to accept reasonable doubt?"

"I bookmarked a page earlier...listen to this:

> *Dr. Cryer, a psychoanalyst called by the defense, testified Mr. Kurtz suffered from the Oedipus complex, a psychoanalytic theory introduced by Sigmund Freud that identifies both positive and negative attributes. Victor's issue was a child's unconscious sexual desire for the same-sex parent and hatred for the opposite-sex parent, leading Freud to surmise this might lead to neurosis, pedophilia, and homosexuality."*

"So what? He hated his mom and loved his dad…how does that support why the little girl was buried inside a concrete block?"

"There's more. He goes on:

Pedophilia is a psychiatric disorder where the subject has a sexual attraction to prepubescent children. Mr. Kurtz's father abandoned the family when Victor was eighteen. Some pedophiles do not molest children. Victor Kurtz is one of them. Consumption of child pornography is a more reliable indicator of pedophilia than molesting a child…and that is the only crime he has committed."

"And, since the love of Vic's life walked out the door, he became a pedophile. So, a jury of his peers bought into the Freud mumbo jumbo but what about his DNA at the crime scene…maybe he has an evil identical twin," sneered Sheriff McAlister.

"Wrap your head around this…his lawyer might be the second coming of Johnnie Cochran. He challenged the collection of crime scene evidence, the probability markers, and the chain of custody, citing a 2001 case where a state crime lab analyst was running tests on a DNA database when she stumbled on two felons with remarkably similar genetic profiles. The men matched at nine of the thirteen locations on chromosomes. The FBI estimated the odds of unrelated people sharing those markers as remote as one in one-hundred-thirteen billion, but the mug shots disagreed. He showed the pictures to the jury…one man was white, the other black."

"Another O.J. moment…to recite Cochran's famous rhyme, 'If it doesn't fit, you've gotta acquit,'" announced the sheriff.

They both turned toward the window as a white Oldsmobile 88 with a rusted top pulled into the gravel parking lot. Climbing out of the driver's-side door was a man dressed in a dingy T-shirt and baggy olive drab cargo pants that looked as though he was carrying fifty-dollars worth of change in each side pocket. His shoulder-length, bleached blonde hair peeked out from under a straw Fedora. Halfway up the walkway, he turned around, retraced his steps back to his car, executed a military-style about face then taking long strides avoided stepping on any cracks in the pavement on his way to the door.

"Well, well, well, look who's here riding solo."

"Victor would make Al Pacino seem gigantic," said Conner.

"You two can look eye to eye my friend."

"God only lets things grow until they're perfect—some of us didn't take as long as others. The ladies call us fun-sized."

Sheriff McAlister opened the door. "Mr. Kurtz, come in. Have a seat. Will your attorney be joining us?"

Victor removed his hat revealing a six-inch part of dark roots running down the center of his head. He clenched and unclenched his hands, his shoulders jerking as if keeping pace with a rapid pulse rate. Inhaling deeply and in a voice as thin as his frame, he garbled, "No...nope...no...not coming."

"No need to be nervous. Would you care for some water?"

"Banana...Copa...Copacabana...banana...Lola. Tourette's tics take over...." Victor looked directly at Conner—his eyes the bluish-steel of a midwinter sky, vacant and chilling. In contrast, between his waggling eyebrows and twitchy grin, one might have mistaken him for a high-school freshman standing in the cafeteria of a new school rather than a Robert Maudsley, the real-life Hannibal Lecter monster.

Sheriff McAlister inserted a tape in the cassette recorder on his desk, pushed record, and said, "Mr. Kurtz, thank you for coming in voluntarily. We're all ears."

Conner jotted in his notebook that Victor's breathing steadied as his motor and vocal tics became less intrusive. *The longer he talked his mannerisms changed from the long-tailed cat in a room full of rocking chairs when he first arrived to now—suddenly he's got the diligence of a squirrel peeling a hickory nut.*

He admitted following the Mackies to Zoar Valley saying he was there for two reasons. Summer's testimony almost ruined his life. The jury believed him, and he wanted her to do the same. "I love little girls and would never hurt them. The special ones get candy hearts."

Conner leaned forward in his chair, a cursory grin lengthening across his flushed face. "Victor, no little girls need your kind of love. By the way, what were you wearing that day?"

"Pink shirt and these pants, I think."

"What was your second excuse for following them?"

Victor's body swiveled from side to side in his chair. "Willa's in danger. The girls—her friends. They're bad to the bone . . . bad . . . sad . . . bad to the bone. I had to warn Summer and give Willa my treat."

The sheriff, glimpsing peripherally at Conner, cleared his throat. "What's that on the knuckles of your pointer fingers, Vic? Looks like a couple of those candy heart sayings. Hmmm . . . there's a *Be Mine* on one and a *Sweet Talk* on the other. I bet little girls love that don't they?" Victor nodded keeping his focus on moving a paper clip with his foot. "How long have you been stalking Willa?"

Victor studied his hands before directing his attention to the ceiling fan whirling above him. "Summer Mackie didn't fall. She was pushed. I hollered . . . then poof, gone." He retrieved his hat from the floor, placed it on his head and stood up announcing he had to check on his mom before his work shift began.

"By whom?" asked Conner.

"There were only three of them on the ledge. I gotta go. . . ."

"Mr. Kurtz, if that's the case, why didn't you call for help?" questioned Conner.

"No one would . . . not one . . . no one would . . . you know . . . believe me. . . ."

Sheriff McAlister opened the door for Victor saying, "Thanks for coming in and we trust you know not to leave the county, right?"

Victor shook both officer's hands before following the same path and pattern back to his car as he had on the way in. He gestured a thumbs up as he pulled out of the parking lot.

"That's one screwy fella but a part of me feels a little sorry for him," said Conner.

"A tender heart doesn't go far in this line of work, son. There's no such thing as a sympathetic pedophile—even one with manners and Tourette's—and this one's a trained actor to boot."

"Why'd you let him walk and not lock him up for violating the protection order?"

"I wanna make sure it sticks. Get a search warrant. We need to prove stalking and I'm sure we'll find what we're looking for at the Kurtz home. Call the clerk in Judge Northland's office—we've got probable cause in the bag."

3

Cracks in the Ceiling

THOUGHTS OF GRANNY Ida flooded Starla's already precarious weepy state when she arrived in the waiting room of Buffalo General Hospital. She closed her eyes inhaling the antiseptic aroma as familiar as the scent of witch hazel that always announced her grandmother's arrival. As she scouted the area a few members of a family in various stages of distress hovered and hugged in a far corner of the room—the atmosphere, a house of stifled anguish. Starla dropped her tote bags on the vinyl sofa at the opposite end before sitting down. Hoping to take her mind off her own tragedies and fretting over having to tell her niece that her mother was dead, she removed her composition book from her bag. Immersing herself in writing, either song lyrics or poetry, was therapeutic similar to the majesty of a sunset transforming the natural world by bidding adieu to another day.

> *Dreams that last hold secrets from the past.*
> *Out of reach. Impossible to breach.*
> *Fragile to clutch. Fleeting to touch.*
> *Like stars and snowflakes and visions all aglow.*
> *Time is endless in our youth. Our dreams are rustproof.*
> *Our time to chase is aloof.*

From the horizon of hope comes the challenge to dare.
Our time to dream has changed in midair.
Dreams that last hold secrets from the past—
uniquely ours to share if we so care.

Starla, absorbed in creative juices, tapped the corner of her mouth with the persistency of a youngster learning to ride a bike when a sudden cough caused her to thrust a hand to her chest. Standing in front of her was a uniformed officer wearing sunglasses with reflective lenses creating a mirror for her to rub a finger over her front teeth... *lipstick has a way of finding a home where it did not belong.*

He removed his shades, hanging them in the neck of his shirt and said, "I didn't mean to startle you. My name is Conner Boyle, Deputy Sheriff, Erie County. You are Mrs. Mackie's sister, correct?"

"Yes, I'm Starla Jordan. Am I under arrest?"

He ran his hand through his military-style haircut, the ruddy tone of his skin spreading into scarlet. "No ma'am, not unless you've committed a crime punishable in the State of New York."

"I apologize. My artist's mind heard a smile in your voice. I didn't mean for my remarks to come across flippant... it's been a rough few days."

"More people should lighten the load with a little humor."

Starla noticed how Conner's mouth upturned revealing dimples in his cheek when he grinned. "Are you here because of what happened to my family?"

"Yes. I need to interview your niece whenever feasible—with an adult present of course. We'll be posting a no visitor sign on her door and one of our deputies will be assigned outside her room while we continue to investigate. And...."

"A guard? What for?...This was a horrible accident."

"We have reason to believe someone might have been stalking Willa. We've got a search warrant for his home, so we'll know more after that."

Starla gasped. "I'm not sure if she knows about her mom, yet. I'm waiting for her doctor to update me on her condition...to see if she is up to the news. How am I going to justify this to her?"

"Tell her it's because of all the media attention and she needs to concentrate on healing, not dealing with reporters."

22

"What about Gabe? Is he in any danger? I'm taking him home today. Matt's parents arrive later this afternoon."

"No, our suspect has a young-girls-only affliction. Here's my card. I'd appreciate a call when I can speak with Willa. Would it be okay to stop by and see Gabe while I'm here...he's a special kid."

"It would do him good to visit with someone other than his inner circle of secret friends."

—∞∞∞—

Dr. Truex, Willa's physician, informed Starla of her progress while walking to her room. "She'll be in a cast for six to eight weeks since the fracture was nondisplaced—meaning the bones are still in alignment. Her ribs are severely bruised causing pain when she breathes, coughs, or sneezes. They'll heal but it might take months. We're alternating five-hundred milligram acetaminophen with Tylenol #3 as we wean her off the codeine."

"What about the concussion?"

"Those symptoms are abating, but she still complains of sensitivity to light and some nausea."

"Has she asked about her family?"

"She knows her little brother and dad are here and asked a nurse if they knew what happened."

"How did the nurse respond?"

"She told Willa they had not been notified yet. Willa drew up her shoulders and said they would freak when they found out. Sounds cold I know, but remember she is still traumatized by the accident."

Parked in a chair outside Willa's room was the deputy assigned to guard duty. As Starla approached he stood up, unfurling a body that would consume twice the space of Conner's, and although a little fleshy around the waistline, his forearms rivaled Popeye the Sailorman. Starla introduced herself, showed identification, and after her bags were searched, opened the door to her niece's room.

Willa, engrossed in a television show, jumped when Starla said, "Hey, kiddo, whatcha' watching?"

"*American Horror Story*...the Harmons have just found out their house in LA is haunted. I'll just die if I miss the end...please."

"I brought your MP3 player."

Willa nodded, flaunting a muted grin, her attention fixated back on her show. Starla popped a piece of Juicy Fruit gum into her mouth, stacked May's *Teen Vogue* with blue-haired Katy Perry on the cover, and the latest issue with a grown-up Miranda Cosgrove on the nightstand alongside Willa's digital music device and headphones. Moving on to the closet she hung up her brown and white polka-dot pajamas under a terrycloth robe and a denim top over a pair of faded jeans. With tennis shoes and slippers lined up on the floor, she closed the door. In the bathroom she unpacked toiletries setting them behind the sink and lined up Willa's e.l.f. cosmetics on the counter.

Starla pulled up a chair beside the bed as the credits rolled on the episode of *American Horror Story*. Willa grabbed the remote flipping through the channels until landing on a rerun of *Beverly Hills 90210*.

"Please turn the television off. We need to talk."

"My ribs hurt. Can't this wait?"

"We've all suffered a terrible shock. I want to help but you've got to let me in."

"Where's Gabe? Is he okay?"

"Yes, he's physically fine but sad. Retreats into his shell as usual. I'm taking him home today. Your grandparents are coming in to help out."

"And, Dad?"

"He's still in intensive care but the doctor says he's improving. They plan to transfer him to a regular room in a day or so."

"Good."

"Tell me what you remember about the day you went to the park."

The timbre of Willa's voice fluctuated from scarcely audible to maniacal while expressing her displeasure of being part of the family outing to begin with. "This was all Mom's idea and it's her fault we got hurt."

"Why on earth would you say that?"

"She was all happy again and we were supposed to just get over how she blamed me for Griff's death. We had to look at the pretty flowers and that stupid waterfall from the cliff." Willa grabbed her headphones. Discussion over.

⸺ ✕ ⸺

Starla left Willa's room holding her own grief at arm's length as she turned down the corridor to Gabe's room. Opening the door, she found her nephew and Conner in a hotly contested card game of Go Fish. "Do you have any fives?" asked Gabe.

"You know I do. Here you go. You're a regular card shark. I need to take you to Vegas with me someday."

"Can we take Aunt Starla with us?"

Conner caught Starla's eye. "I haven't been there in many a moon. That's a story for another day," she said.

"I don't know where Vegas is, but can we go?"

"Let's get you out of the hospital first. You ready to go home? Dude's tail will be wagging so hard it might just fall off and Halle will be meowing a welcome home Gabe song." He sighed, his chin sinking into his chest looking as though every beat of his heart was drowning in memories. Starla wrapped her arms around him, "I promise you we'll all find a way to be happy again...trust me, please." Her nephew lifted his chin, tilting his head as if searching for any sign in his aunt's face to give shape to this optimism.

"Gabe, you up for a madcap ride in this wheelchair? If it's all right with your Aunt Starla, I'll push this brave lad and professional Go Fish player out to the car," said Conner.

The young Mr. Mackie lit up like the brightest star in a constellation and the dark shadows, for now anyway, slipped away as if they had an appointment elsewhere. "Let's go fast."

Starla picked up her bags, heading to the parking lot to meet the wheelchair racers at the front of the hospital. "Thanks, Conner...you're awfully good with kids. Any of your own?"

"No, just nieces and nephews...but they adore me and it's mutual."

"I can see why," she blushed, announcing a clarion call of her fascination with Deputy Sheriff Boyle.

4

Just a Bend in the Road

PATRICK MACKIE'S FAMILY resided in a prefabricated single-story Ranch style home with maize yellow enameled siding, a steel roof that provided a symphony during a hailstorm, and white decorative trim in a working-class neighborhood of Green Tree, Texas. His younger sister, Pamela, was best friends with Margo Tate, whose father owned the local bank, lived in a two-story mid-century modern home with an in-the-ground swimming pool. Economically the families ran in different circles, but since the laws of attraction are often not governed by money matters and aside from a union poo-pooed by some as a royal marrying a commoner, wedding bells rang for eighteen-year-old Margo and twenty-two-year old Patrick in 1970 right before he joined the Buffalo Bills football team.

The elder Mackies, after landing at Buffalo Niagara International Airport, rented a Lincoln MKX for the short trip south on I-90 to their son's home. A laborious silence fell between them like a mantle of uncertainty, the only distraction coming from the tires vibrating against the pavement. "Margo, thank you for coming with me."

She stared at her reflection in the passenger-side window, a vague expression coloring her face as the detritus of over forty-years of marriage, akin to a river overflowing its banks from winter's melt-

27

ed snowfall, inundated her memories. "Where else would I be? Our family is in crisis and our son is and should be our number one priority. Our issues are trivial compared to what he is going through."

"Agree...but this separation...it's been hard for me."

"In a perfect world we shouldn't settle for a relationship that won't let us be ourselves."

"Is that from a book or a shrink?"

"Can we table the sarcasm?"

"I'm sorry...I just wish it was as simple as the Kraft Mayonnaise-Miracle Whip controversy we never resolved."

She shook her head, a thin smile crossing her face remembering that battle. "We were imperfect youngsters making promises to each other in spite of our faults...."

Several years had passed since they visited Buffalo as Matt, Summer, and the kids spent a few holidays with them in Texas, but the drive through the Lakeview neighborhood revived images of a pastoral scene enclosed in a bubble of simplicity. Margo leaned forward in her seat watching as children played a boisterous game of freeze tag, their shouts of "Go" subdued inside the car. The whirring of lawn mowers competed with nesting purple martins and yellow warblers out chirping each other as if auditioning for the Buffalo Philharmonic Orchestra. Patrick parked the car on the street in front of the house.

Before opening the door, he squeezed Margo's hand—a signal both heartening and awkward, one that lingered a hint beyond comfortable. "You ready to put on our happily-ever-after-married-couple faces?" he asked.

"The most important thing is the stability for our son and grandchildren. I'm ready when you are."

The ringing of the doorbell created a barking frenzy as Dude's tail wagged in perfect cadence with every woof as he welcomed Matt's parents to his home. Starla waved at the Mackies through one of the insulated glass panes before opening the carved double mahogany doors. Gabe charged by her yelling, "Big Pop and GoGo," before leaping into Patrick's outstretched arms.

"All that's missing is the cat joining the greeting party...please come in. Let me help with the suitcases."

After a long embrace of shared tragedy, Margo placed her hands on Starla's shoulders, looking into her eyes glinting with sadness, and said, "We are all so shocked, upset, and...angry about what's happened. We're here to make life a little easier. You tell me how."

"Gabe is a priority right now with Willa and Matt still in the hospital. I'm trying to connect with her, but she's throwing up every wall imaginable. I'm sure my teenage years challenged my parents, but she's...I don't know...there's something else going on besides attitude and hormones."

Since Starla occupied the guest room, she suggested they would be more comfortable in Matt's room instead of Willa's. "There's fresh sheets on the bed and towels in the bathroom. I hate to run off as soon as you get here, but I'm meeting the deputy sheriff at the hospital in an hour. He's going to interrogate Willa and an adult must be present."

Margo's eyebrows drew together, coiling her necklace around her finger. "Why would the sheriff want to speak to her...I don't understand...what are you keeping from us?"

"They've posted a guard at her door. Summer testified in court against a man who should have been locked up, but the jury couldn't reach an unanimous decision so he's out awaiting a new trial. He might be stalking Willa. She needs to tell the deputy sheriff what she recalls about that day at the Gorge."

"Then there's got to be more to this than meets the eye."

"They're being very thorough. Listen, the refrigerator has the bare necessities and although Mrs. Brennan next door put together a meal train which has overstocked the garage freezer with meatloaf, chicken and broccoli, lasagna, and spaghetti casseroles, I thought you might enjoy a meal from Fat Bob's Smokehouse...a little Texas-style brisket with all the sides. Gabe loves their macaroni and cheese, so it'll be a treat for everyone. I'll pick it up on the way home...sound good?"

"Patrick will be waiting on the front porch for you! Tomorrow we'll visit Willa and Matt at the hospital. When we get home, I'll send the boys with a list to the grocery store. Gabe knows how to work Big Pop, so there's no telling what'll be in those bags."

Starla waited for Deputy Sheriff Boyle in the corridor several doors down from Willa's room. Leaning against the wall and looking down at her unadorned left hand, she was soaking in self-reflection when a voice forced her back to the present.

"You looked like you uncovered a flaw in the quantum theory."

"I wasn't that intense...just remembering another chapter in my life."

"Maybe we can talk about it over a cup of coffee when all this settles down."

"I was born in Northern Ireland. A beer would be more appropriate. It's a date."

"Let's chat a little about this interview with your niece. It's important that she leads the discussion rather than me asking questions that would only result in one-word answers. This event was harrowing, and I want her to show us some emotion. It might be difficult to witness. Are you up for this?"

"I want her to lose the attitude and mourn the death of her mother with the rest of us."

"I'm asking you to refrain from commenting as the words she uses will tell us a great deal...doable?"

"Again, I'm Irish...I speak in essays...but I'll give it my best shot."

Starla and Conner entered Willa's room to find it vacant. A check with the officer posted at the door revealed a nurse wheeled her down to see her father as he had just been transferred to a regular room.

"Why didn't you tell me that before?"

"Sorry, Sir, but you didn't ask if the young lady was in."

Starla swallowed a giggle as Conner rolled his eyes. Their amusement was short-lived with Willa being pushed back to her room by an orderly. "Hey, kiddo...how's your dad? Glad he's out of ICU and you got to visit him. Let me help you back into bed. This is Deputy Sheriff Boyle, and he wants to ask you about the day at the Gorge."

"Do I have to. I'm tired of thinking about it."

"Yes, Ms. Mackie...can I call you Willa? We're trying to close out the investigation and make sure we have all the facts. You were there so we need your version."

Willa detoured into the bathroom before crawling back into bed, pulling the covers up to her chin. Conner scooted a chair close, sitting down to her right while Starla stood at the foot of the bed.

"I wonder how it was for you after your brother Griff died?" asked the deputy.

"I thought we were going to talk about the day at the Gorge."

"We are. How would you describe your relationship with your mom?"

"She tossed out every piece of candy in the whole house...as if that was going to bring Griff back. It was stupid. She didn't talk to me forever. Like I wanted him to choke on that gumball and die. It's not fair. I was just a kid, too."

"How'd that make you feel?"

"Sad at first, but then I just didn't care anymore."

"Fast forward three years to the day at the Gorge. Were you and your mom on better terms?"

"She acted better—happier—but...it was like she was trying so hard not to hate me, then she'd slip up and say what she really thought."

"Was it the same way with your dad and Gabe?"

"Dad adopted me when I was four. We've always gotten along great, but he's married to her so it's his job to make peace. Gabe is just a super kid."

"Whose idea was it to go to the park?"

"It was hers...all about taking in nature and being a family again...such a farce."

Willa's scripted responses persisted through a series of questions posed by Conner until he handed her a photo. "Have you ever seen this man?"

She stared saucer-eyed at the man in the picture before squeaking out a response. "He's the creepy guy from the park. I'd seen him before though...at school or the mall...somewhere. Who is he?"

"At the park? Where and what did he do?"

31

"It was like he knew Mom...we're on the ledge waiting for Gabe and this guy strolls up, gives me one of those candy hearts, and begins to argue with her...she was waving her arms at him...saying get away from us...he reached for her arm and then we fell."

"Willa, did you see him push her?"

She twisted her earlobe, raised one shoulder and with a jaded smile uttered, "We all went overboard and he didn't...I guess that means he must have...right?"

"If this was a deliberate act then whomever is responsible will be accountable for Summer's death and that of her unborn child."

Willa's posture stiffened as Starla's hand flew to cover her mouth her lips pursed as if waiting for a long heavy wave to break on the shoreline before commenting.

"I'm sorry. I assumed you knew she was pregnant. My apologies. That'll be all for now."

Willa turned on the television, flipping channels to a rerun of *Beavis and Butt-Head,* immediately engrossed in the antics of two acne-ridden moronic preteens. Starla followed Conner out the door glimpsing peripherally anticipating an explanation. She cleared her throat waiting for him to acknowledge her presence. He kept in stride a few more steps before turning around to face her. "I had to know whether she knew about the baby in order to gauge her reaction."

"I wish you'd told me before dropping this bomb."

"I couldn't risk it. Your moral shockwave reaction had to be real, and it was."

"I guess I'm glad I got an 'A' on the test...but this just adds another level of sorrow to all of this."

Conner put his arm around Starla's shoulder. "It does. But I have to expose the cracks in Willa's armor if we're ever going to get to the truth about what happened. If she knew about the pregnancy would she feel threatened and angry that another sibling might push her further down the affection ladder...would it be enough to push Summer off the cliff, risking her own life as well as her dad's?"

"I refuse to believe my niece is a cold-blooded monster."

"I get it. Join me for my chat with your brother-in-law?"

Conner and Starla arrived at Matt's room just as his neurologist, Dr. Thompson, handed the updated patient charts to the nurse. "Excuse me, Doctor, I'm Conner Boyle with the Erie County Sheriff's Department and this is Starla Jordan, Mr. Mackie's sister-in-law. Is he up to a short visit?"

"Physically he has improved. We're not concerned about the residual effects of his mild oxygen deprivation, but as a result of his traumatic brain injury, he's experiencing lapses in his short-term memory."

"Meaning he can still remember how the prime rib from his wedding dinner ten years ago tasted, but not what he had for breakfast this morning. Right?" asked Starla.

"Correct. He is also suffering retrograde amnesia. He remembers backing out of the driveway on the day of the accident and nothing else. There's no guarantee he will ever regain these memories but if he does, they will return in pieces like a jigsaw puzzle and in random order. As part of the neuro-recovery program, we'll get him started with our speech therapist to develop a memory strategy to help regain what he's forgotten."

"His speech is impaired?" inquired Conner.

"No, this therapist not only works with patients with slurred speech, but after conducting extensive testing, she'll develop several plans to help improve verbal and/or visual recall deficiencies."

"Thank you. Has he been told about his wife?"

"Yes, but he seemed to already know."

Starla opened the door. "Who's that hunky guy in the hospital gown?"

Matt turned toward her voice managing a valiant grin. A by-product of his suffering, the wrinkles around his eyes matched his countenance—as buoyant as a rudderless ship tossed into a shoreless sea. He patted the bed for her to sit close.

When he spoke, his voice was gravelly and subdued. "Starla…I keep having the same nightmare. Summer and I are hand-in-hand strolling along Bird Island Pier. Hundreds of geese, gulls, and black cormorants line up on the railing as if paying respects to royalty. Summer looks up as we walk under the Peace Bridge and steps in a pile of bird poop. She shouts, 'Holy crap,' which was right on except the holy part. Our laughter causes the birds to scatter. Anyway, when we reach the end of the walk, we jump into Lake Erie. The water temperature felt as if it was January. Coldness fills my lungs. When I finally break through the surface, I am alone under an overturned canoe. Then Summer's image appears. She blows me a kiss and disappears. I flip the boat over and watch as she follows a path through a cloud. She has a blue blanket wrapped around her."

Starla and Matt clung to each other united by a muddled emptiness as though their emotions were entangled in a stunt kite diving uncontrollably above a windswept city. She whispered in his ear, "Our rock is gone but her legacy lives in your children. We'll help each other get through this...you and me for Willa and Gabe."

"Mr. Mackie, forgive the interruption and know I'm deeply saddened by your loss...please accept my sympathies. I'm Conner Boyle with the Erie County Sheriff's Department and I'm heading the investigation into what happened. Before we go there can you think of anything that has happened at Seasons LXX that might have earned you an enemy...any disgruntled customers or employees?"

"We've had our share of complaints not unusual in this business—the fish was overcooked, the wrong cheese on a burger— that type of thing. A couple of near brawls in the billiards area— mostly as a result of too much alcohol and accusations of a hustler in the house. Tina, my partner, might know of any staffing issues, but honestly I can't remember anyone that might have an agenda against my family."

"I'll check with her. I understand you have no memory of that day, but we have reason to believe this was not an accident. Your late wife testified in a heinous case recently that resulted in a hung jury. The accused was released awaiting a new trial. He violated your family's noncontact protection order and began stalking Willa. He was seen at Zoar Valley Gorge the day of the tragedy."

"Willa...oh my God, is she in danger? Where is she? And my son, where is Gabriel?"

Trying to calm her brother-in-law, Starla tells him, "Matt relax,

I took Gabe home. He's with your folks at the house. And Willa is here in the hospital. She's got a guard at her door. She came to see you this morning...don't you remember?"

Matt violently rubbed his arms, anguish inching across his face, "My daughter was here, and I have no memory of it. What the hell's happening to me?"

"Your short-term memory is affected by the brain injury. It'll come back with therapy, but you have to be patient," offered Starla.

"Not my strong suit. Okay, this scumbag was there that day? What's his name? Have you arrested him?"

"His name is Victor Kurtz and he's disappeared off our radar, for now, but I guarantee the entire State of New York is on the hunt for him. He won't get far," Conner assures the concerned father.

Starla, reliving Matt's vivid nightmare, absorbed a torrent of caged hollowness for her brother-in-law. Conner walked silently beside her through the corridor, alone with his thoughts about the visit with Matt. "You are aware that the FBI considers spousal murder common and both partners are initially treated as suspects. Please understand I have to...."

Starla stopped walking, her mouth falling open as she turned to face Conner. "What...are you nuts? You think that man grieving in the hospital bed for the loss of his wife is a suspect in her death...I can't believe you would even suggest this as a possibility...How could you? I thought you were on our side—someone who was going to find out who did this to my family. We're done, Deputy Sheriff Boyle." Each footstep gained pace as she hurried away from Conner.

"Starla Jordan. Halt. You're under arrest for fleeing the scene of a discussion with an officer of the law." He collided into the back of her when she abruptly obeyed his order. "I gambled you were a law-abiding citizen. Please turn around...hear me out."

She put her hands behind her back. "Either handcuff me or I'm leaving."

"As you wish...but you're going to listen to me one way or the other."

A visit to Siberia in January would feel tropical compared to the distrust and betrayal raging in Starla's eyes when she turned to face Conner. "I doubt anything you say will make a bit of difference...."

"Pipe down and please hear me out. Everyone is a suspect because they were present when one person died and two were severely injured. Each one had the means and opportunity to commit a crime. It all comes down to motive. We have a duty to the public to find out the truth. We'll consider if Summer took her own life...if Willa pushed her mother...if Matt had an agenda that day, and yes, as far fetched as this sounds Gabe is included in this list...did he blame Willa for taking his brother away from him...he might have had motive but it's doubtful a seven-year-old boy could push three adults off a cliff. Among the others at the Gorge that day, we've not identified the person in the navy hoodie eyewitnesses described hollering at the family. Starla, I'm just doing my job."

"Good luck. Now if you'll excuse me, I need to get back to my family."

"You promised me a beer...my treat. There's a watering hole right around the corner. My mom always told me that life was too short to hold on to anger. It's a waste of happiness. Apologize when you should and let go of what you can't change. I've done both. Come on...truce?"

"Simply because your mom is a wise woman."

The Anchor Bar, steeped in history dating back to the 1930s, earned legendary status in March 1964 when a young member of the Bellissimo family was tending bar when later that evening a group of his friends arrived with ravenous appetites. Dominic asked his mother to prepare something for his friends to eat and after surveying the kitchen, Teressa deep-fried chicken wings originally destined for the soup stock pot, added a secret sauce and a franchise was born.

The bartender looked up as the couple entered the birthplace of wings. "Hey, Conner, been a while. Looks like *youse* got a live one tonight."

"Two Blues, Jimmy. And, green is not a good color on you pal."

36

"*Touché*...that's French you know. Miss your folks. Where did they go...someplace in Texas?"

"Ozona. No worries about polar vortex, wintery mix, or shoveling snow in the southern part of that state."

The bar showcased walls lined with celebrity photographs from all walks of life, license plates from all states, flying motorcycles overhead and sports memorabilia. Conner grabbed both bottles of Labatt's Blue Ribbon, pulled a chair out for Starla before sitting down opposite her. "Cheers...here's to the City of Buffalo often coined as a drinking city with a sports problem."

"Were your mom and dad regulars here?"

"Yes and no. She was a waitress and he was a bartender. They've opened a restaurant/pub in Ozona, Texas, now...loving it but working their tails off to make it. How about your parents?"

"I was two when we moved into a large Irish community in South Buffalo after fleeing Ireland. Dad was an ironworker and my mom did domestic work. They died in 1998...a head-on crash with a tractor-trailer on the International Peace Bridge. I remember how excited they were to visit Canada...but they never made it. They're buried at Holy Cross Cemetery...side by side in life and death."

"Coincidence or maybe fate...my grandparents are also laid to rest there—both our ancestors are in good company among those Irish immigrants who dug the Erie Canal, worked the docks, in steel mills, and grain elevators. When I visit, I stroll through the graves—so much of the past buried in the ground. I swear someone is singing 'Danny Boy' from behind one of those headstones."

The tension from earlier eased with each sip of beer, Starla again seeing the side of Conner that piqued her interest before. He experienced a warm glow of relief as her hesitant smile turned radiant and her eyes softened. "So, what's your life story, Deputy Sheriff Boyle...single, married, a significant other?"

"I thought you'd never ask, Ms. Jordan. I'm single...never said I do in a contractual way but was in a relationship. She was young and starry-eyed and had our life all mapped out. I was to quit my job and go to work for her daddy in his furniture store. I told her I was in my dream job and had no intention of giving it

37

up to wear a suit and peddle sofas. That didn't set well. Then of course the ultimatum was delivered—*It's either your job or me.* It's clear what my decision was. She wasn't a bad person...just a bit spoiled, manipulative, selfish...Shall I go on?"

"I think you made the right decision. You had mentioned you're close with your sister's kids."

"Yes, very. They've got alphabet names—Aaron, Barry, Claire, Daryl—easy to remember. Another Blue?"

"Raincheck? I promised Matt's folks I would bring dinner, so I better get going. Thanks for calming my rant."

"No problem...and I appreciate you listening to my reasoning. I didn't want to have to lock you up, but I would have. By the way, you're not married or attached, are you?"

"Only in my memories...a story for another day."

5

G-24

WITH THE NEWLY issued warrant in hand and a day dawning as bright and warm as the sun at noon's high hour, Sheriff McAlister and Conner led patrol cars along historic Stanley Street where remnants of Buffalo's affordable "kit" homes littered both sides of the road. The aftermath of World War I and families hoping to own a home prompted Sears & Roebuck, Montgomery Ward, and the hometown entrepreneur, Ray H. Bennett Lumber Company, to offer catalogues detailing an assortment of styles of ready-to-ship homes. Nestled side-by-side were large cedar-shingled houses and more modest four-room cottages.

"Boy this drive brings back memories. My grandparents, parents, my sisters, and brother lived in one of Bennett's homes called the Potomac Colonial. All the bedrooms were on the second floor, so regularly I had to wad up toilet paper to stuff in my ears. Bennett was a pioneer in this type building—you'd order one of his homes and it came with everything down to the nails—no measuring, cutting, or refitting required...amazingly simple and great quality," said Sheriff McAlister.

"The old houses still look cared for."

"A friend of my folks still lives here. Most residents appreciate the history attached to these places."

In this generally untroubled neighborhood, the presence of law enforcement surrounding the Kurtz home prompted front doors to crack open and drapes to be pulled aside. Victor's automobile was missing in action. Officers searched the perimeter of the home while Sheriff McAlister and Conner climbed the front porch steps, knocking on the door. "Sophia Kurtz, this is the Sheriff's Department. Please open the door. We have a search warrant."

Although they couldn't make out the words, raucous sounds penetrated the barrier separating the officers from the resident on the other side. A few minutes lingered before the door swung open. The sheriff and Conner stood in disbelief at the appearance of a size zero woman with black horn-rimmed glasses covering her face, dressed in a neon green tunic adorned with multiple necklaces, holding a winter-white rodent in her hand. "Excuse me, Sophia Kurtz?"

With speech peppered with exclamation marks, she bellowed, "In the flesh. This is my pal, Mr. Bubbles. He's a Syrian hamster. Wanna' hold him?"

"Is your son here?"

"Victor, that bum. No, he's left his poor mama just like his cockroach of a father did. Haven't seen hide nor hair of him in a week or so. Came in one night after work and was gone by morning. You either coming in or I'm gonna close the door. I need my oxygen, so if you'll excuse me...."

"Mrs. Kurtz, here's the warrant to search your home so let's go back inside where you'll be more comfortable."

"What a nice young man you are...please, Dearie, come in," she said in a voice as harmonious, albeit resounding, as a church choir. Sophia settled into her recliner using her inhaler before fitting the plastic nasal cannula in each nostril and affixing the tube over each ear. With oxygen flowing the rattling in her lungs eased. Sheriff McAlister and Conner surveying the cottage noticed a mansion-sized hamster cage with built-in tunnels and exercise wheels on top of a dining room table. Stacked in a bookcase lining one wall, an eclectic collection of books from *To Kill a Mockingbird* and *Romeo and Juliet* to *Agnes and the Hitman* and *Barely a Lady* resided side-by-side. A tiny television set, angled in the corner beside the literary display, hummed the theme song from the *Young and the Restless,* a prelude to a guaranteed heated discourse between Jack Abbott and Nikki Newman. Five cats lolled on perches of a carpeted cat tower yawning and stretching at the interruption of their naps.

Mrs. Kurtz, regaining the strength of her voice, shouted, "Those three Siamese are my male protectors...Tom, Dick, and Harry, and those other two are my princesses—they're Maine Coons—I named them Sylvia and Virginia after Plath and Woolf—my favorites from my library days. Bet you didn't know that cagey Ms. Woolf dressed up in a beard and robes back in 1910 to trick the British Royal Navy into thinking she was a prince. Takes some brass clankers to pull that off."

"That's quite a home your hamster has," commented Conner.

"It's all the way from Belgium...nothing is too good for my Mr. Bubbles."

"We're going to need to see Victor's room."

"Second door on the left...help yourself."

His bedroom was as tidy as the rest of the house—no dust, no cat litter odors. The closet was empty except for a few wire hangers. Tossing the sheets and bedspread, looking under the mattress and bed, and behind the headboard proved futile. The bureau drawer held a stray sock and a striped pillowcase which they added to the evidence bag. They confiscated an old Dell laptop even though the hard drive was removed. Missing was any proof of Victor stalking Willa...or anyone else for that matter.

"We're striking out here, Sheriff."

"Ask Mama if she's seen any photos of Victor's girlfriends?"

"Mrs. Kurtz, did Victor have lots of friends?"

"Call me Sophia...never met any of them but he had pictures of girls all over his room. They looked younger than him, but I didn't ask...he deserved a life after what his father did and with his Tourette's and all. Anthony leaving defeated my son."

"What about Victor's older brothers. Where are they?"

"They came with the Anthony package...two boys born nine months apart—leftovers from a secretarial fling. I suggested they follow their daddy out the door. Haven't seen them since."

"Did Victor have a secret hiding place? Somewhere he could keep his treasures safe?"

"Not that I knew about."

"Sophia, here's my card. Please call if you think of anything or if Victor returns."

"What's my boy accused of now?"

"I'm sorry, but we can't discuss it with you."

The officers met on the lawn to review the findings. The search of the garage turned up a shelf of empty paint cans, a bicycle pump, a few tools, and a wheelbarrow sized tire. "Hang on a minute Sheriff." Conner knocked on the front door again and when Mrs. Kurtz opened it, he apologized for disturbing her, but asked if she had a wheelbarrow.

"Why no...why would I need one?"

"Thanks...by the way without Victor here how do you get around...grocery store, appointments?"

"My charming neighbor, Mr. Samples...he's a widower. Joseph takes care of all my needs." Conner, shaking his head while walking back to the group, shared Sophia's answer to the wheelbarrow issue and a snapshot of her personal life.

"Slice the tire open."

"Bingo. Ziploc bags full of Victor's obsessions—Willa with friends at Auntie Anne's Pretzels at Walden Galleria Mall...on the balcony of Seasons LXX...walking into City Honors School...posing by the cross in front of the Christ Chapel beside Trinity Episcopal. Mr. Kurtz just thought he was up shit creek without a paddle before. Issue an APB on him," Sheriff McAlister whooped as he swaggered past Conner.

6

The Way We Were

IT WAS DUSK when Starla arrived home with bags of take-out. The vibrant rays of the departing sun danced through the treetops bathing roofs in gemstone shades of citrine and ruby. Patrick and Gabe sat on the front porch so engrossed in a game of checkers they jumped when Starla said hello. "Sorry, you guys, I didn't mean to sneak up on you. Gabe what have you got on?"

"We're superheroes, Aunt Starla. I'm Captain America—that's why I got this red, white, and blue cape." Gabe held up a berry-berry juice box declaring, "I drank this secret serum that turned me into a super soldier and Big Pop is my sidekick, Bucky. I got a shield to protect us from the bad guys."

"Very creative...a pizza pan with an aluminum foil star in the center. I suspect GoGo had a hand in this."

"Between battles we decided to play a game," added Patrick. "Gabe always has the black checkers, so he gets to go first. He's winning of course."

"I trust you superheroes have worked up an appetite. Come in and wash up for dinner."

Starla opened a bottle of Windsor Vineyards Cabernet Sauvignon, pouring a glass for Margo and herself while Patrick opted for Johnnie Walker Black on the rocks. They joined Gabe at the breakfast

43

nook table while he polished off his macaroni and cheese, chicken fingers, and fruit cocktail—*evidently Captain America had worked up an appetite*. Starla served the smoked deviled eggs topped with bacon in a fluted crystal dish especially designed to hold these treats, delighting Margo as she had given this mainstay of the south to Summer and Matt several years ago. They sipped cocktails, sampling the appetizers while the brisket and baked beans warmed in the oven and the creole salad chilled in the refrigerator. With impressionable and sensitive ears within range, the dialogue addressed benign subjects.

Patrick popped a deviled egg in his mouth before offering a preview of the London Summer Olympics marveling at the continued excellence of one of the greatest sprinters of all time, Jamaica's Usain Bolt. "He could give a cheetah a run for his money." He added the United States had plenty to shout about with Misty May-Treanor and Kerri Walsh Jennings in beach volleyball and Michael Phelps trying to be the first man to defend an Olympic swimming title twice and break his own record for the number of medals won at the games.

Margo tilted her head toward her husband asking, "What is it about beach volleyball that captures your attention?"

"More than anything I'm amazed how they're able to keep everything in the proper place when spiking the ball. Makes me want to invest in spandex...and of course, their fitness is enviable," he said, his face broadening into a playful smile.

Margo told a humorous story about her book club co-chairman, a bona fide Southern belle with high expectations of literary excellence and the background to back it up, surprising everyone by choosing to read the erotica romance novel *Fifty Shades of Grey* while recuperating from knee replacement surgery. "We all roared at the meeting when I told the ladies, concluding there must have been some high dosage of pain medication involved for her to slog through the trilogy."

"I've never been in a book club. I love to read, but the idea of someone telling me what to read doesn't appeal to me," said Starla.

"Some in our group felt that way in the beginning, but we've gently persuaded them to try it...we've had more join than quit, so it's working for us."

"GoGo, can I be in your book club?"

"I doubt you'd like our books, but we can form one for you and me and Aunt Starla if she wants to join."

"We can't leave Big Pop out."

"Thanks, little guy, but I'm a western junkie...super fan of McMurtry and McCarthy. I've read *Lonesome Dove* and *All The Pretty Horses* so often the pages are dogeared and the margins are filled with notes. When there's no more sports on television, it's the recliner with a dog on my lap, a bag of Cheetos, a cold beer and *Shane* and *High Noon* on DVD."

"As you can see, his life is full," observed Margo.

"I'm done. Can I watch *Tiny Wings* on my iPad? I wanna dream I can fly."

"Yes, but take your plate to the kitchen for us first. Patrick, your drink appears to need a doctor-up and our wine could use refilling if it's not too much trouble."

"I'm at your beck and call."

"Great answer," quipped Starla.

Margo raved about the Buffalo versions of Texas staples, prompting Patrick vowing to visit the eatery to track down which cook had defected from the Lone Star State to the Queen City with homegrown recipes in his pocket. With the leftovers in the refrigerator and the dishwasher loaded, Margo served homemade banana pudding, and they returned to the table to savor the semi-healthy high potassium concoction.

Gabe, still curled up on the couch hypnotized by the reverie of soaring through a fictional world created just for him, bobbed his head with the motion of the game, a look of delight covering his face. With his attention clearly indifferent to the adult discourse, Starla gingerly recounted the agonizing events of the day to the Mackies from her visit with Willa in the company of Conner, to Matt's profound despair and memory loss, saving the most unnerving news that Summer was pregnant as the final blow. Suddenly a household that had adopted a semblance of routine dissolved—all the positive energy and silliness exited stage left.

Margo's hand clamped over her mouth, a snarl of agony spreading over her face, her eyes panicky and darting from side to side in search of an explanation. Patrick shot from his chair, wiping his face on his sleeve before standing behind his wife, hands kneading her shoulders. He took a deep breath trying to find a word…something to ask to make some sense of this latest revelation, but a mental numbness kept any coherent thoughts at arm's length.

"I'm sorry. There wasn't an easy way to tell you this."

"Does Matt know? What did he ever do to deserve all this heartache?"

"Yes, he does…he's having a recurring nightmare about Summer and the baby. It was another little boy."

Margo's voice creaked like a rusty gate. "They'd just gotten their life back on track after Griff and now this…."

Gabe tore off the couch to his grandmother's side. "GoGo, what's the matter…don't be sad. Mommy says hugs fix everything, even boo-boos. You got a boo-boo?"

Margo used her napkin to dab her nose, looking into the face of her young grandson thankful for his innocence and grateful he remembered his mother's words of wisdom. "Your mommy was right. One of your hugs will do the trick."

Starla tousled Gabe's hair saying, "It's bath time and then off to bed."

"Do I hafta take a bath. Superheroes press their bellybutton and we're all clean. Right, Big Pop?"

"I think Gabe's on to something here, ladies. But I think the clean button works every other day, so tomorrow both of us will take a bath…deal?"

"Deal."

"Done. Now it's off to bed for Captain America. Bucky will read you a story and then lights out. We've got a big day of crime fighting and grocery shopping."

Gabe kissed Margo and Starla on the knee before Patrick scooped him up on top of his shoulders for the march to bed. He waved farewell as they headed upstairs.

"That little boy has a way of bringing joy even if you don't want it. Wonder what's up with the knee kissing," chuckled Starla.

"No idea, but I suspect it's part of his insulated universe. His world seems less complicated than ours, doesn't it? Must be a nice place to visit."

Gabe, falling asleep in his grandfather's lap, remained down for the count, shifting to face the wall when Patrick pulled up the covers from the end of this bed. He murmured, "Sleep tight, little man," before closing the door. The house was dark except for a glow from a lamp in the living room when he descended the stairs. Starla, seated on the couch scribbling in a notebook, looked up as he approached. "Gabe all tucked in?"

"Sawing logs. Did Margo go to bed?"

"Yes, it's been a long and stressful day for her...and you, too. Can I get you anything before I go up myself?"

"Go ahead, we don't need a thing. I'll turn the light off when I go to bed."

"See you in the morning. Hopefully tomorrow will bring nothing but good news."

Starla, unable to shut down the heartache coloring her life, wrestled with the duvet, tossing and turning until sleep was beyond reach. She threw on her robe, stepping barefoot onto the hardwood floors which chirped from the weight of her footsteps, reminiscent of the dulcet trill of a Japanese nightingale. Memories took her to a castle she and husband Thomas visited on one of his band tours where they were introduced to a type of flooring designed to warn sleepers of an intruder with the subtle creaking sound that mimics the twittering of birds.

Starla gripped the banister steering her path down the dark staircase, reaching the last step without tripping. Dude, in his bed beside the Birdseye maple curio breakfront, raised his head feebly wagging his tail at the prospect of an early breakfast. Halle, lounging on a cushion on the fireplace hearth, arched her back, curling back into a ball, satisfied a few more hours remained before any kitten chow would be served. Starla switched on the light, turning to grab her tote bag she had left beside the couch to find Patrick covered from tip to toe in a quilt, his breathing robust and grating before jolting to attention with the sudden glare. "I didn't mean to wake you. Is your room uncomfortable?"

"No, not at all. I must have dozed off. What time is it?"

"Three-fifteen. I couldn't sleep. I just came down to get my tote. I'll head back upstairs. You go back to sleep."

"I'm up now...how about I make some coffee?"

"A caffeine kick in the pants sounds lovely!"

Patrick and Starla sipped their brew at the breakfast nook table, appreciating the hot liquid as much as the camaraderie. The in-laws had not seen each other very often since the Mackies moved back to Texas, so they were curious about each other's lives. Starla relived her life after marrying Thomas Jordan, ten years her senior and lead singer and founder of the rock band, Tommy. They resided on Hudson Avenue in the predominately Irish American district of Vinegar Hill in Brooklyn's East River waterfront area. Their union produced a hit record, "Let Go," which she wrote, becoming the signature song for the band. She was comforted by the recollection of happier days but shook her head at the cruelty of a full life cut short through senseless violence. In the early morning hours after the band performed for a private event, they were walking home when gunshots ricocheted off the flagstone street killing him instantly on the steps of their apartment, leaving Starla a forty-two-year-old childless widow. "That was four years ago...I'm still in shock."

"How horrible for you."

"Let me get us some more coffee and tell me about life in West Texas."

Their chat took flight on an air of easiness, confiding in each other as if lifelong friends. Patrick spoke passionately of transforming a tract of land on the property set aside as a refuge for abused animals to live out their lives. "I was inspired when Tony La Russa, manager of the Oakland A's baseball team, coaxed a terrified stray cat into the dugout that somehow got onto the field during a game, starting his crusade to champion saving animals' lives. We're a nonprofit no-kill shelter, home to sheep, llamas, goats, donkeys, and dogs from puppy mills. There's even a couple of peacocks."

"Who would have thought I would be having coffee with the patron saint of animals. I'm humbled in your presence St. Francis of Assisi. What's Margo into these days other than book club. She still a CASA volunteer?"

"She stays enthusiastic about that organization—in the same

vein as Summer's advocacy for sexual assault victims. Both noble women standing up for noble causes." Patrick stared into his cup and when he looked up, moisture welled in his eyes, a shroud of regret dangling in the air. "She's moved into The Murphy Hotel—we're separated. I had to tell somebody. Please keep this confidential. We're here as a couple to help our son and grandchildren get through this tragedy."

"You have my word. That explains the couch bed. I can't believe this. You two epitomize what marriage stands for."

"We support different causes. Even in our spare time we have other interests. I play golf. Along with book club and CASA, she's helping with the renovation of the hotel."

"You're both putting on Oscar-winning performances, which tells me there's plenty of love still there."

"She's been the most important part of my life along with Matt. Maybe we'll find a way back to each other."

Margo, after noticing a light under her bedroom door and hearing contained voices coming from the breakfast nook, decided to investigate, finding her husband and Starla sharing coffee and more. She lingered before stepping into the room, having heard enough to know the cat was out of the bag. "Is there room for one more forsaken soul at this table in need of a caffeine fix? I'm glad Patrick and I are better actors than we are husband and wife. Starla, we didn't want to add burden to the family. Our issues are minor considering what's happened. I hope you won't think less of us for not being truthful."

"Don't be silly. Grab a cup and sit."

Dude had given up the *I'm starving* lobbying falling asleep on Patrick's feet and Halle fled to the catbird seat on top of the refrigerator, huddling with an array of stuffed animals until the food train was in the offing. The Mackies and Starla brewed several pots of coffee while catching up and all were shocked when dawn inched across the sky casting a still life of a harvest of goldenrods through the windows. With the start of a new day upon them, each adult retreated to their rooms preparing for what events might rumble in, longing for the sky to clear with rays of hope flickering on the horizon. The plan was for Patrick and Margo to visit Willa and Matt at the hospital while Starla entertained Gabe at home.

Starla, dressed in black jeans and a long-sleeved polka-dot top, opened her bedroom door just as her nephew streaked by on his way downstairs saying, "Mornin' Aunt Starla. I'm hungry."

"I'm right behind you." When she reached the bottom of the stairs Gabe had already dumped his partially constructed LEGO City Hospital in the center of the living room floor. He placed the ambulance with a patient inside on a stretcher to one side and the helicopter with spinning rotors on the helipad. Because one story of the main hospital was finished, he bundled some of the mini-figures—the doctors, hospital workers, and paramedics—inside the building. Starla paused at the eerie familiarity of this set to the events of the last few days, watching for any reaction from Gabe.

"Look, Aunt Starla, that's me on the stretcher, and that's Willa and Daddy in the helicopter." He picked up the woman mini-figure..."and Mommy—where do I put my mommy?"

Starla looked into Gabe's cherubic face, the dark night of his being unlocking acute lacerations in the heart of a motherless child—unreleased grief had gotten in the way of an ordinary morning. She sat on the floor beside her nephew. "Honey, come here I need one of your magical hugs." Gabe, still holding the mom mini-figure in his hand, curled up on her lap. "Let's do what turtles do when they're sad. They go into their shells, close their eyes, and take three big breaths. Ready?"

Gabe nodded.

Starla pulled a throw off the couch, putting it over both their heads. "Now we're inside our turtle shell...one, two, three...deep breaths." After uncovering she took the mini-figure from Gabe. "You know where I think we should put Mommy—how about right here in front of the hospital—in the flower bed. We'll pretend it's full of blooming white larkspurs in honor of her July birthday. I'm pretty sure she's got an angel job now where she plucks a large handful of flowers and carries them up to God where they will bloom even brighter than on earth."

"Can we ask God to bring her back home?"

"You know what, she's already home." Starla patted her chest. "She'll always be right here in our hearts."

"But I can't give her a hug."

"Yes, you can...if you hug yourself or me or Willa or Daddy or Big Pop or GoGo you're hugging her because she's a part of us."

"Aunt Starla, what's for breakfast and after I eat, will you play Minecraft with me? We need to build our world."

"Waffles with syrup, orange juice and bacon first...then playtime."

"No syrup, please, just butter and Mommy always made my bacon real crispy."

Margo and Patrick, dressed for the visit to the hospital, joined Gabe and Starla in the breakfast nook. The sideboard, set with two boxes of cereal, pitchers of juice and milk, and blueberry muffins, was void of fresh fruit. "I'm afraid these are our choices—Cheerios and Shredded Wheat."

"I've been making a grocery list for Patrick and his sidekick, so we'll be restocked by this afternoon," said Margo.

"I'm not much of a breakfast eater. Any leftover brisket and beans from last night in the refrigerator?" offered Patrick.

"The health fairy doesn't visit West Texas often."

"Meat's loaded with iron and beans have fiber...I'll have a little banana pudding—bananas have eleven different vitamins."

"Big Pop, ya want some of my bacon?"

"Gabe, that's thoughtful of you to share, but your grandpa doesn't need to add slices of fatty pork belly cured in salt, nitrates, and sugar to his morning banquet, although he aspires to be Garfield the cat, lazy, fat, and cynical," kidded Margo.

"See what I have to deal with. GoGo is a restrictor plate in the car of fun."

Halle, dragging a stuffed elephant in her mouth, nonchalantly strolled by the table, a muffled meow announcing her presence. She bounded up the stairs, disappearing into Gabe's room, later returning with a bunny rabbit to add to the farm growing on top of the refrigerator.

"What's she doing?" quizzed Starla.

"She sleeps in my room at night a lot. She picks a friend from my stuffed animals. I think she's lonesome," said Gabe.

"That makes sense...I guess," said Starla.

Patrick and Margo arrived at the hospital making Willa their first stop. The uniformed deputy screened both identifications and bags before allowing entry into their granddaughter's room. They knocked on the door before opening it, "Willa, sweetie, it's Big Pop and GoGo. Can we come in?" No answer. Patrick verified with the guard that she was in the room. They called out again. Still no response. A breakfast tray sat beside the bed, untouched. A box of candy hearts rested on her pillow. Margo wiggled the bathroom doorknob, banging on the door and calling Willa's name. Patrick's eyes widened in alarm as he again grilled the guard responsible for his granddaughter's safety.

"I guarantee you, Sir, the only person in and out of this room was the orderly bringing her breakfast."

"Then where the hell is she, Officer? If you've not left this post, tell me how it's possible that her room is vacant? And we need a key to the bathroom. It's locked."

Margo peeked her head out the door saying, "Honey…she was in the bathroom with her headphones on so she couldn't hear us."

Willa was visibly shaken, her lips trembling and voice breaking as she tried to detail what had happened. "I was in the bathroom when the guy brought breakfast. I came out just as he was leaving and saw those candy hearts on my pillow. Freaked me out so I locked myself in the bathroom and was afraid to come out."

"Could you describe him, Ms. Mackie?" asked the police officer.

"I just saw him from the back. He had dark hair in a ponytail."

"Officer, did you recognize the orderly?"

"No, but he was dressed in white as are all of the food service attendants. I was on the phone when he arrived, and I motioned him through. He was done and gone before I hung up."

Margo put her arm around Willa's waist guiding her toward the bed, reaching down to remove the box of candy from the pillow. "Ma'am don't touch that or the breakfast tray please. We need forensics to check for fingerprints. I'll call it in."

Willa pleaded with her grandparents to take her home prompting Patrick to ask the on-duty nurse to arrange a meeting with her physician to see if she could be released into their custody. "I bet

52

you're starving. How about we all go visit your dad and we'll get something to eat from the cafeteria while we wait for your doctor?" said Margo.

The speech therapist hurried by the family as Patrick opened the door to Matt's room. "Hey number one son...up for some company?" Matt broke into a broad smile when he turned to see his parents and daughter standing at the door.

"I've lost some of my memory, but I definitely know who you all are!"

"Good—that way we can skip the pleasantries," teased Patrick.

After a round of embraces with each one harboring moments of melancholy and joy, Margo disclosed the latest on Willa's scare earlier that morning and the efforts made for her release today. He squeezed Willa's hand, promising they would find this nut and lock him up. Patrick, concerned about Matt's memory loss, asked what the speech therapist recommended.

"I wish I could remember what she said...I'm just kidding...She said think of memory as a muscle...the more you use it the stronger it gets. Also, get organized, write everything down while it's fresh and use associations...If I can't remember who quarterbacked the Oakland Raiders to victory in Super Bowl XI, I'd trigger it by picturing a snake—Kenny Stabler's nickname."

Matt, unsure about when he would be released, expressed worry that his absence was burdening his parents and Starla, but his most pressing concern was a memorial for Summer. "I've asked Dr. Thompson if I can see her—to say goodbye—but he doesn't think I'm strong enough, but I'm not leaving the hospital until I see my wife."

"Son, your mother and I are doing fine. Starla is a tremendous help. No reason to worry about us. We've got it all under control until you come home. I know you want to see the love of your life. I would feel the same," Patrick said locking eyes with his wife.

Willa's physician, although reluctant due to her reliance on pain medication for bruised ribs, agreed to release her but stated he would not prescribe the opioid she was taking in the hospital after she left. "We've been weening her off this, but she still asks for it, especially at night. Willa, do you understand that over-the-counter Tylenol will be the strongest drug available to alleviate your pain?"

"I guess."

"Then I'll sign your papers and you may go home today. It'll take a little while to get all the discharge information in order. When we're done, we'll get someone to wheel you out of here."

Patrick headed to the cafeteria for some sandwiches, chips, soft drinks, and cookies to bring back to the room while they waited. The guard outside Willa's room informed them the forensics team had finished collecting the items of interest and they were free to go back in. Margo called Starla to let her know the latest. Willa pulled on her faded jeans, buttoned her denim top, and slipped on her tennis shoes, emptying the rest of the closet onto the bed. A trash bag found in one of the drawers would accommodate the overflow—magazines, MP3 player, etc. Willa packed up her toiletries and cosmetics from the bathroom. While they were waiting for her walking papers, Margo surprised her with a new iPad and iTunes gift card. "We thought you might appreciate the new technology...Gabe has one too, so you're both up-to-date on the latest and greatest. His is loaded with a couple of games and Minecraft, but we thought you'd have fun filling yours with your choices."

"Very cool. Thanks, GoGo and Big Pop."

"You're welcome, Sweetheart."

"Willa, if you want to say goodbye to your mom, I'll go with you," offered Patrick.

"Please, Big Pop...don't make me. I don't want to see her."

7

Keep on Hoping

SHERIFF WARREN MCALISTER, channeling his roots on the family farm trusted the proverb about early to bed, early to rise, makes a man healthy, wealthy, and wise, arrived at the office before the rooster thought about crowing. He unlocked the door, turned on the light in the break room, hanging up his jacket before brewing a cup of Bigelow Green Tea with mint. He opened his lunch sack, curious as to what healthy option his wife of fifty years, Sherry, had packed today, snickering when he saw a package of Twinkies on top of the salad bowl and carrot sticks. Since his grade four B prostate cancer diagnosis she was on a mission to provide the proper nutrients to help him live longer, but she also threw in an occasional high calorie, fatty, salt-laden, carb-heavy treat to let him know he was loved.

Today's first order of business—transfer the deputy assigned to guard Willa Mackie at the hospital to permanent desk duty, living out his tenure as a paper-pusher until retirement after allowing a fugitive into her room. The forensic report on the fingerprints collected from the candy hearts and food tray in Willa's room proved an inconclusive match to Victor Kurtz, but no one doubted he posed as the orderly in white, sending a message that he was fearless, rash, and a Janus-faced criminal. The sheriff picked up the latest edition of *The Buffalo News*, a jaunty smile traversing his face as the front page featured an article about the Mackie family along with a photograph of Mr. Kurtz, labeled as a person of interest in the case.

We at the Erie County Sheriff's Department plead with the public to come forward if they recognize the suspect and/or know his whereabouts. And, if anyone at the Gorge the day Summer Mackie lost her life witnessed anything or saw anyone that might add to the on-going investigation, please contact us.

The morning clamminess promised a sultry afternoon driving the prelibation of autumn's petal fall forward a few months. Conner checked his watch when he parked his vehicle next to the sheriff—6:40 A.M.—both men predictable in their daily routines. His boss lowered the paper to greet Conner when he opened the door. "Mornin', young man."

"Sheriff, anything earth-shattering on this fine day? I still can't believe what happened at the hospital yesterday and thankful Ms. Mackie is home and safe. Have you decided what to do with our real-life Barney Fife?"

"He's lucky not to be in the unemployment line this morning. I spent the night wrestling with everything that could have gone wrong. Oh, by the way, our Mr. Kurtz must have worn gloves when he delivered Willa's breakfast and box of candy...fingerprints are inconclusive."

"I'm going to stop by Seasons LXX today to talk with Matt's partner to see if she recalls anyone who might have an ax to grind. Also, will check on Willa to reinforce she knows not to go anywhere alone."

"And, what else?"

"What do you mean?"

"I suspect there are other reasons for stopping by to chat with Ms. Mackie. As my cousin in Mississippi would say, I might have been born when the Dead Sea was just sick, but I do see a spark at the mention of Starla Jordan's name."

"Guilty as charged, but I also bought Gabe a LEGO Las Vegas set. It's our little joke. Not to mention meeting the man behind the Seasons LXX name. I've always been a Bills fan.

Conner arrived at the restaurant as it was opening finding an elf-in-sized redhead wielding a mop like a hockey stick grumbling about a no-show cleaning crew. "Excuse me, Miss, are you Mr. Mackie's partner?"

Without looking up she asked, "Who wants to know?"

"Conner Boyle, Erie County Deputy Sheriff."

Tina whipped around, missing swabbing Conner with a wet mop by inches. She removed her wire-rimmed glasses, tucked her curly hair under her baseball cap, sheepishly fumbling with her response. "I'm so embarrassed, please forgive my rudeness. It's been one of those mornings."

"Is there somewhere we can talk—without the mop machete?"

"Of course, my office. Mops and other weapons are checked at the door," she gently giggled.

Tina opened the refrigerator offering Conner his choice of beverage, which he declined. She opted for a can of pop. "We make a mean Beef on the Weck if you're low on nourishment—my treat."

"Sounds good, thanks. Let's get this done first."

The initial dialogue examined the beginning of their relationship. Tina said she and Matt had met in school, both attending the University at Buffalo, and both in the School of Management. She admitted being part of the majority in the accounting class carrying a torch for him from day one. "He had girls falling all over him, but he was too shy to notice... an endearing quality in someone so handsome. We went out in groups and our only real date was a disaster. We were invited to a party hosted by the infamous A-team, H.R.I. group and since we all were under twenty-one, we went to this bar in Canada."

"H.R.I. stands for?"

"Hell-Raisers Incorporated... We should have taken that as a hint. Anyway, neither of us drank alcohol, but we caved to peer pressure both ending up wrapped around our dorm toilets for the most part of the next day. Born from a fierce hangover, we jointly decided we would be lifelong friends and leave the dating pool to others. We're closer than siblings and have a wonderful working relationship. One of my happiest days was when he found Summer. I can't imagine his life without her."

"Are you still single?"

"Yes, Mr. Right always seems around the corner, but he seldom walks through my door. Plus, now, with running the place by myself, there's not enough time or strength for romance."

"Matt mentioned a few customer complaints and a couple of alcohol-pool-hustler-related incidents but couldn't recall anything specific that might cause someone to seek revenge on him or his family. Can you?"

"I've been thinking about it since the accident and the only thing I can think of that might be of interest are recent visits from Summer's first husband—Willa's biological father." Tina, opening another pop, recalled seeing him recently. She remembered him sitting at the bar ordering a Blueberry Gin and Tonic. "I thought he looked familiar, so I asked him if he was somebody. He laughed and said he guessed so. His name was Bradley Anderson and he had been on the soap, *Another World*, and was opening in November on Broadway playing a preacher in *Scandalous,* I think he said. We talked awhile before he asked if Matt was in. I questioned how he knew Matt and he said the weirdest thing... 'We have a daughter together.' I told him he was due in about an hour and he said to keep the drinks coming. He would wait."

"What did Matt do when he saw who was sitting at the bar?"

"It didn't appear he knew the guy. I told him he was waiting for him, so he put his paperwork in the office and headed to meet him. They shook hands and although I couldn't hear their one-on-one, the more they talked, the redder Matt's face, neck, and ears got. He looked ready to explode. Bradley threw his arms in the air, paid his tab and left. I'm not sure on the dates, but he came back several more times and the chats were always heated."

"I need to interview Matt about this. I'm surprised he didn't mention it, but he's had a lot on his plate lately. Thanks, Tina. Here's my card if you remember anything else."

"What about your lunch?"

"Thanks. Can't beat rare roast beef on a Kummelweck roll... add extra horseradish if you don't mind... my sinuses could stand a good cleansing.

Conner rang the doorbell at the Mackie home and was met by a barking tail-wagging Dude. Margo, holding on to the dog's collar, warily opened the door realizing this same uniform allowed a stalker into Willa's hospital room. "Can I help you?"

"You must be Matt's mom. Nice to meet you, Mrs. Mackie. I'm Deputy Sheriff Conner Boyle. May I come in?"

"Could you come back later, this isn't a good...."

Starla rounded the corner just as the door was closing. "Conner, wait...please come in." She patted Margo's shoulder saying, "He's one of the good guys."

"Mrs. Mackie, I applaud your caution. The officer responsible for guarding your granddaughter has been removed from active duty. Please accept apologies from our entire department for his lack of professionalism and judgment."

"He was supposed to keep her safe. I've still got goosebumps at the thought of what might have happened."

"Perfectly understandable. I wanted to stop by to make sure Willa knows the house rules until Mr. Kurtz is in custody and hoped to see my little friend. Is Gabe here?"

"He and my husband have gone to the grocery store. They should be back soon unless there's too many groceries to fit into the car. Gabe has a way of pulling Patrick's strings. What's that old saying, that children are spoiled because no one spanks grandpa."

"I guess that applies to me as well. You might think it's a bit odd to bring a seven-year-old a LEGO Las Vegas set...you had to be there," he said with a wink thrown Starla's way.

Conner, Starla, and Margo gathered in the living room awaiting the shoppers' return. Willa, after being summoned, descended the stairs with her best friends, Jackie and Misty, playfully bumping into each other, their giggle-fest contagious and missing any remnants of angst. Sitting on the floor whispering in secret code, Margo commented they looked more like kith and kin, as they would say down south, than a circle of teenage friends.

"Girls, listen, this is important. Willa, under no circumstances, are you allowed to leave this house without an adult. And neither of your friends are old enough to be considered an escort. Is that understood?" said Conner.

"I guess, but when are you going to catch that creep that's been following me?"

"Soon...but until we do, you're in danger."

"Wow, Willa, this would make a good novel. You need to write this down," said Misty.

"Except this story's not fictional. This is serious, girls," warned Starla.

Willa inhaled and exhaled a lungful of air that would register a 6.9 on a *Sigh Richter Scale.* "Are we done?"

"Here, take this with you when you go up," said Margo handing her a journal entitled, *Same Questions Every Day.* "It should be fun. It asks the same one every day for a year...so by the end of the book your answers will show how you've changed and grown—say you had to pick one friend as your best friend forever, who would it be and why; who's your favorite teacher; what made you laugh today; who's your celebrity crush and why; if you get married, what qualities must he have."

Jackie, whose mouth formed a permanent oval, crinkled her freckled nose, and said in an authoritative undertone, "You better pick me as your BFF today."

The corners of Misty's angelic smile turned down. "Hey, what about me?"

"You can be tomorrow," announced Willa as they romped back to her room, hollering "Thanks, GoGo," before again insulating the friends inside their youthful milieu.

With the girls out of earshot, Conner asked Starla and Margo what they knew about Bradley Anderson. They both acknowledged few details, but knew he had given up his parental rights, allowing Matt to adopt Willa when she was young. Starla recalled he had moved to Los Angeles to further his acting career. "Well, he's back and according to Tina, he has visited Matt at Seasons several times recently, all encounters resulting in heated exchanges."

"Where are you going with this and what does it have to do with my sister's death?"

"I won't know until I speak with Matt, but it just adds another piece to the mystery."

"By that you mean another suspect?" said Margo.

"That and maybe another target...Summer died but Matt might have been the intended victim."

"That means Bradley would have been there that day."

"Correct...we can't say for sure he wasn't...we do have an unidentified person in the hoodie according to a witness at the scene."

"How are we going to prove anything...it seems the whodunits are multiplying. And, what about Victor. I find it hard to believe he's not the number one suspect in Summer's death," said Margo.

Patrick and Gabe loaded with grocery sacks entered the side kitchen door just as Halle, with a stuffed Tuxedo cat in her mouth, leaned back on her haunches in an attempt to land atop the refrigerator. She aborted in mid-flight, dropping her treasure on the floor, and hissing her displeasure at the intruders before scurrying into the living room. "That's one helter-skelter cat," said Patrick.

Hearing all the commotion, Margo and Starla arrived in the kitchen to help unload the groceries. "What did you do to Halle? She almost knocked us down on her way up to Gabe's room."

"Big Pop called her a bad name and she took off."

"Patrick Mackie?"

"I said she was a helter-skelter cat...Gabe, that's not a bad word...It just means she's a little wacky."

"You're not supposed to say hell, Big Pop. If Mommy were here, she'd wash your mouth out with soap."

"I'm sorry, Gabe. I won't do it again. Forgiven?"

Conner's face illuminated in wonderment at the simplicity, the honesty, the unaffected clear line between right and wrong of a child under the umbrella of innocence. *If only life was that simple.* When he stepped into view, Gabe's infectious nature filled the room with wonderment. "Conner, when'd you get here?"

"A little while ago. I needed to talk to Willa, and I want to show you Las Vegas."

Gabe, running in place, grabbed Conner's hand insisting they start packing for the trip. "Hold on, buddy. Come on. Let's go into the living room."

"LEGOs. Thanks, Conner. After I build it can we go there for real? Aunt Starla can go, too."

"We'll talk about it for sure, Gabe."

Patrick, finishing unloading the groceries, suggested Starla invite Conner to stay for dinner noting enough food to feed Patton's army and an obvious attraction brewing amongst the two. She blushed at the accuracy of his observation saying she would ask him. Conner and Gabe sat on the floor—Gabe pointing out his hospital LEGO set. "This's where Mommy belongs...see she's in this flower bed and now that she's an angel she'll fly down and pick the pretty flowers to decorate heaven."

Starla cleared her throat before speaking, hoping to keep Gabe's keen sense of intuition from noticing the soreness in her heart. "Conner, please stay for dinner. As you've seen, we have plenty of food."

Gabe jumped in insisting he should stay.

"How could I say no but let me call the office to make sure everything is under control, otherwise, I'd love to."

A household mired in shadowed light with a family existing in a gap between two trapezes, suddenly felt ordinary as though the newel anchoring their stability was back in place. With no mention of the discomfort associated with her bruised ribs or her fractured arm, Willa convinced a reluctant Margo that the absolute best medicine would be if Jackie and Misty spent the night. Gabe dominated Conner's attention, while Patrick tuned into the nightly news on television. Starla helped Margo prepare dinner for eight. With everyone seated at the dining room table, wordless bliss filled the canyon of hopelessness as if their prayers were answered by God's wink until the phone rang. Matt was in surgery.

Margo and Patrick rushed to the hospital leaving Starla and Conner to supervise Gabe, Willa, and company. Dr. Thompson greeted them when they arrived in the surgical waiting room expounding on what had transpired earlier that evening.

"Matt had been complaining of headaches and double vision. He had no appetite and was generally lethargic. We ordered an MRI, which showed a fluid build-up on the brain called acquired hydrocephalus. It's one of the side effects of his injury."

"So, surgery will fix it?"

"It should, as frightening as the procedure sounds, it's generally routine. The surgeon will make an incision in his scalp, drill a minuscule hole in the skull, insert a shunt—basically a drainage system that will redirect the fluid to another part of his body—probably to the abdomen. This usually takes care of the problem."

"What if it builds up again."

"The brain shunt is permanent so it should take care of it. The recuperation is minimal with a few restrictions on things like exercise for a while. This shouldn't delay his full recovery."

"When can we see him?"

"He'll be back in ICU for the night. You can go in, but he'll still be sedated."

The elder Mackies, unwilling to leave until they knew their only child was out of surgery, sat on the couch in the surgical waiting room. Patrick mindlessly flipped through a tattered copy of *Sports Illustrated* while listening to the recap of world developments. His attention was drawn to the television as the weekend anchor for *ABC World News Tonight,* David Muir, reported the U.S. death toll in Afghanistan since October 2001 nearing two thousand soldiers. "Also, breaking just now, Captain Francesco Schettino, who allegedly steered the *Costa Concordia* cruise ship off course, grounding it on a jagged coast off a Tuscan island which caused the ship to capsize, resulting in the deaths of thirty-two people continues to be under house arrest until formal charges of manslaughter are filed. He is accused of causing the wreck and abandoning the ship before the evacuation was complete." Patrick shook his head muttering in sympathy for the sacrifices of our military families and the inequity of families torn apart due to the incompetency of one man.

Margo rummaged through her purse finding an old grocery receipt and a pen to copy down a recipe from a *Better Homes & Gardens* magazine. "The restaurant at our Murphy Hotel has to put this on the menu for winter. It's Brown Ale and Cheddar Cheese soup!"

"It's soup for goodness sake...you'd have thought you had discovered a Honus Wagner baseball card."

"Mickey Mantle is the only baseball player I know of. Did they play on the same team?"

"Not even close—different generation, different teams, different positions. The speedy Wagner who they called 'The Flying Dutchman,' played twenty-one seasons in the majors in the late 1800s almost all with the Pittsburgh Pirates. He won the batting title eight times, a record that still stands and matched only once in 1997."

"Well, this delight should have its own collectible *soup-card*—any recipe that uses bacon pan scrapings as one of the major flavoring agents for a liquefied Welsh rarebit has winner written all over it. Savor this…the finest cheddar available, brown ale, garlic, onions, sautéed smoked bacon pieces in a cream sauce topped with more bacon, diced jalapenos, and fresh tomatoes. Add crusty French or sourdough bread and put on your sweatpants."

"I'm guessing you wouldn't want to eat this for dinner the night before your first day of basic training for the Marines, but count me in as your go-to guinea pig."

Margo stowed the recipe inside her purse before removing a copy of one of her book club books, *Unbroken*, by Laura Hillenbrand, the story of Louis Zamperini. "Patrick, you might enjoy this one. It's nonfiction."

"Like *Seabiscuit*. Great story."

"You actually read the book?"

"I'm a closet bibliomaniac."

"You've done a good job of hiding your addiction."

"So, what's this one about?"

"As a youngster Louis was cunning and an incorrigible delinquent…his words…but his incredible life journey took him from a world-class Olympic runner to a World War II bombardier on a doomed flight where he spent over forty days on a raft in the ocean before his capture by the Japanese Navy and held as a prisoner of war. He faced and survived incredible odds, but his biggest challenge upon his release was learning how to forgive those responsible for his injured soul."

"Can I borrow your copy when you're finished? Surely there's a movie in the works too."

Groaning she said, "Yes, it was optioned, but in my humble opinion, few books-to-movies do the books justice. I'll hand it over when I'm finished...you could probably read it before it's available on the big screen...especially in our neck of the woods."

"Variety keeps us on our toes. Here's how I see us—you're the sea salt and I'm the coarse pepper, but you do know, Margo, salt and pepper shakers are packaged together."

"You've developed a James Bond charmer personality."

"Is it working?"

She tried to keep a straight face, but a flicker of tomfoolery reduced her poker face to rubble. "I'll keep you posted."

Still sitting on the couch beside her husband, Margo felt the pull of grogginess creeping into her weary bones, her body stiffening as if she had trudged through molasses wearing a pair of Tony Lama boots. Attempts to stay alert were unsuccessful as she rested her head on Patrick's shoulder, her eyes closing as if packed with wet sand. It was after midnight when Dr. Thompson informed them the operation went well and Matt was in ICU until tomorrow. After a brief visit to their son's room, the Mackies returned to a quiet home, grabbing a few hours of sleep before the start of a new day.

8

New York, New York

BRADLEY ANDERSON, IN the role of holy roller Brother Bob, was in rehearsals for *Scandalous*, a musical co-written by Kathy Lee Gifford, set to open on Broadway later in the year. The show documented the life from childhood to the death of an early twentieth century evangelist, broadcasting pioneer, and pop culture icon, Aimee Semple McPherson, whose passion for saving disbelievers was matched by her passion for making headlines. Instead of driving six hours from Buffalo to Manhattan, Sheriff McAlister booked a flight to LaGuardia for he and Conner, justifying the expense as Summer's ex-husband and Willa's father was a person of interest in the Mackie family's tragedy.

A dark-haired man wearing a baseball cap backward driving an unmarked black four-door sedan rolled to a crawl a few yards away from where the duo waited outside the airport terminal. Conner raised his arm to flag him down at the same time the sheriff signaled for him to pass on by.

"The only trustworthy rides in the City are Yellow Cabs, although we might have to wait a bit. You ever been to the Big Apple, Conner?"

"First time. Might be my last...everyone looks like they're late to their own funeral."

"It's a city on steroids. I started my career with the NYPD—a beat cop in Precinct 109 in northeast Queens. Married the love of my life and our daughter was born here."

"I thought you were a born and raised Buffalonian. Your daughter?"

Sheriff McAlister's face paled. When his eyes locked into Conner's, they were barren as if haunted by an inner pain too unfathomable to summon. "Lily just finished her first semester at NYU. Her goal was to work for a public relations firm after graduation. She was walking to a coffee shop in the middle of the day when three young boys stabbed her multiple times in an apparent robbery gone bad. The boys pocketed twenty dollars and left her to die. A blood trail showed she crawled for help, but it was too late. Sherry and I couldn't stay in the City after that and when the opportunity opened in Buffalo, we jumped at it."

"What a tragic story...I'm so sorry. What happened to them?"

"Put in a Juvenile Detention Center in the Bronx. One of the boys was from a prominent family. He died under suspicious circumstances. Rumors swirled that he was negotiating a deal and suddenly he's found unresponsive in his bed. The other two were released when they turned eighteen. I've made peace with the justice of them spending every minute of every day for seven years living with the fact they took an innocent life. I don't know how the oldest one turned out, but maybe he's helping at-risk youths by sharing his tragic story. The youngest of the boys wrote a letter to us every month he was incarcerated. Sherry kept them in a box unopened until we could face his words. Incredibly, his soul-bearing was a source of healing for us knowing how remorseful he was for taking the life of our Lily. He didn't pull any punches, didn't blame anyone but himself for his stupidity, and asked for our forgiveness. Guess it was therapy for him also."

"How can you be so forgiving?"

"A wise man, my father, always said, a bitter root bears bitter fruit and then he'd point to the crucifix on the mantel adding...he's the only one who had the right to be bitter and wasn't."

Conner hailed the appropriate cab and he and Sheriff McAlister settled into the backseat for the ten-mile ride to their destination. After exiting the airport, Mani steered onto Grand Central Parkway, the traffic moving along at snail-speed pressing the sights and sounds of the City into full display. A metallic lunar blue Mercedes-Benz SL 550 convertible driven by a permed redhead with lavender highlights and a Great Dane occupying the passenger seat dived in and out of traffic, waving excuse-me at everyone she cut off oblivious to the arm gestures from incensed drivers and deaf to the chorus of brakes squealing and horns honking.

"Eating chicken soup with chopsticks would be quicker," joked Conner.

Twenty-five minutes later the two-level double cantilever Ed Koch Queensboro bridge connecting Queens with Manhattan loomed over the East River and the narrow tract of land within its waters. This island, named after the thirty-second President of the United States, FDR, runs from the equivalent of East 46th Street to 85th Street in Manhattan and features a community full of parks and landmarks making up the one-hundred-forty-seven-acres of Roosevelt Island. Conner was about to ask when the sheriff morphed into a tour guide walking him through the folklore of this unique piece of land. "Back in the day it housed a smallpox hospital, a prison with its own medical facility, and the New York City Lunatic Asylum. In the late sixties the urban development corporation divided the land into three residential communities and forbade automobiles. Only two car-free zones still exist—on the northern and southern tips of the Island."

"Seems like it would be a great remedy for the hustle and bustle of the City."

With a slowdown on the bridge, Mani turned around to offer his two cents into the chitchat. "Tons of diplomats live over there. You could toss a Frisbee from here to the U.N. Headquarters. Also, lots of creative types—actors, singers, authors—those kind—live on Roosevelt. "My brother-in-law played a parking attendant in one of those Law & Order television shows...he's a big burley guy you can't miss him...maybe *youse* seen that one—Detective Briscoe and the gang uncovered some bones on the Island getting a new trial for a crooked Wall Street Junk Bond broker."

"I don't tune into crime shows on the tube. We get enough of the real thing just doing our jobs," said Conner.

"So...hot on the trail of a perp I guess."

"Just an interview...for now. Is Ellen's Stardust Diner still going strong?" asked Sheriff McAlister.

"Totally—still the home of the world famous singing waitstaff and the finest diner food in the country."

"How far to walk to the Neil Simon Theatre from there?"

"Three minutes tops—take Broadway to West 52nd. My niece works at Ellen's when she's not in a show...they shuttered *Baby It's You* so I'm sure she's slinging, singing, and still waiting for her big shot at stardom."

Horns honking ended the chitchat as Mani's attention was again on his job. The sheriff mouthed to Conner, "All New Yorkers say they either know everybody or are related to everybody. It's a town full of name-droppers and everyone has a story to embellish. It's in the DNA of the City."

The bright red and yellow neon signage announced Ellen's Stardust Diner on 51st Street and Broadway, a curb-to-door canopy shielding customers as a light drizzle began to fall. The outdoor analog clock ticked eleven-forty-five while the design of the eatery celebrated the 1950s retro dining experience. After bidding Mani farewell, Conner and the sheriff stood in line for almost thirty minutes before they were ushered to a red vinyl booth. Standing on a platform behind the table, four young men crooned Frankie Valli and The Four Seasons' hit, "Walk Like a Man," their movements synchronized with marching arms waist high front and back as they traveled the length of the stage. An animated young waitress, dressed in a black felt poodle skirt and white blouse, introduced herself as Flossie handing them menus and taking drink orders. She bounced away, her ponytail secured by a forty-five-record swaying back and forth reminiscent of a cow's tail shooing flies. Sheriff McAlister decided on *Gene Kelly's beef stew* while Conner joked, he might go with the *Homer Simpson burger* made with glazed donuts, American cheese, and bacon—finally choosing the *Love Me Tenders*. "We can't leave here without having the *Corvette* for dessert since my Sherry isn't here to overrule me."

Their food was delivered with more fanfare as one of the waiters broke into "Hakuna Matata" from the *Lion King*, the young warthogs' version of don't worry, be happy, prompting the lunch crowd to sing along. After polishing off the malt made with coffee ice cream, hot fudge, and chocolate milk Conner remarked, "We might need to jog back to Buffalo."

On the short walk to complete why they were in the City to begin with, the sheriff offered a little more to the history of the Stardust Diner and its owner, Ellen Hart and the Miss Subway title that was bestowed on individual New York City women from 1941 to 1976. Posters with their picture and a brief description of the women were placed on the City's subway trains with about two hundred Miss Subways crowned during the program's run. All the straphangers on the commuters had to do was look up to see their smiling faces. He added, "Miss Hart won the title in 1959 and holds annual reunions at the diner for the former Miss Subways. The feminist movement axed the contest in 1976."

The classic-styled red brick exterior of the Neil Simon Theatre featuring three double height arched windows appeared as the sheriff and Conner maneuvered around sightseers heading down 52nd Street. After several minutes of knocking on the front door they caught the attention of a uniformed staffer who, after inspecting their credentials, allowed them into the lobby. He introduced himself as Rupert, a proud usher for a playhouse rich with history, who failed to match the stereotype of a university student or wannabe actor working a summer job as a mass of white hair covered the nape of his neck. The air that Rupert breathed was thinner than that of the average person and his Paul Newman sapphire-blue eyes, shaded behind tortoise-shell framed glasses, penetrated like a gas laser when he asked, "What can I do for you young men?"

"We're here on official business and would like to talk with one of the cast members, Bradley Anderson. Is he here?"

"We're always aware when he's in the building these days and I mean that in a positive way...the old version wrapped himself inside his enormous talent, but his antics played out as a sideshow and he took no hostages."

"What happened to change him?"

"When he first joined us again he announced he had finally

71

realized how smart his grandfather was about life and about people—he said, the wheel is always turning and you'd better be nice
to those on the bottom of the wheel because at some point you'll
be there yourself."

"Thanks for your insight. Could you show us where to find
him?" said Conner.

"They're all in blocking rehearsals right now. Follow me." The
trio walked toward the spacious auditorium, their shoes rapping
against the black marble floor like a musicians' metronome measuring beats per minute. "Wait here please, while I check to see
where they are in rehearsals." Rupert walked down the aisle toward the stage, stopping to shake hands with a group seated in
the audience. After a brief talk with the director he reported they
would be taking a break in ten minutes making Bradley available
for a chat.

While they waited the senior usher of the Neil Simon Theatre
reached into the bowels of his personal nostalgia to share some of
his favorite memories of his time there. "After my wife passed—
she'd been ill for a while—the cancer you know...I had to come
back home—and this place is home to me. I'm too old to sing and
dance anymore, but too alive to spend my days rocking on my
porch, so I pushed management to let me volunteer for anything
they needed. This is in my blood...I love what it takes to put on
a performance and the nuts and bolts of the production. So, I'm
an usher and/or a tour guide. My favorite story is of the booming mezzo-soprano voice of Ethel Merman. When she opened her
mouth you just knew what you were about to hear was special. I
was there when she held a high C note in the second chorus of
"I've Got Rhythm" for sixteen bars—unheard of in the business.
We lost another one with the same vocal range this past Febru-
ary...tragic—Whitney Houston died so young."

"My wife dearly loved Ms. Merman especially when she sang,
'There's No Business Like Show Business,'" said Sheriff McAlister.

"Another Ethel moment was when she and Ernest Borgnine
got married and separated after eleven days...seems he got more
fan attention than her and she didn't like it one bit. The divorce was
bitter, each one claiming mental cruelty. In her 1978 biography,"

Rupert chortled, "she devoted a chapter to the marriage—one blank page." The doors swung open and some of the actors spread out in several directions. "Looks like it's interview time with Mr. Anderson. Follow me."

Inside the auditorium, a few dozen individuals, all in street clothes, congregated in the orchestra section, each in different stages of animation while reading a bound script. On stage the star of the show sang the last chorus of "Stand Up"... *high enough...to touch what you dream.* Far removed from the rest of the audience, a mother breastfed her infant while intently highlighting sections of the script with a yellow marker.

"Let me get the director for you guys."

Sheriff McAlister, after identifying himself and introducing Conner, asked the whereabouts of Mr. Anderson, saying it was urgent they speak to him privately today. In a short while they were seated across from Bradley in his dressing room.

"What's this all about, Sheriff?"

"When's the last time you were in the Buffalo area, Mr. Anderson?"

"Why?"

"We'll ask the questions, son. Again, we already know the answer, so it doesn't take a rocket scientist to know to be careful with what you say."

"Sometime in June I believe."

"June 20... Zoar Valley Gorge... sound 'bout right? Tell me, you own a navy hoodie?"

"Since when is it crime to appreciate a beautiful day at the Gorge? Look, this has been fun, but I have to be back at rehearsals, so if you'll excuse me."

"Mr. Anderson, who was supposed to die that day... Matt or Summer?"

"What the hell... should I call my attorney?"

"We know you were there... we have witnesses who place you at the scene... who heard you shouting at the Mackies and, as chance would have it, we have a photo courtesy of the New York State Department of Environmental Conservation who filmed a promotional video that day. Any guesses as to what it shows?"

Bradley's face turned from pallid to flush. "I didn't think so...we have a closeup of a man with a prominent cleft chin just like yours sporting a five-o'clock shadow and wearing a navy hoodie over a Bills baseball cap."

He lowered his head picking at his fingernails while pondering the scales of honesty versus duplicity. "The truth is never simple...but all right, I've had several conversations with Matt at Seasons LXX. I thought I could appeal to his paternal instincts. I begged him to let me see Willa. But he wouldn't budge. He said I had my chance to be a father and I threw it in the garbage."

"How did you know where they were going that day?"

"It was pure luck. I was going to their house to plead my case, hoping Summer would be more reasonable than Matt. I was two houses away when I saw them backing out of the driveway, so I followed them."

"What were you hoping to accomplish by doing that?" said Conner.

Bradley's uneven smile lingered beyond necessary looking as if he had just accomplished a rare four-move checkmate while playing the black pieces in a chess game. A swagger in the texture of his voice melted into scripted mawkishness as he spoke. "I have no idea...maybe I naively thought if Willa saw me, she would run to her daddy...I'd tell her I had made a foolish mistake...that I'd always loved her mother and her, but I focused on the wrong things...I was wild and unpredictable, and everything had to be about me. I lived to work and loved to work—and still do—but my perspective has changed. I am her biological father...doesn't that stand for anything?"

Sheriff McAlister stood, applauding the performance. "It's obvious you're a gifted actor, Mr. Anderson. Tell me, if you can, how and when did this fatherly epiphany strike you?"

"With a brain and spinal cord MRI and a spinal tap confirming that I had primary-progressive Multiple Sclerosis, the second stage of the disease. It explained my headaches, dizziness, and difficulty walking, but more importantly, put a timeline on my life expectancy. I want my daughter to be a part of the time I have left."

"I'm sorry to hear that, but I have one more question. Why

didn't you call for help when they tumbled off the ledge...what'd you do just walk away when the love of your life and your daughter disappeared?" said Conner.

"I swear I didn't see them fall. Ask Matt. I flipped him the bird when I took off and he reciprocated. How are he and Willa by the way—still in the hospital?"

Conner's deadpan stare drilled into Bradley's eyes. "Your concern is touching. I'll convey your best wishes. By the way, if they were still on the cliff when you left, how did you hear of the accident?"

"All the New York papers covered it."

Rupert rapped on the dressing room door announcing that rehearsals had resumed, and Bradley was due on the set. Conner robustly suggested Mr. Anderson stay in New York, as he was, best case, a witness in an ongoing investigation and possibly culpable in Summer's death. The sheriff shook his hand, thanked him for his time, adding *break a leg* as they say in the business.

"You know where to find me. If you're back in these parts when the show opens, I'd be happy to comp your tickets...it's guaranteed to be a smash."

"Let me show you out, Sheriff," Rupert said as the trio walked back to the lobby. "I hope you got what you came for. As I mentioned before, the Bradley we used to know, shall I say, manically focused...some might say a handful, but I admire his grit. His voice is a gift, although he can't read a note of music and he's been nominated for a Grammy and two Tony Awards...the man has talent!"

Sheriff McAlister and Conner thanked the friendly usher for sharing his story before hailing a cab for the airport. As they traversed back over the Queensboro bridge, their driver, Jada, asked if they knew the background of Roosevelt Island. Before either could respond they had the tutorial on the earlier trip, she launched into more details without taking a breath. The backseat duo looked at each other and shrugged knowing they were at the mercy of their cabbie hoping for a little extra fare for her history lesson. Pointing to the lighthouse on the northeast tip, Jada remarked it was built from stone mined from the Island by penitentiary inmates in

1872 by the same architect who designed St. Patrick's Cathedral then added, "See those two red gondolas. That's the aerial tram that runs about every fifteen minutes connecting the Island to the Upper East Side of Manhattan. They rise two-hundred feet in the air and the views of Midtown, Long Island City, and the East River are worth the cost of a ticket. If you look to the southern end, that's Four Freedom Park designed around FDR's State of the Union speech in 1941. It's set to open in October." With a lengthy pause, the passengers supposed class was dismissed, but getting a second wind, the cabbie inquired if either gentleman was familiar with Fitzgerald's novel, *The Great Gatsby* to which they both acknowledged, however, it had been a while since either had read it. "My mother taught American literature and I remember in chapter four when Nick and Jay drive into Manhattan via the Queensboro bridge and Fitzgerald describes how the City looks from this view. It's just perfect. I'm an aspiring author and if I could write one sentence like Fitzgerald my life would be complete. I remember he said not to write because you want to say something, write because you have something to say. Forgive me...I get a little long-winded. My boyfriend says not everyone cares about my passion. I might just dump him. Not to worry, gentlemen, LaGuardia is in view...and thank you for letting me ramble on."

Sheriff McAlister paid the fare and a little extra. His eyes glistened remembering how his own father had forbade him from leaving farm life as it was his legacy, his destiny. "Good luck. At times we need to ignore what the world expects us to be and be who we are." He added, "I'll look for author Jada Nelson on the bestsellers' lists. And, I'd definitely find a new beau."

9

Tears in Heaven

VICTOR PARKED HIS Oldsmobile a block from his former residence crossing his fingers that his mother would be out, asleep, or otherwise occupied. He had not seen her since he loaded his possessions in the trunk and bid her adieu to focus on his mission—to ruin the idyllic life Summer Mackie had built for herself—mostly, in his mind, at his expense. Being born under the sign of Taurus the bull and a zealous disciple of the zodiac and its influence on daily life, Victor chose this day seven hours after sunrise to visit Sophia Kurtz. He opened the back door leading into the kitchen. His plan, open the freezer, unwrap the package labeled *cookie dough,* pocket several Franklins from the cash stash, and rewrap the bundle. Next on his agenda was to confiscate her cell phone that she kept in the knife drawer, which offered another treat...a recent letter from his long-lost father with a return address on the envelope. He left his calling card on top of the freezer package and was hardly out the door when he heard muffled laughter coming from the kitchen. Sneaking a peek in the window provided a glimpse of two people, one dressed as Catwoman in an all-black body suit carrying a bull whip, the other as Batman wearing cape and tights. Victor deduced the archenemies appeared to be settling their comic book feud. He felt both a tinge of approval that Mama Kurtz had found someone to appreciate her zest for life and an aching that he failed at being a better person and son. Since narrowly escaping discovery, Victor proceeded to the carport to remove the photos of Willa he had hidden in the wheelbarrow tire to find it slashed and empty. He kicked it to the driveway, cursing under his breath knowing who now had possession of his prizes. Once back in his vehicle, he cruised in front of his house blaring the horn as a mock goodbye to his mother, certain she would notify the sheriff of the stolen property as she was not one to be duped and keep silent even for her flesh and blood.

Matt, scheduled for release from the hospital as soon as his physicians signed off on his discharge, had one more thing to do before going home in his new role as a widower. Summer was still waiting in the hospital mortuary for him to say goodbye and recognizing, like ink in water, he would have to find a way to stabilize and find a new pathway. Patrick, arriving to escort his son to see his wife, helped Matt into a wheelchair. The clacking of the wheels on the vinyl sheet flooring carved up the quietness like a foil in the hands of a fencer, neither man able to find a word to soothe the other. Matt looked left and right as they passed framed photographs of snow-capped mountains, hammocks tied to palms on a white sandy beach, canopies of cherry and magnolia trees in full bloom, and an image of an empty canoe gliding on a tranquil lake.

"Dad, can we stop for a minute. I want to look at this picture." Patrick turned the wheelchair to face the photograph of a child with flaxen tousled hair kneeling in a parched cornfield, her head lifted to the sky, hands folded in prayer.

"What is it, son?"

Matt, in his aphonic voice, mumbled, "Image in its simplest form, so powerful…feelings without words. This must be what my boy, Gabe, sees when he withdraws inside his mind."

"It'd be nice to be in that world at times…like now. You ready to see Summer?"

"I think so."

They were joined in the foyer by a member of the medical examiner's staff who had worked with Summer on several cases. He handed Matt a plastic bag containing her personal effects, offering condolences on behalf of the entire office before escorting them into the chamber where bodies awaiting identification or burial are secured inside vaults. When Summer's body was removed from her resting place, Patrick wheeled Matt beside her, retreating to a far corner as not to intrude on the privacy of the moment.

Matt shivered unable to control the heightened sense of mourning and finality as he stared at the lifeless corpse that was once his wife. "You've left this earth, but never my heart. I'd like to believe you and Griff, and our unborn child are in the peaceful arms of God...but I'm not on speaking terms with Him right now so I can't pray that you are. I feel like a recorded episode of myself...I need a place to hide and heal, but I can't, and I won't because you've left me in charge of Willa and Gabe. I took normal for granted...Dude and Halle begging for food every time we stepped one foot into the kitchen; us doubling over with laughter reading Erma Bombeck's book *The Grass is Always Greener over the Septic Tank*; and you sitting beside me on the couch watching the Super Bowl when the Saints beat the Colts when all you cared about was halftime and the Budweiser commercials...remember you loved the one with the Clydesdale and the Longhorn steer." Matt's face plunged into his hands, overwhelmed by the intimacy and snapshot of homelife, his sentimentality whipsawing from the low wail of a violin to R. Kelly's inspirational lyrics "I Believe I Can Fly."

Patrick moved quickly to his son massaging the back of his neck trying to calm his suffering. "Matthew, you have to believe Summer heard your words and felt your devotion...but I think it's time to say goodbye."

"I'm just so afraid, Dad. Afraid of my life without her...scared that I'll fail our children...."

"There's an old Japanese proverb that says if you fall nine times, stand up ten. We'll be there to pick you up until you can manage by yourself."

Father and son, each internally digesting the intensity of the morning, rolled back to Matt's room to await another MRI scheduled for later that afternoon to complete his release papers. Patrick, helping him settle into a recliner, witnessed Matt's body sagging inside the arm rests, his eyelids drooping involuntarily. "Rest, son. I've got an errand to run but I'll be back after lunch and maybe we'll be on our way home after that." Matt, supporting his head with his hand, fell into the arms of Morpheus, the Greek god of slumber, before his dad was out the door.

One of Western New York's most iconic architectural landmarks, the Hotel Henry Urban Resort Conference Center located at the corner of Rockwell Road and Cleveland Circle, was originally built in the late 1800s as the Buffalo State Asylum for the Insane. Two original decorative towers, each one-hundred-eighty-five-feet tall, function as symbols for preservationists and holistic mental health treatment. It now operates as a full-service hotel with eighty-eight rooms and suites, the property surrounded by galleries, cultural institutions, and nearby parks.

Patrick entered the hotel's glass vestibule on the north side of the building, following the grand staircase to the second-floor registration and front desk. He requested separate suites on the private floor. The concierge peering over rimless bifocals showed him a brochure showcasing the two-level suite. "This jewel features a separate sitting area with dining table, a European style free-standing soaking tub, and oversized shower."

"This will be perfect for my wife, Margo. I would like another suite on this floor if possible."

"Certainly, Sir, we have one available. Mr. Mackie, when will you be checking in?"

"Later today, but I'm not sure when."

"Not a problem. The suites will be ready by four o'clock."

Patrick left the hotel satisfied Margo would be pleased with the arrangements. With Matt coming home from the hospital and the iceberg melting a bit between them, he wished they could share a special evening along the lines of a couples "date-night." There was a spring in his gait anticipating the possibility, but he remembered what great-grandma Trudy used to warn, *Don't sail out farther than you can row back*. He arrived back at the hospital making his way to Matt's room to find it empty. According to the nurse he was still in radiology. She said, "It could be a while as a school bus overturned sending several children here for x-rays."

Starla answered the phone when Patrick called with the news there was a real possibility Matt would be released today, promising to keep them posted. "Is Margo handy?" The couple had discussed moving to a hotel when this day arrived enabling their son to sleep in his own bed. They had reservations at the Henry Hotel beginning tonight, suggesting she pack their belongings to be ready to leave whenever feasible.

Starla stripped the bed, remaking it with fresh linens, propping extra pillows against the headboard. Margo dusted a framed photograph taken at their home. Summer and Matt sat atop Starless Night, her prized Friesian, his flowing mane, and tail as glossy as a cut black diamond. Looking into the idyllic innocence of her son and daughter-in-law produced a surge of wistfulness as if the couple deduced this mount was nothing more than a carousel horse at the New York State Fair. Suddenly, years of remembered joy curdled into a throbbing loss of a beautiful spirit.

The bathroom, following a thorough scrubbing, sparkled, a whiff of warm vanilla sugar hung in the air from an uncapped scented candle setting the senses on an excursion as pleasing as the first rain after a long hot dry spell. Burgundy towels with golden threads woven into a pattern of interconnecting circles were draped over the fixtures. With Matt's homecoming imminent, the ladies moved to the kitchen. A crockpot of homemade spaghetti sauce simmered while a large cauldron of water awaited the noodles. Margo sliced a loaf of French bread, brushing each piece with olive oil, sprinkling with Parmesan cheese, and garlic salt. Washed Romaine lettuce, grape tomatoes, sliced avocado, and red onion were stored beside the raspberry vinaigrette dressing in the refrigerator. All that remained was dessert...brownies topped with chocolate mousse and crushed English toffee candy layered in individual goblets.

———— ∞ ————

The Mackie household buzzed with excitement and activity as Willa insisted everyone write a message on her purple cast, saving a space for her dad when he came home. Starla and Margo watched as Gabe sketched a picture of floating feathers and peppermint candy canes. Margo tugged on her ear before asking for an explanation. He said, "Well, now that mommy's an angel, she has wings, and wings have feathers and I know when she comes to check on us because I smell peppermint."

"Very sweet…makes perfect sense to me," Starla said with a nod.

Margo, sitting on the floor beside Gabe, looked down and off to one side beaming at the tenderness of his heart before dragging his attention to the book she brought for him titled *Me, Myself, and I,* an imagination builder guaranteed to engage children for hours on end. As she detailed it, her doe-eyed grandson devoured every page of interesting things to draw or write about. Gabe, dashing upstairs to get his crayons and colored pencils, took two steps at a time on the way back down to snuggle against his grandmother ready to dive into this project. Talking nineteen to the dozen he exclaimed, "After I draw what my hair looks like, I'm going to think about lizards and outer space…but I don't know about lightning and pickles…they both scare me."

"Lightning can be scary…but pickles?"

"They're all bumpy like a crocodile…and green too. I just can't love 'em."

"But, Gabe, what about lizards…they look pretty scary, too, but you're okay with them?" Starla asked.

"Yeah. They live outside, not in a jar in the fridge."

Starla and Margo agreed they may never look at a gherkin again without thinking about reptiles.

Gabe and Willa, after tying balloons to the mailbox and front porch, fled upstairs to practice the surprise for their dad when he came home. Margo and Starla acknowledged neither knew what to expect or what to say when Matt arrived at the house he once shared with Summer.

Gabe bounded back into the living room, iPad in hand, capturing Starla for a tutorial of Minecraft. They sat on the couch listening as the narrator, in a toneless voice, depicted it as a three-dimensional sandbox game with no specific goals to accomplish. "This allows the players a large amount of freedom in choosing how to play it." The game world consists of "blocks" representing materials such as dirt, stone, tree trunks, water, and lava and the players move these objects around to build things in a world divided into deserts, snowfields, jungles, each with terrain that includes mountains, forests, and caves.

"Minecraft follows a day and night cycle where players encounter passive nonplayer characters called mobs, such as cows, pigs, and chickens during the daytime," the narrator added.

Starla concluded his tone could induce a hypnotic state, but the description of the hostile mobs that appear during the night, spiders, skeletons, zombies, and an exploding creature called a creeper that sneaks up on the players, would test the resolve of any Stephen King fan. Margo noticed Starla biting her thumbnail knowing that a spate of worry over this game's content might be the culprit. "I checked and Minecraft is age-appropriate for seven-year-old children, especially those with creative minds like our Gabe. And parental controls to alter the settings are available. You okay with that?"

Before she could answer a car pulled into the driveway with a ballyhoo of horn honking. Gabe scurried to the door hollering, "Big Pop and Daddy are home. Willa come on...come on everybody...we hafta sing our song." Patrick opened the passenger door helping Matt out of the car. He leaned on his cane managing a demure smile while looking like a comet pulled from orbit. Gabe, taking control of the Daddy's-home celebration took center stage with Willa.

The song and dance duo began sidestepping in unison before breaking out in song. "Ready...One and two and three....

Daddy—Daddy—we're glad you're home.
Cuz if you weren't, we'd be all alone....
ABCD, chickadee boom.
Daddy—Daddy—we're glad you're home.
Uh-huh....Oh yeah....
ABCD chickadee boom....
Pat the dog....Feed the cat....Hug the folks....
We're glad your home.

Ta Da! The end."

"Wow, guys, what a reception. You're awesome," Matt said embracing his children before they romped back into the house. Margo moved forward to meet her son's open arms. With his head buried in her shoulder, she gently rubbed Matt's back while speaking soft- words of comfort hoping something might unfasten the deadbolt on the serenity gate padlocked when Summer died.

Gathering his composure, he pulled away from Margo sniffling, "I think I'm ready to go inside now and you need to change your blouse."

Starla opened the door for them teasing, "Don't I get a hug from my hunky brother-in-law?"

"We wouldn't want your boyfriend to get jealous, now would we?"

Patrick chimed in, "He wears a uniform if I'm not mistaken."

"Stop it you two. Conner is investigating this case and he adores Gabe. End of story."

Matt elbowed his Dad saying, "The lady doth protest too much, methinks."

"And you read *Hamlet* when?" baited Starla.

"Willie and I spent a heap of time together in college," countered Matt.

Starla, pressing her lips tightly desperately trying not to laugh, reveled in the flicker of Matt's sense of humor that had escaped. Once anchored in his recliner, he surveyed the scene in the living room, realizing the new definition of home was being played out in front of him. Willa and Gabe huddled in front of the television to watch the early rounds of season seven of *America's Got Talent* where judges, Howard Stern, Sharon Osbourne, and Howie Mandel, commented on a variety of contestants including a clogging dance troupe, a mariachi band, parrot trainer, and several singers and comedians. One of the acts featuring dog tricks prompted Dude to howl while pacing back and forth in front of the set. Halle, curled up on Matt's lap, opened one eye at the disturbance. Patrick sat on the couch reading the newspaper. Margo finished preparing dinner and Starla set the table for six. With the family congregated, an aura of intimacy engulfed the scene as the small talk eddied between the courses. Starla insisted she should be the one to move to a hotel instead of the elder Mackies. Matt contended no one should have to move as he would be comfortable sleeping on the couch or in the recliner. Patrick played his *paterfamilias* card effectively arguing he stole a march on everyone because he was the oldest and the wisest manly man among his tablemates. Margo declined to challenge the imperial edict issued by her husband, tilting her head to one side in wonderment as to what part of his psyche harbors this minutia.

Gabe and Willa, ignoring the adults, giggled through a spaghetti slurping contest resulting in their faces looking as though they had developed the measles. Table etiquette, for that evening at least, curtsied to the entertainment value of two children able to cope with sorrow, while inadvertently lightening the load for the rest of the family. Margo used a wet washcloth to remove the red splotchy contest evidence from the children's faces while Starla refilled their milk glasses. Patrick, as a toast to Matt's homecoming, poured an after-dinner cocktail into four stemless tumblers. "I bought this for a special occasion and now we have one. The owner of the liquor store raved about how it helps digestion. An Italian Barolo wine soaked in cinnamon, coriander, mint, and vanilla has gotta be tastier than popping Pepto-Bismol tablets, and as they say in the romance language, it's *eccellente* with chocolate, which I'm told is our *pièce de résistance* tonight."

Matt cleared his throat and raised his glass. "A round of applause for my bilingual dad. Big Pop is full of surprises. Here's to the love in our hearts. The Mackies love strong, long, and for all time. *Salute*...and before I drink all of this, I need to know who volunteers to put me to bed."

Gabe jumped out of his chair bringing his right hand up to his eyebrow. "Daddy, who're we saluting?"

A wide grin emerged across Matt's face. "Come here, doodlebug. In Italy when they toast something or someone, they say *Salute* instead of cheers."

Gabe scratched his head and wrinkled his nose before patting Matt on the knee. "It's okay, Daddy, I know you got your brain hurt but we're not in Italy...we're still in New York."

Willa chimed in, "Gabriel, duh...I think he knows that...it's because we had spaghetti for dinner, like they do in Italy."

"You're both right...and thanks for reminding me how smart you are. This dessert might be too pretty to eat, but let's give it a shot."

Patrick polished off the remnants of Gabe's brownie before clearing the table. He and Margo looked like a skillful assembly line scraping plates, rinsing the dishes, and loading the dishwasher. "You outdid yourself tonight."

"Thanks, I'll take that with a grain of smile," she hummed.

"Isn't that supposed to be a grain of salt?"

"Not according to my mom...she put her own twist on the tired cliché. She called it God's pearls of wisdom."

Willa and Gabe scurried off to the couch instantly immersed in their iPads. Matt's eyes involuntarily drifted shut while stifling a yawn. Starla laid her hand on his causing him to jolt to attention. "I'm sorry. Are you all right?"

"I'm all in but for my shoestrings. I need to get the kids to bed before I fall over."

"Matt, just kiss them goodnight. Your folks and I got this."

Without argument Matt retired to his bedroom. Through the open drapes behind the nightstand, moonlight pouring through shadowy leaves fell haphazardly on the plastic bag full of shattered memories of his wife. He sat down on the bed, a dark silent gaze spreading over his face. Opening the bag released the flowery scent of licorice and violets—Summer's signature perfume, Lolita Lempicka. He remembered she always said the aroma reminded her of childhood lullabies, fairies, and magic kingdoms. Matt buried his face in the tattered polo shirt she was wearing that day inhaling the faint trail of his lost love.

Starla, with Gabe and Willa engaged in their evening routines and Matt calling it a night, urged Margo and Patrick to check into the hotel before it gets any later. "Get a good night's sleep and we'll see you in the morning. I've got some ideas for Summer's memorial service I'd like your opinion on."

"I've been dreading bringing that up, but we do need to take care of this as soon as possible for everyone's sake," said Margo.

Suitcases in hand and goodnights spread all around they were almost out the door when shattering noises escaped from behind the closed doors of their son's bedroom. Patrick dropped his bags sprinting to Matt's door, knocking before sticking his head in. Slivers of glass covered the top of the dresser, fragments scattered around and on top of Matt's walking cane.

"Son, are you all right?"

Matt looked up into his father's eyes, his face sketched in sorrow. "No," he said. "I can't breathe without Summer, Dad," his voice breaking with every word. Patrick sat on the bed rocking his only child in his arms as a paroxysm of sobbing fueled by the lonely tone of his aching heart offered an acute silhouette of Matt's loss. An hour passed before his body uncoiled and suddenly the bungee cord stretching between mental collapse and physical lassitude slackened. Patrick laid Matt's head on the pillow, removed his shoes, covering him with the comforter draped over the oversized wicker Papasan chair next to the window. He retrieved Matt's cane, leaning it on the nightstand beside the bed, inching by the dresser on his way out delaying the cleanup until the next day. Margo and Starla were seated in the breakfast nook when Patrick peered in.

"What on earth happened in there?" Margo inquired.

He ran his fingers through his hair before commenting, "Matt's asleep now, but the magnitude of Summer's death just beat him up. He cried until the well dried up."

"Is he hurt?"

"Only his heart."

"What was all that noise?"

"He must have hurled his cane. The dresser mirror is shattered. Starla, promise you'll leave the broken glass to me in the morning, but I think the missus and I should get checked into the hotel."

The hush inside the car as the Mackies drove away felt weighted, their thoughts residing inside a vast buried chamber, anchored in place by self-reflection. Margo crossed and uncrossed her legs, smoothed and re-smoothed her blouse under the confines of the seatbelt while Patrick tapped his fingers on the steering wheel. She turned to the profile of her husband of over forty years, his sideburns and swept back hair reminding her of a fresh blanket of snow on a hilltop and his complexion, although wizened with time, still radiated a warmth as if kissed by the sun. Although seemingly absent in thought he turned to meet her gaze.

"What?"

"Nothing. . . ."

"I've seen that look before and have never known it to be nothing. So, fess up." Patrick rubbed the scar across the bridge of his nose, a trophy of the ferocity of playing the game of football and a visual reminder of the incident. In the dwindling minutes of a close game against the New York Jets, a charging defensive back trying to block his punt instead ran full force into him grazing his face with his cleats as they both tumbled to the turf. A penalty flag awarded the Bills another chance to win the game, but their punter was taken to the locker room to stitch up the damage.

Margo, seeing the ever-present sensitivity and calmness in his slate-colored eyes, recognized how capable he was of seeing clearly through any misty cauldron regardless of the density of the fog ahead. "Honey, I can't get past the enormity of what our son has lost . . . doesn't that put in perspective what we have together . . . I'm probably not making any sense."

"You are to me," he said reaching out to squeeze her hand as he pulled into the valet parking of the hotel.

A bellman carrying the luggage ushered them down the corridor lined with modern artwork and featuring a plush carpet, looking as if a can of blue-gray paint spilled causing the irregular patterns.

"That's livid," said Margo.

"She knows her colors," commented the bellman.

"That's good to know," ribbed Patrick. "I thought I was in trouble once again."

"Here we are. Mrs. Mackie, I hope you're pleased with the accommodations and don't hesitate to call the concierge if you need anything at all. Mr. Mackie, your suite is just a few doors down."

Patrick, after tipping the bellman, blew a kiss Margo's way and closed his door. Ten minutes later he answered the phone. She said, "Sweet Love . . . I need a spoon."

"You haven't called me that since high school. So, do you need a tablespoon or teaspoon?"

"Human."

A few minutes passed before Margo opened the door to find Patrick holding a fork and knife sporting a sheepish grin and dressed in pajamas and a bathrobe. "Where did you get the utensils?"

"Room service tray...no spoon though...so here's the Homo sapien version as requested."

"I couldn't be alone...not tonight."

10

Leaning on the Everlasting Arms

HOURS BEFORE NIGHT succeeded to dawn tiptoeing across the horizon, Starla sat alone with her thoughts surrounded by stacks of papers, the Dalai Lama's book, *The Art of Happiness* with pages earmarked with post-it notes, and an open King James Bible covering the breakfast nook table. Steam, spiraling from her coffee mug, presented a hypnotic backdrop as the murmur of Summer's life intruded on Starla's ability to find words to render the emptiness brought on by her death. The burden weighing profoundly in her heart faintly lifted with insights from the spiritual leader of Tibetan Buddhism who believed suffering can strengthen us by testing our faith, the result bringing us closer to our maker fundamentally and intimately. This fresh vision guided her thoughts, continuing until a passionate tribute to her sister filled the pages of her notebook. With the house still quiet, Starla prepared a fresh pot of coffee, heading upstairs to get ready for the rest of the day.

A ringing phone jolted the couple awake. A pleasant voice on the other end reminded them this was the requested wakeup call, offering the local weather forecast and hoping they have a joyous day. The married duo locked into each other's eyes lingering at the edge of uneasiness at last night's sleepover. Patrick cleared his throat contemplating the implications of the arrangements and ahead to any collateral damage caused by the impulse. Margo reached for his hand saying, "Thank you for coming to my rescue and before you say anything, this was not a mistake…we've been soul mates for a long time, but.…"

"Before you say any more, I want this to be a beginning point for us to solve our differences and I'm willing and able to be patient—so how 'bout a quickie to start the morning off."

"You're incorrigible, Patrick Mackie…can't you ever be serious?"

"When necessary. I'm just teasing you, Margo. I get we have a lot of work to do to repair our differences. But I'll be your spoon anytime day or night."

"I'm hungry and need some coffee…the room service menu looks wonderful."

With a peck on her cheek he said, "I'm going to trek back to my room to shower. I'll meet you back here in a half hour for breakfast and then we can head over to Matt's."

When Patrick and Margo arrived at the house the noise level rivaled a birthday party of preschoolers armed with plastic kazoos. The front door was open, their calls of hello absorbed within the commotion. Halle with a stuffed treasure secured in her mouth rounded the corner into the foyer followed by Gabe in hot pursuit who almost upended his grandparents. Dude followed the chase barking feverishly at being excluded from the game.

"So much for a quiet morning. Our son certainly couldn't sleep through all this," said Margo.

"Only if he was in a coma. Make a run for the kitchen while the path is clear."

Matt and Starla, in consultation at the breakfast nook table, looked up when Patrick and Margo appeared. "Mom, Dad…we didn't hear you come in. Welcome to the asylum."

"Would you like some coffee?" offered Starla. "We've had breakfast, but I can scramble some eggs and we've got English muffins."

"Thanks. We had room service at the hotel, but more caffeine is needed. Keep your seat, I know where it is," said Margo.

Patrick pulled up a chair next to his son searching his face for any signs of last night's torment. Matt said, "Dad, don't worry. I'm okay. Thanks for helping me. Starla and I are working on the memorial service for Summer. Wait 'til you hear her plans."

Cars snaked along Delaware Avenue, sunbeams carving slivers of daylight through the leaves of variegated maple trees lining the path to Trinity Episcopal where the memorial service for Summer Mackie was scheduled for eleven o'clock. Mourners from all walks of the family's life—neighbors, friends, colleagues, and victims moved by Summer's unyielding quest to right all wrongs mixed with plainclothes law enforcement officers interested in who might be in attendance in this high-profile case—filled over half of the eight-hundred pews.

The steel casket, adorned with a pearl white cross, occupied the center aisle in front of the altar, the nectarous scent of lilacs blended with the creamy bouquet of lilies embodying first love and hope eternal.

After everyone was seated, the choir tenderly harmonized the poignant lyrics of "Footprints in the Sand," ... *I'll carry you* ...as Father Ireland waited at the raised pulpit for the family to be seated. An usher escorted the Mackie family to the front-row pew—Matt, steadying himself with a cane; Starla holding Willa's hand; and Matt's parents with Gabe in tow.

"The shortest verse in the Bible, yet one that holds such great power, allows us to see straight into the very heart of our God whose heart beats for us. John 11:35 tells us, 'Jesus wept.' With those words we know He understood extreme sorrow. He wept. He hurt. He grieved. He experienced loss. He felt compassion. He understood this path of suffering. With all the tragedy in today's world no single gunman, no hand of a terrorist, no disease or cancer, no tragic accident, or even the final days of our old age can ever separate us from the love and sheer grace of God. For He has set eternity in our hearts. We are set free by His power. One final breath here on earth is just the beginning of life evermore. We never have to fear. Let us pray. May God's comfort and peace cover all those who grieve. He weeps and is with us for those who are suffering great loss right now. And He's here. Still. With us. Close. In the Mighty name of Jesus and the name of Summer Sullivan Mackie. Amen."

Starla slid out of her seat clutching a notebook in her hand as she walked to the lectern. Father Ireland stepped aside, mouthing something in her ear before taking his seat behind the altar. Bright sunshine poured through the La Farge and Tiffany stained-glass windows casting a heavenly illumination of rainbow colors on the chancel walls as though the spiritual lives depicted in the artwork sent a message of hopefulness into an otherwise somber day.

"If you're wondering how Father Ireland just made me smile... he said, 'Just breathe.' I'm going to try. For those of you who don't know me, I'm Starla, Summer's older sister. From the looks of this crowd I was not the only one whose life was shaped by this re-markable woman. I'm certain she would demand our memory of her to be a happy one, leaving an afterglow of serenity for a life well done. Her legacy will shine despite her physical absence—leaving her daughter, Willa, and son, Gabriel, in the trusted care of the love of her life, Matthew."

"Our parents, Dillion and Colleen Sullivan, fled Northern Ireland in 1968 during the *Troubles,* the conflict centering on whether to remain a part of the UK or leave to join a united Ireland. I was two when we settled in a large Irish community in South Buffalo. Dad joined the apprentice program of Ironworkers Local No. 6 while Mom took in ironing to help pay the bills. Summer was born on July 24, 1975. She never just walked...she was always sashaying with a flair for the dramatic at an early age, adoring the spotlight so much she created her own paracosm full of singers, dancers, and magicians. It was no wonder when she saw her first Broadway show, *Ragtime,* her fantasy world premiered on that same stage, feeling empathy and adoration for the actor, Bradley Anderson, whose gut-wrenching portrayal of rejection was aimed directly at her heartstrings. Twen-ty-one-year old Summer married her Broadway actor in the fall of 1996, their daughter, Willa, born three years later. The combination of being a new father and his obsessively intense personality led to a divorce with Summer and Willa moving back to Buffalo."

"Matt would probably rather tell us the rest of the story, but

A KIND OF HUSH

since he's still mending from the fall, I'll summarize the happiest part of Summer's life—beginning when she pranced through the doors of Seasons LXX, the only woman in a group of men, sidled up to the bar, batted her long eyelashes at her future husband, ordered a tequila shot, and commenced to dominate the billiards table with her skill—a talent drummed into us by our dad who was bent on making sure his girls would be able to hold our own in anyone's world. I must admit I was more interested in music than racking billiard balls and chalking pool cues, but I guess we all have our individual talents. Matt and Summer married in 2002, he adopted Willa and they added son Griff the next year, and another lad Gabe completed their family in 2005."

"Our families have suffered great loss in the last decade, beginning with the deaths of our parents. A heartbreaking accident took the life of Summer and Matt's six-year-old son Griff...and now...our beloved Summer." Starla bowed her head grasping the lectern with both hands strangling on the emotion welling in her throat. Time became immaterial as she fought to regain her composure. Suddenly she felt an inpouring of support as Matt wrapped his arm around her shoulders.

"Folks, I think Starla just quit breathing. So, it's Matthew to the rescue. She just conveyed all the love she can muster into this tribute to her sister, her words drawn from the depth of her soul. We all feel a part of us has been yanked away and it's easy to ask if the price we pay for life is just too high. I'm guilty of falling into that mindset, but I know my wife would find a way to make my life miserable if I didn't look at the big picture—the fact that two young lives depend on me. How can I let Willa and Gabe down? I can't. So, let's cry until we're empty and take our anger out on a punching bag...let's dive to the bottom of the pity barrel and when we emerge, we'll find a way to take two steps forward without taking four steps backward. We all have been given a gift—the gift of life—so as Lee Ann Womack's song says, *I hope you dance.*"

Starla and Matt, clutching each other paused, gently patting Summer's casket before returning to their seats. Father Ireland motioned for everyone to stand as the choir sang "Amazing Grace," before leading them in a final prayer.

95

"We know there are no guarantees in life. The Mackie family and everyone here confesses their need for you today. We need your grace to cover every broken place, every wound, every heartache. We need hope restored. Forgive us our doubts in face of tragedy—as we know healing must be found first in you. We come to you because we are hurting. You stand as our lighthouse. In Jesus' name, Amen."

"The family invites you to join the procession to Forest Lawn Cemetery for the interment of Summer Sullivan Mackie."

The crowd filed out of the church, some dabbing the corner of their eyes, others detached and staring straight ahead, uncertain how to help a family torn and unable to give into the tenuousness of life. Matt emerged from the church, removing his sport coat, rolling up the sleeves of his oxford shirt before putting on his sunglasses. Starla and Willa remained inside, both numbed by a hollowness—the air too thick to swallow, each waiting for the other to gather the might to move forward.

Willa touched Starla's hand, her voice quavering as she said, "Where's the baby?"

"Oh...Willa, the baby died when your mom died."

"I guess I thought there'd be another casket...Aunt Starla, do I have to go to the cemetery? I want to go home. My ribs are hurting."

Starla studied her niece's face. "Yes, sweetie, you need to be with the family."

"I've never been there. Mom didn't ever go, either."

"This is the cemetery where Griff is...and now his mom and his unborn brother. I'll be right beside you."

Margo opened the church doors for her husband as he held Gabe to his chest, the little boy's face buried in his granddad's shoulder blade as if he had lost the pacifier of boyhood. Gabe's head jerked abruptly in the direction of a noise.

"What's the matter, buddy?"

"I heard my Roy Rogers you brought me."

"Your cap gun? Where?" He followed where Gabe was pointing, locking into the angular face of a man dressed in a tight mortician-quality black suit whose eyes, as arctic as a Siberian winter, were the kind that would not invite an exchange of words.

Gabe's legs tightened around Patrick's waist. "Don't be scared. Big Pop's got you."

"I heard that sound at the park... *click-click-click*... when Mommy died."

Patrick searched the crowd outside the church finally catching Conner's eye, waving him over to share what Gabe had said and what he had seen. Margo shepherded the children inside the family limousine while Starla and Matt waited for Summer's casket to be loaded into the white hearse before joining the rest of them. The funeral procession escorting Summer to her final resting place was led by the Erie County Sheriff's Department. Conner, riding shotgun with the driver of the Mackie's black town car battled a plethora of feelings, ranging from anger that a spiritual observance of a human life would be subjected to the immorality of a merciless criminal to the disbelief of Victor flaunting his illusiveness in plain view. The atmosphere in the backseats dangled from outrage to bereavement and anxiety as each occupant struggled to rectify the frailty of a world that could shatter with each turn of the car's steering wheel.

The procession entered Forest Lawn Cemetery welcomed by the electronic ringing of the Oishei Memorial Bell from the Paris Exposition in 1867. The property, with over two hundred professionally landscaped acres, was home to thousands of residents including U.S. presidents, foreign royalty, and veterans of every conflict since the Revolutionary War. It was also an important arboretum replete with three thousand trees and two hundred permanent birds nesting in specially designed houses located throughout the grounds. The motorcade wound along the paths coming to a stop by Mirror Lake surrounded by flowering trees and starring a bronze statue of a little girl standing on an island in the water dedicated to the memory of all children.

Summer's coffin, removed from the hearse, was placed on the straps above the burial site awaiting the family to make their way to the front row seats. Matt lingered at the grave of his son, Griff (Boo) Mackie, using his finger to trace the epitaph inscribed on his headstone... *So young, so loved, so soon.* His shoulders bowed trying to regain composure, but the depth of his pain was vibrant with the colors of grief. He stood motionless until Gabe grabbed his hand. "Come on, Daddy. I'll help you." After being led to his seat by his young son, Matt inhaled trying to concentrate on Father Ireland's words.

"This incredible daughter, sister, wife, and mother had light in her soul and beauty inside and out. Her legacy lives in everyone she touched. She has challenged us to carry on with purpose and grace. Let us pray. Almighty God into your hands we commend Summer Sullivan Mackie in sure and certainty of resurrection to eternal life through Jesus Christ our Lord. Amen. This body we commit to the ground—earth to earth, ashes to ashes, dust to dust."

He invited mourners to share a story or remembrance of the deceased. A dozen victims of sexual assault, both women and men wearing teal awareness ribbons, stood arm-in-arm with one spokesperson, Judith Sands, echoing all their voices attributing their productive lives to Summer's unflinching dedication to the preservation of justice. "She told us our bodies were crime scenes...just like those surrounded by yellow tape...holding key pieces of evidence of a crime committed and she would find the truth. Mrs. Mackie said that truth would heal our internal wounds, the scars would be symbols of a fight won as we move the blame elsewhere. She gave us all a reason to believe our lives were just beginning...not ending."

Father Ireland shook the hands of each victim. "Thank you for your courage. She would be proud! The family is grateful for each of you here today. You are all invited to a private celebration of life at Seasons LXX at 6:00 P.M. this evening. There will be plenty to eat and drink and, in her honor, you'll witness an exhibition by some of the premier nine-ball billiard players in the country."

Starla looked into Matt's glazed eyes circled with unrest and filled with pain, but unable to shelve her own concerns. She grumbled that Willa had refused to attend the graveside service, whining about a headache and being frightened of "her creepy stalker," staying in the car with the driver. "I need a few minutes of deep breathing alone with my sister to calm the anger I feel...Willa is complicated, but right now I see a disrespectful bitch. It's her terms or no terms. Matt, I'm sorry. This is not what you need to hear right now."

He squeezed her hand. "We'll try to figure out what's going on with our teen but not today. I'm bled dry as I'm sure you are, too. We'll wait for you in the car—no hurry."

The funeral home's staff backed away granting Starla privacy to say farewell. She fiddled with the flowers covering Summer's casket before kneeling beside it. Speaking in hush tones to the sister she adored, she confessed her fear of crumbling under the millstone of responsibility. *I have to be strong for Matt, Gabe, and Willa and yet my loss is as devastating as theirs. Please guide me.* She smiled through the ache of hoping her beloved Thomas might be singing a favorite tune while Summer danced a jig. *If I picture you and Mom and Dad sitting on a porch swing while Boo finds the right pieces to fit into a heavenly puzzle, I might be all right. Talk to me often. I love you Summer.*

The only intrusion to the quietness of the landscape ensued when one by one mourners departed the gravesite after paying their respects. Starla stopped for one final glimpse as the staff lowered Summer into the ground. When she turned around, Conner was waiting for her. A collective moment of genuineness flowed between them, Starla noticing more profound lines around his eyes as if nurturing a roadmap of empathy. He opened the car door, extending his hand to help her inside, his kindness acknowledged by her slight nod.

A raw numbness lingered inside the family's car. Outside, the day that began cloudless turned pensive as prowling clouds lurked in the distance and a light mist peppered the windshield as they followed the road away from Summer. Scalloped shadows reflected in the nearby lake and a tour around the numerous statues provoked excitement from Gabe. They passed a bronze sculpture of a woman in a robe, her right arm extended upward, her expectant face tilted toward the heavens surrounded by a multi-figure composition of eight human figures.

"Daddy, I want to do that."

"What, son?"

"Make angels out of metal 'cause that's what Mommy is now."

11

I'm Moving On

VICTOR KURTZ SCURRIED to his car after being spotted at Summer's memorial service amplifying his brinkmanship by his self-proclaimed ability to disguise his appearance. His mother, as a former librarian, relished the works of Charlotte Bronte introducing him to the antics of Rochester when he dressed up as a Gypsy woman in her novel *Jane Eyre*. What he failed to remember was the vocal tics caused by his Tourette's disease was like waving a red flag at a bull. Victor left his identifiable white Oldsmobile 88 in a parking lot of a closed automobile dealer, hot-wiring his new home-sweet-home, a 1975 black Buick Century GS. With a trunk loaded with clothes, he tossed his suit jacket in the pile, tucked his hair under a black braided Fedora, covered his eyes with cat eye dark sunglasses and joined the long processional from Trinity Episcopal to where Summer would be laid to rest. He wasn't bold enough to join the gravesite ceremony, dawdling within audible range beside a monument to another cemetery resident. As the procession left the burial site, he stood on the bridge overlooking Serenity Falls, genuflecting as the family limousine passed by, an act not lost on Conner who peered over the rims of his shades mumbling under his breath, *Who does that?*

Victor, puffed up like a male red howler monkey, flounced back to his car. He relished a heightened sense of invincibility after recording another notch in his cat and mouse game with law enforcement. Two weeks ago, he had answered a flyer for the Lust for Dust Cleaning Company, specialists in commercial sanitation in need of a temporary employee. A fortunate stroke of serendipity arrived in an emergency call from Seasons LXX in need of services to ready the establishment for an event. He had just enough time to change into his navy work uniform and report for work as Frances Carson. He parked his car in the lot across from the company's Clinton Street office, taking a final look in the rearview mirror before reporting to duty...beard cover neutralizer applied under his mother's alabaster foundation, a special razor used to thin his eyebrows, brown contact lenses, neutral lip gloss, and an auburn wig styled in a long braid down his back, the company's logo ball cap firmly planted on his head. Satisfied at his feminine appearance, old Victor posing as the new Ms. Carson strode across the street.

"Since you have your own transportation meet us at Seasons LXX in an hour. The owner is throwing a shindig in honor of his wife that just died. We need to be done and out of there by 4:30," instructed his supervisor.

Ms. Carson nodded, offered a thumbs up and turned to leave. "Boy are you a quiet one. I like that in a worker. I've got enough *kibitzers* on the crew." The comment was met with a cheeky wink and then he added, "And, oh, Frances, please tell me your temperament doesn't match your hair color if you know what I mean."

Victor parked his car around the corner from Seasons LXX ensuring he would not be interrupted later. If there was ever a sign that this was a good time to purchase a lottery ticket, it was today. His motive for taking the cleaning job was money and the reason for the disguise as a woman was to hide in plain sight from the police, but this Plan A provided an opportunity to implement a Plan B. His assignment was to clean and sanitize the bathrooms adjacent to the restaurant, sports bar, the facilities servicing the arcade and outdoor patio. He worked solo, quietly, and efficiently until everything was as clean as a hound's tooth. The rest of the cleaning crew finished their assignments, packed up the equipment, and loaded back into the company van. Frances Carson exchanged the uniform for her paycheck—in cash—gesturing farewell to her fellow workers as she walked to her car where she retrieved a large tote bag before striding back inside the Mackie family business.

———⊗∞⊗———

Arriving back at Trinity Episcopal, the Mackie family gathered in the vestibule of the church for a briefing from Sheriff McAlister. He instructed one of his deputies to escort Gabe and Willa to the Christ Chapel while he addressed the adults. "Kids, there's juice and homemade chocolate chip cookies for you next door. We won't be long here. You remember Axl. He helped you at the park that day. He can tell you all about the last bad guy he nabbed. I promise you won't be bored."

"This is just an update on Mr. Kurtz. We have verified he was at the memorial service today as suspected. He left his calling card—boxes of candy hearts—in the collection plates, and he must have gone somewhere that has public computers—maybe the library—at any rate he offered his condolences online saying he was sorry *Starla quit breathing*. And, of course, there's Gabe's testimony of hearing the clicking noises just like the day his mom died. He's obviously feeling brash, but he will slip up, I promise. And, I'm almost positive he was at the cemetery...on the bridge as we were leaving."

"Of course, we'll be all over Seasons LXX this evening, but be on the lookout for anyone suspicious," added Conner.

After leaving the church, the family returned home for a few hours of rest before heading to Seasons LXX. Patrick and Margo offered to stay home if Matt was uncomfortable with the children attending the celebration, but it was unanimously decided they would be safer at the restaurant with the law enforcement presence. Plus, neighborhood friends and classmates would be attending, and it could be cathartic to be around groups their own age, especially for Willa who seems to blossom in the company of her *besties*.

Conner and the sheriff briefed the officers assigned to the evening's event stressing diligence in following up on anyone or anything questionable. "It's going to be crowded. If Victor is there, his vocal tics might be undetected with the noise so we may have to rely on instinct and his physical description, although he's probably in disguise, so hair and eye color will be irrelevant but take notice of his hands as he does have those candy heart quotes on the knuckles of his index fingers. Beyond that he is slightly built and about Conner's height—or fun-sized as Deputy Boyle calls it. Half of you in uniform will be stationed around the inside perimeter including the billiards room, the other half on the patio and in the arcade. Officers from the Buffalo Police Department's Districts A and E will be in plain clothes mingling with the guests. Pay special attention to Willa and Gabe Mackie as Victor might approach the kids. If there aren't any questions, we'll see you at 5:00."

With the destination less than two miles away, Patrick chauffeuring Margo and Matt left the house at 5:45 P.M. driving south to the waterfront restaurant and sports bar located in the Erie Basin Marina that he opened in 1995 after leaving the Bills organization. Starla followed in her car with Willa and Gabe. Upon arrival at Seasons LXX they pulled into the reserved spaces near the front door. With the parking lot near capacity and a ruckus emanating from the outdoor terrace, the celebration of life for Summer Mackie was off to a roaring start. Conner met Starla as she came through the door with Gabe and Willa whisking them off to the arcade which was closely monitored by parents and security. Tina, upon spotting Matt, rushed to embrace him fighting back a torrent of emotion for her long-time friend and partner.

"I owe you big time," he said.

"Some of us just know what it means to be a friend. You would have done the same for me."

"I hope you never have to go through anything like this, but you're right, I'd be Johnny-on-the-spot."

"There's lots of people here to see you...go mingle. I've got work to do."

Matt slowly made his way through the gathering accepting condolences and heartfelt remembrances of how Summer affected their lives. He spotted his mom and dad chatting with a couple he knew well. His dad and Jim Kelly had been with the Buffalo Bills during the same time...Jim the quarterback and later a Hall of

Famer, Dad an ex-punter and kicking coach. Jim and his wife, Jill, paid a visit to Matt and Summer shortly after Griff's death. They had buried their eight-year-old son, Hunter, a few years earlier and knew first-hand the agony of losing a child. The visit helped Summer realize that although the loss of Griff was monumental, it would get more manageable in time and that sunshine would again brighten the Mackie household. *And, now here we are again.*

Victor, still in the persona of Frances Carson sans the navy uniform, rode the wave of guests pouring into Seasons LXX, her gaze ping-ponging to avoid any direct eye contact. She drew in a deep breath trusting the newly prescribed antiseizure medicine, Topamax, to work keeping the Tourette's vocal tics in check. However, a fluttering stomach and a mind visiting the worse-case scenario of being discovered, prompted her to beeline to the women's restroom behind the pool tables where she had stashed a sign announcing the bathroom temporarily out of order. After hanging the notification on the door and locking it, she unloaded her tote bag filled with necessities for the transformation of Victor from Frances Carson to Samantha Franks. Padded panties and silicone breast plates transformed a slightly built man into a Rubenesque woman, and the addition of a baby bump prosthetic completed the illusion. Donning the platinum blonde wig with bangs covering the forehead with one stray piece falling over the corner of the left eye and fusing with thickened lashes, puckering the lips to make sure mother's Jungle Red 4ever lipstick was not smeared, covering both knuckles with concealer, pulling on the long kimono floral maternity dress...and *voila*, Samantha was ready for her close-up.

Margo, after excusing herself from the conversation with another group of longtime Buffalo friends, zigzagged through the billiard room heading to the restroom to discover the out of order sign on the door, visiting the one in the arcade instead. The area was saturated with boisterous children of all ages playing air hockey, bumper pool, and arcade games. Gabe, standing on a stool to reach the controls of Pac-Man, was so engrossed in providing his friends a tutorial of how the game was played, his grandmother's presence was unseen. "Here's what you do...see all those dots in that maze...you gotta eat all of them, but be careful of these four colored ghosts…but you get extra points for eating the big blinking dots—they're called power pellets and turn the ghosts blue."

Margo decided not to interrupt Gabe and his captive audience, electing to find Tina to report the bathroom issue. Matt, seated at the bar, waved at his mom as she made her way through the thirsty guests lined two-deep behind the bar stools while Starla helped Tina with the drink orders. "Matt, you look a little pale. What's wrong?"

"A bit overwhelmed at the attendance, but happy so many loved my wife. It's more than the free food and booze."

"It is an outpouring, isn't it?"

"Have you seen the kids?"

"Yes, Gabe is showing everyone the art of winning at Pac-Man and Willa is huddled in the corner of the arcade with her girlfriends. She waved at me when I came out of the restroom. Which reminds me that I need to tell Tina the ladies' bathroom in the billiards room is out of order."

"I'll tell her for you. Your job is working the room," he joshed.

When Tina came up for air, Matt informed her of the restroom issue. There was not a sign on the door and upon investigating inside, the toilets flushed, the soap and paper towel dispensers were full, and the air hand dryers worked. The only thing out of place was a mascara wand left on the counter.

Samantha circulated among the other guests ordering a bottle of water from a waitress serving the patio. A radish pink and orange sherbet sunset reflecting in the waters of Lake Erie took center stage telegraphing a sense of cordiality amongst the crowd. She maneuvered unnoticed through the throngs like water filtering through the cracks in a sidewalk with each step bringing overweening mannerisms to her mission. Samantha, sipping her water gingerly as not to disturb any facets of her makeover, moved into the arcade area locating Willa and friends clustered in one corner while children of all ages capered around the room creating ear-splitting noise levels as if announcing a battle cry of youthful stimulation. Groups of parents either leaning against the walls or seated on couches attempted to converse with each other while keeping an eye on the youngsters and their activities. Samantha gulped down breaths trying to stay quiet and calm when Gabe looked up locking into her eyes before turning back to his game with a little boy from his class. Patrick arrived in the arcade, much to the delight of his grandson, insisting he and Willa eat dinner before the billiard exhibition.

Gabe said goodbye to his Pac-Man pal, leaving in the arms of his grandfather with his sister following close behind. "Big Pop, there was this lady that came in the room. Ya know when GoGo puts that finger on her mouth for us to shush. She did that. I got butterflies in my tummy."

"Gabe, it's probably your tummy saying how hungry you are."

"No...but, Big Pop, I got one of those *uh-oh* feelings that Mommy always talked about."

"Okay, little guy...we'll check it out right after dinner. We don't want any big worries going on in your head."

The fortunate timing of the Mackie children's departure was crucial to Samantha's plan because with them out of the area, the focus of the police officers stationed there should be less intense.

Samantha scanned the room before moving closer to the young boy Gabe had been playing Pac-Man with. "Hi. I used to play this with my son. What's your name?"

"Derek."

"Hi, Derek. I'm Samantha. Your folks here?"

"No. I'm with my sitter."

"Where is she?"

"She said she'd be right back."

"Are you hungry? My baby is kicking so that means he's hungry for some chicken nuggets and fries. How about you?"

"A Happy Meal?"

"I love Happy Meals. Wanna come with me to get one?"

"No, you're a stranger."

"But we're not strangers...we're Pac-Man pals now. We'll be back before anyone notices we are gone. Okay?"

"I guess."

Samantha took Derek's hand saying, "I bet you'd like a vanilla ice cream cone too."

"Strawberry is my favorite."

12

Little Man

IN ANTICIPATION OF the exhibition of two of the world-re-nowned nine-ball champions, the billiards area of Seasons LXX overflowed. Pitted against each other was Earl "The Pearl" Strickland and Ewa Laurance, "The Striking Viking" and sports commentator for ESPN. "In honor of my wife who we secretly called Summer Shark, we're so grateful these outstanding players agreed to enter-tain us tonight. They'll play four racks and will lag to determine who breaks first—the closest to the top rail will have the honors."

Starla, amazed at the display of talent with a cue stick, thought of her sister's acumen with the same instrument and her dad's in-sistence on teaching the nuances of the sport to both girls. Having seen Summer in action she could appreciate the skill of these pro-fessionals and the fun they had competing.

Sheriff McAlister and Conner, also enjoying the exhibition, caught the eye of one of the deputies motioning to them. His face, flushed and drawn with a rising storm of concern, echoed his magnified arm movements as he spoke in thick undertones to his superiors. Starla, after accounting for Gabe and Willa's where-abouts, noticed as the Erie County Sheriff's Department hurried out of the billiard room. She slid past the rows of enthralled spec-tators finding a path to the arcade area where an officer attempted to calm a hysterical young woman whose face was a mask of terror, staring catatonically as if watching in numbed horror *The Girl Next Door* in real time.

"I told him not to move. I told him I had to go to the bathroom. He was playing Pac-Man with another little boy. The place was full of people—parents and kids—there's cops all over the place. How did this happen?"

"Ma'am, what is his name?"

"Derek Brighton. His parents are Alesha and Greg. Why are you just standing here? You've got to find him."

"Have you called his folks? Could they have picked him up? We need to rule that out before we go any further."

"I just spoke with them. They're on the way here."

"Can you describe him?"

"He's seven. Brown hair short on the sides and kinda spikey in the front, hazel eyes, and cute little freckles on his nose. Oh my God...what if something happens to him!"

"Height? Weight?"

"Well, he comes up about to my chin—four feet tall maybe and probably weighs forty-five pounds or so."

"Thank you, Miss...?"

"Abbott, Beth Abbott."

After briefing the other officers, he suggested Ms. Abbott take a seat and wait for Derek's parents to arrive. Sheriff McAlister radioed the information into headquarters instructing an Amber alert to be issued for the abduction of Derek Brighton. Conner motioned for Starla to join him. His gaze flitted around the room as if trying to land on anything that might make sense of this latest development while recapping the news. Although he avoided sharing his instinct that Victor Kurtz somehow had to be connected to this, Starla read the signs loud and clear. She said, "I thought he just liked little girls...if it's him maybe Derek will be safe."

Samantha, holding Derek's hand, briskly walked to the car, opening the passenger side door for him. "Mommy won't let me ride in the front seat," he said.

"Get in, Derek, let's get you buckled in," her tone hoarse and resolute.

Samantha shifted the car into gear pulling away from the curb arriving at the McDonald's on Niagara Street in less than twenty minutes. She looked at her watch, a rascally grin spreading across her face in anticipation of the frenzy playing out at Seasons LXX upon discovering Derek was missing. They entered the near empty restaurant just as a busload of teenagers fresh from a baseball tournament playfully pushed and shoved their way into the dining room for the game-day meal. Derek, sitting by himself, bounced his knees under the table while Samantha placed their order. In a few minutes she unloaded a tray with two Happy Meals, napkins, and extra ketchup. "Here we go, son."

"I wanna go home."

"Eat first."

"I'm not hungry."

"Derek, eat your nuggets or you don't get ice cream."

In a pitch that would shatter glass he wailed, "I said I'm not hungry."

Samantha watched as the reaction to his outburst was akin to spectating a car wreck with heads rubbernecking in their direction to witness the commotion. A spasm of irritation crossed her face, her eyes narrowing as she tried to find a way to calm the tension without calling more attention to them. "Ladies room then we'll go. All...all...right, okay...? Wait here." Samantha opened her purse, put a box of candy hearts on the table, caressed her belly and walked out of McDonald's.

The scene at Seasons LXX resembled a flash sale on the Saturday before Christmas. The Erie County Sheriff's Department coordinated the search from a command center set up in the back of the arcade, ordering officers to scour the property inside and out, the boardwalk and businesses along the lakefront for evidence of the abductor and the whereabouts of the missing child. Forensics bagged the mascara found in the bathroom and dusted for fingerprints, but outside that area would be useless due to the number of people attending the event honoring Summer Mackie. When Alesha and Greg Brighton hustled in the front door, Beth collapsed into the outstretched arms of the mother of the son she had neglected to keep safe, her gasping wails echoing the nightmare caused by her recklessness. Conner assured them every resource was being utilized, every available officer was combing the area, a nationwide alert was broadcast for Derek, and an APB has been issued on a person of interest.

"Derek will be found," Conner reassured the boy's parents.

"You know who might have done this?"

"We believe it might be the work of someone with a vendetta against the Mackie family."

"But why our son…he's just a classmate of Gabe's."

"We'll know more after we find him. Now, in the meantime, go home in case the abductor contacts you. This could be a ransom case. One of our officers will stay with you in the house in case this happens. Do you have any other children?"

"No…not yet. We're in the process of adopting a little girl from Guatemala."

"We'll need the name of the U.S. agency acting on your behalf with the attorney for the referred family agreeing to the adoption. These issues can be sticky. We'll look into this as it might be connected to Derek's abduction."

Greg, taking a breath and holding it, stopped short of directing his criticism to the person solely responsible for Derek's disappearance, but his forced smile and the cords pulsating in his neck told a different story. He and Alesha held opposite opinions of Beth Abbott. She was the daughter of one of Alesha's law partners whose ambition in life was to marry wealth, be society's darling, and exploit her carnal desires regardless of any moral code.

His wife dismissed her immaturity as fostered by the success of her high-profile parents, but Greg had seen first-hand her unscrupulousness when she paraded naked in front of him one night when Alesha was out of town. Granted, she possessed the whole package if a person was in the market for the fling of a lifetime. Her appeal however was lost on a man unwilling to upset the blissful apple cart he shared with his wife of twelve years.

Beth pleaded to wait at the Brighton's for news of Derek. Alesha said, "Of course" as they walked out of the arcade arm-in-arm. Greg remained silent following alongside the officer assigned to their home.

Tina and Matt were huddled at the bar when Sheriff McAlister approached. He requested the names of the distributors, food vendors, and cleaning crews...anyone who had access before opening for the private party tonight. Tina provided the list, pointing out to the sheriff the regular cleaning crew was not available, but they had recommended a twenty-four-hour-a-day company, Lust for Dust, who did a thorough job and were out of the building by 4:30. The sheriff handed the list to one of the deputies to follow up, and after speaking to the owner, passed on the following statement:

> We had the regular crew with the addition of one woman; Frances Carson filled in for an employee recovering from surgery. She was smallish, brown eyes, long braided red hair, very quiet. She met us at Seasons LXX, was assigned to the restrooms, did a good job, turned in her uniform and was paid in cash. I didn't see a car in the lot so don't know how she got there. And, unfortunately, the uniform has been laundered.

13

Before and After

THE GLITTER PATTERNS triggered by a dappled sunset looked like fairy lights strung on a Christmas tree as they danced across Lake Erie before being overtaken by nightfall. As Matt sat on a bar stool by the front door of Seasons LXX, illuminations brightening the darkness flickered from the marina's waterfront establishments. As guests filed past him on the way out, he thanked each person for helping celebrate Summer's life, accepting comforting words from friends and acquaintances until only the staff and Starla remained.

Margo and Patrick, escorted by a uniformed officer, whisked Gabe and Willa home shortly after Derek disappeared, both children succumbing to the gentle sway of the car's lullaby and an emotionally draining day until arriving home. With nighttime rituals set aside, Willa climbed into bed, kissed her grandmother on the cheek, falling into a dreamland before Margo shut the bedroom door. Patrick carried Gabe up the stairs into his room, helping him put on his pajamas and into bed. Halle rubbed her head on Gabe's hand before curling up on top of the stuffed animal shelf.

"Big Pop...do you think God is still up? I need to talk to Him."

"Okay, buddy...."

Gabe sat up, folding his hands in prayer, "Dear God, it's Gabriel Edward Mackie and I'm not mad at you. But now you have my

115

mommy and you hafta promise she's goin' to be one of your favorite angels and help others... 'cause that's what she did here. Amen."

Patrick bowed his head closing his eyes tightly in awe of the depth and simplicity of his young grandson's wisdom. "I'm sure He heard you, Gabe...now get some sleep and don't let the bed bugs bite." Gabe mumbled a few words before turning over and covering his head with the bedspread.

Dude, pacing back and forth in front of his empty food dish in the kitchen, whined with each unfruitful pass by Margo ignoring his pleas. Snaking in and out of her feet finally produced results as she scooped some food into his bowl, patting his head apologetically. Feeling lightheaded and remembering her meal was disrupted by the chaos at Seasons LXX about the missing boy, she opened a can of toasted almonds tossing them in a bowl with edamame pods, a dash of olive oil and sunflower seeds. Balancing a glass of wine in one hand and the high protein snack in the other, she waited in the breakfast nook for her husband to join her. He descended the stairs carrying a heaviness in his gait, a slouch visible in his shoulders, and the oomph of a deflated football.

"Let me fix you a scotch. You look like you've been crushed by a steamroller."

"I'll get it. It's Gabe. My God, he's so young and has the vision of a John Rockefeller. I'm not sure what you call it...but some people have strength of mind...his is of the soul."

Patrick, with drink in hand, kissed Margo on the cheek before sitting down at the table. She passed the snack bowl his way, and after scrutinizing the ingredients, he relented and tried a handful. "Not bad, but why ruin a bowl of almonds with some green veggie looking thingy?"

"You are aware that you're a food snob, right? The green thingy as you call it is chocked full of low-fat soy protein."

"I rest my case."

"Let me see if we have any Fritos and refried bean dip," she said with a wry grin and a dust of lighthearted sarcasm.

"Bean dip might be a little too heavy for this late in the evening. How about big scoop Fritos and ranch dressing?"

"Have I mentioned lately that you're hopeless?"

"Not in the last ten minutes."

Margo and Patrick slowed into a reflective undertone of intimacy sipping drinks and snacking on their respective munchies waiting for Matt and Starla to arrive from the restaurant. As if experiencing a simultaneous moment of recollection, the Mackies revisited a wedding reception on the south quad of the Hotel Henry for one of the tight end coaches on the Bills' football team who married the daughter of the general manager. It had been one of those affairs that was like entering an elegant Victorian armoire, the bride and groom both outfitted in white, the guests contrasting in all black. With most behaving with polished courtesy and refined behavior, it was as shocking as Pluto being demoted from a full-fledged planet to a dwarf planet, when the bridal toss melted into melee.

"What happened next was certainly gasp-worthy," said Margo.

"I can just see the bouquet in slow motion headed toward the bridesmaids when the recently divorced mother of the groom intercepted it in midair. She made an all-pro move on the flowers."

"I loved when the bride came to her rescue, embracing her new in-law, muttering something in her ear that made her happy. Bet the family reunions are going to be interesting."

"Speaking of family, if we're going to try to convince Matt to come home with us and he agrees, we'll have to tell him about our living arrangements and I'm not sure it's a good time to add any more to his plate," said Patrick.

"What living arrangements?"

The couple followed the voice to find their son and Starla standing just inside the kitchen door. "Matt, we didn't hear you come in. Did they find Derek?"

"No. What living arrangements?"

Patrick looked at Margo exhaling, "Your mother and I have been going through some things and we've separated for a little while so we could work through the issues."

"So, you've been living apart trying to work on things…for how long?"

"Matt, I know this is none of my business, but maybe we should save the interrogation for tomorrow. We're all exhausted and worried about that little boy," offered Starla.

"Mom, how long have you and Dad been separated?"

"A year. I'm living at The Murphy Hotel in town."

"I'm your only child and you chose not to tell me about this for a year. What the hell is wrong with you two?"

"That's enough, Matthew. I don't like the tone you're using with your mother."

"Fine, but you know what pisses me off? Being kept in the dark when it comes to the people that I love and that I thought loved each other. I lost my wife and now the relationship that I patterned my own life after was a lie."

"It has never been a lie and it's not a question of loving each other. That has never been an issue," implored Margo.

"I'm going to wait in the den for word on Derek and I'd like to be alone. Why don't you take off to your hotel...two rooms I suspect."

The chiming of the doorbell halted the discourse. Starla, looking into Conner's face for some positive news, saw a wave of relief in his expression. After joining the rest of the family seated in the den, he erased their fears by announcing that Derek was physically unharmed and at home. "The little boy willingly left with a pregnant woman named Samantha who promised him a McDonald's Happy Meal and strawberry ice cream. Evidently, Derek sensed something was wrong and when he made a scene at the restaurant, she abandoned him. The employees called us. As scary as it was, Derek was never in harm's way as Victor Kurtz, aka Samantha, was only making a statement. He was in our face once again with his bold actions. Earlier that day he was Frances Carson with the cleaning crew, then pregnant Samantha Franks at Seasons LXX...right under our noses."

"How can you be sure it was him?" posed a worried Margo.

"He gave Derek a box of candy hearts and he said *she* had kind of a stutter."

Throwing his hands up and in a stilted voice Patrick demanded, "When is this nut case going to be caught? Why can he torment all of us and all law enforcement can do is follow two steps behind his antics!"

"I realize how frustrating it has been for you, Mr. Mackie, but

I assure you we are using every avenue available to us to bring him in. I promise, he will screw up and when he does, it will be over for Victor Kurtz."

"Sounds like hollow promises, Deputy Boyle."

"Please...they're doing everything possible. There's no need to be rude," offered Margo.

"My dear wife has her typical Pollyanna answer to all that's wrong in the world."

"Mom, Dad...please take a breath. Conner, thank you for bringing us up to date. If you all will excuse me, I'm pretty spent so I'm going to bed." Matt closed his bedroom door needing some escape from the evening's marmalade dropper about his parents. He steadied himself on the dresser, pulling open the top drawer to find the bits and pieces of Summer's life residing in jewelry compartments. He examined her watch, the one she had coveted—a two-toned gold and stainless-steel Omega De Ville—the one he had surprised her with on no particular occasion—now with a shattered face from the fall. He twirled her gold wedding band examining the inscription, *For starters with love Matt.* They had recently chosen a halo setting encompassing his grandmother's diamond solitaire with micro-pave stones and a matching delicate wedding band extending around her finger. He closed his eyes firmly against a torrent of regrets and sadness upon opening a box that held a gold "baby feet" charm...for their unborn child. Summer always wore her gold rope-link mommy bracelet with three hearts, each engraved with her child's initial...W, G, and G. The latest charm, etched with the letter M, would be added after the birth of their son to be named Mack. A good night's sleep seemed as unthinkable as putting the past few weeks behind them, but when he climbed into bed every muscle in his body slackened as if a storm hewed a carvel-built vessel into planks setting them adrift in the sea.

Margo and Patrick, after saying goodnight to Starla and Conner, walked hand-in-hand to the car, each silently digesting the emotion of the evening. Their relationship, presumedly faded with time, now somehow felt fresh and unfinished like a deserted campfire with enough fiery hot embers to warrant a call to Smokey Bear. On the way through the lobby to their suites Margo said, "Do you think we should keep both rooms?"

"Yes."

Her eyes widen. "I thought we...I mean I hoped we had taken an important step."

"Honey, I would tee off with my regular golf group dressed in tights and a tutu with a tiara on top of my visor if I thought this was more than our son guilting us into reconciling."

"What time? I'll make a point of being there with the camera. Seriously, I understand what you're saying, but I think we both have taken a step toward rekindling what we've meant to each other. I'm not suggesting a quick tumble under the sheets for old times' sake."

Patrick hooted at his wife's use of a euphemism for sex.

"Why are you laughing? I'm serious," she declared.

"You just have a way with words that's always entertaining and sometimes surprising. It's Margo unplugged."

"So, here we are." She kissed him on the cheek before opening the door. "Sleep well. See you in the morning."

"I'm certain we're headed in the right direction—toward each other, not away." He was almost to his suite when he turned around. "I've never stopped loving you, Margo Tate Mackie. Sweet dreams."

Conner, officially off duty, popped open a beer while Starla poured a glass of wine. She laid the almond/veggie snack bowl on the table before sitting down on the couch beside her deputy. They snuggled close enough for the redolent bouquet of her cabernet to mix with the malt and hops of his beer. She cleared her throat. "This is going to sound weird, but have you ever wished you could get to know someone faster—like you could exchange your darkest secrets first then ease into spending weeks of small talk?"

"That makes perfect sense to me. Here's my darkest secret. I've wanted to kiss you since the day I laid eyes on you in the hospital. Now...your turn."

"When my husband died, I vowed never to let myself love so intensely that the loss of that person would almost destroy my desire to live. But I must admit your incredible cuteness has worn me down."

"So, if I'm reading the signs correctly, you wouldn't call the police if I kissed you?"

"Calling the law to arrest the law seems pointless...what would be the charge—assault with deadly lips?"

The banter mixed passion with moments of gentleness filling the air around Starla and Conner, fueling the fires of desire that had lay dormant for too long. Both confessed not wanting to live a life of could haves, might haves, or should haves. With the realization that two children were asleep upstairs down the hall from Starla's bedroom and with her mourning brother-in-law around the corner, the next phase of their passion would have to wait for a more appropriate time and place. She laid her head on his shoulder, his kisses staying on her lips as she dozed off with illusions of silent verses of a poem gliding as noiseless as an oar passing through the surface of a glassy fishpond. It was after midnight when they untangled from each other saying goodnight with a leisurely embrace and promises to pick up where they left off.

14

He's Gone

WITH FRANCES CARSON and Samantha Franks stowed away in the trunk of Victor's stolen Buick GS and after affixing a Michigan license plate to the back bumper, he revved the engine to a pitch equaling the king of the jungle announcing his prowess to his pride. He rumbled out of a vacant lot puffed-up and full of bluster at hoodwinking the local police at the church, cemetery, and the most satisfying of all, his *coup de grâce* at Seasons LXX. Knowing he had padded his criminal record with the abduction of Derek Brighton, it was time to physically leave Buffalo and the torment of the Mackies behind, at least for the immediate future. Crossing state lines would add consequences, but a desire for a warmer climate and spicier cuisine directed his automobile westward.

Sheriff McAlister convened a meeting with his staff updating them on the Mackie family and their number one suspect. Summer's cell phone had been turned over to the forensic technicians. Since service providers sell access to databases and cell tower dumps to law enforcement, they will have every phone number, website, text, and location associated with the number at their fingertips. "We're hoping to tap into a treasure trove of information like in the Darryl Littlejohn case in '09. His cell revealed he made multiple calls after raping and murdering a young girl while traveling from Queens to Brooklyn where he dumped her body. He's serving life without parole," said the sheriff.

"What's the time frame for this process? Days, months?" inquired Axl.

"With any luck, days. Guess it depends on how much data is stored. So, in the meantime let's move on to Victor Kurtz. His latest stunt with Derek puts him closer to the bottomless pit—one that I doubt he'll be able to climb out of."

"Sheriff, we've got a bead on his car. Lakefront Autos reported a stolen car, a black 1975 Buick GS with temporary dealer tags number 17694. Left in the lot was an old white Oldsmobile with no plates or registration," reported Conner. "I sent a patrol car to check it out."

"Sounds like he's on the run. The fresh pursuit law is our friend. No warrant required. We're preventing his escape. Although Vic is who he is today because Daddy Dearest abandoned him, he still might try to re-bond with his father. What's the last address we had for Anthony Kurtz, Conner?"

"Beaver's Bend Resort Park in Broken Bow, Oklahoma. Handling cabin rentals."

"Axl broadcast this information now."

"Anything else, guys? If not, get to work. Conner can I see you in private?"

"Sure, what's up?"

Settling into the chairs in the break room, the sheriff fidgeting in his seat asked Conner if he remembered the best advice his dad ever gave him. Without hesitation he replied, "Don't fall in love with anyone who won't help with the cat litter box."

"Sound guidance for certain. So, speaking of relationships, how are you and Ms. Jordan getting along?"

"Fine. Why do you ask?"

"I know you are attracted to each other. My concern is professional not personal. There might be a conflict since the Mackie case is an on-going investigation. If I recall you voiced doubts that Starla's niece might not be telling the truth about the fall that resulted in her mother's death, right?"

"I still think Willa is either hiding or suppressing something. Vic is probably our guy, but dang if I know...."

"You see where this relationship with her aunt might cloud your judgment. All I'm suggesting is that you put it on hold until we solve the case. Fair enough?"

"This timing sucks!"

"I agree, but we've got a job to do. My grandmother once told me that relationships are like moving planets—sometimes they are in sync and other times they are so far away that you never think they will reconnect, but if you have faith, are patient, and it's meant to be, you'll find a path back to each other."

"So, Starla is Mercury and I'm Neptune—a safe distance of billions of miles apart."

"Just for now."

Conner returned to his desk, an inside storm of disappointment coursing through his thoughts. He recalled two occasions when Starla showed her fixed side, thrusting her chin upward and walking away from him. Both times Willa had been the issue. He could only pray that last night's vibes would survive the setback. He reached for the phone to call Starla just as it rang. The caller was Sophia Kurtz requesting to speak to that nice young man Deputy Boyle.

"Ma'am, this is Conner Boyle. How can I help you?"

"My home has been burglarized and I know who did it—my son."

"Victor?"

"He's the only one I've got."

"Can you come to the office this afternoon so we can take your statement, Mrs. Kurtz?"

"No, Dearie...I'm not well with my COPD, you know."

Sheriff McAlister and Conner, agreeing to meet her, arrived at her home on Stanley Street mid-afternoon. They climbed the front porch stairs, knocking several times and announcing their identities. A bellow on the other side of the door instructed them to come in, the door was unlocked. Sophia, seated in her recliner, was surrounded by her cats all in various degrees of dozing except for one feline hypnotized by the antics of her hamster diving in and out of his plastic tunnels and vaulting into the exercise wheel for a spin or two before launching onto a platform and into his house. "You remember my Mr. Bubbles, don't you?"

"He would be impossible to forget."

"Take a load off, Sheriff. And you, young man, pull up a chair by me."

"Tell us what happened, Mrs. Kurtz," said Conner.

"Sophia, please. Well, I'm not sure exactly when I was violated, but today I discovered some money missing from my freezer."

"How much?"

"Seven one-hundred-dollar bills. And that's not all. I kept my little phone in the knife drawer, and it's gone too."

"By little phone you mean a cell phone?"

"Yeah, the one that's not attached to the wall."

"We can probably track it. What's the number?" asked the sheriff.

"It's written down on a recipe card in the one-dish meals section of my Betty Crocker cookbook on top of the refrigerator. I put it there cause I thought it would be safe unless a thief wanted to whip up some dinner before he stole my stuff," she chortled until her body shook triggering deep rales from her diseased lungs.

"Tell us why you think Victor is responsible for the theft," said Conner.

"Well, first I thought I heard a noise in the kitchen a few days ago, but me and Joseph were playing Halloween. He was so foxy all dressed up like Batman. I was Catwoman...I even had a bullwhip—but he only got a few lashes on the tushie—not enough to break the skin—just enough to get his full and rigid attention."

Sheriff McAlister cleared his throat. "Mrs. Kurtz, so you didn't see anyone in the kitchen?"

"Nah. The backdoor was open a little, but I thought the wind must have blown it. Besides, me and Joseph had business to take care of while the iron was hot."

Conner pulled at his collar as the temperature in the room had increased two fold. "So, back to Victor. If you didn't see him, how do you know it was him?"

"He left a candy heart on top of the frozen money package."

Conner left the grilling to retrieve the phone number from the cookbook while Sheriff McAlister resumed conversing with Sophia. When he returned, she had removed Mr. Bubbles from his cage, handing his boss the rodent to pet. He squirmed out of the sheriff's hand, causing five cats to assume chase positions scrambling in hot pursuit of an appetizer.

Amid the chaos the deputies promised they would follow up with her on the progress of the investigation, suggesting for her safety she lock her doors, and to please call if she remembered anything else. On the ride back to the office, neither could shake the images of the clash of the Superheroes as narrated by Sophia Kurtz. "I guess interrogating Batman wouldn't be worth the effort," said Conner.

"I'm not sure I can take another recounting of their escapades," said the sheriff.

"They're obviously kindred spirits."

"On another note, maybe we'll get lucky with her phone. And, with this latest antic, Vic is looking at adding a Class A Misdemeanor to his rap sheet."

Victor, cruising down Interstate 90 from Buffalo in his newly acquired muscle car, rolled down the windows, cranked up the radio jamming with Buffalo's own Goo Goo Dolls to their hit tune "Iris" followed by Queen's "Bohemian Rhapsody" and "Back in Black" by AC/DC. Drumming the tunes out on the steering wheel, he glanced in his rearview mirror, spotting a highway patrol car behind him. He slowed down although the speedometer registered sixty miles per hour, well within the limit, turned the volume down on the radio, hoping the Michigan license plate would deter any interest. Sirens blared. The car pulled up to his back bumper before speeding around him in pursuit of another lawbreaker. Victor breathed a sigh of relief and continued to his destination, *The Rock and Roll Capital of the World,* and then on to *River City.*

15

Together Again

MARGO, AFTER A fitful night of unrest was startled by a clap of thunder, the rain pattering on the window sounding like someone's muffled gossip just out of earshot. She rolled toward the clock on the nightstand. It read 5:00 A.M. She propped herself up in bed soaking in the character of the suite with its attic-style vaulted twenty-foot ceilings, exposed brick, and original bargeboard beams with industrial truss plates. She scolded herself. *It's all my fault that my life right now is like a book with a senseless wandering plot featuring a troupe of unlikeable characters, none more imperfect than Margo Mackie.* She picked up the phone dialing Patrick's room before she remembered the time. It rang several times before he gruffly answered. "This better be life or death."

"Sweet Love...I'm sorry I was awake and forgot how early it was...go back to sleep and call me when you're ready for the day."

"Margo? What's wrong? I'll be right there."

"No, I'm fine! The storm woke me up. Couldn't go back to sleep so instead I decided to parade through a guilt trip. Are we putting our faith in the wrong dream—thinking we can mend all fences in a blink of the eye. Is this because Summer died...I'm just rambling."

"Do you have a date for breakfast?"

"What kind of question is that—of course not."

"Yes, you do—with your husband...you know the guy down the hall," he said with a flicker of mischief. "Shall we say room service in an hour—your place or mine?"

"Mine. Coffee, two fried eggs, extra bacon, biscuits, and raspberry jam. Anything else?"

"A little vitamin C watered down with champagne."

During their leisurely breakfast Patrick and Margo agreed they would suggest or if needed, insist, their son and grandchildren join them at home in Texas, at least temporarily or until Victor Kurtz was apprehended. Around 9:00 they were in the car on the way to Matt's hoping he was in a more amenable mood than the night before. Their concerns were answered upon arrival at the house. "A wise woman taught me never ruin an apology with an excuse...so Mom, Dad, I overreacted, and it wasn't any of my business in the first place."

"We were going to tell you, but the timing wasn't right given what you all had been through. On a positive note this tragedy has helped both your mother and me put things in perspective. Which brings us to what we want to discuss with you. Is everyone still sleeping?"

"So far, it's just Dude, Halle, and me. Grab some coffee and pull up a chair."

Matt listened with a keen level of interest to the proposition offered by his parents, acknowledging Seasons could continue in Tina's capable hands and Gabe and Willa's well-being trumped any other considerations Matt might have. The elder Mackie's Sky Island Retreat, located in the heart of Big Bend Country, would provide an auspicious change of scenery. Starla descended the stairs stumbling into the discussion offering to stay at Matt's house and helping Tina, if she needed an extra hand. The plan was taking flight until Willa bounded into the breakfast nook.

"Morning, sweetie. Did you sleep well? How about I make you some breakfast? What would you like?" said Margo.

"What's with all the questions, GoGo? I just got up."

"Willa...rudeness is not becoming," barked Matt.

"No worries, son. Although it's been decades since I was a

teenager, I remember my mom firing a barrage of questions at me before I rubbed the sleepy sand out of my eyes. Give her a little while to wake up and we'll start again."

"I need some coffee," announced Willa.

"When did you start drinking coffee?" asked Starla.

"This morning," she said with an exaggerated groan, her eyes rolling back into their sockets so only the whites were visible as she trudged into the kitchen.

A feather could have knocked over those gathered in the breakfast nook. Starla shot straight up in her chair. "Drama, puberty, and the teenage girl...my heavens. I hate to think that I put my parents through this, but they probably got a double dose from Summer and me."

"Matthew was no peach if I remember correctly," said Patrick. "An unmoored buoy in a tsunami was more stable than him."

The discussion resumed with Margo commenting how wonderful it will be to have their son and grandchildren at home in Texas followed by Matt asking when the school year begins. Willa breezed by with a mug in hand stopping short of her den destination, swooping back into the room smirking in defiance of what she had overheard. "I'm starting the ninth grade—HERE—in Buffalo with my friends. I'm not going to be stuck in the middle of nowhere."

"With your creepy stalker as you call him still on the loose, we're trying to protect you and your brother," offered Matt. "It's a temporary move, Willa."

"I'll stay here with Jackie or Misty...or go live with my real dad," she said huffing out of the room.

A vein in Matt's forehead throbbed as he pushed his chair back from the table. Starla put her hand on his arm. "Let me talk to her."

Willa, in the midst of a mini workout of contempt starring head tossing, hand wringing, and mumbling, was sitting on the bottom step of the staircase alongside her brimming caffeinated drink. Starla sat beside her. "How's the coffee?"

"Cold."

"Here, let me nuke it."

"No, it's perfect."

Starla, leveling her eyes on Halle curled up in the wingback chair across the room to prevent transmitting any judgmental opinions in her niece's direction, cleared her throat. "Okay...You're smart, so you know words can hurt and once said you can't take them back. Matt will forgive you because he is your father, legally and emotionally, and he loves you."

"I don't care. I'm not going to Podunk, Texas."

"I'm afraid you are whether you like it or not. Do you honestly think Bradley Anderson will give up his Broadway show to care for the teenage daughter he gave up when she was four?"

"Why can't I live with one of my friends?"

"Many reasons—the most important one is Victor Kurtz—how would you feel if he went after Misty or Jackie just to get back at your family?"

"What about you? Are you going to Texas, too?"

"No, I'll stay at the house and help Tina."

Willa's glint of hope quickly turned into a frown of disappointment when Starla declared that her staying in Buffalo did not change the situation. "I'm counting on you to take care of your little brother. He sometimes acts all grown up but he's just a kid. He's lost his mom and needs a strong family unit around him. He'll get that with Big Pop, GoGo, you, and your dad in Texas."

"Why can't you be our mom, Aunt Starla? Everyone else hates me. I know they think I pushed Mom."

Starla observed her niece's profile, searching for any visible signs of guilt, loss or sorrow for actions Willa could not change. The scrutiny revealed nothing more than an odd serenity and stillness as if holding her breath against the truth. Starla asked, "Did you?"

Willa hesitated just long enough to toss doubt on her denial. "No. They said it was that stalker guy. You're just like everybody else...you think I'm a monster. I'll be in my room while you all plan my life."

Starla retrieved Willa's untouched cup. Goose bumps dotted her arms as a splinter of alarm united with hollowness as though beams of light from the setting sun had gathered somberly on her heart. Willa's mindset was tenuous and Starla needed to discuss a Plan B with the rest of the family. Without detailing the chat with her niece, she proposed accompanying them to Texas, if Matt thought Tina could do without her help at Seasons.

"If you're sure you want to do this, Starla, Tina is more than capable of running the show," he said.

"Not that we aren't thrilled to have you, I'm just wondering what brought on the change of heart," said Margo.

"I just feel I can be of some help with the transition, especially with Willa. She'll come around but it might take all of us to keep from locking her in the bedroom until she's twenty."

"That brings up another issue—what about Conner? I thought there was a spark developing between you two," said Patrick.

"It's no secret there's a mutual attraction, but he'll understand what I need to do and it's only until Matt and Willa get settled in Texas."

They all turned around when a voice as soft as a down feather pillow whimpered, "Why can't I go to Texas, Daddy?"

"Gabe, we're all going to Big Pop and GoGo's house. Why would you think we would go without you, son?"

"Aunt Starla said you and Willa."

"Gabe, of course you're going. I just mentioned your sister because we were just talking about her. Understand?"

"Can Conner come too?"

"He's got to stay here so he can round up all the bad guys and keep us safe," said Patrick.

"When he gets them all in jail, then can he come to Texas?"

"Next time we see him we'll ask."

"I'm hungry. I need breakfast before we go to Texas."

Gabe's timeline produced some essential laughter with his grandmother escorting him to the kitchen to choose his morning sustenance.

"If the bottom line is what you're interested in, my grandson is the man. What a kid," said Patrick.

"My son does have a knack for cutting to the core of things."

Starla excused herself to call Conner from her bedroom saying, "We need to talk." They agreed to meet at Betty's, a fixture in Buffalo's eateries on Virginia Street, for dinner at 7:30. She was seated in the outside dining area sipping a glass of California Merlot when Conner scurried in. He apologized for being late as he had to park several streets away. When he leaned in to kiss her cheek, she traced the curve of his jaw with her hand noticing his skin was tightly drawn around his eyes as though weighted down with uncertainty and blazing with questions. By contrast the set of her face was of someone wreathed in smiles exuding good cheer. "You look like you were inside the outhouse when lightning struck," she teased.

"I guess I can't hide behind my tough guy image anymore especially when I'm dating Lisbeth Salander."

"*The Girl with the Dragon Tattoo* fame, correct?"

"Yeah, we actually had a hacker with a photographic memory like in the book. Amazing stuff. They can recall in a matter of seconds everything they ever did in their life."

"So, we're dating?"

"You tell me. Is that what we need to talk about?" Conner signaled to the waitress, suddenly feeling as though Death Valley National Park had relocated to his oral cavity. She recommended one of the specialty beers, a fan favorite being Samuel Smith's Nut Brown Ale.

"It's an English ale, rich in walnut color with hints of hazelnuts. We serve it in a souvenir dimpled British pint glass."

"I can't possibly turn down a glass filled with the Nectar of the Gods. And, bring the young lady another Merlot please."

"Conner, first you're the one that has gotten me through this terrible time with Summer dying and then all the bedlam about who did what to whom, but...."

"I knew there was a but coming. I guess the other night meant more to me than you."

"Would you please let me finish. I wanted to tell you in person."

Conner pushed his chair back from the table. His voice was taut and his words clipped as if trying to extricate himself from further embarrassment. "Ms. Jordan, you don't owe me anything. I was just doing my job and I am guilty of misreading our connection."

He abruptly stood as if he had been on the receiving end of a bullet and was waiting to fall. Starla grabbed his hand trying to stop him from leaving. "Since we're being formal now, Deputy Sheriff Boyle, Ms. Jordan requests that you please sit your adorable ass down."

Conner, speechless with astonishment, obeyed the order but doubled over in laughter.

She giggled, "What's so damn funny?"

"You are. There're daggers in those beautiful blue eyes. Murdering an officer of the law will get you serious prison time."

"Take another sip of your nutty beer and let me finish. I am going to the Mackie's place in Texas—temporarily. Patrick and Margo thought it would be a good idea for Matt and the kids to visit for a while, especially since Victor is still on the loose. I was going to stay in the house while they were gone, but Willa is just a mess and I think I can help her. As far as we are concerned, our budding romance will have to be put on hold until I get back, if you'll wait for me that is."

"You've managed to make me look like an idiot...and I deserved every bit of it. Can you forgive me?"

"I'll give it my best shot."

"Excellent...and after dinner maybe we can swing by my place for dessert."

A moist wind swirling as if trapped inside a cave guided Conner from the parking lot to his job with the Erie County Sheriff's Department. He bounced into the office with ample air between the floor and his footsteps to create a crawl space. As he proceeded to his desk humming Bruno Mars' "It Will Rain," Sheriff McAlister looked up from the stack of paperwork shooting a wondering glimpse at the rest of the deputies.

"So, Boyle, care to share why you're beaming like a groom on his wedding night?" said Axl.

His response, "It's just a beautiful day," signaled the query was as futile as trying to capture a tornado. "Sheriff, are we ready for our morning briefing?"

"No time like the present. First on the agenda, Victor's great escape. We know the abandoned Oldsmobile at Lakefront Autos was his and we assume he is the one who stole the 75 Buick GS. A car matching the description was reported by the Cleveland highway patrol, but the license plates did not match so they didn't follow up. The car was later found by an Amtrak security guard in the parking garage. It was empty except for women's clothing, a long platinum blonde and braided auburn wigs. Looks like he deserted Frances and Samantha opting for a train ride as Victor or disguised as who knows who and who knows where he's going."

"We have to assume he boarded one of the trains, so he had to purchase his ticket in person—cash I would imagine. The agent would ask for a photo ID and might remember him. We faxed a description and photo to Amtrak so if he boarded as Victor, we might get lucky," said Axl.

"Don't forget his vocal tics. We have to trust that Tourette's will be his downfall," offered Conner.

After the meeting Conner invited Sheriff McAlister to join him for lunch at Imperial Pizza so they could talk privately. They each ordered slices of one of the specialty pies—Conner opting for the Reuben with sauerkraut, swiss cheese, corned beef, and Thousand Island dressing; the sheriff choosing the Stinger with blue cheese, chopped steak and chicken fingers with melted cheese. "I've got to swear you to secrecy. My lovely wife must never know what I just ordered. Breaking the promise is an automatic demotion...got it?"

"Yes sir. You've got my word. Now for the reason for our little meeting."

"I suspect by your mood this has to do with Ms. Jordan."

"You're very astute, Sheriff."

"I didn't get this far by not recognizing the obvious. I thought we were clear on the issue. I have to say I'm disappointed in your actions."

"Before you scold me, let me assure you the situation has been taken care of."

"So, why are you so damn happy?"

"Because it solved itself. We had dinner last night and she is going to Texas with the family for a while. So, I didn't have to bring up the conflict and the mandatory *no-Starla-zone*."

"Glad it all worked out. When are they leaving?"

"Not sure, but I am going to talk to Matt before they go about Bradley and why he didn't mention his visits to Seasons LXX. I'm certain he will not be able to collaborate Bradley's story about the day at the Gorge though unless he's regained some memory since the fall."

"Keep us posted. You ready to waddle back to the office?"

"Like a duck."

With the family's plans to visit in place, Margo called her housekeeper, Concha, to ready the main house and the pool house with fresh linens and bath towels. She also asked her to gather some of her clothing and personal items from the suite at The Murphy Hotel and put them back into their bedroom. Starla's announcement to Willa of her decision to join them in Texas was the recipient of a blank stare into space, a nod toward feigned enthusiasm, instead of a *Thank you Aunt Starla for saving me from this horrible plight.* She plonked down on the couch donned her headphones, escaping into a world without relatives.

Matt discussed with his physician about going to Texas, asking if there were any restrictions on travel due to his recent traumatic brain injury. Dr. Thompson warned of the risks involved in air travel as patients often experience headaches, fatigue, and nausea due to decreased oxygen levels and changes in pressure. They are also exposed to an overwhelming amount of stimulus from the general busyness associated with airports, such as noises, lights, people scurrying to and from gates, and loud flight announcements. He stopped short of forbidding Matt to fly, but strongly advised against it. As far as travel by car, he was cleared as a passenger and reminded to check in at radiology tomorrow at one o'clock for a his follow-up CT scan. With Matt's "no-fly" zone in force, Starla offered to take the reins of designated driver on a road trip with Patrick proposing he and Margo fly with Willa and Gabe. With everyone in agreement the plan was in motion with the elder Mackies booking a flight from Buffalo back home. Dude and Halle, huddled together under the breakfast nook table, must have sensed they were left out of the equation as each bid to make their presence known by rubbing their heads on Matt's legs.

"Guys, I see you. Starla, what about the pets?"

"It's over eighteen-hundred miles so you're looking at probably three or three-and-a-half long days. That could be monstrous with a dog and cat," said Patrick.

"Tina's probably not an option. I can't ask her to take on any more responsibility. Seasons already takes most of her time."

Dude hightailed it from his station heading for the front door when the bell rang while Halle sauntered into the kitchen to see if there was a spare morsel left in either food bowl.

A moonstruck smile on Conner's face extended from one ear to the other when his *inamorata* opened the door. Starla returned his gaze with a flash of affection lingering from the previous night. The mood was interrupted by an excited Gabe seeing his buddy. "Conner, we're going to Texas. I wish you could come with us, but Big Pop said you have to stay here and catch bad guys."

"He's right. My job is to serve the community and protect. Is your dad here?"

"Conner, come in. Yes, Matt is at the table in the nook. Could I get you anything to drink?"

"No thanks, Sweet...I mean Starla."

"Conner, here take my chair. I've got some chores to do in the kitchen," said Margo.

He inquired about how Matt was feeling and whether he had been able to recall any memories from the day of the fall. He voiced frustration that the last day of his wife's life was a complete blur and waited every day for something to surface. Conner informed him of his talk with Bradley and his admission that he was at the Gorge that day, but he swore when he left everyone was still standing on the ledge. "He said you two exchanged hand gestures. Ring a bell?"

"I assume you mean more than a friendly wave?"

"I'm just saying there were a couple of birds involved if you get my drift."

Gabe popped up from drawing his picture asking wide-eyed, "Conner, were they bald eagles?"

"Maybe, Gabe. New York State has restored the Hudson River and its estuary which means the bald eagles are back, but they also gather on the upper reaches of the Delaware River near Niagara Falls in the winter," deadpanned Conner.

Gabe returned to his project apparently satisfied with the answer as Conner moved on to another inquiry asking Matt why he didn't mention Bradley's visits to Seasons LXX. "I've never been a big fan as I can't imagine being so selfish that you leave your wife and child to fend for themselves while you focus on your acting career. And now since he's got a life-threatening disease, he wants to be a father to Willa. It's just BS. Another minute spent on this jerk was one too many."

"Understand, but we have to rule out every scenario. Because of your past connection with him and the fact that he was at the Gorge, you might have been the target, not Summer. When are you all headed south?"

"Mom and Dad are flying home Tuesday and taking the kids. I'm having a CT scan tomorrow and as soon as I'm cleared, Starla and I are driving to their home. Our pressing problem is the dog and cat with that long of a road trip."

"I'd take them, but my place doesn't allow pets," said Conner.

"Could you stay here while we're gone?" asked Matt. "That would solve the animal issue, and law enforcement would be in-house to keep an eye on things. It'd be like our own private security detail. What do you think?"

"Conner, sleep in my room so Halle won't be lonesome," squealed Gabe.

"Matt, is there somewhere we can speak privately?"

"Sure, my bedroom."

Matt closed the door after Conner, motioning him to sit in the chair by the window while he sat on the end of the bed. Conner removed a piece of paper from his shirt pocket, looking directly into Matt's eyes said, "We retrieved some data from your wife's cell."

"You sound serious. What is it? "

Conner detailed the number of calls and text messages to the same number belonging to Assistant District Attorney Randall Reid's office and to his home number. "When we questioned him about what we had found, he admitted the connection to Summer was more than work related. They were spending long hours on cases, but he broke it off before the relationship was *consummated,* as he put it. I'm not judging, Matt. I felt like it was my duty to share this with you."

"Conner, thank you. We were going through a rough patch. I resented every minute she spent with Randy and was so threatened and jealous of the time she devoted to work and to him."

With Conner's new job detail as the official pet sitter, he excused himself needing to get back to work. Starla walked him to the door, stealing a hug and kiss along with a promise to talk with him later before waving goodbye. When he arrived at the office, it was abuzz with news from Cleveland. An agent with Amtrak reported selling a man a one-way ticket to Omaha, Nebraska, departing at 2:00 A.M. He remembered the man because he presented a card indicating that he was a mute. He paid $138 cash for his fare and took a seat near one of the vending areas to await the train. He said he was puny, brown eyes, dishwater blonde hair tied back in a ponytail, and would never be a center on a basketball team—even at middle school. "The agent said he reminded him of one of those fellas that would sip tea with his little pinkie in the air," said Axl. "I then asked if he noticed anything unusual about his hands." He said, "Yes, he had on leather gloves and although it's not as hot today as it was in 1988 when it got to 104, it's way too warm to wear those things."

"How long of a trip is it?" asked the sheriff.

"Twenty-plus hours. There are no direct routes, so passengers have to disembark and board a connecting train. If they're on time Victor should be arriving in Omaha sometime between 10:00 P.M. and midnight day after tomorrow," said Axl.

16

Come Fly with Me

HEAVEN'S NIGHT LIGHT blazed in the starless sky while the only sound breaking the resplendent quietude of the darkness came from the backseat of the rental car as the Mackies and their grandchildren headed to the airport for the trip to Texas. Since Willa's ears remained closed to her brother's nattering, Gabe responded by informing his overstuffed turtle, Wiz, of the details of the excursion. Margo and Patrick, both holding in laughter, listened with interest as Gabe chatted to his uncommunicative reptile about their first airplane ride. By the time they arrived at the rental car return, Wiz was well versed in the excursion plans. As all their luggage would fit in the overhead compartments, the family proceeded to the security checkpoint for clearance to the gate area. Gabe held Wiz close to his chest before being instructed to put him in a plastic bucket for a ride inside the x-ray machine. Gabe, chewing on a fingernail, stood on his tiptoes on the other side of the tunnel waiting for his pal to appear. Once back in his possession, Gabe mouthed an upward thank you for his safe return.

Willa, having already experienced the excitement of flying and still reeling from the unfairness of being forced to leave her friends, sulked inside her cocoon of silence. Margo tried futilely to pull her granddaughter out by soliciting her opinions on fashion, movie star crushes, artists and their music, and favorite books. But, Willa's one-word responses continued as snappy as the jaws of an alligator at lunchtime. When time to board, Gabe, pulling his granddad's hand, skipped the length of the jetway until greeted by the flight attendant welcoming them on board.

"We're on row four Gabe. The window seat is yours if you want it." Patrick, stepping inside the galley, asked the flight attendant if it would be doable for Gabe to visit the cockpit. She said it would only be allowed while on the ground and if the Captain approved it, promising to ask him. While a steady stream of passengers located their seats and stored their carry-on luggage in the overhead bins, Gabe's eyes glistened with desperation as he searched his backpack, the seat pocket in front of him, on both sides of his seat and the floor around him.

"Big Pop...help me, I can't find Wiz."

"He's got to be here, buddy. Didn't you have him when we boarded?"

"I don't remember. I was so excited to get on the airplane. I gotta get off and go find him."

"Gabe, they won't let you off once you've boarded. Let me ask the flight attendant if she could call the gate agent and ask them to check around where we were sitting."

Gabe curled up in a ball, leaning his head on the window, tears inching their way down his cheek. Margo unbuckled her seatbelt and slid into Patrick's seat wrapping her grandson into her arms. She caught her husband's attention who shook his head side to side fearing Gabe's inanimate companion was lost for good. Watching the scene unfold across the aisle, Willa took off her headphones, tossing Gabe's turtle into his lap.

"Willa...you found him. You're the best. Where was he?"

Margo's eyes narrowed. She moved back to her seat.

"What? GoGo, why are you looking at me like you hate me?"

"Why did you put us all through this when you had Wiz all along? Are you so cruel that you enjoyed seeing your little brother in pain?"

"I saw that Gabe left him behind, so I picked him up. He has to learn to keep up with his stuff."

142

"So, that was your idea of teaching him a lesson? Willa, I'm speechless."

"Can we just drop it? He's got his stupid stuffed animal back so the little prince will be all happy again."

Conner arrived with suitcases in hand to begin his house and pet sitting assignment. Much to his regret, he had missed saying good-bye to Margo, Patrick, Willa, and his little pal, Gabe, as the flight to Texas departed that morning. Matt, after receiving an all clear on his CT scan, was released to travel and he and Starla were set to start their driving excursion after lunch. Matt handed Conner a notebook with emergency numbers for the veterinarian, neighbors, and Tina's home number along with feeding instructions for Dude and Halle, security codes, breaker box location, and lights and sprinkler system timers. "This is probably more information than you need."

"I read Michener's *Space* in college. This looks doable," Conner joked. "I'll just drop my stuff in Gabe's room and be on my way."

Starla and Conner ambled to his car, knowing each deliber-ate footstep meant the road to parting was nearer. He leaned his back against the door pulling her within inches of his face, their personal space evaporating like dew steeped in the warmth of the morning sun. She tilted her head sideways, searching his eyes with hers. Straightening the collar of his shirt she said, "If I'm too bold forgive me, but you fill a void in my life...you're like finding that stray earring I've been trying to find for ages and now that I have, it scares me."

"Me, too."

She reached in her pants pocket. "I brought you something." She handed him a sterling silver pocket coin with an inscription, *Please don't ever leave me*. My dear sweet Thomas gave this to me for when he would go on road tours alone. It always kept me close to him. I want you to have it, Conner."

He cupped her face in his hands, gently kissing her nose, then eyelids and cheeks. "You do realize that you make me feel like the inside of an oven on broil. Please tell me you're coming back soon."

"The colors of life disappear when you shut down emotions. You've reawakened desires that I had buried long ago, and I promise to be back here as soon as possible."

Conner rubbed his finger over the inscription on the coin before putting it in his pocket. "And, thank you for this. Me and the oven will be on delayed start until you get back."

Starla waved as her deputy pulled out of the driveway, a fervent bouquet of joy and yearning welded together. Her thoughts flowed to a song lyric she composed after Thomas died that plumbed the intensity of her despair... *How can we go on...how can we be so bold...when love is like a dandelion seed blown by the wind to unknown places.* As Conner's car disappeared around the corner, she wondered if those dandelion seeds would return, or would they remain buried under a pile of external circumstances?

Starla rang Mrs. Brennan's doorbell while Matt loaded her Range Rover with the necessities for the road trip to Texas. When she opened the door the friendly neighborhood watchdog insisted Starla come in as she had just taken a batch of double cherry hot-chocolate cookies out of the oven. "I can't stay. Matt and I are leaving in a few minutes joining the family in Texas and Deputy Sheriff Conner Boyle will be staying at the house taking care of Dude and Halle."

"Did they ever catch that guy that caused those poor kiddos to be without their mother?"

"Not yet. That's one reason we're leaving. I gave Conner your phone number, but if you need anything, holler at him."

"Well, you can't go without some cookies for the road. Give me a second and I'll get you a tin ready."

Starla thanked Mrs. Brennan, promising to see her again soon and left to help Matt with the rest of the preparations for their extended journey, but he was waiting beside the car when she returned. With Starla in the driver's seat and Matt buckled up in the passenger side, they backed out of the driveway for the first leg of the trip, taking Interstate 90 West to U.S. 40 headed to the state capitol of Ohio and the home of the Buckeyes—Columbus. In a little over five hours they pulled into the valet parking of The

Blackwell Inn, a craftsman designed hotel on the campus of Ohio State University. After settling into their rooms, the travel companions convened for drinks in the fireside bar in the lobby before early dinner reservations at Bistro 2110 overlooking the football stadium. Day two would be longer and more taxing making a good night's rest important.

———— ∞ ————

The flight attendant motioned for Gabe to come with her. Patrick followed as she opened the cockpit door. Captain Maverick turned around to shake Gabe's hand, asking if he would like to sit at the controls. A wide grin covered his tear-stained face as he climbed into the seat. The captain showed him which ones enabled the aircraft to fly, asking if he wanted to be a pilot when he grew up. "No, I'm going to make angels out of metal," Gabe said in a booming tone. Captain Maverick looked to Patrick for an explanation.

"Our boy here was a little architect but since he saw bronze sculptures, he's decided that will be his calling. He's one worldly seven-year-old."

"Impressive."

Gabe leaned in holding up the little finger on his right hand, his eyes piercing into those of the pilot. "Pinky promise you won't let us crash. My mommy is one of God's favorite angels now, and my daddy would be so sad if he were all alone in the world."

Captain Maverick linked fingers with Gabe, shaking twice to seal the deal. "When I leave for a flight, my daughter makes me swear the same thing, so, young man, I know how to fly this big airplane carefully. Don't worry. I won't let you or my little girl down. Now, me and First Officer Bolten need to get ready for takeoff."

Patrick thanked him for allowing Gabe into the cockpit and for how he handled the anxiety of his grandson. "Maverick huh...shades of Tom Cruise in *Top Gun*?"

"You should have heard the razzing I got in the Navy."

Patrick and Gabe returned to their seats fastening their seatbelt ready for the next adventure. The safety instructions appeared on the inflight monitors as they taxied before takeoff and as the captain guided the plane around a corner barreling and bouncing down the runway, Gabe reached for Patrick's hand. "Is Captain Maverick goin' over the speed limit?"

"Feels like it, but we've gotta go super fast to lift this big bird in the air." As if on cue, American Airlines Airbus Flight #1021 carrying the Mackies to Texas ascended over Buffalo heading to Dallas-Ft. Worth International Airport where they would board another flight to Midland and resume the journey by automobile to the Sky Island Retreat.

Gabe, glued to the window, commented, "Look, Big Pop, all the houses look like LEGOs."

As many times as he had flown, Patrick was seeing a city constructed with colorful plastic interlocking blocks for the first time. Margo tapped his arm. "You're deep in thought. Care to share?"

"It's Gabe. He might look at an iceberg floating on the sea and wonder what was under it where I would only be interested in how cold the water must be to keep it solid. He's pointing at the moon and I'm looking at his finger."

"He's a little boy and an old man in the same body." She turned to gaze at Willa, headphones on and eyes closed. "Then we have the cross between Sara Crewe from *A Little Princess* and Maleficent of *Sleeping Beauty* fame sitting to my right."

"Complicated youngster for sure. We'll get through this as well and Starla will be reinforcements."

The flight attendants, in response to the first ping on the intercom indicating the plane had passed the ten-thousand feet mark, began moving about the galleys in preparation of food and beverage service. Patrick and Margo both ordered mimosas, Gabe opted for a glass of orange juice while Willa ordered a cup of coffee. After snacking on a granola mix of dried cranberries, pineapple and almonds, a flight attendant handed out warm towels with most passengers using them to wipe their hands, except for Gabe who covered his head with it. "Look, GoGo...have you met Gabriel McTowel?"

Patrick snatched the covering off his grandson's head, amusement traversing from one ear to the other. "You're as goofy as Goofy."

"Woof."

Willa added sugar and cream to her hot beverage before taking a sip. When asked if she would prefer a fresh fruit yogurt parfait and English muffin or a cheese omelet with tater tots and sausage for breakfast, she exuded the politeness of a Mary Poppins with her choices and requesting, "When you have time, I would love another cup of coffee."

Margo passed a box of raisins and a package of Goldfish crackers to Gabe in case he was less than enchanted with the breakfast selections. Patrick shrugged his shoulders nodding in Willa's direction after witnessing the granddaughter he would like to see more of.

After finishing breakfast Gabe rested his head on the tray table. An oversized yawn caused his eyes to water and shut signaling his early morning wakeup call had caught up with him. Patrick closed the window shade, shifted Gabe's body back into the seat, tucking a pillow under his head and covering him with a blanket as the rhythmic whirr of the plane's engines cruising above America's fruited plain sang a slumberous refrain.

Gabe, alarmed by the noises associated with the descent of the aircraft, peered at Patrick for reassurance that everything was normal. "Hey, Bud, we're going slower because we're getting ready to land. You're hearing the landing gear go down and we should be on the ground in about five minutes."

"My ears are stopped up."

"Mine too. GoGo brought us gum which should help. One piece or two?"

"Two, please."

While the aircraft taxied to the assigned gate, a flight attendant announced, "On behalf of your cabin crew, Captain Maverick and First Officer Bolten, we know you had a choice today and thank you for flying American Airlines. If this is your final destination, we will be deplaning in Terminal A, Gate 14. If you are connecting, please refer to the flight information board or ask one of our customer service representatives for assistance. Please remain seated with your seatbelts securely fastened until the aircraft is parked at the gate."

On the way out, Gabe was presented with a *First Flight* certificate detailing his trip and signed by the captain and the flight attendants. He asked if they would give the pilot a message from him. "Tell him our pinky swear worked."

The family caught a SkyLink train for the short ride to Terminal B where they boarded a CRJ-900, a smaller regional aircraft operated by American Eagle. Gabe, at ease with his recent flight operations acumen, settled into the window seat in row two beside GoGo with Willa and Patrick occupying the seats directly behind them for the hour and fifteen-minute flight to Midland. Gabe, after taking inventory of his fellow passengers, motioned for his grandmother to come close. "GoGo, do you think these people wonder where Mommy is?"

She examined his long face carting a myriad of emotions, none more prevalent than his half-hearted smile. "Well, Honey, maybe, but what they probably see are two adorable children on an adventure with their grandparents. They might just think your mommy and daddy are on a special trip of their own." The genuineness of youth in his expression suggested her answer was suitable as he turned his attention to the view outside his window. However, once again his questions seem to sink to the bottom of all feelings and thoughts.

Patrick's attempts to engage his granddaughter in conversation resulted in dispassionate boredom furthered by the tapping of her feet and refocusing her attention on a YouTube music video. He listened as Alexis Jordan, dressed as a high schooler eating an apple, belted the lyrics to "Good Girl." Willa noticed him watching and listening.

"She looks like that young gal who was on *America's Got Talent* a while back," he said.

"It's her. She got cut from the show but posted a bunch of covers on YouTube and some record producer signed her. How did you know that?"

"Contrary to your opinion, Big Pop does not live in a cave. It's a catchy tune."

Willa suppressed a giggle at her grandfather's phrasing. "It's a girl's anthem about bettering yourself even if you've been bad before."

Their eyes joined in a moment—a moment of breathing a glimmer of hope into each other of a shared trust and respect. He said, "The message is a keeper." She nodded, thankful that the generational barrier waned enough for this dialogue.

On approach to the airport Midland's skyline rose out of the southern edge of the vast Llano Estacado, a successful small city of over one-hundred-thousand residents that began as a dusty railroad stop built on the dreams of land speculators, ranchers, financiers, oilmen, and engineers who placed their own brands on the landscape. Over time the area earned a variety of monikers including the Tall City as office buildings of glass and steel could be seen for miles by travelers on U.S. Highway 80, and later Interstate 20. After deplaning, the Mackies caught the shuttle to the long-term parking lot to retrieve their Escalade EXT, and with everyone loaded into the vehicle and bags stored in the covered truck bed, they followed the Interstate west to Monahans, then veering south to home-sweet-home located between Green Tree and Marfa.

17

Running Away

JUST AFTER MIDNIGHT when the air was thick and cloaked in a murky brume, Axl and two other deputies from the Erie County Sheriff's Department were stationed to meet the train from Cleveland when it arrived in Omaha to arrest their fugitive felon when he disembarked. Victor Kurtz did not get off and the passenger manifest revealed he missed the connecting train at Chicago's Union Station. Amtrak officials in the Windy City verified no one by that name purchased a ticket to anywhere in the last twenty-four hours.

"We'll fax a photo and description of him to the ticket agents there to see if anyone recognizes him," said Axl.

"Don't get your expectations up, Deputy. Union Station serves one-hundred-and-forty-thousand passengers on an average weekday. It's our fourth busiest terminal."

"This is turning into a live Tom and Jerry video game. Our Mr. Kurtz is no Frank Abagnale Jr., but right now we look like the Keystone Cops," scowled Axl.

Meanwhile Victor munched on a Jersey Mike's turkey and provolone sub at the food court on the Mezzanine of Union Station before exiting the Beaux-Art beauty through the bustling Great Hall bathed in sunshine from the vaulted skylight. A walk-in at Funk's Barbershop landed him in Berto's chair who unsuccessfully talked Victor out of shaving his head. Sporting a new look and a new identity courtesy of a driver's license found on the counter in the men's bathroom, Victor, aka Lou Knight, launched into a fast-paced strut in a southwesterly direction after learning the propitious location of the Greyhound bus terminal for the next episode of his great escape. The ticket agent, half-comatose and itching with boredom, read passenger Knight's *mute card,* squinted through tinted fingerprint laden glasses at his identification, exchanging cash for a ride to Kansas City, Missouri. The trip would allow Victor to expend eight more hours of anonymity to formulate the next phase of his escapade.

Back in Buffalo it looked like a game of musical chairs as Sheriff McAlister and Conner awaited news from Omaha. They both had shuffled, stacked, and restacked the case files on their desks, brewed another pot of coffee, refilling each cup with the hot liquid, and stared down the slow-moving clock. "When's the last time we changed that battery?" said Conner.

"A three-toed-sloth moves faster. I'll get a new one if you'll grab the step ladder." Conner opened the battery compartment, removed the old battery, used a damp swab to clean the loose corrosion from each terminal, letting the area air dry before inserting a new battery. He was reaffixing the clock on the wall when the phone rang. The sheriff scurried to answer, hanging up after a few seconds.

"That was a representative from the New York Sheriff's Association asking for a donation to help disabled officers. I wonder how fast he would have hung up if he knew who he was speaking with. For every law passed against this type of bogus solicitation, new loopholes surface."

"Legitimate organizations in dire need of funds lose, the criminals win."

The call from Omaha came in around one o'clock, the news disappointing everyone involved except Victor who no doubt was as chirpy as an uncaged cockatiel. Axl reported the improbableness of him standing out among the masses at Union Station, but they were checking the bus terminals, O'Hare Airport, and any reports of stolen cars on the outside chance someone in the third most populous city in the United States might remember an un-memorable pedophile.

—⸻⸺—

The bus carrying a handful of passengers pulled out of the station following Interstate 55 south before heading westerly on U.S. 36 to their destination. Victor, now temporarily able to table the persona of Lou Knight, occupied a window seat across the aisle from a mother with a young child. The mom carried the loneliness of an old bluegrass tune, dejection filling her vacant eyes when she glanced over the head of her daughter in Victor's direction. Under a Kansas City Chiefs ball cap was a rawboned woman whose malnutrition presented in every ounce of her being. Her daughter wearing a tiara on top of her curly brown hair was podgy with a glint of mischief puddling in her ingenuous smile. Victor checked his tote bag to make sure he had a stockpile of candy hearts and drifted off to sleep. He was relishing in the sanctity of never-never-land when a prickling inside his nose prompted a series of sneezes, the culprit secreting from his aisle-mate who now occupied the seat next to him. She pointed to her daughter sprawled across both seats in slumberous bliss. Victor inhaled slowly, his focus on squelching the sound of his heartbeat roaring in his ears.

"I didn't mean to move into your space, but when my lard-butt young'un is ready for a nap, movin' a mountain would be easier." Victor responded with another round of forceful *achooing* motivating his seatmate to ask, "Allergies?"

His head bobbed up and down between sneezes. She moved to a vacant seat one row behind her daughter. The little girl, awakened by the commotion, cried out with the velocity of a wild screech owl before her mother stroking her hair repositioned her crown that had slipped off her head. Her temperament softened at the offerings by the bald man across the aisle. Victor, managing a guarded smile, passed a box of candy hearts to the little girl. Her mom mouthed a thank you his way. The rest of the trip proved uneventful until they pulled into the terminal at their destination. The mom gathered their belongings while the little girl plopped down beside Victor chewing on her bottom lip, her eyes disappearing in the folds of her cheeks akin to a toasted marshmallow on a s'more. "Hey, Mister...got any more candy?"

"Charmaine Jones leave the poor man alone. You don't be needing no more sugar."

"Pretty...witty...kitty...city," stuttered Victor. "Pretty name... from Shakespeare...buccaneer...disappear—Shakespeare...."

"Mama," she thundered. "What's wrong with him?"

Grabbing her daughter's arm, she pulled her back to their side of the aisle, whispering strong words in her ear. "My name is Sally and all I seem to do is apologize but, well, there's no excuse for rudeness in my book. And by the way, I didn't know her name was from Shakespeare."

"Yes, Cleo...Cleo...Patra...Sorry...Tourette's tics...."

With the dialogue waning, the Jones' family and Victor stepped off the Greyhound one behind the other. Sally's attention turned to a voice calling from the parking lot across the street. A woman dressed in a sleeveless house dress frantically waved her under-toned arms catching the attention of her granddaughter who giggled, "Look Mama. Mamoo's here."

Victor's mood darkened watching the cheerful family reunion playing out in front of him. He cradled his tote bag with both arms as he began walking away from the terminal, stopping suddenly when Charmaine pulled on his sleeve. "Bye bye, Mister Candy Hearts Man," she said before skipping off to catch up with her mother.

Sally could not dismiss the feeling that she and the strange man on the bus shared the same baggage, both losing their footing—both with fists clenched against the world. Mamoo, shaking her head at the number of times she had picked up the pieces of her daughter's misguided trust, recognized that look in her eyes. "Sally, you can barely save yourself much less every poor sap with a sad story. The latest example is the little munchkin standing right beside you. Do you understand me, child?"

"This one has a kindness buried inside. I can see it. He doesn't look like he has anywhere to stay. You've got that apartment above the garage."

"Yes, and he could be a serial killer."

154

"He's not. Serial killers don't carry candy hearts to give away to kids."

"Gee...I guess I musta missed that class at Harvard. Why do you do this to me?"

"Because behind all that bluster, you're as soft-hearted as I am."

Victor, staging a brief hemming and hawing, accepted the offer, below the skin jumping at the opportunity to have a roof over his head, a bed to sleep in, and a break from looking over his shoulder for a little while. The cherry on top was being close to a young girl with an affliction for candy.

18

The Road Less Traveled

PATRICK TURNED ON to the private road leading to their four-hundred acre *gentleman's ranch* as his foreman called it. The tires of the sport utility truck crunched as they traveled on the crushed rock for a quarter of a mile before arriving at the black hand-forged wrought iron security gate announcing the Sky Island Retreat. He lowered the window of the crew cab, entering the code activating the dual gates to swing open inviting the New Yorkers into a slice of Texas heaven. Lanterns atop a bricked half-wall and barking escorts—birddog Sadie, German Shepherd rescues Bonnie and Clyde, and yellow Labrador Magnolia—guided them to the Austin stone, two-story main house nestled among a landscape of native live oaks, Shumard red oaks, and desert willow trees wafting the sweet scent of their pink and violet orchid-like flowers. The rolling countryside with acres of fenced Bermuda pasture dedicated to hay production bordered the stable and corral, home to Margo's cherished Friesians and adopted Clydesdales. Four one-acre, stocked lakes with fishing piers and wooded creek bottoms offering no hunting zones for "pet" wildlife allowed whitetail deer and waterfowl to roam carefree while over one-hundred fenced acres at the back of the property was dedicated to Patrick's rescue animals. Ornate coping circled an intricate patterned European-styled

157

Alpine stone fountain, its central tiers featuring lion-head spouts cascading water into the seven-foot basin below.

As the car passed through the *porte cochère,* the front doors swung open with the housekeeper, Concha, her husband and ranch foreman, Donny, with his sidekick Corgi, aptly named Squat, serving as the welcoming party. Patrick, exiting the truck, shook hands with his foreman noting he was sporting a new 'stache. "You ditching this gig to be Tom Selleck's double my friend?"

"Nah…I was looking like a walrus. *Mi esposa* found a dried-up pinto bean hidin' in it one day…that was enough for me to hightail it to the barber."

Margo, with the grandchildren in tow said, "Concha, Donny, you remember Willa and Gabe—she's our teenager now and he's seven–going on thirty."

"Oh, my goodness…*son tan adultos*…what happened to my babies?"

Donny shook their hands and handed each one a quarter. A puzzled Willa asked, "What's this for?" while Gabe turned it over and over in his hand.

"Good question," he said. "The fountain is new since you were here last. Now guests who visit Sky Island toss a coin into it. Back in the old days water was considered a gift from the gods, so this is kinda like thanking those spirits for what we couldn't live without—water. And, you can make a wish too."

Gabe sprinted over to the fountain hurling his quarter over the top on to the grass. Scurrying to find it, he again launched his coin in the air, this time it ricocheted off the upper tier and into the bowl. "That's what I'm talkin' about," he hollered before throwing both arms in the air and mimicking Michael Jackson's moon walk.

His performance, albeit acknowledged only by an eye-roll from his sister, drew laughter from the rest of his audience, with Patrick commenting, "Our grandson might not have the accuracy of a quarterback or a baseball pitcher, but he's got the makings of a mighty good team mascot. Hey gang, grab your stuff. It'll be cooler inside."

Suspended from the recessed ceiling in the foyer was a rustic two-tiered weathered oak wagon-wheel chandelier, diffusing radiance from nine cylinders of clear seeded glass. A chair made of drop-forged steel horseshoes sat in the corner beside a matching magazine rack. The centerpiece of the area was a round table, hand carved with the names of the stable of horses. The sudden parade of commotion upended Richard Parker, Margo's bushy striped tabby, who was in the midst of his daily fourteen-hour nap emitting his happy-cat *squunk* (a cross between a sigh and a purr) while upside down on top of the den sectional. He executed a perfect four-paw landing, mewed his displeasure, skulking off to safety underneath the king bed in the primary suite.

"Ms. Margo, I got your things from the hotel like you asked. They're in your room," offered Concha.

Patrick opened his mouth, but no words fell into a comment while hauling his and Margo's luggage through the downstairs den to their bedroom on the far corner of the house.

Margo, with Willa and Gabe toting their luggage and backpacks, opened the door to the elevator. Once loaded inside, she latched the gate, pressing the button for the second floor where the children would occupy bedrooms down the hall from their dad when he arrived in a few days. "Remember what we say about the elevator?"

"It's not a toy," recited Willa and Gabe in unison.

"Good job. Now, we're off to your rooms."

On the way to Willa's, Margo expressed her efforts to fine-tune her decorating skills in line with more of the modern trends which was verified when she opened the door exposing the floor-to-ceiling windows overlooking one of the lakes. The wall behind the queen-sized bed was covered in lava red vertical shiplap planks contrasting the canopy bed with a geometrical black and white spread with mulberry red and autumn yellow accent pillows. Willa gave her grandmother a quick peck on the cheek. "GoGo, this is so cool."

"It's a little more contemporary than some of the other décor. I thought you might like it. Do you need help unpacking?"

"Nope, got it covered."

Gabe grabbed her hand saying, "GoGo, mine next!"

"It's right down the hall. Come on."

Gabe's room, decked out in royal blue and white striped wallpaper and matching throw rug, was furnished with a chair-and-a half recliner, a queen-sized platform bed, and an armoire stocked with children's books, a television, and a Xbox 360 S gaming console ready for players. "Can we play a game on that, GoGo?"

"We'll have to get Big Pop to do that with you, Gabe. GoGo doesn't get all that techie stuff. We'll get you situated first." With Gabe's belongings tucked away, they headed back to Willa's to see if she was ready to go back downstairs. Margo knocked on her door. After no answer, she peeked inside. Willa was sitting on the bed, headphones on, singing along with tunes playing on her MP3. Gabe rushed in startling her into a frown. "I'll be down later," she said, returning to her music. Gabe skipped down the hall to the staircase where he and his grandmother followed the animal print stair runners to the living room.

Patrick huddled with Donny in his office, the duo catching up on business since he had been in Buffalo with Magnolia and Squat curled up under the desk. "I've got some sad news about our favorite yellow Labrador. As ya know, she's recovered from tons of issues in her short life but this one will take some adjusting. She's been tripping over things, so we took her to a veterinary ophthalmologist in San Antonio. She's not in any pain, but she's going blind."

"Poor girl. What's the treatment?"

"Afraid there's not anything we can do other than watch her closely. We might get some baby gates to put in front of the staircase and make sure she has on her life jacket when she's around the water. Squat and Sadie know something's different. They're like her escorts, one on each side when she decides to go somewhere. The timing of this sucks on top of Summer's tragic death. Man, I don't have words, much less the right words...how's everyone holding up?"

"Numb, sad, angry, frustrated...but trying to make things as normal as possible for the kids. Matt is physically recovering, although he still has no memory of the day she died...the police haven't caught the nut-job they think was responsible...so we're all just in limbo."

"We're glad you brought them here. They'll be safe and maybe this'll be a good change. Could it be a permanent move?"

"I don't know. Margo and I selfishly hope so. We're just goin' to take it one day at a time."

"Speaking of the missus. Concha told me she's moved back in—where she belongs."

"I didn't know until we got here. In a way, it was our beautiful daughter-in-law's death that made us realize what we had to lose. The reason doesn't matter...it feels right Margo's back home."

The men turned toward the door when a gentle voice called out, "Did I hear my name?"

"Guilty. We were just saying how good it is to have you home."

She tilted her head in a gesture of introspection, "I really never left."

Gabe, dragging Concha by the hand, interrupted asking if he could have another quarter to make a wish in the fountain, then go swimming, and take a hike, and fish, and play golf, and make friends with the horses, and...."

"Whoa, little pal, we'll do all of that, but not all of it right now," said Patrick.

"But, Big Pop, can Concha take me just one of those places?"

"Mr. Patrick, I've already fixed my specialty enchiladas for dinner so let me take this bundle of energy for a swim." Gabe was already sprinting up the stairs to get his bathing suit before the permission was given. Margo agreed to go along counting on fatigue to creep into his little body sooner than later.

Concha and Margo returned from the pool winking *mission accomplished* to each other as their yawning *boy-fish* fought to keep the sandman at arm's length. Patrick, taking Margo aside, suggested their grandson might be ready to eat dinner before the rest of the family. "Gabe, honey, we won't be eating dinner for a little while. We've had a long day and I bet you're tired. How about Concha's macaroni and cheese, some fresh fruit, and for dessert, a big bowl of chocolate ice cream. Sound good?"

"But I hafta find out what's in her special enchiladas."

"Change out of your swimsuit, come back down to eat, and I'll tell you what it is. Deal?" promised Concha.

"Come on. Big Pop, will help you change."

With his wet bathing suit off and his pajamas on, Patrick and

Gabe came downstairs. Concha, after draining the pasta, added butter and a mix of cream cheese and sharp cheddar for the sauce. Margo prepared a tray of strawberries, watermelon, and sliced peaches, setting a place for Gabe at the dining room table. He refused to sit down until Concha told him the secret. After she whispered in his ear, his mouth formed into a Cheerio and his eyes broadened. She leaned in again and this time he nodded, executed a pinky-swear, and began eating his fruit. Concha returned from the kitchen with the rest of his dinner which he devoured. After licking the last remnants of chocolate ice cream from his bowl, Gabe joined Willa in the den armed with his iPad for a game of Minecraft while his sister, curled up in one of the cowhide covered barrel chairs, was absorbed in a musical trance, headphones on, her body moving in a succession of dreamlike illusions as she listened to her favorite tunes.

Margo removed place mats from the marble sideboard in the dining room, setting the table on one end for five. She reminisced about the many dinner parties that had filled the room with all fourteen leather chairs occupied with guests. Inlaid in the center of the table under beveled glass was the ranch logo extending from armchair to armchair. The texture and shades of the setting sun reflecting through the windows in the ornate mirror on the wall tossed a luminous stillness throughout the room. She was home. It was ordinary and as wonted as a baby clinging to her favorite blanket.

Concha brought Mexican pine wooden bowls filled with homemade tortilla chips, pico de gallo, and guacamole to the table. While in the kitchen, Patrick rimmed frozen glasses with salt as the blender whirled together the ingredients for margaritas. Willa's request for a sip earned a frown from her grandfather inquiring how many years until she was of legal drinking age. Margo completed the table setting with hand-painted Talavera ceramic plates at each place. Once seated at the table, Donny offered a welcome home toast before the family indulged in the feast. Rave reviews tumbled into a halo of praise as they all applauded Concha's culinary skills. Then the talk turned to the secret ingredient in her specialty enchiladas. She whispered what she shared with Gabe, "I told him it was rattlesnake meat, which explains his reaction and he promised not to tell anyone."

Willa's nose wrinkled in disgust, "Gross. Ew... Please tell me that's a joke."

Donny threw a wink her way confirming the shaggy-dog-story but did confirm there was a secret ingredient in her enchiladas. "She's protective of that recipe handed down from her great-grandmother. The only thing I know is that they're different from any others I've tasted."

"My *Bisabuela* would excuse herself from her heavenly kitchen to have some choice words with me about revealing a sacred trust."

"What if we guess it?" said Patrick.

"How long have you known me? It might be easier to go with the snake story."

"But would you tell me if I guessed, right?"

A hint of a grin tiptoed across her face before she replied, "No."

"Dear, you're not going to win... let it go," suggested Margo. "Concha, I'll help clear the dishes. Boys refill your margaritas and enjoy the porch while we get this cleaned up. Looks like Squat is waiting for you, Donny."

Willa took her plate to the kitchen, excusing herself to go to her room. Calls of sleep tight followed her path upstairs as she gestured a hand of dismissal toward the family. Margo shrugged her shoulders, mumbling under her breath at her granddaughter's progression of one step forward, two steps back. Concha squeezed Margo's hand, signaling that she understood how difficult Willa's lack of decorum was to witness.

With the kitchen spotless and the dinnerware handwashed and stored in the cabinet, Concha hollered at her husband that it was time to say goodnight. Their house, located in the most southern portion of the property, was at the end of the gravel road leading to the private entrance. It was the perfect size for a childless couple—the housekeeper/chef, the ranch foreman, and their stubby legged, rodent terminator. It was rustic, private, and went along with the other perks of taking care of the Mackie family. A large metal barn used for hay, equipment storage, and a separate bunk house for a tired ranch-hand to use was within walking distance of the Rodriquez's home.

Margo settled into the rocking chair next to her husband on

the wraparound covered deck overlooking one of the lakes. The sky, as sooty as the inside of a chimney flue, served as the backdrop to a scattering of stars twinkling in the distance over the mountains, while a mild dry breeze prompted leaves to rustle like a songbird's musical trill. Patrick grasped his wife's hand, sighing as if unwinding in the familiarity of home. She locked hers in his. "You look like the Thinker statue."

"Except I'm not nude, but I can make that happen," he teased.

When Margo laughed, her heavy-lidded eyes brandished an unforgettable sultriness in his direction that never failed to capture his heart as it did over forty years ago. Her manner brimmed with contentment as though a tide of joy had washed any doubts out to sea. She was close to suggesting they turn it in for the night when a sleep-walking Gabe sauntered out. "Gabe, you're dragging. Come on. Big Pop will take you upstairs."

An argument was not in the mix as Gabe hugged and kissed Margo goodnight. She said, "I'm going in, too. Patrick, I'll see you in a little while."

Margo finished unpacking the suitcases placing their toiletries above the honeyed-wood floating cabinet in the bathroom. She turned down the spread on the antique white four-poster king bed, using the remote to lower the shades on the sliding glass doors overlooking the veranda. A smoky-paneled wall emitted a subtle glow behind a loveseat accented with burgundy leather throw pillows adorned with snowflake crystal conchos. A hot soaking bath in the freestanding claw-foot tub was next on the agenda before curling up to devour Pat Conroy's *Beach Music*, a masterpiece of words constructed by the author that invites the readers to cry, laugh, see, and feel his every emotion. The bedside light was still on when she awoke alone. Margo grabbed her robe, climbing the stairs to Gabe's room where she found Patrick asleep in the oversized chair and her grandson sprawled sideways across the bed. Although disappointed at spending another night without him by her side, better sense prevailed knowing that nudging her husband out of his concentrated slumber might startle him enough to wake Gabe. She covered each with a comforter, softly retracing her steps to her bedroom, turning off the light and crawling back under the covers.

19

Walk On

STARLA AND MATT, heading south on Interstate 71 toward Louisville, planned a stop there for lunch as one of Matt's suppliers recommended Shenanigans Irish Grille if he were ever in the area. The outdoor courtyard, lined with hanging baskets of ferns, their fronds stirring like a wind soughing through a canopy of loblolly pines, embraced the warmth of the season postponing a preview of cozy socks and fireplaces. They were seated at a table in the corner and after perusing the menus, Matt ordered sweet tea and a Deerwood Black and Blue burger with fries while Starla opted for a Hi-C pink lemonade and Dutch's thick fried bologna sandwich on Texas toast mentioning this should satisfy her *fried-food* quota for several days. On the way out, a force beyond her control directed her to the gift shop where she purchased a pair of sweatpants with the restaurant's logo and motto, *One more and I'm outta' here*, stitched on the back pocket.

"Is it your goal to grow into those pants?" Matt asked.

"Mom always said, measure a thousand times, cut just once. I'll be prepared when my Achilles' heel for chocolate martinis captures my willpower."

The duo strolled back to the car, buckling up and heading south to Nashville with their sights on the destination for the day,

Memphis. On the road trip to Texas, they would have many hours to spend in quiet reflection, sharing each other's music genres, the scenery, and occasionally a self-cleansing confessional. Starla had suffered all stages of grieving with the death of her parents, her husband, and young nephew but after countless therapy sessions and time, she reached the final plateau of acceptance. With Summer's tragic death she was again experiencing the infinite agony of loss, but knew recovery was possible. Her mindset was that life was only a reflection of what we allow ourselves to see, and she chose serenity. Matt, having lost a son and his wife to catastrophe in a three-year time span, was in the early stages of grief. His pain was raw and unbridled and subject to fits of agonizing outbursts, especially with the solitude afforded by his role as a passenger on a long haul. Starla tuned the satellite channel that played a collection of melodic songs designed to feed her love of storytelling and adventurous personality. "The Long and Winding Road" by the Beatles led off, and by the time the sweet strings of the Fender guitar solo of Led Zeppelin's "Stairway to Heaven" finished, she embraced the deliberate spiritual liberation of her soul. Her rosary beads might have undergone a workout if she had not been at the helm of the automobile. Her eyes wandered for a moment at Matt who had reclined his seat, intoxicated by the purr of the engine and his body's necessity for repose. He yawned and straightened his legs just as they crossed over the Cumberland River.

"How long have I been out?"

"Couple of hours or so. We're about to Nashville."

"My heavy lunch clobbered me."

"You need your rest, Matt. I've been just fine, just grooving to my favorite tunes."

They merged with Interstate 40 east of downtown, Nashville's skyline looming with several skyscrapers, none more conspicuous than the AT&T Building nicknamed the "Batman Building" towering over the city. The moniker fit as its style was similar to the fictional character's mask, including two points extending from the top of the building like bat ears. "The District" was the heart of the city, featuring many nightlife staples like Tootsie's Orchid Lounge, the Wildhorse Saloon, and B.B. King's Blues Club and Restaurant, all located within blocks of the world's largest music museum, The Country Music Hall of Fame. Matt and Starla veered west on Interstate 40 for the remainder of the second travel day to the home of the *King*, rebranded recently as *The Grind City* after their NBA team, the Grizzlies.

Matt covered his face with his hands as if blindsided by the reality that he not only buried his six-year-old son but was now a widower in the prime of his life with the responsibility of raising two children alone. When he spoke, his voice was thick and opaque like turbid water churning in a sea of ambiguity. "Starla, tell me how you or anyone can blindly trust in the love of a higher power, of a God that allows innocent people to just die for no reason?"

"You know I've traveled that road and the simplest answer I can give you is the one my priest gave me after Thomas was gunned down. He said, 'I don't know. Cries of why go unanswered—look back at the Holocaust, the killing fields of Cambodia, September 11. Horrific events happening to the most vulnerable of mankind.'"

"How was that possibly comforting? Sounds like a cop out scripted answer."

"I felt the same way. Fire must have been spewing from my ears. He patiently let me seethe until I was ready to listen. Then he said, 'Although we can't comprehend everything about why He allows suffering in our lives, we can understand some things.' Then he told me a story about driving along a dark highway in winter. It started to pour and a heavy fog rolled in. He could hardly see the white stripe on the road but was afraid to stop, fearing someone might come along and rear end him. Out of nowhere a big rig appeared in front of him. He could clearly see the taillights and knew all he had to do was just follow and he'd be headed in the right direction."

"So, a truck's taillights will help me with...what? There better be more to the story or you've lost me."

"We're not able to make out all the details of why certain things happen, but there are some points of lights that can illuminate us—if we follow them, our hearts will stop bleeding."

"How long did it take you to buy into that?"

"Many therapy sessions and introspection led me to the realization that I had a choice." Starla explained she could live a bitter life by running away or she could run back to her faith for peace to deal with the present and the courage to deal with the future. She said, "Think of it like this—one mother loses a child to a drunk driver. She turns inward in chronic rage for a life of never-ending despair. Another mother experiences the same loss, but she turns outward establishing an organization to help others suffering the same type of agony. Those are choices. I found comfort in composing lyrics that addressed the inner pain of losing a loved one, offering a ray of hope to anyone suffering from a devastating loss."

"After Griff died, I felt as helpless as a rabbit in the jaws of a starving Doberman, but I couldn't let myself mourn. Summer was falling apart. Willa was a mess with lots of guilt and resentment aimed at her mother, and poor little Gabriel...Who would take care of them if I fell apart? And now...I've been an Episcopalian my whole life. We went to church. I never questioned why bad things happen to good people and now I feel like a hypocrite asking God's help because I know I wouldn't believe the answer."

Starla grew melancholic as her losses multiplied, the sorrow buried under layers of drowned memories. Her empathetic ear turned toward her brother-in-law. She mustered, "Matt, grief is medicine. It's necessary to heal. It's the price we pay for love according to Queen Elizabeth II...there's reasoning in her words...there's a why."

"We could've had a picnic in the backyard, but oh no, I was hellbent on proving we were back to being a regular family again, doing normal stuff." He punched his fist into his open hand. "Now, I can grieve, and I don't know how."

Starla encouraged him to be patient and recognize there was no one-size-fits-all and to start by finding words for his loss, then by saying them out loud you know they have been heard. "It sounds simple but to vocalize what losing Summer means to you and the kids is a step in the right direction."

"Expressing my feelings in words is not my strong suit. How 'bout you give me some to chew on and I'll try," he said as the edges of his mouth curved into a smile.

With the somberness of the mood lightened Starla ribbed, "My thesaurus is in my carry-all bag."

"Bet you didn't know you signed up as chauffeur and whipping post. Seriously, thanks for listening."

"Been there. Bought the T-shirt. It's a good thing we're almost to Memphis. I'd hate for you to have to thumb a ride."

A brick red pyramid roof protected the apartment above Jasmine Jones' two-car garage that would serve as an asylum for a felon on the run. Victor followed Sally to the top of the outside staircase where she opened the door to the well-appointed guest quarters bathed in contemporary black and vanilla-cream tones. She noted this had been her mother's pet project, dabbling in interior design from her *Modern Apartment Style* magazines. Until now, no one had stepped one foot inside. Street-side windows invited the afternoon sun to toss particles of dust through the room. A filigreed black room divider with a cherry blossom motif separated the bedroom and bath from the small den and kitchen. With all his worldly possessions stowed inside his large tote bag, unpacking would be swift. Victor promised himself to be on his best behavior as he suspected his nemesis lurked in the ample physique of his landlady. As if on cue, the elder Mrs. Jones arrived to set the ground rules for his stay. "Sally, I'd like to speak with our guest in private. You go tend to your little one who's waiting in the kitchen for her afternoon snack."

"I gave her some Fruit Loops before I came up here."

"She's pouting at that choice. Now, go on...give that poor child what she wants."

Sally's grumbling was indistinguishable as she scooted out the door leaving her mother and their guest alone. Victor's facial muscles twitched while using his sleeve to wipe the beads of sweat that had formed on his lip. Mrs. Jones raised one eyebrow, cautiously summing up her houseguest before saying, "My name is Jasmine like the vine, sweet if you follow the rules, uncontrollable if crossed. Understand?"

Victor acknowledged her comment with a nod.

"You're a quiet one, huh, Mr....What's your name?"

"Kurtz...I mean Knight. Lou Knight."

"All righty, Lou Knight. Sally says you've got a stutter."

"Yeah. Tourette's vocal tics. Meds help some."

"You'll pay your rent while you're here by doing yard work and any other chores that need doing. Our day starts with breakfast at seven, lunch is at noon, the dinner bell rings at six. Nothing fancy, but you're welcome to join us. If not, so be it. Don't care either way. Any questions?"

Looking down at his feet he shook his head from side to side. "Weeds...got to pull weeds."

"Then you best get started...Mr. Kurtz."

An immobilized stare passed over his face landing in Jasmine's direction, each summing up the other as if in Tombstone wit-matching instead of gunfighting at the O.K. Corral. He licked his lips before speaking, "Lou Knight, Mrs. Jones. Lou Knight."

Lou in Victor's body established a comfortable routine within the Jones' home, darting upstairs every evening after playing charades and dress-up with Charmaine. It was as though he finally had a playmate. After finding a boom box stowed away in one of the hall closets inside the home, he asked Sally for permission to use it to help entertain her daughter, who under the guidance of her new pal, the candy man, had devoted every waking minute to singing, dancing, and pretending. Sally also offered her collection of CDs to him to assist in the development of their little starlet. They were a pair, both plagued by unworldliness, uncalloused by expectations, and oddly incurious to the world around them. One night, Charmaine dressed in a wedding dress crafted from a white sheet belted with a golden rope and wearing her signature tiara and Lou shirtless and barefoot thrashed about to the mournful theme from *Schindler's List* emoting the eternal yearning and sadness dictated by the song. His young protégé, too immature to appreciate the depth of the emotions, followed Lou's lead parroting the drama in his body language as much as a six-year-old could accomplish. As Jasmine circumspectly watched the production, her eyes narrowed with uneasy puzzlement while every cell in her body registered a high alert as her granddaughter and their houseguest acted out the emotion of the piece. She jotted down a mental note—the old saying that butter would melt in his mouth—innocent he is not.

Each evening after the Jones family retired and within the confines of his room, he began writing a play—a dream dashed when his father walked out of his life and Tourette's walked in. One night, after many rehearsals, *The Devil in Lou's Town* starring Charmaine Jones debuted in front of an audience of two. He had used his tattoo markers to draw new candy hearts on his knuckles, one saying *Cool Cat,* the other *Purr fect.* Lou was dressed in all black and instead of a speaking role, he held up story boards introducing a simple plot—a desperate family bargains with evil, leaving a sick child's rescue in the hands of the muted storyteller—the devil.

Sally wildly clapped as Lou introduced her daughter, the star of the show who curtsied, waving at her mother and grandmother. Her hair was pinned with a large red bow and she wore a sleeveless red, white, and blue pair of Hello Kitty pajamas, her mouth covered with a piece of white tape. She assumed her position laying on a cot in the center of the "stage." Lou knelt beside her bed his head bowed in prayer. He kissed her hand before turning to the audience and through a series of cardboard signs began the tale of a young girl dying of oral cancer. He paced around Charmaine's bed in the character of the distraught parent, chin tight to his chest, hugging his shoulders, and as a last resort, made a pact with the devil himself to save the child. The devil wanted one thing—for him to create a character, likeable by everyone and famous all over the world so he could gain worshipping followers who would do anything he asked. Lou drew a picture of a mouthless kitten with pointed ears that resembled Satan's horns. As on cue, Charmaine on all fours crawled around the room, smiling and purring. Lou held up the final story board displaying, *The End . . . Wasn't our starlet the cat's pajamas!* After many bows and encores, the production shut down and the stars and the audience retired to the kitchen for refreshments. Charmaine sat on Lou's lap while they snacked on potato chips and onion dip.

"It was clever to tie in a cat with the devil—they've been linked to witchcraft for centuries," said Jasmine.

"Kitty . . . ditty . . . kitty . . . means demon in Chinese," stuttered Lou.

"So, Hello Kitty means Hello Demon. Didn't know that . . . kinda weird," said Sally.

Lou kissed Charmaine on the forehead, giving her a box of candy hearts before excusing himself, feigning exhaustion from the performance, heading up to the quietness of his apartment. Sally and Jasmine moved to the den after putting Charmaine to bed, each wedged amidst skepticism and certainty about the houseguest's influence on their youngster.

"Sally, I know you believe in the goodness of this man, but...."

"Before you say any more, I see my child happy and enamored with him...that means lots to me and to my daughter."

"There's just something not right about him. It's not his speech problem. He relates to children on their level...he's almost like the Pied Piper and I smell a rat."

"What on earth has he done other than be a built-in companion to your granddaughter? Let's forget about this before I get mad."

"I asked him his name and he said Kurtz...then corrected it to Knight...Lou Knight. I thought that was odd."

"You're just looking for reasons not to trust him. I'm going to bed. Goodnight, Mama."

After the intensity of the soul-searching earlier, Starla tuned the satellite radio to the year's top forty singles flavored with the best of Britain, America, the islands of Barbados, and Trinidad and Tobago. Highlights of the playlist included the genius of Maroon 5, Coldplay, Rihanna, Nicki Minaj, and Jessie J., but the lyrics of Kelly Clarkson's "Stronger (What Doesn't Kill You)," and Ellie Goulding's "Lights" touched a nerve with both Starla and Matt as the vibrancy of the artists voices filled the car with a powerful mantra of standing tall against all odds facing the whispering hymns of loss with the grip strength of an eagle's talon. A brief gaze between the two lay bare a transcendent moment of kinship and an unspoken promise to be each other's life jacket if either slips off the dock.

Starla, having been to Memphis while on tour with her late husband's band, had booked two deluxe rooms at the River Inn of Harbor Town, the Tennessee boutique hotel with twenty-eight guest rooms overlooking the Mississippi River. After exiting the Interstate and successfully navigating the roundabout, they arrived at Harbor Town Square with their overnight haven in full view. Upon arrival in the lobby, they were treated to a glass of champagne while waiting for the final touches to the rooms to be finished. Although summer was in full swing, the wood-burning fireplace crackled, tossing flames in perpetual motion as if applauding the arrival of guests to Southern ambiance. An ornate 1850s New Orleans mantel and a baby grand piano added to the coziness of the setting, prompting Matt to comment, "Starla, that keyboard has got your name on it."

The rooms overlooked the river, the décor, European, featuring a four-poster bed beautified with signature crisp white luxury linens. After unpacking and freshening up from the nine-hour journey, they met at Tug's Casual Grill outdoors to toast the sky unfolding into a mosaic of pale pink quartz while a flock of prothonotary warblers migrating north from wintering in South America eclipsed the setting sun. They moved to the rooftop terrace for dinner where the folding windows were open to the river breeze suppressing any lingering humidity. Spanning across the Mississippi, the blue bulbs illuminating the Hernando de Soto Bridge, also known as the "M" bridge because of its double arches, drew attention to the riverfront area reflecting colors onto the water surface as if paying tribute to the birth of blues music. After being seated at a table by the window, Matt, feeling adventurous, ordered the bartender's surprise dubbed, Gentleman's Treat, a mix of Jack Daniels, freshly squeezed lemon, splashes of sweet and sour and Coke. "And for the Missus?" the waiter asked.

They looked sheepishly at each other before Starla remarked, "Oh, the gentleman was married to my sister."

To which Elvis the waiter smirked, "Sweet...keeping it in the family. Now, what would you like to sip on tonight?"

"No, you don't understand...."

"Sir, it's not my job to understand."

Starla, experiencing a slight warmth radiating in her cheeks, ordered a Blackberry Julep made with bourbon, blackberry puree and mint. Dinner consisted of small plates of Mojo shrimp, lamb sliders, and fried panko-breaded pimento cheese balls served with Louisiana hot sauce. After dinner Matt and Starla sauntered through the lobby filled with patrons delighting in a singalong of "Do Wah Diddy Diddy Dum Diddy Do..." led by the evening's piano-man on the baby grand.

With a seven-hundred-fifty-mile leg planned for day three, Matt and Starla retired to their suites agreeing on an early breakfast at Paulette's before hitting the road with Midland, Texas, targeted as the destination after eleven or so hours of travel. By nine o'clock that morning they passed through Little Rock, heading west on Interstate 30 to Dallas then Interstate 20 toward the energy hub of West Texas. The Lone Star State being the leading producer of wind power electricity in the United States—the fruits of then Governor Bush's labor in 1999—was evident by a landscape strewn with wind farms, their turbines rising three-hundred-forty-five feet in the air. The duo arrived around six that evening at their accommodations, the Hilton DoubleTree, located in the heart of downtown providing a shelter for the weary travelers. A hot shower and room service made a strong case for the pair, but at the recommendation of the concierge and an iconic restaurant within walking distance, they decided Italian food was on the dinner menu. A whiff of garlic trickled into the air when Matt opened the door to Luigi's. The atmosphere smacked of a time-capsule of old-world charm complete with red gingham tablecloths, wicker basket wine bottles dripped with candle wax, warm breadsticks, and freshly grated Parmesan cheese on each table. Once seated, the waiter informed them of the two-drink per person limit and took their orders—Veal Parmigiana for the lady and a glass of Chianti, Pinot Grigio and Fettuccini Alfredo for the gentleman. After savoring the meal, Matt and Starla, thankful for burning a few calories on the walk back to the hotel, retired to their rooms anticipating a much shorter day tomorrow and looking forward to arriving at Sky Island Retreat by noon.

20

The Candy Man

CONNER STARTED THE day as normal since occupying Matt's home. Dude and Halle, loyal to their internal early morning *pay-attention-to-me* clocks, sat beside his bed hoping he would respond to the stare-down technique. If unsuccessful, the wake-up call fell to Halle, a maestro of the loud purr followed by a gentle nip on any piece of Conner's exposed skin. Even the slightest movement by the lump curled up in the bed signaled it was Dude's turn to rouse the sleepyhead by jumping on top of him. Conner quickly learned he was no match for his housemates who possessed the persistence of a blue heron with a frog in its mouth. The animals led the race downstairs to the kitchen and once fed, they scurried to their beds for a morning nap while their *fill-in-skipper* readied for work. He resisted the temptation to razz them awake on his way out the door recalling his father's words when he was bound to repay his sister with some of her own medicine . . . *the axe forgets what the tree remembers*. Backing his cruiser down the driveway he paused before pulling on to Prospect Avenue to wave at Mrs. Brennan who was in her usual position rocking away on her front porch.

Sheriff McAlister received a grim report after his six-month checkup with his oncologist, his prostate cancer had metastasized to his bones. Although there was no cure, he would begin systemic radiation therapy where radiopharmaceuticals are injected into a vein, the path targeting cancer in the bones, killing the cells in numerous affected spots at once. His first treatment required a day-long stay in the hospital that he shared with no one except his wife. She called Conner with the cover-up that he was taking a personal day to spend with her celebrating their wedding anniversary.

When the sheriff arrived late the next day for the regularly scheduled morning briefing, Conner saw Atlas carrying the weight of the world squarely on his shoulders as he pushed through the front door. "Morning, let me toss my lunch in the break room and I'll be right with you guys."

Conner and Axl gazed saucer-eyed at each other, both noticing the sheriff's voice sounded as though it was hanging on by a thread unable to get enough air from his lungs to form the words. His gait on the way back to his desk was a slow awkward motion—shambling like a man twice his age.

"Sir, are you all right?" asked Axl.

"Of course, why would you ask? Now, what's the latest on our runaway felon?"

"We're still waiting for the tracking information on Sophia Kurtz's cell phone that Victor stole from her. I've got a call into the technicians, but nothing yet," said Axl.

"Our hands are tied until then. Anything else on this case? If not, let's move on to the rest of the stack," said the sheriff.

The deputies filed out of the office, dispatched to uphold a presence in the community and answer any calls for assistance. Conner's fingers drummed on his desk while observing his boss and mentor out of the corner of his eye. Sheriff McAlister's hand shook while rubbing his forehead and his expression appeared and disappeared in a jerky motion as if struggling to retain his composure. "Warren, how long have we known each other?"

"Long time, why?"

"Basic training as an officer of the law demands recognition of body language signs. Wanna tell me what's wrong? Your brave front is not working."

As Sheriff McAlister detailed his diagnosis and treatment, Conner's heart ached with each word. Their relationship had always been special, but this moment felt familiar as if a father and son were having one of those big talks neither ever wanted to have with Conner's emotions spiraling downward like a slinky on a staircase. "Your strength has been tested before. There's not a give-up bone in your body," Conner said, the catch in his voice, thick and uneven.

Tears welled in Warren's eyes. "I'm worried about my sweet Sherry. I'm the only family she's got...since we lost our daughter, Lily."

Their mood, consistent with introspection, dissolved with the ringing of the telephone. "Hello...Yes, this is Deputy Boyle." Sheriff McAlister's ears perked up when Conner mouthed that the call was about Mrs. Kurtz's cell phone.

"So, please tell me we know where Victor is."

"Kansas City, Missouri. Residence on Fairmount Avenue. At least that's where the phone is."

"Put a call in to our counterparts in Jackson County. Finally, we may have caught up with the dirtball."

After a lengthy briefing with the deputies and emphasizing that he is a flight risk, Conner faxed all Victor Kurtz's information including his profile photo to them. Sheriff McAlister returned from the break room with his lunch, taking a seat at his desk. "We need to finish our little talk."

"I'm going to grab another cup of coffee. Can I get you a refill?"

"Just a bottle of water if you don't mind. Doc is encouraging me to cut my caffeine intake and eat kale chips instead of Pringles. I'm not sure why that'll make a difference, but I'll play along for a bit."

"What can I do to help you, Sheriff?"

"Take over my job."

"You mean until you get through these treatments?"

"No, permanently. I have to retire. I need to spend as much time as I have got left with Sherry."

"I can't replace you. This is crazy."

177

"You're right," he said with a wry grin. "It's not about replacing me. It's about your accepting a promotion to sheriff."

"You can count on me taking over your duties while you're going through these treatments—until you're strong enough to take back over."

"Conner, I'm not coming back."

A brick to the forehead would have been easier to digest than Sheriff McAlister's revelation and proposal. Granted, Conner aspired to be sheriff, sometime, not now and not because of his mentor's medical crisis.

After discovering her husband, Sally's father, was married to four other women at the time of their nuptials, Jasmine Jones retained the only blessings from his deceitfulness, her daughter and a prized possession housed in the garage below their guest's quarters. When she backed out of the driveway to go to the grocery store in her robin's egg blue 1969 Volkswagen Thing four-door convertible, Victor aka Lou watched from his apartment window. His life in the company of this family had developed into a mixture of guarded security, although relentlessly under the vigilance of the elder Mrs. Jones. The giant anteater, the fiercest mammal-mama in the kingdom with her newborn pups, failed to compare with the tenacity of Jasmine as related to her granddaughter, a threat not lost on their houseguest. Sally, the antithesis of her mother, possessed a blend of jauntiness and mischief-making, feeding into Victor's commitment to dysfunction. She also was not shy about taking advantage of his kinship with her daughter, handing off parenting challenges in favor of settling into her beanbag chair in front of the television, plopping in a VHS tape to binge watch every season of *Alfred Hitchcock Presents*, her favorite one about an unmarried ugly-duckling sister infatuated with her movie-star brother.

Jasmine returned from the store with several weeks supply of food. Lou, trailed by Charmaine, sprinted downstairs to help carry the sacks to the kitchen. "Come here, pumpkin. Look what Mamoo brought you—your favorite lemon meringue cookies." After hugging her grandmother's leg, she caught her toe on the throw rug while pirouetting causing her to tumble to the floor. Before the squealing began, Lou rushed to her side, kissing her wound, and tickling her into fits of giggles. Drama avoided with a box of cookies soothing any woes.

"My Candy Hearts Man fixed my boo-boo, Mamoo."

Jasmine had a way of looking at Lou like she was sucking the juice out of a lemon. "I can see that he did. Now, why don't you and your hero go outside and eat your snack."

When Charmaine and Lou were together, he felt his landlady's guarded eye permeating through his skin, especially after the premier of his play. After sharing the cookies, he began pulling weeds in the front flowerbed while his young friend sat cross-legged on the sidewalk drawing pictures with colored chalk. Lou looked up at the electric-blue sky sprinkled with pearlescent clouds listlessly in abeyance until a breeze floating by reshuffled the creations into new shapes. *What a perfect day for a photo shoot,* he thought. He bolted upstairs to retrieve his beloved companion, a Fujifilm Fine-Pix digital camera. Charmaine, always ready for playtime, jumped up and down when she saw what was in her friend's possession.

"Whatcha got on your fingers today, Candy Man?"

"Today we have *Dream* on the left and *Diva* on the right," Lou said, mimicking how she should strike various poses while he snapped pictures of her. Mamoo, walking by the window, stopped to view the antics going on in her yard. Her granddaughter, hand on her hips pouting; puckering her lips; tucking her hair behind her ears; gazing over her shoulder with a come-hither look; blowing kisses; performing cartwheels; and pulling a straw hat down where only her eyes were visible. The blood drained from Jasmine's face as her attention was transfixed on her granddaughter and the resident photographer. It was as though she was frozen inside a horrible nightmare unfolding in slow motion. The trusting innocence of her sweet little girl was on full display as she frolicked, playing to the lens of the camera as Lou clicked away. He looked up catching Jasmine's eye through the front window. He waved. She looked away then glanced back before disappearing to another room to answer the phone.

21

Wishing on a Star

MATT AND STARLA'S road trip presented a wide range of topography leaving the eastern shore of Lake Erie passing by rivers and tributaries, hundreds of horse farms of the inner bluegrass region of Kentucky's "gateway to the south" to Nashville, sitting on the start of the Highland Rim, and Memphis rising from a bluff on the Mississippi River as if overseeing the multicultural mix of blues, country, rock 'n' roll, soul, and hip-hop. After navigating through Little Rock, on the south bank of the Arkansas River, the lush foothills surrendered to the tall skylines of the Dallas-Fort Worth Metroplex situated in the Texas Blackland Prairie region with a few rolling hills dotted by man-made lakes, cut by streams, creeks, and rivers, surrounded by forested land. Saying farewell to Midland after a night's stay, the travelers found themselves near the home of a West Texas curiosity, the Monahans Sandhills State Park, a desert-like oasis with wind-created, seventy-foot sand dunes. Fort Stockton, rich with large private ranches, was next on the agenda, in close proximity to Patrick and Margo's hometown of Green Tree situated on a high plateau in the Chihuahuan Desert—the Davis Mountains to the north and the southernmost mountain range in the mainland United States, the *Chisos*, fully contained within the boundaries of the Big Bend

181

National Park. In a few more miles the duo arrived at the gated entrance. It was lunchtime at the Mackie's abode.

Gabe bounced from one foot to the other waiting for the car, an energized grin spreading from one ear to the other when it came into view. He bolted toward his dad when Matt climbed out of the passenger side of the Range Rover, father and son's bond bookended by love. Margo aimed a weak smile at her granddaughter who stood immobile on the porch, her eyes wandering to the skies and exhaling a big breath as if she had somewhere else to be. Starla greeted the welcoming committee noting her niece's lack of enthusiasm. "Willa, how is it possible that you've grown in the last week? Come give your aunt a big hug."

Willa's embrace held a touch of affection before dropping her head and pulling away saying, "I'm not taller, just fatter."

"Honey, I don't know what your definition of fat is, but I promise you're far from obese."

"Seriously. . . ."

Gabe pulled Starla and Matt to the fountain handing each a quarter insisting they make a wish. "Daddy, it's a secret, but I wished Aunt Starla and Conner would get married. I need an uncle to go with my aunt."

"That would be great, but, son, that's up to them, understand?"

"But I already threw my money in and Donny gave me this rabbit's foot and I wished on a star like Pinocchio."

Starla, eyeing the private father-son chat, shot a wondering glance in Matt's direction upon hearing Conner's name. "Starla, Gabe was just telling me we couldn't go inside before making our wishes. Ladies first."

"He's right and Concha's preparing barbecue brisket and grilled cheese sandwiches for lunch. Hope you're hungry," hollered Margo.

"Fire away, Aunt Starla."

Willa's little brother's appetite for life and his universal appeal, although infectious and pure, drained her temperament into a glowering missile of resentment. At times, especially recently, his *golden-boy-wonder* persona triggered a numbness mended only by flight. During the coin tossing she turned to flee, instead encountering the cast-iron level stare of her grandfather. "I think it would be an excellent idea if you stayed put to say hello to your dad."

"Big Pop, he's busy. I'll catch him later."

"No, you'll see him now. Clear?" The sternness in Patrick's voice matched his eyes, leaden like the gray of the ocean before dawn's first rays strike the water.

Willa's life had troubling issues beyond her age, but she was smart enough to recognize when the line in the sand was drawn. Starla announced her arrival back on the front porch by clearing her throat interrupting the atmosphere suspended as taut as a lanyard used in a sailing vessel's riggings.

"Patrick, this place is unbelievable. I can't wait to see the rest of it."

"Hope the long drive was worth it. Margo and I are excited to have you here. How's my son?"

"He had lots of time to beat himself up, but he let go of some of the anger, which is good. Clearly, he is going through a faith crisis. There were many *Matt moments* full of silliness and laughter, too."

"Do you charge by the hour?" retorted Patrick.

"No, just room and board in a luxurious oasis."

Father and son made their way to the front porch. Willa stepped forward, "Hi, Dad," her voice as hollow as an echo bouncing off the walls of an empty house.

"Let me look at you—a gangly teen left Buffalo last week and now you've grown into a beauty. Must be something in the Texas water."

Margo put her arm around Willa's shoulders in agreement with Matt's assessment. "Y'all follow me and I'll show you your rooms."

Margo, cognizant that Matt might be bombarded with memories of the room he and Summer shared when they visited, prepared two options for him upstairs. Without hesitation he opened the door to reminiscences of his past. The peaked ceiling featured exposed wood beams with a studded upholstered headboard framing the king-sized bed accented with sage green pillows and throw. A small fireplace occupied the corner and sliding doors opened to a private terrace. "Honey, are you sure the other room wouldn't be better?"

"Positive, Mom. Starla said I have to find words for my loss. This might help me do just that."

"We all want you to heal. If the room does that for you, then that's where you should be. Promise you'll tell me if it's just too much too soon. Can I help you unpack?"

"I got it. I'll be down in a few minutes."

Patrick offered Starla a rendering of the property on the way to her accommodations just a short walk south of their home which featured five bedrooms and bathrooms upstairs while the primary suite was in the corner of the first floor alongside two full kitchens and a massive dining room. The Mackies hosted many large groups utilizing the numerous separate residential buildings scattered through the acreage including a multi-story, four-bedroom party barn with indoor/outdoor event and dining areas; a two-bedroom farm house, a three-bedroom cottage, and a secluded stone exterior one-bedroom cabin with separate bunk house.

"If you've never ridden a horse you're in for a treat as Margo's prized possessions are her majestic Friesians and a stable of Clydesdales. We've got six par three golf holes that we can set the tee boxes from sixty to two-hundred-thirty-five yards to the pins. We can play golf, hike, ride all-terrain-vehicles or horses on the trails, fish, or take the chill off at one of the fire pits. Believe it or not the night air around here can be a bit nippy."

"I can't imagine why you would want to go anywhere else."

"Sometimes you leave one paradise for another. Here we are—your home away from home." The pool house, a one-bedroom, one-bath bungalow with a partial kitchen with retracting doors opening to a large, covered deck and pool area. "Margo and I thought you might enjoy the privacy and quietness for your song writing. If it isn't acceptable, we've got more choices."

"Hmmmm...so I get to relax in a lounger, put my drink on the natural stone cocktail table, and overlook the swim-up grotto, waterfall and slide. Somehow, I'll manage," she wisecracked.

"I'll wait for you and we can walk back to the house. Concha is probably pacing around the kitchen."

"Let me just drop my bags and I'll be right there."

Starla and Patrick arrived back at the house where an airstream of busyness greeted them. Concha wiped her brow with a hand towel while flying around the kitchen tending to griddles of toasted beef and cheese sandwiches; Margo, with the help of Willa, set the table for lunch while Donny engaged Gabe in a tickle game of *mercy*, with giggle tears running down Gabe's face and no surrender in sight. "We should sneak out before we're put to work," said Patrick.

"Honey, could you help Matt with the drinks? Pitchers of sangria are in the other kitchen's frig," said Margo.

"GoGo, can I have a sip?" asked Willa.

"It looks like fruit punch, but it's made with red wine. I don't think you'd like it."

The kitchen flurry dissipated, replaced by a hint of geniality as the family congregated around the table. Donny, offering a toast to Starla, said, "Let's raise our glasses in honor of our Irish-born New Yorker. Welcome to Texas. As a proud native of the Lone Star State, you might notice we are a mix of valor and swagger, but we tend to park our bluster on the side when welcoming guests to our state. Our arms are as open as our big hearts!"

"I had forgotten how much I love this place. Dad, do you think Green Tree might be ripe for Seasons LXX South."

Willa fired her father a dark smoldering look, tossing her napkin on the table before pushing her chair back. Margo squeezed her granddaughter's knee, returned the serviette to her lap, issuing a stern visual warning to reconsider her actions.

The blood drained from Jasmine's face as she listened intently to the police officer on the other end of the line—her instincts regarding their houseguest verified. They asked about his whereabouts now, ordering her to calmly remove the family from the residence. Fortunately, a neighbor was picking Charmaine up for a birthday party at the local zoo. She and Sally would ride along. Victor watched from his bedroom window above the garage as the Jones trio loaded into the van for a fun day in the KidZone with its peek-a-boo tree and endangered species carousel. As the car disappeared, his escape plan kicked into high gear. His possessions were packed, and with the key he had stolen to Jasmine's car in hand, he took one last look around one of the happiest places he had ever experienced—even under the extreme scrutiny of Mama Jones. His pal, Charmaine, in possession of his cell phone, would play a role in his vanishing act. He would leave her the rest of his candy hearts. She deserved a reward for being his playmate.

One police unit continued to track Victor's cell which led them to the zoo, finding it in the child's care. Confiscating it caused hysteria as she ducked in and around the carousel screaming "no—mine—no—mine...mine." A tag team of Sally and Jasmine corralled her, prying her fingers off the phone, handing it to the officers. A promise to return it to her received louder protests, only pacified by an extra slice of birthday cake.

While this pursuit was unfolding, law enforcement, accompanied by the SWAT team, swarmed the Jones' residence. Victor, sporting a Kansas City Chief's ball cap borrowed from Sally, was cruising southbound on Interstate 35 in Jasmine's prized Volkswagen Thing, top down and Willie Nelson's "On the Road Again" blaring on his way to his next destination. When the zoo birthday-partygoers arrived back home, they were met with the bad news that not only was Mr. Kurtz one step ahead of them, but he stole Jasmine's car to make his getaway. Making matters worse, they were forced to break down the doors to gain entrance to the home and the apartment leaving extensive damage to both. The searches revealed little, but officers dusted Victor's residence for fingerprints and bagged the boxes of candy hearts.

"So, now what? What are you doing to find my car? And, what about all this damage?" a frustrated Mrs. Jones asked.

"An all-points-bulletin has been issued. Law enforcement across the country will be on the lookout for your car. It'll stand apart. There aren't a lot of them on the road these days. Mr. Kurtz might have stolen the wrong mode of transportation to just blend in with traffic."

"Mama, you were right. Can you forgive me?" begged Sally.

"Mamoo...where's my friend Lou? I hate you. You made him leave," whined Charmaine.

Jasmine looked into the teary eyes of her granddaughter clinging to her mother's legs. "Honey...listen to me. Your friend Lou stole my car. He lied to us and took advantage of your mother's kindness. Now quit crying."

"Mrs. Jones, forgive me for interrupting and for all the mess. My name is Hazel Stockman. I'm with Child Protective Services and I need to speak with Charmaine."

"Wait just a minute. She's in a loving home—the last thing she needs is to be protected from her family. How dare you insinuate our little angel is in danger."

"Please, let's find somewhere to speak privately."

"Sally, entertain your daughter while I talk with this lady."

"But, Mama...."

"You heard me, now go on."

Jasmine's hackles rose to exaggerated heights as she listened to Ms. Stockman detail the sordid life of Victor Kurtz, their Lou Knight. "I'm sorry, Mrs. Jones, but with his track record, we must make sure your granddaughter did not experience any inappropriate behavior from this man. Don't worry, we're trained to deal with children."

"My God. I was right. I knew something was off with this guy. My poor baby...."

"Sometimes it's easier for a child to open up without an audience—especially family. There may be more criminal charges filed depending on what she tells me...and counseling might be necessary to work through the issues if...but let's don't get ahead of ourselves before we know what we're dealing with."

"Okay."

Charmaine's hands were covered with different colors of chalk dust as she drew pictures on the sidewalk in front of the house. Hazel sat down beside her. "What a beautiful name."

"Lou said it was from Shake somebody...I don't remember, but he said it was pretty—just like me."

"What color hair did he have?"

"None—he said he looked like a bowling ball. He was funny like that," she moaned. Her face sagging like the jowls of a basset hound as she turned back to her chalk masterpiece.

"Sounds like he was your best buddy. What kind of things did you do together?"

"Sing and dance and put on shows. He took lots of pictures of me."

"Did you get all dressed up for the pictures?"

"Nah...just put on hats."

"What other fun things did you do?"

"Running through the sprinkler. He didn't have a bathing suit, so he just wore his undies."

"Charmaine, he sounds like he was a good playmate. Bet you got lots of hugs and kisses huh?"

"And candy. He drew hearts with markers on his fingers. Lots of tickling, too. I miss him."

"I bet you do. You know when you were playing together, did he accidentally touch you in your swim-suit area...do you know what I mean?"

"Where I wipe after tinkling?"

"Yes, there."

"Nope, that would make him bad...he said so."

"So, you talked about that?"

"Kinda. He said some people might try to do that and I should run away fast."

Hazel asked Charmaine to draw a picture of herself with her friend Lou on the sidewalk. The tribute was filled with candy hearts surrounding a stick figure with a big red heart on his chest holding the hand of a smaller stick figure with a heart with a *Cutie Pie* message. "I'm going to talk with your mom and grandma. You goin' to stay here?"

"I'll come with you. It's time for a snack. Lou always liked snacks."

Hazel briefed the family on her visit, concluding that she found no evidence that Charmaine encountered any inappropriate touching from their houseguest, although acknowledging their connection was undeniably odd, and in her words, "borderline creepy." She advocated keeping a vigilant eye on her for any changes especially behavioral extremes—overly aggressive or passive. And, to take notice if she flinches at sudden movement, shies away from affection, or reverts to thumb-sucking or temper tantrums. "These might be warning signs that she has repressed abuse anxiety. Because of her age, she might not have the words to express what she's feeling."

When the officers finished the investigation at the house, Jasmine, Sally, and Charmaine were left to pick up the pieces of Victor Kurtz's departure. The outer doors suffered the most damage and although the interiors of both the house and apartment were tossed, they were fixable. Putting their lives back into some sense of normalcy might be the challenge at least in the short term. Jasmine swallowed the urge to rub salt in the wound by playing the *I-told-you-so-card* as Sally was already back to biting her nails down to the quick. The recovery of her car and the capture of Victor/Lou took top priority on her calendar.

22

Life's a Dance

MARGO RELEASED THE grip on Willa's knee when she physically acquiesced to the heavyweight signal issued by her grandmother, although bellyaching, "Whatever," and picking the melted cheese out of her sandwich. Matt's attention, drawn to his pouting daughter, directed a deadpan stare her way, sarcastically adding, "I missed you, too, sweetie."

"May I be excused. I'm not hungry and my ribs hurt," she whined looking around the table for a sliver of pity for her plight. The reception, reminiscent of a cold wave breaking on a deserted shore.

Patrick cleared his throat, aiming his displeasure at his granddaughter by playing an air violin. "I think you should wait in your room while we finish the delicious lunch Concha prepared for us."

"But, Big Pop...I didn't mean to make you mad."

"What did you mean to do then?"

Willa's body slumped, strands of hair crisscrossed her face, her emotional vault emptying into a monsoon of tears tumbling into her lap. Patrick pushed back his chair from the table, kneeling beside his granddaughter and taking her hand. "Come on...let's walk."

Quietness escorted Willa and Patrick as they strolled past one of the lakes on the property. Willa's petulance, consistent with unsettled feelings of shame combined with anger, was on display as she took inventory of each step she took. "Mocking you was childish and uncalled for," he said. "I'm just trying to understand what you're going through. And it's a lot. You were injured in the same accident that took the life of your mother. You're a teenage girl who has been uprooted from your friends and school. You're a victim of a stalker. We all get that, but that doesn't excuse your thoughtless behavior."

"Big Pop, I'm sorry. I am. I just feel like whatever I say or do is judged...like being under a microscope. I just get fed up with it and I don't know...just act out."

"I know it seems that way, but your grief is not any bigger or smaller than ours. Your dad is without the love of his life and he's responsible for raising two kids on his own. Margo and I are mourning with our only child and feeling helpless."

"Don't you ever just want to scream or hit something?"

"Yes."

"So, what do you do?"

"I find a place to let it out and get rid of it."

"Where?"

"Could be in the shower but most of the time it's on the golf course. I love the game, but it can bring a grown man to his knees sometimes. We could help each other with the hittin' and hollerin'...how 'bout a code to let each other know we're about to explode...."

"Girl's anthem?"

"That song we heard on YouTube, right? Let's put it on your purple cast as a reminder."

He put his arm around Willa's shoulders as they renewed the *therapy* session walking back to the house. A shared flicker of the eyes unearthed a deluge of understanding, breathing hope back into each other that the days and nights would get better and a level of peace amid the heartache was attainable.

Laughter, one of life's sweetest and most contagious creations, greeted them as they returned to the house. The family, still seated at the table and immersed in a game orchestrated by Gabe, paused to acknowledge the arrival of Patrick and Willa. "What in the world are you all giggling about and Starla, why are you wearing oven mitts?"

"We're playing the saran wrap game. Starla patted the vacant seat beside her. Willa, come sit...it's lots of fun."

Patrick nudged her gently toward the invitation, taking his seat between Margo and Gabe. "Big Pop, here's what you do. There're treasures buried inside that big ball. Whoever has the ball has to wear the mitts and tries to unwrap the ball and get the presents before someone rolls doubles on the dice...got it?"

"Absolutely," Patrick shrugged.

Concha refilled the Sangria glasses, mentioning to Willa she might like a soft drink and some cheese, crackers, and fresh fruit since she missed lunch. She dropped her head before looking up, offering a gracious smile for Concha's nonjudgmental gesture, "Thank you. That sounds great."

Matt caught his Dad's eye mouthing appreciation mixed with confusion for the change of attitude in his daughter. Margo, with a backhanded toss of the dice, rolled two fours passing the dice to Willa, receiving the mitts and saran wrap ball to unravel. Willa's first toss was double sixes taking possession of the ball and mitts before Margo had unwrapped a single layer. The game ended with Willa being the big winner taking possession of two five-dollar bills, a pack of gum, wrapped peppermint candy, and a dozen lottery tickets, which she honored her little brother by insisting he scratch off all the numbers, much to his delight. Margo, pulling Patrick aside, thanked him for whatever he said to turn around their granddaughter's caustic behavior.

"I just tried to walk in her shoes. We've got a signal now if things get too overwhelming for her. She's still going to have her teenage girl moments, but they might be less dramatic."

"Did anyone ever tell you what an intuitive man you are?"

"I have other qualities, too, in case you've forgotten."

"Bottlenose dolphins and I have excellent memories," she said.

"I thought elephants ruled the memory kingdom."

"Nope, dolphins each have a unique whistle instead of a name. They can remember the whistles of the dolphins they have lived with even after twenty years of separation—just like me."

"I might have to learn to whistle better," he teased.

"Not necessary—you have a name my love."

Later that day the group gathered poolside for a swim and a friendly-turned-competitive game of "horse" basketball pitting Patrick and Starla against Matt and Margo. Willa, wearing a waterproof cover over her cast, indulged Gabe in his speedy duck game, launching rubber ducks from the top of the waterfall and careening into the pool, the goal to move them to the opposite side without touching the buoyant yellow waterfowl. The activities died down as the world became bathed in a soft golden haze, leading Patrick to preview the show expected to debut when the sunset yielded to nightfall.

"Because we're so far from urban centers and light pollution, we're a certified dark sky park, meaning lots of stars and most of the time the Milky Way is visible."

Gabe, hopping around the patio with a foam ball between his knees, dropped it inviting the resident furball, Richard Parker, to bunt it under the couch. "Wait, Big Pop. There's a candy bar in the sky? That's Mommy's favorite treat," he said, his eyes gleaming like a jeweled Fabergé egg.

Patrick patted his lap for Gabe to sit. "I'll try to explain. Ya know those pinwheels we blow so they'll go round and round...well this Milky Way is like a giant pinwheel in the sky and it's called that because it looks like milk. But it's just a galaxy made up of billions of stars, not the Mars Company candy bar."

"Hey, my planet book says Mars is the red planet...so maybe Mars has a candy shop in heaven so Mommy can have a Milky Way."

"Anything is possible," said Matt, a blissful smile tossed at his high-spirited son.

"GoGo, could we eat one while we watch the galaxy twirl?"

"I'm afraid we don't have any. The best I can do are some M&M's."

"Okay...but I only like the green ones 'cause they make me happy like Christmas trees, peas, and those little green lizards...but I don't like tree frogs or grasshoppers."

"Do I dare ask...Gabe, tell us," razzed Starla.

"Frogs give you warts and warts are nasty. My science book says hoppers have ears on their tummies. We couldn't talk unless I flipped him over."

Willa tussled Gabe's hair saying, "That's my little brother's logic on full display, folks." The moment of love was not lost on the family as each one caught the other's eye at the chance that the teenage corner on the behavioral scale might have tipped in the right direction.

Gabe batted his sister's hand away, smoothing his locks back into place, the gentleness of the sibling's playfulness infectious and ordinary.

From their vantage point they watched the sun's fiery kiss to the day guiding the path for a countless fleet of stars illuminating the sky now draped in Phoenician purple as if clad in Her Majesty The Queen's cape. The quietness, garnered by the behemoth pageant playing out in the sky above, was disturbed by the neighing from the horses prompting Donny to excuse himself to make sure they were in their stalls for the night. Before leaving he kneeled beside Gabe who was laying on his back, hands behind his head, continuing the hypnotic trance produced by the magnetism of the night.

"See all those lights? They look like pinholes in a blanket, don't they?"

Gabe nodded.

"Well...they're for our angels in heaven to look through to make sure we're doin' all right down here on earth."

Gabe threw an inquiring glance at Donny, searching his face for any signs of pretense. After a few minutes, convinced that Donny's nose was not going to grow, Gabe blew a dozen kisses and waved to the celestial city above.

The congenial and unruffled aura of life at the Sky Island Retreat persisted for the family, each discovering a new passion for simplicity. Patrick assumed the role of golf pro teaching the basics of the game to Gabe who was equipped with a set of junior customized clubs and adjusting Matt's ball positioning, alignment, and tweaking his rusty swing amongst exploring the hiking trails and fishing the stocked ponds. Margo escorted Starla and Willa to the corral to meet her highly intelligent six-foot, four-legged loves.

"Donny's working with my one-ton gentle giants, youngsters Calamity and Dale, who are about four now. Look at their feet— they're the size of a dinner plate and watch how they lift each hoof off the ground during regular movement." Willa jumped back when the stampede of adult Clydesdales spotted Margo. Handing a carrot to each horse, she commented, "Ladies, I'd like you to meet Queenie, Ruby, and Duchess. When you adopt these magnificent animals, you do so for life as they live thirty-years."

"They have such sweet faces, but I bet they would send you flying if they just bumped into you," said Starla.

"Look how their ears are pricked forward. They're hanging on your every word."

"GoGo, do they like people?"

"Yes…they're social and love attention. Queenie is our prankster. Last month she held her hoof up for her shoe to be inspected then leaned back on that hoof putting some of her weight on the person handling the examination. Then she lifted her head, snorting as if laughing at her own joke."

"I've never ridden and honestly cannot say it was on my bucket list…until now. Can we ride them sometime?" asked Starla.

"Of course, Donny will saddle them up whenever we want."

"Now, follow me. Let's meet my Friesians."

Margo, Starla, and Willa made their way to the fence bordering the pasture where four stately horses eclipsed the view of the sun dipping behind the elevated peaks of the Chisos Mountains in the distance. Two chestnuts engaged in an affectionate game of nip and shove, biting around the neck and head, and leaning their bodies into each other while the jet-black stallion cantered behind the fairest of them all, a mare the color of eggshells mottled with streaks of silver.

"What we're seeing is horse-play at its finest. Shows the diversity of the personalities of these animals. Watch the bond between the chestnuts. Allegro is our dancer. She's rhythmic, powerful, and graceful when she moves—like Baryshnikov. Sergeant Pepper on the other hand is fiery, independent, and loyal to one person. If you make the mistake of paying attention to another horse, his ears will slap back, tail will swish, and often he'll raise his hind leg threatening a kick if anything gets too close."

"Who's his person?" asked Starla.

"Donny. Sometimes Concha comes with him and the *Sarge* loathes sharing."

"GoGo, what about the black and white horses?"

"My prize, Starless Night, has a good solid heart. He's faithful and reliable with impeccable integrity. He's Prince Charming to Lady Joan who is part Arabian. She's calm, wise, and noble. They'll make beautiful babies together."

"Is that why he's chasing her—to mate?" asked Starla.

"No, they're just doing the first-dance-tango at the moment," said Margo, laughing.

Conner, conversing daily with Starla, updated her on how things were going at the house, work, and with the hunt for Victor. Mrs. Brennan religiously left cookie tins on the front porch, resulting in a loosening of his belt buckle by two notches, and he admitted a growing fondness for Dude and Halle as they provided constant entertainment especially as early morning alarm clocks. He shared Sheriff McAlister's grim health news and his reluctance to assume the job formerly held by his esteemed mentor and offered an update on the hunt for Victor which she relayed to Matt and his parents since Gabe and Willa were under the tutelage of Donny who was showing them the nitty-gritty of riding a Clydesdale.

"Our *stalker-felon* was tracked by the phone he stole from his mother to Kansas City, Missouri. He'd been staying in the garage apartment above a house occupied by a woman, her daughter, and young granddaughter. When police and a SWAT team swarmed the home, he was gone. Stole the woman's car."

Matt's strained voice echoed his frustration as though his life was nothing more than a pus-filled boil, excruciatingly sore and painful. "How can this jerk persist in outfoxing the police? If it wasn't so fucking serious, it might be comical...sorry, that word doesn't come out of my mouth often."

"Son, your father's been mumbling that word under his breath for weeks now."

Attempting to calm the atmosphere, Starla explained, "The good news, if you can call it that, is Conner said the car he stole would not fade into traffic unnoticed. He likened it to going to a disco party dressed in a sheet with an olive branch wreath on your head."

"That's a pretty big red flag waving...surely it will be the downfall of Mr. Kurtz," said Margo. "On a cheerier note, Concha and I have been busy planning a *meet-the-family* party for next Saturday."

"Matt, you haven't seen your grandparents in a while...particularly since the changes to their lifestyles," commented Patrick.

"What do you mean. They're not ill, are they?"

"No, far from it," Margo paused. "You know our families have been friends for many years and after my daddy died from being struck by lightning on the golf course, and your dad's mother died of ovarian cancer, it seems my mom and Patrick's dad moved in together."

"Surely you're kidding. We've got our own version of *Bob & Carol & Ted & Alice?*"

"Except this didn't happen until both spouses passed...so now Betsy Tate and Sid Mackie are cohabitating."

Matt glanced from his dad to his mom trying to gauge any misgivings about the bombshell, but both faces held an outward veneer of acceptance. "Guess a toast is in order for our super-senior-teenagers."

"It's a wonderful time in their lives—they are active, enjoy a lot of the same things, travel with friends, and don't suffer from any let's say...performance anxieties," coughed Patrick. "Except I think my dad might have a jealous streak as Betsy is what he calls a looker. He sometimes complains he has to compete for her attention...aw...puppy love in full bloom."

Margo continued the guest list which included children in both Willa's and Gabe's age groups with her book club gals bringing their grandchildren, her dear friends Lovey and Morris Kirkman and their daughter Aria, a few of her fellow CASA volunteers, the superintendent of the school district and her husband, and Patrick's golf buddies plus his animal shelter board members and their spouses. She estimated fifty people would likely R.S.V.P. yes to the invitation.

Saturday arrived with a warm glow of excitement mixed with a flurry of last-minute details consuming the hostess. Matt offered to fill in for the bartender who reportedly imbibed too much during Friday happy hour at the Last Call Tavern, landing a reservation in the county jail for settling a dispute with an off-duty police officer by ramming his truck into the hood of his car. Margo's expression hardened into a frown upon hearing the overgrown boys were discussing the over and under toilet paper debate.

Margo, determined to find a replacement to tend bar instead of one of the guests of honor, called on Donny to round up an able body to fill in, which he did. Having solved that problem, she recruited Starla with her outdoor checklist for the deck overlooking the pool while she finished the preparations around the dining room table. Patrick busied himself making sure the bars were stocked and the tubs of bottled water, beer, wine coolers, and soft drinks were iced down. Concha and Margo flew from one kitchen to the other adding final touches before filling the stainless steel covered chafing dishes for transportation to the buffet tables located in the dining room and throughout the outdoor venues.

Willa ran her fingers through her hair sending a silent thank you to her grandmother for finding a milk protein and olive oil conditioning shampoo that tamed her naturally curly hair. After emptying her closet, she twirled in front of the mirror offering a thumbs-up with her choice of tunic, shorts, and sandals. Gabe, having knocked on her door five times, gave up, sprinting down the stairs wearing his bathing suit, a Buffalo Bills T-shirt and carrying his flip-flops.

The automated gate remained open as cars streamed in, parking on both sides of the road. Golf carts patrolled the line of cars, offering guests a ride to the *porte cochère* where Gabe was stationed with a sack of quarters for guests to toss into the fountain for good luck. Everyone found it impossible to dampen a young man's insistence of the protocol to first make a wish, toss the coin into the fountain, high five the financier and then receive clearance to proceed to the party. Patrick, stationed at the front door, introduced Matt to their friends, thanking each one for coming and indulging in Gabe's credo, *If you wish hard enough, it will come true.*

The party held an air of congeniality with bubbly laughter spilling into jubilant squeals from Gabe and his new-found buddies playing water tag. Pockets of conversation among the ladies praised the creativity of the hostess for her use of canoes sitting atop hay bales, planked from one end to the other, displaying charcuterie boards filled with prosciutto, sharp white cheddar cheese, cream cheese with jalapeno jelly, an assortment of crackers and baguettes, fresh fruit bowls, toasted almonds and vegetables, all underneath mesh umbrella covers.

Sid, with his arm draped around Betsy's shoulders, sat poolside enjoying the antics of their great-grandson, keeping an interested eye on the relationship developing with the teenage girls. Willa, sitting in a chair encircled by three others, looked from one girl to the next, her face emitting a cheerful glow as giggles mutated into hilarity. "These girls remind me so much of your Pamela and my Margo when they were that age," whispered Betsy.

"I miss Pamma. When is she going to come to her senses? She's hooked up with a kook hawking the voluntary extinction of humankind as the only thing that will save our planet. Hogwash. I'm glad her mother is not here to witness this."

"Sid, I understand but your daughter was always a passionate kid. Remember she started a 'friends of the tarantula campaign' because she thought the spider was misunderstood. Come on let's quit dwelling and go mingle."

Starla and Matt, grazing around the *southern-specialties* appetizer table, sampled the fried green tomato sliders spread with horseradish sauce, the pulled pork bathed in a spicy peach sauce, and grilled jumbo shrimp on top of cheesy grits. Starla watched with interest the dynamics between her niece and the other girls bringing back memories of her high school clique, the thespians consisted of good students interested in theater, song, and dance led by the queen bee and her sidekicks. The euphoria riding the jet stream from Willa and her newly found friends rippled through the atmosphere from the pool deck causing her dad and aunt to share a jaunty smile and crossed fingers at the semblance of a positive attitude adjustment.

"My mother could be the next Joan of Arc if this continues."

"Speak of the devil...wait isn't that an oxymoron...Saint Margo is headed our way," bantered Starla.

As she strode toward them, Margo's demeanor radiated a closeness with the couple who accompanied her. The gentleman clad in dark skin, a color impossible to achieve by a glancing sun, displayed a silver cross tattoo on his lower arm, the bald spot on the top of his head reflecting a blinding light. The full-figured woman by his side bore resemblance to a harvested pearl, her fairness glowing with a hint of rose in her cheeks. "Matt, honey, there you are. And, Starla, perfect. Meet our dear friends, Morris and Lovey Kirkman. This is my son and his sister-in-law. You remember I told you about losing our precious Summer."

Morris extended a comforting hand to both Matt and to Starla expressing his sympathy, "You must feel like God has abandoned you. I've been where you are. The woman who gave birth to me wrapped me in newspapers the day I took my first breath and flung me in a dumpster. It took me a long while to reconcile how a loving God could let that happen. Over the years I've realized that I'm strong because I've been weak. I'm fearless because I've been afraid. I'm wise because I've been foolish. You'll be just fine...give it the time it needs. Think of me as your lighthouse, your red door, your own beacon of hope. If I can help you in any way, I'll be here in a flash."

"Thank you. I assume it's Pastor Kirkman then?" asked Matt.

"Just Morris will do. Not an ordained cleric. Just a lay preacher with a daily radio prayer hour, a wicked sense of humor and a child's sense of mischief. I owe my life to the woman who pulled me out of the trash. Mama was the happiest person I ever met because she was helping someone else doing a job someone couldn't or wouldn't. She believed we all need help physically or spiritually and she was put on the earth to do a service to others. If ironing sheets helped, then she paid back her place in the world and never doubted someone would do the same for her."

Lovey stepped in to add another layer to her husband's story. "He gets teased constantly about having a Bible in one hand and a joke book in the other. When he'd act up his Mama would say, 'How do you expect to get into heaven, young man?' Of course, he had an answer...he said he'd just run in and out slamming doors until someone says, 'Oh for heaven's sake, either come in or stay out'...then he'd go in."

Morris removed his glasses using the earpiece to scratch the inside of his ear. "Laughter heals the soul. It's the sun that drives winter from us. Matt, Starla...one thing is for certain, the sun will come out."

Margo caught her husband's eye motioning him to join them. He was in the company of the Kirkman's daughter, Aria, whose vivacity flashed like a bolt of lightning escaping through the prowling clouds of a thunderstorm dominating Patrick's attention with her beatific smile. There was a swing in her gate as she walked with feline grace toward the group, striding up to Matt. "Hi, I'm Aria Spencer. Your enchanting son said you needed a friend. He could get a job in public relations when he grows up. I'm truly sorry about your wife."

"Thanks, and, yes, my youngest seems to be the one looking out for the rest of us. This is Starla, my late wife's sister. Summer's tragic death blindsided all of us."

"Nice to meet you, Aria. Cool name," said Starla.

"You're the songwriter, right? Gabe told me about his talented aunt."

"I am. Sounds like you and my nephew already have a bond."

Patrick commented the instant connection between Aria and Gabe comes from sharing the same love. "She owns an art studio in Green Tree and is a sculptor who studied under legendary Charles Umlauf, the first professor of sculpture and life drawing at the University of Texas. Remember, Gabe told us at the cemetery he wanted to make angels out of metal. Aria has invited him to take part in her beginner classes which are starting in a few weeks."

As she spoke, her deep brown eyes glittered as though bursting with fireflies, darting from one person to another while twirling a strand of hair falling on the nape of her neck. "He's young, but I sense he has vision beyond his years. I can't wait to witness his imagination and see what he can do."

The host and hostess whisked Lovey and Morris away to visit with some of the other guests, encouraging Matt, Starla, and Aria to try one of the frozen vodka and mango cocktails. Willa and her cohorts bounced over to her dad announcing they were going upstairs to her room to change into bathing suits. "Why don't you eat first...GoGo and Concha have outdone themselves...there's shish kebabs and shrimp, roasted chicken, sliced rib-eye steak and all the fixins."

A group moan followed the suggestion, but after a stern eye directed their way, they realized this battle was not one they could win. One of the girls grabbed Willa's hand hollering, "Come on, Buffy, let's eat."

Starla glanced at Matt at the same time he threw a puzzled look her way. "Buffy?"

23

The Road Goes on Forever

VICTOR'S *LOANER* SPUTTERED and died on the side of the interstate just outside the cultural center of Kansas—Wichita. He was standing beside the car when a fire-engine-red big rig pulled in behind him. Emerging from the cab was a compact middle-aged woman dressed in overalls wearing spiked silver-foil sneakers and reflector aviator sunglasses with side shields. "Had to stop. Never seen such a cool car. Where you headed?"

"Oklahoma...homa...city...Sorry, it's Tourette's."

"Wanna hitch a ride with me?"

Victor nodded in agreement, grabbing his bag of worldly possessions and headed for the truck.

"You just gonna leave your car on the side of the road?"

"Yep, no, no, no, choice."

"Shame. I could call in a 10-37 for you." Lines formed between Victor's eyebrows. "That means a wrecker."

He shook his head from side to side.

"All righty then, let's get rollin'. Leaving Air Capital traveling on the *boulevard* to Okie City. My CB handle is Flaming Chick, but name's Melba—dry and crisp like the toast. Meet my co-pilot, Spark Pug," she snorted, "Most people walk their dogs, but he's so old I take him out for a stand...it takes all he's got to lift his leg.

205

Sometimes he just falls over and pees. You'll have to share a seat with him. You got a name, sonny boy?"

"Vic...Vic...Rick...Dick," he stammered.

"That's quite a handle VicVicRickDick," she hooted. "How 'bout I just call you Vic?"

His head bobbed in agreement. Victor stared into the expressive eyes of the wrinkly muzzled-faced dog with a curled tail whose head tilted in stupefaction as if sizing up the stranger invading his home. Melba unfastened his harness from the seatbelt before instructing Vic to sit down, placing the dog on his lap before buckling them up together.

A long-haul trucker's life has more than a fair share of monotony as evidenced by Melba's nonstop storytelling, every exaggerated word rejuvenated by the adrenaline of having a captive audience in the passenger seat of her cab. She exploded into fits of maniacal laughter, her hands slapping the double-pistol chrome steering wheel as she related how once she was driving a truck in Canada. "I was stopped at a red light and this blonde scurries up to my window to let me know I was losing some of my load. I thanked her but it happened four more times. Finally, I pulled over, ran back to her car. She lowered her window and I said, 'Ma'am, it's winter in Winnipeg and I'm driving a salt truck.'"

Victor offered a subtle chuckle, his vim and vigor dwindling as spasms crossed his face. He tried to calm himself by patting the dog's head which shocked Spark Pug into polluting the air inside the cab with a cloud of rotten eggs.

"Wow, dog, now that's downright nasty." The unpleasantness seeped out of the windows prompting Melba to launch into another tale from the road.

"Another funny one for ya. Was carrying a load of canned whipped cream topping through the Rockies when hunger drove me to my favorite little hole in the wall for a bowl of elk chili and corn muffins. Seems I was at a high enough altitude to cause the lids to pop off all the cans of aerosol cream. When I got back from dinner the entire trailer was covered in Reddi-Wip. You talk about a mess. Spark Pug tried to lick it clean, but a dog's tongue couldn't fix it. I got a million stories. Too bad we don't have a longer haul together."

Victor, attempting to quiet the jabbering, nodded before closing his eyes and resting his head on the window. Melba turned her focus back to driving the road until the CB radio squawked with fellow trucker High Plains Drifter announcing, "Back it down, Flaming Chick, there's bears in the air." She peered upward out her window to see black police helicopters, the pulsing noise from the choppers' blades causing her passenger to jerk awake as though struck by a bolt of lightning. "Looks like a manhunt...prison escape or a fugitive on the run."

The choppers, zigzagging across the sky above the Interstate, appeared to be chaperoning the fire-engine-red big rig to Oklahoma City, a detail not lost to either occupant inside the cab as they exchanged interrogative stares. Melba broke the silence, "I hafta ask, but I already know the answer. The cops lookin' for you?"

Victor focused his gaze on the scenery rocketing by his window while stroking his *lap-mate's* head. Slowly turning toward his questioner, his shoulders lifted as his arms and upward palms signaled his answer.

"I'll take that as a not guilty. Just as I suspected. Spark Pug likes you. He's my personal alarm system for stranger danger. Funny story...that I'm not particularly proud of. I only drink when I dance. Undoubtedly, shots of Black Velvet Whisky and two-stepping to 'Past the Point of Rescue' affected my good sense, so I invite my drinking/dancing partner home. About four in the morning, Spark Pug vaults into my bed, jumping on top of me whining like a grounded teenybopper. He wouldn't go away so I got up, looked around my bedroom and bath, but there were no signs of my guest. I found twinkle-toes halfway out the door with my television."

Spark Pug, relishing his role as a star in his mistress's story, tilted his head from side to side with each punctuated syllable. Victor closed his eyes thankful for the clear-sightedness of his unforeseen furry ally.

"So, what are your plans when we get to Okie City?"

He took a deep breath, "Hitch...hitch a ride."

"Oklahoma City's not your final destination I take it. What is?"

"Lake Texoma...family there."

"You can ride with me to the border. I got a hot date with my biker friend at the casino. I bet I could sweet talk him into taking you to Texoma...it's about fifteen more miles from there."

A slow smile escaped the corners of Victor's mouth in silent gratitude for this stranger who acted like a friend—the type who would ignore your broken fence but admire the flowers in your garden. He also saluted the *kismet* that introduced the strange bedfellows to each other under inexplicable circumstances. Melba, after pulling into the parking lot adjacent to the Borderline Truck Stop and Casino, leashed Spark Pug, cradling him in her arms for a ride to the nearest tree. Victor, after a short break to the men's room, climbed back into the cab, babysitting the dog until Melba and her date resurfaced. Just as dawn cracked, bleeding an iridescent kaleidoscope of favrile glass in shades of flamingo pink, sandstone, and wisteria onto the early morning panorama, inaudible muttering stirred Victor awake, causing his *lap-mate* to snort. He peered out the window to find his driver and his next ride waltzing out of the casino headed to the big rig. Her friend sported a salt-and-pepper neatly trimmed beard that fell onto his bare chest and dangling from his mouth was a calabash pipe drawing images of a leather-clad Sherlock Holmes. She opened the door to the cab introducing Victor to Doyle, also called the Concrete Cowboy, his moniker embroidered on his jacket.

"Now, Doyle, this dude doesn't talk much, but he's an okey-dokey guy...seems down on his luck. Spark Pug loves him so that's good enough for me. Victor, meet your ride to Texoma."

Victor looked around the parking lot for another big rig, but the only mode of transportation was a pinstriped deep burgundy motorcycle with a sidecar. "It's a '73 Harley Touring bike. You ever ride in one of these, Bud?"

Victor shook his head no.

"Well, don't worry, it's safe and the sidecar rides pretty smooth. Strap on your helmet. Let me say farewell to my main squeeze and then we'll rock and roll."

Victor shifted his weight from side to side holding Spark Pug while Melba sprang, wrapping her legs around her biker man's waist, the intimacy of the bear-hug and the deep open-mouth smooching most assuredly would unnerve the most calloused of onlookers, much less Victor. He was considering skedaddling when Melba dismounted, Doyle slapping her on the behind before firing up the Harley and taking off with his passenger. She loaded a whining dog back into the cab before heading in a westerly direction taking Interstate 40 through the Texas panhandle on her way to Phoenix, Arizona.

Doyle and Victor Kurtz arrived at the Grumpy Point Marina, a large full-service facility with over eight-hundred boat slips, cabin and boat rentals, a restaurant, RV and campgrounds nestled in a private channel twenty-five minutes after leaving the border separating the Lone Star State from the Sooner State. Lake Texoma, one of the largest reservoirs in the country, is the most developed and popular lakes in the region boasting six-million yearly visitors enjoying fishing, sailing, water skiing, and windsurfing.

The Concrete Cowboy taking Melba's assessment of Victor wrote down his telephone number. "Melba likes you so that's good enough for me. If you need any help, give me a call," he said before dropping his passenger off within walking distance of the marina. Acknowledging Doyle's parting with an appreciative salute, Victor tucked the small scrap of paper with a phone number inside the lining of his tennis shoe in case things did not go well with the family reunion.

The bell rang when he opened the door to the minimart at the fuel dock, the clerk looking up from restocking the beer aisle. Victor pulled out his mute card, writing the name of his father on a piece of paper, asking how he could locate him. Rattler directed him to Cabin 216.

From behind a closed door, Anthony Kurtz grumbled, "Coming...for the love of God hold your horses...do you have any idea what time it is..." before swinging the door wide open and staring into the face of the son he walked out on years ago. "Jeez...Shit...Victor is that you? What'd you do to yourself?"

"Surprise."

Anthony's gaped mouth could have accommodated a giant jackfruit. He raised his hand as if warding off evil spirits, looked over his shoulder and began closing the door. "I'm a little busy right now," he snapped.

Victor, grim-faced with somber purposefulness driving his headstrong boldness, forced his foot inside the door refusing to accept another rejection, especially now. He had come too far and risked too much. It was time to flush the debris that ruled his existence down the sewer where it would feel right at home. "I need. I need...truth," he said daggers shooting from his eyes.

"What about? Is that stutter for real? What did your loony-tune mother do to you?"

Father and son sat on opposite sides of the kitchen table, Anthony softening his guise as Victor recalled the end of his Broadway dreams and the onset of his Tourette's when he walked out on them. He described the arrest for possession of child pornography requiring him to pay a fine and register as a sex offender, but his father leaned away from the table when he began the tale of an innocent man being arrested for sexually assaulting an eight-year-old girl and burying her in a concrete block. He paused for the ta-da moment before saying the trial ended with a hung jury. Anthony blew out a noisy breath, his voice pitching an octave above normal range. "Boy, you dodged one there. Prison is no place for someone like you."

"I didn't do it. I look...I don't...don't...ever...never touch."

"Look, good to catch up but I need to get ready for work. 'Member I was always good with fixin' things. Got me a cushy job now as a marine mechanic—do lots of sterndrive work." Victor raised an eyebrow. "Some boats have a combo of indoor power with outboard drive. Your brothers handle boat detailing...we're the Kurtz team. So, where you off to now?"

"Nowhere."

"We gotta a couch...you're welcome to spend the night. Your ol' Pop's not into charity cases...even for family."

24

That's What Friends Are For

MATT, STARLA AND Aria, after draining the recommended mango infused specialty drink, agreed it was refill worthy. While Matt was taking care of the cocktail reorders, the exchange turned to marital status. Starla wiped away a lone tear from the corner of her eye as she recounted the details of her husband's death, but her cheeks flushed as she spoke of her newly found love interest, Deputy Conner Boyle. "How about you, Aria?"

"Divorced. He's from billionaire-type money. Family empire is tourism, and they own several vineyards in France. They live on Corsica, a French island in the Mediterranean Sea. Our son and daughter were born there, and their father and I have been embroiled in a custody battle for years. Add distance and unlimited resources to the mix, and he's successfully kept me from my children. The last time I saw them they were ten and twelve...that was two years ago."

Starla covered her mouth. "How incredibly sad for you."

Matt, carrying a tray with the frozen drinks, bowls of salsa, queso, and tortilla chips, hesitated sensing Aria and Starla's high spirits now held a trace of quiet sadness. "I hope I'm not interrupting...is everything all right?"

"No. I mean, yes, we're fine. It's just that the past never stays where we put it…we think we've got it tucked away under an immovable rock only to find it creeping out when we're not looking. A hunky waiter with fresh drinks and snacks will fix what ails us," said Starla throwing a serendipitous smile at her brother-in-law.

"You two are the cutest. I love your bantering," commented Aria.

"My sister was a lucky woman."

"Enough pseudo-Matt-worshiping. Let's toast Sky Island Retreat and the company it keeps."

"I'll drink to that…but would someone please explain the island part. My mind conjures up flower leis, hula girls, rum drinks with umbrellas, and pig roasts…unless I'm missing something, we're in a desert."

Aria agreed it is a little confusing. "Think of it as a mountain island in a desert sea—true anomalies—our Davis Mountains rise more than eight-thousand feet above sea level out of the Chihuahuan Desert." She further explained the drastic differences in terrain between the surrounding arid desert and the high mountain peaks forested with a temperate climate. "Plants and animals living in the mountains could not survive in the dryness."

Inside around the dining room table, the noise level bouncing off the walls certified the festivities were in high gear, the draw, plates loaded with chocolate mousse cupcakes, lemon meringue tarts, and peanut butter fudge. Willa and her friends, after changing into bathing suits, were part of the kitchen congestion as a line formed in front of Concha who scooped vanilla, peach, or coconut homemade ice cream from the churns into cones rimmed with brown sugar. Margo motioned the girls over. "Y'all look like you're having fun. I'm Willa's grandmother—GoGo, and you are?"

Linley stepped forward extending her hand, saying, "Mrs. Mackie, thank you for inviting us to your beautiful home to meet Willa. She's part of us now."

"Wonderful…but what do you mean, part of us?"

Willa jumped in squealing the announcement that she had been invited into the N.K.I.T. group. "We have nicknames and everything."

"Yep, we're the *New Kids In Town*. We're calling her Buffy—

get it...for Buffalo," said Linley. "And mine is Holly because I'm from California, and this is Dana but we call her Dolly because she's from Tennessee and can sing and she's kinda built like Ms. Parton if you know what I mean, and this is our Deanna who we call, Yo-Yo 'cause she's always dieting. We're all going to get perms so we can look like Buffy."

"I see, how exciting," Margo said with a slight break in her tone.

It was midnight before the festivities began to wind down, finding Gabe and his friends in his room captivated by the antics of "Phineas and Ferb" and their pet, Percy the Platypus, while Willa and the other members of the N.K.I.T. huddled around one of the firepits, giggling and babbling in a language foreign to anyone over thirteen. After all the goodbyes, hugs, and promises to visit their parents soon, Patrick humming the Beach Boys' "Good Vibrations," led his sleepwalking wife to their bedroom. Any tingles of romance skated out the window, kissing Margo's cheek right before her face became one with the pillow.

On the agenda at the end of the following week was the girls-plus-one trip to Green Tree while father and son headed westward to the nine-hole Marfa Municipal Golf Course for a round with Patrick's regular group. "Hope you're not prone to nose bleeds. The course sits at the highest elevation in Texas. It's flat as a pancake, but one day a guy in the group ahead of us had his superglued toupee ripped right off his head. Rumor was it rode the Rio Grande River all the way into Mexico," Patrick said with a wink and a nod.

Father and son met the group on the first tee, the camaraderie surfacing as if their friendship had begun in the womb. "Matt, let me formally introduce these scoundrels to you. Meet Robert Engle Samson III...*Bobby-Three-Sticks* to us. And we call these two *Chunky* and *Skippy*. You'd think they had stock in Smucker's. This tall drink of water is *Draw-Shank*—that moniker will become obvious with his first swing."

Matt shook hands with the group and apologized for his rusty golfing skills which garnered some guffaws. "Skills...whatever do you mean? All of us except your dad, who we call *Hitch* as he does a mean imitation of Arnold Palmer's signature pant hiking, feel we've won the lottery if we get off the tee box without pulling a muscle."

"Hazards are almost nonexistence—no sand and one pond. The fairways are wide open, but the greens are the size of a postage stamp. Keep the ball low or it'll join the tumbleweeds on the other side of the fence," offered Bobby. "And, Patrick, hated we missed your get-together. The wives had booked a romantic weekend at Lajitas Golf Resort...we thought we'd be playing Black Jack's Crossing, but oh no...we were on the Flying Goat Zip-line tour followed by couple massages and a sunset horseback trail ride."

"I warned you against robbing the cradle."

Margo with Starla in the passenger seat and Willa and Gabe buckled into the backseat of her car pulled out of the driveway heading in the opposite direction from the golfers for the short drive to her and Patrick's hometown of Green Tree with a population close to six-thousand residents. On the outskirts of town, the road divides around a small tract of land scattered with grave markers. "Wait...Margo, is that a cemetery in the middle of the road?"

"Yes. The locals got up in arms when the highway department planned to move the graves to put the road in. It's obvious who won that battle."

"Who's buried there?"

"Green Tree founders and their descendants, and one other interesting grave. The marker says, *Let 'er rip!* which has fostered speculation that it's the final resting place of Texas outlaw James Brown Miller. Deacon Jim is what they called him. He was a regular church goer, didn't smoke or drink, just assassinated people including his grandparents. He was lynched by an angry mob. Witnesses said he hollered *Let 'er rip!* and jumped off his hanging platform voluntarily."

Margo, the acting tour guide, continued to offer the origin of her town's name as they approached a ninety-foot native cedar elm

214

tree showcasing a spectacular display of light green blossoms and dark green leaves forming an excellent canopy from the blistering summer heat. "This tree was growing in the center of the proposed town. One of the founding fathers was Samuel Green, a Baptist minister, who kept cutting the tree down and it always grew back, so everyone started calling the mighty elm, Green Tree. Samuel began to look at the tree as a sign from above citing a passage in Proverbs that mentioned the fruit of the righteous being the tree of life. So now, we make a pass around it to get to Main Street."

Nestled among the antique stores, custom jewelers, leather and silverwork shops, western-themed clothing, and gift shops, were art galleries and artist's working studios including *Serenity by Aria* located on the corner of Main and Third Avenue. The bell dinged when Starla opened the door as Gabe barreled in hoping to find her creating a masterpiece but instead, they found it vacant. He collapsed onto a bench, his chin dipping to his chest. Starla sat down beside him saying, "She didn't know we were coming today. We'll come back when we're sure Aria will be here."

"I just wanted to start my metal angels."

A voice from the back room broke the disappointment as Aria hollered, "I'm here. If you'll wait until I wash my hands, I'll be right with you."

Deputy Conner Boyle unofficially assumed the lead operations of the Erie County Sheriff's Department while Sheriff McAlister, after requesting medical retirement to deal with the advanced stages of his prostate cancer, awaited the official paperwork. At the recommendation of Conner's mentor, friend, and boss, he was the heir apparent to assume the role of sheriff for the remainder of McAlister's four-year term. But until things were finalized, he continued in his role as a subordinate except in the eyes of his fellow deputies. The regular morning briefing revealed the recovery of Jasmine Jones' convertible broken down on the side of Interstate 35 near Wichita, Kansas. "We assume Mr. Kurtz, or whatever he's calling himself these days, snagged a ride with who-knows-who to who-knows-where. His fingerprints were the only things he left behind in the snazzy little VW. It was returned to its owner who was still fuming about the damage to her home in the failed attempt to arrest her weird tenant."

"Have we located his dad and two brothers yet?" asked Axl.

"They're not in Broken Bow, Oklahoma, anymore. No forwarding address so a dead-end there."

"We need a break...he snagged a ride with someone and he's not an easy person to forget."

25

A Voice in the Dark

WHEN ARIA APPEARED from her workroom, Gabe, in a bubbly voice announced, "I'm ready to make my metal angels."

She knelt searching the eager face of her young prodigy, the delight in his eyes as transparent as a cloudless sky. "Margo, why don't you and Starla join me for lunch. I'm meeting my folks at The Murphy at one, and in the meantime, I'll show Gabe the sculpturing ropes and we'll meet you there. Willa, why don't you stay too...it'll be fun."

"I don't know...I'm not artsy."

"We'll start with a hunk of clay. I think you'll be surprised what you can make. Sound good?"

"Come on Willa...we can learn together," begged Gabe.

After Gabe and Willa donned aprons to protect their clothing and Aria wrapped Willa's cast in plastic to protect it, she explained original designs for bronze sculptures are most often created from another medium. Oil-based clay is the go-to material because it remains flexible for adjusting the piece if necessary. "Today, Gabe, since it's important to learn the basics of working with clay, we'll use stoneware clay which is generally used for pottery-type pieces like bowls or plates."

"But I can't make metal angels out of a bowl."

"No, you can't, but for you to make your bronze sculptures, you've got to start from the beginning. Okay, kids, the first step is getting the air bubbles out of your piece of clay. There are two ways to do it...wedging and spiral kneading...both are kinda cool. You can bang your piece of clay on the table, or you can knead it like you're working with a hunk of yeast bread dough."

Willa chose pounding her clay on the table, each bang increasing with intensity as if exorcising demons instead of air bubbles. Gabe hopped around the table executing the consistent excellence of quiet slam-dunking superstar, Tim Duncan of the San Antonio Spurs, while Aria twisted her piece into a spiral shape. "You guys ready for the sixty-four-thousand-dollar question? Do you like to play in the mud?"

They glanced at each other, then back at Aria, their uncomprehending looks wrapped in puzzlement at the lack of puddles in the studio.

"We'll have to take turns on my pottery wheel, but that's where we get our hands dirty."

Mastering the wheel is a trained art as the wedged clay is placed in the center of the metal plate attached to the wheel. Water is applied to the clay while pushing the mass down and pulling it up until it is centered perfectly. Gabe led off with the enthusiasm of a seven-year-old boy with a chance to play soon realizing his expertise in keeping the clay from wobbling was going to require more time and patience. Willa watched with amusement at her little brother's determination, trying to muffle any laughter but when his last piece of clay flew off the wheel and on to the floor, she burst out giggling as he looked like a statue himself covered from head to toe in clay.

The first stop on Margo and Starla's shopping list was Bound Together Bookstore, where she ordered ten copies of *Cold Sassy Tree* by Olive Ann Burns for the next book club meeting. As Starla had not heard of the novel, she asked Margo to fill her in on the story. "It's one of my favorite books, set in a small Georgia town in the early 1900s featuring a crusty old widower who marries a young Yankee milliner three weeks after his wife died...and the scandal becomes the focus of Cold Sassy, but the real story is the relationship between grandfather and grandson. The characters are unforgettable, and I guarantee you'll laugh and cry in the same sentence."

"Sold...could you add my order to yours?"

The next stop on the circuit was a unique jewelry store, *Life Force Gems*, featuring hand crafted pieces adorned with natural healing stones. The proprietor, Lovey Kirkman, jitterbugged at the sight of her dear friend and Starla. "What a nice surprise to see you two. Where's the rest of the Mackie clan today?"

"The boys are playing golf and your beautiful daughter is entertaining the grands. She's invited us to join you and Morris for lunch."

"Wonderful. Starla, if you're unfamiliar with the magic powers of these stones, let me give you the cliff notes. Each one has its own healing properties." She handed her a wrap bracelet pointing out that the largest stone, a lapis with the intensity of a bin of fresh picked blueberries, promotes tranquility and peace much like a calm sea. "It also pushes you in the right direction to see what your essence already knows," she said.

Lovey wrapped it around Starla's wrist who extended her arm to examine the craftsmanship of the piece, her demeanor holding an aura of ecstasy discovering each detail of the design. "Well, clearly I have to have this...the bracelet itself is fabulous, but I can feel the spirit of the stones. I'd like to get something for Willa...Lord knows she might benefit from some positive energy," she said tongue-in-cheek.

Lovey removed a delicate sterling silver amethyst bangle bracelet from the display case. "I just finished this one...the stone's powers promote happiness and absorb negativity. What do you think?"

"I should probably purchase one for each wrist, a ring for each finger and toe, a necklace, and anklets if it will help turn *Willa-Attila* back into *Willa-Vanilla*."

Starla's mission to stimulate the Green Tree economy continued as she browsed through an art gallery specializing in local scenery, choosing framed prints of native cacti, one of a sugar-plum tinted purple prickly pear, and the other, hundreds of clusters of springtime's jewels, the orange-red claret cup cactus.

Armed with shopping bags, the ladies on their way to lunch passed by the campus of the Ross Shaw Sterling College of Engineering, named in honor of the founder of Humble Oil Company, the precursor to ExxonMobil, and the thirty-first governor of Texas. During his term, the East Texas oil fields experienced rapid and uncontrolled expansion in which the Railroad Commission attempted to manage with proration, which was struck down by the courts. "Because of the chaos, Sterling declared martial law in four counties for six months, deploying the National Guard. Many felt he was out of touch with his constituents, more comfortable inside his personal residence, a mansion perched on a hilltop near Houston, which he built as a scaled down replica of the White House."

"Guess he still had enough cronies to get an institute of higher learning named after him."

"Not to mention Sterling Avenue, Green Tree Sterling High School, Ross Junior High, and Shaw Elementary."

Fronting Main Street, The Murphy Hotel, one of the masterpieces of architect Henry Trost's Spanish Colonial Revival design with its stucco exterior from the late 1920s, cast a block-long shadow over the sidewalk. Opening the lobby doors transported guests back a century to enjoy the opulence and uniqueness of the décor with intimate vignettes scattered through the area encouraging patrons to visit. Although midway through a renovation project to update the restaurant and bar, the outdoor courtyard remained open. Morris, seated at a table, rose when he saw Margo and Starla, a princely smile crossing his face. "What a nice surprise to see such lovelies. Aria didn't tell me you were going to grace our presence today."

"She didn't know we were in town until we popped into her studio earlier. Gabe pressured her into an early sculpting lesson and of course she graciously accepted. They even got Willa to participate. I'm assuming you haven't seen them yet."

"Not yet. My bride is not here either."

"Our fault. We just left her store. She said to tell you she's putting her *Closed for a Rendezvous* sign on the door and would be here shortly."

"Code for long lunch followed by a siesta," he said, an impish twinkle brightening his eyes. "Let me grab a bigger table and an extra seat for the packages."

While they waited for the rest of the group to arrive, Morris shared that he grew up in the small community of Songbird located in the Mississippi Delta, a region known as "the most southern place on earth" because of its unique racial, cultural, and economic history. "Before the Civil War, this was one of the richest cotton-growing areas in the nation saturated with plantations along the riverfronts, but when our little piece of heaven turned dangerous, Mama gathered me up one day sneaking out of Songbird in the dark with no destination in mind other than westwardly. How we ended up in Green Tree, Texas, is still a mystery, but I'm glad we did."

"Glad you did what, fetching man of mine?" asked Lovey.

"There's *ma chèrie*. We were just talking about how I got from Songbird to Green Tree."

"Forgive my tardiness. Last minute customer—a sweet woman but one who believes why use one word when ten or twenty will do. Aria not here yet?"

"No. Our grandson has a way of captivating time. Should I go check on them?"

"I'm sure they're fine. Our daughter can lose track of time, too," said Lovey.

After learning Morris had graduated with a degree in petroleum engineering from the local college, Starla said, "If it's not too personal, how did you go from an engineer to a lay preacher?"

"One day I could speak and the next day, not a peep. Vocal cord paralysis—the nerve impulses to the larynx were disrupted but test after test revealed no scientific evidence of why. It wasn't a viral infection, it wasn't cancer or herpes or Lyme disease. We went to every specialist known to man and no one could figure it out."

"Then someone knocked on our front door and when I opened it there was a package addressed to Morris with no return address." Lovey placed her hand over her heart, her eyes softening as if filled with an inner glow as she nodded to her husband, "You tell the rest of it...."

"Inside was a pewter coin inlaid with a mustard seed. The front was inscribed *All things are possible with faith.* And on the reverse side, it said, *If you have faith as small as a mustard seed, you can say to this mountain, move from here to there and it will move*—Matthew 17:20. I originally thought losing my ability to speak was some kind of punishment...as it turned out it was a sign I was in the wrong profession."

Back at the studio, the question was how to get Gabe's clay bath out of his hair before heading off to lunch. Willa and Aria agreed a shower was the better option over Gabe's objections. The battle lines were drawn...it was two against one. His clothes mostly had been spared thanks to the apron, so after showering, the only residual from his sculpting experience was a wet head. And they were off to meet the rest of the group at The Murphy.

They arrived at the midpoint of a story—Lovey recalling the Saturday night ritual on the square in Green Tree...where she met her intended. "The boys in cars circled the square on the outside while the girls circled on the inside. If you saw someone you liked, you would leave the formation and go to the *wall,* which was a vacant parking lot around the corner."

"Sometimes there would be multiple attractions going on at the same time, so it was competitive until the boy or girl picked who they wanted to leave with. The ones left out would resume circling the square," said Morris.

"It was pretty embarrassing when you spent the whole night circling," said Lovey. "My girlfriends and I camped many a night at our house trying different hairstyles and makeup certain that had to be the reason we weren't one of the chosen ones."

"Boys are intimidated by beauty. How did you not know that?"

"My hubby, the flatterer. Morris thought I was more worldly since I'm a little older than him," Lovey said tapping him on the shoulder.

"That tradition wasn't going on when we were in high school.

Patrick and I met because I was best friends with his sister, so when I visited their house, I spent most of the time sneaking peeks at him. He was on the football team but also played drums in the band. For me it was love at first field goal, drool, and drum roll," joked Margo.

Gabe sprinted to the table, hungry and anxious to tell anyone who might lend an ear, his adventures while Aria and Willa visited the restroom before joining the group. As most young boys full of snips, snails, and puppy dog tails, he wore his heart on his sleeve, but no one could dampen his nature—a maturity that allowed him to touch the world of wonderment with pure joy radiating from his face. Gabriel Mackie defined the quirks and quiddity of little boys, although void of the masculine badges of honor tied to home run hitting or fascinations with guns and fighting. He was in the right place for the right reason with his role in the universe. His job...make angels out of metal.

Margo finger-combed her grandson's hair asking, "Why is your hair wet?"

"They made me take a shower."

They all looked over upon hearing, "Yes, we did. Gabe looked like a clay statue himself after working on the wheel," Aria said, smiling.

Morris, a foodie by reputation, offered his overview of the menu, asking who in the group were PB&J aficionados prompting Gabe to fervently wave his arm. "You're in for a treat, little buddy. This delicacy is made with crunchy peanut butter, homemade strawberry jam, rolled in frosted flakes and deep-fried to golden perfection. It's my all-time favorite treat!"

Margo ordered the grilled avocado Caesar salad and Lovey and Starla opted for bacon cheeseburgers.

"Willa, honey, have you decided?" asked Starla.

"Is there anything low-cal on the menu? Holly says I could drop a few pounds."

"That girl doesn't know what she's talking about. How dare her say something like that to you," chided GoGo. "As you go through life, there will always be someone prettier, thinner, smarter, richer, funnier, or kinder. Perfection is not the goal."

"But when I look in the mirror all I see is a dumpy kid and Holly is like this Barbie doll. It's just so unfair."

"Trust me she has her own fears and insecurities and she's hiding behind them by making you feel bad about yourself."

"So, what do I do, Aunt Starla. I'm afraid they won't want me in the group anymore," moaned Willa.

"I remember not belonging. I was always Summer's older sister—the plain one with the red hair and a gap between her front teeth. The first boy I had a crush on said my teeth looked like piano keys. My smile hid behind by hand until one day the captain of the hockey team said I looked like Madonna. It was like instant validation. Mine wasn't a flaw, it was a feature...my unique trademark. I knew then I didn't want to be perfect nor was my self-esteem tied to any clique."

Gabe jumped in the conversation giving Willa a bear hug and saying, "Nobody's supposed to make my sister sad. I'll kick 'em in the shins next time I see those girls."

"That's sweet to defend your big sis, but we don't lower ourselves to that level," said Margo.

"The burgers are huge. How about I split mine with you, Willa?" asked Lovey.

"I guess. Thanks."

26

Truth?

MELBA, VICTOR'S RESCUER, confidant, and transporter from his broken-down stolen car on the highway just outside of Wichita, Kansas, was cruising down Interstate 40 across the Texas Panhandle mumbling while blowing her cheeks out and swallowing the air. She had always prided herself as being able to quickly gauge a person's nature with a few exceptions. A sinking feeling in her stomach told her she had missed something by taking *VicVicRickDick* under her wings although Spark Pug loved him, and he had proven to be an astute judge of character even though he was just a dog. Requiring a physical and mental break from her qualms she pulled into Love's Travel Stop in Albuquerque, New Mexico. While she waited for her to-go order of fried chicken for the dog and beef tips with corn-bread for herself, her attention gravitated to a news story airing on the television above the counter about a fugitive wanted by Buffalo, New York, law enforcement. A photo of Spark Pug's buddy scrambled her thoughts upon hearing... *arrested for possession of child pornography; pedophile and registered sex offender; suspect in death of Buffalo mother of two Summer Mackie; violation of noncontact protection order; stalking; crossing state lines; child abduction; two counts of auto theft. ...*

Melba paid her tab escaping to the sanctity of her cab, her

225

furry companion waggling his backside like a bowl of gelatin and with a combination of a yap and a whine expressed his delight at the odor emanating from the box of fried chicken. She looked into the furrowed brow and doleful somber eyes of her trusted pal, shaking her head saying, "How could we be so wrong? Tell me dog…how could we be so wrong. What are we goin' to do now?"

———— ✺ ————

Two weeks passed since Victor arrived at Grumpy Point Marina and although his dad offered him a bed for one night, he was still sleeping on the couch. After Anthony's shift he bounced on the balls of his feet on his way to his cabin anticipating opening the door to find his boarder gone. His troubled son was casting a damper on his mood, not to mention his social life as his girlfriend refused to be in the same room with him. In this case, blood was not thicker than water. His other sons, Raymond and Floyd, treated their younger half-sibling like the lobster boy in the traveling carnival—a curiosity but if you've seen it once, that's enough. Their lone interest in him was trying to guess what he wanted. They witnessed how antsy their dad acted in his presence, delighting their sadistic personalities. The television Waltons and the Kurtz families were not in the same galaxy with good night *Victor-boy* or *Raymond-boy* or *Floyd-boy* never to be uttered inside intimate quarters.

"So, Victor, it's been nice catching up, but I think it's time for you to move on."

"As soon as I get the truth about the girl…the girl in the concrete."

Anthony pulled out a chair, removed a pack of Newport 100s menthol cigarettes, placing them on the kitchen table beside his Zippo lighter. His face reddened as if suppressing a cyclone of alarm with his son's innuendos followed by a quick high-pitched burst of laughter solidifying his anxiety. He offered Victor a smoke before lighting one himself breathing nicotine into the depth of his lungs.

"What's that got to do with me? You're the one they arrested."

"Yep. My DNA matched."

"Shut and closed case. What the hell happened to your stutter? Texas air clear it up?"

"Medicine's working better and I found the reason the Tourette's started...you. Now, back to the DNA recovered at the crime scene—I didn't do it which leaves a relative with at least a fifty percent match...which would be you, Daddy."

Anthony rose from his chair lighting another cigarette, pacing from one side of the room to the other. The door opened abruptly with Raymond and Floyd stumbling into the interchange, a case of beer under each arm, and reeking as if fermented in hops. "Hey bro..." Raymond slurred. "What's goin' on?"

"Me and the old man were chatting about DNA. He killed a little girl, and I got the rap."

"Wow...that's heavy. The one in the concrete block?"

"Shut up, Floyd. You and your brother get your drunken asses out of here. Victor and I are talking."

"Nah...this's goin' to get good. We're staying right here."

Anthony's eyes wielded poison at his sons before grabbing them by the shirts. They pushed back knocking their dad into the chair.

"All right, you two losers. Stay...you might enlighten old Vic on your part of the story."

The elder Kurtz lit cigarette number three before giving Victor what he coveted—a confession, but also implicated the brothers in the crime. "This is hysterical...my little odd Victor, the actor, accused of a crime I committed. I always wanted a little girl, but you Victor was the closest thing to it. Poor sugar-pie Nancy lived in the neighborhood. Parents were never home—think they were dealing drugs. Anyways, she used to sit on my lap if I gave her candy. One day my manhood was on full alert if you get what I'm saying, and she tried to run away but tripped and hit her head. I didn't want her to die, but she did. I left these stooges in charge of taking care of this and they came up with the concrete idea."

"Then when was she sexually assaulted?" quizzed Victor.

The elder Kurtz boys aimed warning glances at each other before breaking the silence. "She was already dead," declared Raymond.

227

"We didn't see any harm," crowed Floyd.

"What's the matter, Vic, cat got your tongue? You got what you wanted, now beat it."

After soul-searching and much discussion with herself and Spark Pug who tilted his head from one side to the other with the delivery of each word, Melba vowed to contact the authorities upon her arrival in Phoenix. The seven-hour drive from Albuquerque offered ample time to reflect on her choices and to weigh her culpability in aiding and abetting a fugitive. She mentally berated herself over her decisions, trying unsuccessfully to justify her role by blaming the dog and Victor for the deception. She was the one who picked up the poor soul, took the dog's confirmation that he was an okay guy, and unwittingly harbored a criminal, providing him with an escape route—all because she was lonely. After dropping her cargo at the warehouse, Melba steered her eighteen-wheeler into the driveway that circled behind her small modular home on San Miguel. Unfurling her achy body from the cab and gathering Spark Pug in her arms she opened the screen door and unlocked the back door. The house was as dark as her mood, failing to brighten even as she turned on the lights. The refrigerator was stocked with essentials including a 1.5-liter bottle of Woodbridge Chardonnay, thanks to her baby sister. Tonight's agenda would include a hot bath, at least one glass of wine, and a bowl of tortilla soup in front of the television tuned to reruns of *The Statler Brothers Show.* She succumbed to the Sandman sprinkling *la-la-land dust* in her eyes as the chords of the gospel song, "I'll Fly Away" ended the show as she muttered, "Hallelujah" before falling into a deep slumber with her companion curled up beside her on the couch.

Melba, awakened by a stream of sunlight piercing through the open drapes, stretched causing Spark Pug to leap into action pawing her arm, finally resorting to face licking.

"I know dog...you're hungry and you have to go out. Give me a few minutes." His face contorted in confusion followed by a series of whines and woofs as Melba rolled onto her stomach.

She had procrastinated enough. It was time to make the call.

She got dressed, loaded the dog into the car, driving to the lone pay phone still in the area, outside a convenience store between the ice machine and the newspaper stands. The operator connected her to the Erie County Sheriff's Department, reaching the voice mail of Deputy Sheriff Conner Boyle. Melba, without identifying who she was, said she picked up a stranded motorist near Wichita, Kansas. He was driving a pretty blue Volkswagen convertible. He was a funny fellow with a stutter, but her dog loved him, and he had always been a good judge of character. "His name was Vic, and I didn't know he was a fugitive until I saw his rap sheet on the television. The last I saw him he was headed to Lake Texoma in Texas. Said he had family there. That was a couple of weeks ago."

With Anthony's admission hanging in the room, Victor had accomplished what he set out to do, but queasiness in the pit of his stomach churned causing bile reflux to lodge at the back of his throat. Beads of sweat glistened on his forehead and upper lip. Victor covered his mouth with his left hand, taking deep breaths to quash the feeling he was going to vomit. He stood up, his knees buckling under the weight of the truth. Anthony grabbed Victor's tote bag slamming it into his son's chest, his face erupting in rage. The duo stood within inches of each other, Anthony's breath sour with nicotine, spitting threats at Victor. "It's time for you to *adios.*"

"We're all born different, but I never thought people were born evil, until now."

"You never met your grandmother. At least Lizzie Borden murdered her family with an axe. Your grammie tortured us daily."

Raymond popped into the discussion, "Dad, we can't just let little bro walk out of here now that he knows about the girl."

"Who would believe Victor? Just look at him...he's a pathetic excuse for a human being. I'm beginning to wonder how he could possibly be my son. His mother wasn't exactly sainted."

"I'm gone. Forget you have another son. I'll forget I have a father. So, we're even. Goodbye, Mr. Kurtz." Victor walked out slamming the door behind him.

Anthony threw a pillow at the door mumbling good riddance,

escaping to his bedroom. Raymond and Floyd caught each other's attention, neither one convinced Victor would pose no threat to them but lost as to what they should do. Knocking on their dad's door resulted in an X-rated rant leaving the boys to continue what they do best—drink more beer.

Victor's pace gathered steam as he fled Cabin 216, looking over his shoulder with each step not believing his family would let him walk out knowing they had committed monstrous crimes. He reached the fuel dock without incident begging to use the phone. "It's an emergency—a matter of life and death. Rattler, can you help me?"

"Whatcha need?"

"I have to get back home to my mother. She's terminal. I lost my cell phone. I have to make a collect call…please."

"I hafta finish stocking but use the phone in the back office."

"Thanks." Victor closed and locked the door, connecting to area code 716.

"Erie County Sheriff's Department. This is Conner Boyle. How can I help you?"

27

Boys Will Be Boys

THE KURTZ BROTHERS flew into the fuel dock minimart causing Rattler to stop stocking the shelves, his face growing chalky
at the sight of the duo who once held his head in the dirty mop
bucket because the shipment of Pabst Blue Ribbon was delayed.
He cleared his throat saying, "Hey boys, we got a cooler full of
PBR. Need a couple of cases?"

"Yeah and put it on the old man's account. Have you seen the
weird little prick with the stutter?" slurred Floyd.

"Nah...not recently...been a few days I think."

"What's behind that door over there?"

"Shh....my boss's doin' some business in there with the bru-
nette he just hired...showing her the ropes so to speak. It'd be a
mistake to interrupt him. Now, let me get your suds and you can
be on your way."

The *click-tock* of beers being opened accompanied the brothers out the door, continuing the search down the ramp toward
the boat slips. Victor warily opened the office door looking from
side to side for any sign of his kin before stepping in behind the
counter. Rattler had returned to stocking, looking up when Victor
approached. "Why'd you do that?"

"When those two are liquored-up, they're dangerous. Hard to believe you're related to them. Don't know where you are going, but it would be a good idea to get as far away from here as possible."

"I gotta wait here for my ride."

"You got any cash? My aunt runs the Super 8 Motel in Sherman. It's cheap and about twelve miles from here. I could take you there after my shift."

"Still got some money but have to find somewhere to hide here until he arrives."

"You didn't hear this from me, but there's an unoccupied boat slip at the end of Landers Pier. The couple that own it divorced. She inherited the slip when her dad died, and they've been fighting over it for years. You'd have to be super careful cause it's close to where your brothers detail boats."

"Thanks for everything."

"Good luck."

"This place is goin' to light up like the 4th of July soon."

Of Patrick's regular golf buddies, Robert Engle Samson III, *Bobby-Three-Sticks* to the group, was the most distinguished, professing to be a descendent of the Superintendent of Railroad Construction for the Southern Pacific route through far West Texas. One of the superintendent's responsibilities was naming the different stops in the region, which he delegated to his wife. As an educated reader, she declared the remote railway water stop Marfa, after a heroine in the Russian novel, *The Brothers Karamazov.* Also, under her influence the towns of Feodora, Longfellow, Emerson, and Marathon carried her literary acumen facilitating Bobby's claim of the region's honorary Mayor.

After finishing the round of golf, the *Mayor* suggested introducing Matt to the Where's My Horse Saloon. They pulled into the parking lot paved with bottle caps, the crude limestone building identified by the red neon sign advertising "Beer" with a bullet-riddled truck parked in front. Stepping inside the iconic bar immersed guests in the ambiance—a little rough looking, dim as a cave, and reminiscent of a B-Western movie starring John Wayne prior to his role in *Stagecoach*—a natural fit for the current proprietor.

The group bellied up to the bar sitting on mismatched stools, ordering beers and brisket sandwiches before the owner, sipping a Lone Star Light, moseyed up to greet Bobby and his group. He was tall and weathered looking like a cowboy-swashbuckler with a leather patch over one eye. "Well, if it's not the Mayor and his posse. Did you bring a designated driver? Who's the young'un?"

"Mitch, meet my son, the New Yorker and a bar owner like you."

"Sometimes northerners get a cool reception down south but not in my establishment. After all, Jerry Jeff Walker was a New York transplant and we adopted him as our own. Remember the rules gents...have fun and behave. Shenanigans will not be tolerated."

"No Jameson this fine day, Mitch?" asked Bobby.

"Don't quote me but there's drummin' goin' on between my ears telling me it might be a tad early for Irish Whiskey." The cerebral side of Mitch continued to shine as he outlined what he would and would not put up with in his establishment. "I welcome intellectual conversation. If you don't keep a civil tongue, I'll show you out and it's against my saloon law to make someone else uncomfortable because they're rooting for the other thing."

"Trust me you don't want to get on this guy's list unless you're cruisin' for a bruisin'. A night of drinking with him might land you on the back of a steed, catching the sun rise over the desert, or belly-up in the Rio Grande. Give your beautiful wife a kiss for me," Patrick said dryly.

"I'll do that, but it won't be from you, Mr. Mackie," he said, employing a sideways grin as he took his leave.

"Matt, how much do you know about our little corner of the world?" asked Skippy.

"Probably as much as you know about Buffalo, except for this saloon and the movie *Giant* was filmed in Marfa, right?"

"Yep, in the summer of 1955. It was James Dean's last movie. He died in a car crash that September. Twenty-four-years old. Rock Hudson played rancher, Bick Benedict, and his socialite wife was

Elizabeth Taylor. They all stayed right here at the Hotel Paisano. Can you imagine that happening today with the paparazzi?" said Skippy.

"Margo's parents were members of the Green Tree Country Club and in the 1950s it was the only place to buy liquor in the area. They hobnobbed with the movie stars back in the day," said Patrick.

Marfa continued to be the subject of the conversation with the focus shifting to the seemingly sourceless mysterious lights frolicking on the horizon southeast of town in an area that was nearly uninhabited and difficult to traverse. Tourists, ranchers, Native Americans, teenagers, and meteorologists have all claimed to see the phenomena that appears randomly throughout the night regardless of weather or season, sometimes in red, sometimes in white, and sometimes in blue as if paying tribute to America's flag. "The naysayers claim they are car lights and campfires. I've seen them. They're the real deal," argued Patrick.

"You probably saw them with Mom, so odds are you already had stars in your eyes."

"And there was a heart shaped moon that night too," teased Bobby.

"We should go before Mitch tosses us out for not respecting each other's opinions. I'll spring for the check this time. One of you jokers can pick up the tab when we dine at one of the high-dollar joints."

Morris and Lovey excused themselves for their afternoon *rendezvous*. "My parents believe like Ghandi, where there's love there's life. They've always been each other's light. It's a relationship to envy."

Aria and Margo agreed that Big Bend would be a must see for Starla and the rest of the Mackie family, suggesting that not taking in all its glory would border on criminal. Geographically, the area is where the Rio Grande makes a one-hundred-mile end-around of the Chisos Mountains on its way to the Gulf of Mexico. Big Bend National Park covers over eight-hundred-thousand acres— big enough to swallow Rhode Island and caters to different types of adventurers—the *windshield tourists,* often first-timers who enjoy the sights from inside their cars spending a day or two traveling the basin, or those opting for a multi-day river trip in a designated wild and scenic area. "There's an unexpected stillness here. All you can hear is a birdsong and your thoughts."

"Aria, have you been to its little sister?"

"Big Bend Ranch State Park? Yes, I have in my more adventurous days. It's definitely more rugged. Only one paved road with primitive campsites, and mountain biking trails. If you want to get lost among the rocks and spikey things, this is the place for you."

A stress line formed on Willa's brow as she shifted in her chair. "GoGo, I'm not going somewhere full of cactus and rocks and I can't imagine what might be crawling around in the desert."

"Me neither. My sense of adventure doesn't include roughing it. The National Park sounds more up my alley," said Starla.

Gabe burst into the discussion asking if they could go to the park now, his face darkening into a stony expression at the answer. "We can't go without Big Pop and your daddy and they're playing golf. We'll plan it soon, I promise...when we can all go," offered Margo.

Aria said goodbye before heading back to her studio as Margo suggested they swing by Ross Junior High, home of the *Coyotes,* where Willa would be enrolled and Shaw Elementary that would house Gabe if the Mackie children remained at Sky Island. Willa, despite her initial reluctance to the idea of not returning to Buffalo for school, acted mildly interested in the possibility of being with her newfound friends.

The journey home wound them within viewing distance of one of the largest ranches in the Trans Pecos region with over three-hundred-thousand acres grazed by thousands of heads of red Angus and white-faced Hereford cattle. "Each year the owners tie in an auction with lots of fun activities for kids of all ages. There's a painting contest where paintbrushes are made from straw; stick horse, wheelbarrow and sack races; horseshoes, square dancing, and line dancing contests. But the one that causes the most giggles are the corn races where you put an ear of dried corn between your knees and race to the finish line without dropping it.

There's even a beauty pageant for teens. They auction off upward of six-hundred head of cattle that day," said Margo.

In the backseat Gabe and Willa exchanged glances and shoulder shrugs before Gabe popped the question, "GoGo, how many cattle are in a head?"

Pulling off the road, Margo clenches her jaw and dabs at her eyes.

"Why are you crying, GoGo? I didn't mean to make you sad. I'm sorry."

"Gabe, honey, I'm not crying... I think I might be allergic to something floating around in the air. Let's let Big Pop answer your question when we get home."

Once back home, they gathered around the dining room table sharing their purchases with Concha and Donny who admired the framed Big Bend prints and commented they could feel the spirit of Starla's bracelet oozing positivity in the room. Richard Parker, the Mackie's cat who possessed a combination of noble indifference dashed with folly, must have sensed a common temperament denominator with Willa as he had been weaving in and out of her legs ever since they got home, curling up in her lap as soon as she sat down.

"Looks like Ms. Willa has a fan club," commented Concha.

"GoGo, I don't get his name. It sounds like a person not a cat."

"It's from one of my favorite books, *Life of Pi*, a magical tale about a boy named after a Paris swimming pool, a four-hundred-fifty-pound Bengal tiger named Richard Parker, and an orangutan co-existing in a lifeboat bobbing around in the Pacific Ocean. They're making the movie version due out later in the year. I can't wait to see how they pull that off."

Donny asked if they saw the old metal desk sitting atop Hancock Hill directly behind the college dorms while they were in Green Tree. "That must have happened after Patrick and I left," said Margo.

"It was around 1979 and one of the distance runners on the track team loved chugging up the hill which was over three-hundred feet higher than the campus below." Donny went on to say one of the athlete's campus jobs was to cull outdated dorm furniture and since he had already made trails up the hill running it several times a week, he thought it would be cool to have a desk up there. "He and a couple buddies, who were sworn to secrecy, lugged it up the hill one night."

"I guess I don't understand the reasoning behind putting a desk on the top of a hill," questioned Starla.

"That's where the story gets interesting. Originally, he stashed a notebook in the drawer so he could record his run times and now and again he would jot down a thought or two on the pages. Word got around and people started writing in the journal and before long journal after journal were filled with people spilling their guts—connecting with each other and to nature. It was like it grew into a cult following full of BFFs, inside jokes, rough sketches, declarations of forever love, and a refuge from grief."

"I guess the desk must represent to so many the opportunity to share glimpses into their lives without judgment. To embrace the vastness around you and be able to write candidly about the human experience," said Starla.

"Well said. It's no wonder you're such a good songwriter," Margo said tendering enviable admiration on their houseguest.

"What do they do with the journals, GoGo?" asked Willa.

"Good question. Donny?"

"They're safe and sound in the Big Bend museum archives...for all eternity."

Richard Parker scampered off Willa's lap at the sound of the front door opening letting in roars of hilarity from Patrick as he badgered his son about a bet he made. Matt, taking the ribbing in stride, playfully slapped at his dad's shoulder on the way to the kitchen.

"You two know how to make an entrance. What's so funny? Or is it an inside joke?" asked Margo.

"Just golf stuff, Mom. Nothing you'd be interested in."

"If it's something that causes your father to split a gut laughing, I most definitely want to know the cause. Patrick?"

"All right but you had to be there. Matthew had been playing pretty good golf until he flew one over the fence into the tumbleweed exhibit, prompting the group to access the standard penalty."

"Dad, there are impressionable ears within range."

"Gabe's got his headphones on absorbed with his iPad and Willa will probably find this funny, too. Anyway, at Marfa Muni, our rule is when you hit a ball out-of-bounds, you incur a stroke penalty, and your next shot must be taken from the ladies' tee with your pants down."

"Patrick, what are you guys, children?" Margo asked, stifling a grin.

"No, just competitors. Now, let me finish. The only other option is the bets are doubled on the remaining holes. It's kinda like lettin' it ride on every roll of the dice at the craps table in Vegas. Money bags here chose option number two hoping to take us to the cleaners and let's just say he had to borrow a little cash from his ol' Pop to settle the bets."

"Yes, and wise guy here offers me some sage advice after the fact, saying the quickest way to double your money is to fold it over and put it back in your pocket."

"I didn't realize that gambling was a big part of playing golf," said Starla.

"It's the best way to make the game fun. Golf is not for the faint at heart. Now, how did you gals enjoy your trip to Green Tree?"

"We had a great time. Which reminds me, Willa, I bought you a bracelet. I hope you like it. The stone is guaranteed to bring you happiness."

"Thanks, Aunt Starla, purple is my favorite color. It matches my cast! Wait 'til I show my N.K.I.T. gang."

"You're welcome. I'm going back to my room. Anyone up for a dip in the pool in a little bit?"

"Great idea. We'll meet you there in fifteen," said Matt.

Forty minutes passed and while everyone was enjoying the pool, Starla was nowhere. Margo toweled off, throwing on a bathing suit cover on her way to make sure she was all right when she appeared. "We were getting a bit worried. Is everything okay?"

With a degree of excitement in her eyes, Starla announced, "I was talking with Conner and guess what—Victor has been located."

Newly-appointed Sheriff Conner Boyle gathered the deputies to bring them up to speed on Victor Kurtz's whereabouts and the admission of guilt by Anthony and his sons regarding their involvement in the sexual assault and death of the young girl several years ago—the crime that Victor was on trial for that resulted in a hung jury. "One of you notify Judge Northland that I'm on my way with a written affidavit establishing probable cause for the arrest of Anthony, Raymond, and Floyd Kurtz. Custody of Victor won't be an issue."

"Isn't there a statute of limitations on these crimes? And all we have is hearsay by a fugitive felon."

"Twelve years I think, but since they have been hiding out of the state where the crime was committed, the statute of limitations restarts when they return to New York. As far as their confessions go, we'll let the lawyers and the courts figure that out," said Conner. He and Axl would be flying into Dallas in the morning and he had alerted the Coast Guard Auxiliary Patrol and the Texoma Police Department to be cognizant of the whereabouts of the Kurtz brothers and Anthony but not to approach them. The Texas Rangers, the criminal investigative branch of the Department of Public Safety with statewide jurisdiction, would meet them to assist in the apprehension of the dad and brothers while he escorted Victor into his custody.

"Conner, what's the latest on Sheriff McAlister?"

"I stopped by to see him the other day. He had taken a tumble and fractured his elbow. He asked about all of you and seemed glad to have some company. Sherry said the radiation therapy was taking its toll as he was battling chronic fatigue."

"Maybe when we get back with Victor, we can tell him the good news in person," said Axl.

"That should cheer him up."

Conner notified Mrs. Brennan, Matt's neighbor, that another deputy would be staying in the house taking care of Dude and Halle in his absence with her promising to bring the nice young man a meatloaf and a batch of homemade fudge.

Axl and Conner boarded the flight to Dallas the next morning. After deplaning they scoured the area outside the terminal for their transportation to Lake Texoma spotting two candidates, each dressed in straw Resistol Cattleman western hats, starched collared white shirts with ties, khaki dress jeans and .45 caliber Colt semi-automatics holstered at the waist. "That has to be our Texas Ranger escorts," said Axl.

Lieutenant Trisha Minton and Field Major Denny Garver of Company B, headquartered in Garland, Texas, introduced themselves to Conner and Axl loading into a white Suburban for the two-hour drive to Lake Texoma. A private prisoner transport vehicle that will house the elder Kurtz and his sons after their capture followed behind.

28

Happy Days Are Here Again

STARLA DANCED AN Irish jig on her way to the pool, glee streaking through the air like a comet, and a grin on her face impossible to contain, while the others looked from one to the other at the jaw-dropping news. Although still in street clothes, she executed a cannonball in the deep end stirring a wave of disbelief mixed with frivolity. Upon surfacing, she stared into the dumfounded faces of Matt, Patrick, Margo, Willa, and Gabe, announcing, "I believe this calls for champagne."

"Aunt Starla, you can't go swimming without a bathing suit. That's a rule,"

"I know, buddy, and I promise not to do it again."

"That's great news about Victor. Tell us the details," pleaded Matt.

"The first call Conner got was a message on his voicemail from an anonymous big rig driver who picked up a stranded motorist matching Victor's description. She claimed she didn't know he was on the lam until she heard a news report, also saying he was headed to Lake Texoma in Texas, where he had family. Conner was alerting authorities there when he answered a call from Victor himself." Starla further detailed that when he stole his mother's cell, he found a letter from his father with a return address at a marina at

241

Lake Texoma. Victor showed up there to find Anthony and his two half-brothers employed and living at a cabin on the property.

"Evidently Victor forced a confession from them about the girl in concrete...the one he was on trial for that ended in a hung jury."

"That's the one where Summer testified against him," added Matt.

"Yes, Victor told Conner they let him leave because no one would believe a fugitive. But he said the brothers weren't going to trust anything to chance and were combing the area for him. Conner promised to come in person if Victor would stay put."

"Oh boy, Conner's coming to Texas," Gabe beamed.

"We're five-hundred miles from Dallas and Conner has to take his prisoner back to Buffalo. He won't be able to visit this time," said Patrick.

"But, Big Pop, there's plenty of bedrooms for them here."

"Yes, there are but it's sheriff business, Gabe. You know Conner's job is to catch the bad guys."

Fragments of solace floated between the group as each one digested the magnitude of Starla's announcement while discomfited enthusiasm accompanied a sense of disbelief that the end to the nightmare may be foreseeable. Donny and Concha answered the call for a proper toast, popping the corks on bottles of champagne, passing glasses to the adults before offering strawberry-peach spritzers with club soda to Willa and Gabe.

"Does this mean we have to go home, Daddy?"

"Willa, it means we can go home and not have to worry anymore about your stalker."

"But what about school...and making my metal angels...and we haven't been to the big park yet...and I want to ride the horses...."

"Gabe, relax. We just heard this good news so for now let's just celebrate that. We'll figure out the rest later."

"Patrick, Gabe has a burning question for you. He asked me on the way home today, but I knew you'd be the one to address it for our inquisitive grandson."

"Gabe, come here. GoGo says you need an answer to something. What is it?"

Gabe climbed onto his grandfather's lap, his jaw set and eyes growing brighter and rounder telegraphing the seriousness of his inquiry. "I just wanted to know how many cattle are in a head!"

Patrick cleared his throat trying to stifle a chuckle and while humming softly he said, "Well, that's a good question. Why did you ask?"

"We went by this ranch and GoGo said they sold six-hundred head of cattle...then I asked her that question and she pulled off the road and had an allergy attack."

Patrick avoided making eye contact with his wife who leaned forward in her chair. "I see, well, yes she unexpectedly has bouts of *hoot-a-titus*. Now, to your question. When we talk about cattle, sometimes the words head and herd get mixed up. A herd of cattle is generally one bull and twenty-five or thirty heifers...so there would be twenty-six or thirty-one of them in a herd."

"But how many in a head?"

"Each cow has a head, right?"

"Yep...unless it's in the circus it might have two."

"Okay, but let's say this cow is just a regular cow. So, if you have eighty of these normal cows, and each one has one head, how many heads would you have?"

"Eighty."

"Exactly. You have eighty head of cattle. Understand?"

"Thanks, Big Pop. I don't know why GoGo couldn't just tell me that."

Patrick, anxious to check in with the on-site manager of his animal refuge, asked if anyone wanted to join him riding the ATVs on the trails leading to the fenced acreage on the back of the property. Gabe saddled up with his grandfather, both strapping on protective helmets, while Starla and Willa did the same teaming up on another vehicle.

Margo sat beside her son on the couch who was staring down at his hands, the profile of his ageless face now veined with abstraction. The elation that his family's nightmare might be over that had spread through him like soaking in a warm bath had now plunged into a vacuous ravine of bereavement. She took his hand in hers. "Matthew, talk to me."

He turned his face toward his mother, his eyes once alive and bright were murky and remote telling the story of a lost soul trapped in a maze of regret. "Mom, I'm fine. It's just the news of Victor's whereabouts was like we now have permission to turn the next page of our lives. The problem is I don't want to do that without Summer."

"I know. Tell me what we can do, son,"

"I wish I knew. I need answers to why I'm here and my wife is not. My guilt is just overwhelming sometimes."

"It's all still so fresh for you. Not being able to remember that day has to haunt you. Has anything come back?"

"A few flashes but nothing I can put in order."

"Honey, that's a good sign. I know it's hard to be patient."

"Mom, thanks for the pep talk. I have to call Tina. I hope she doesn't feel I've abandoned her."

"I'll be in the kitchen helping Concha with dinner. Join us when you want. Love you."

"Love you, too. I'll see you in a little while."

With Patrick and Gabe leading the ATV caravan, they wove in and around the timbered paths heading to the animal refuge. They parked the vehicles and helmets at the gate and were met by Patrick's live-in caretaker, Crooks—a robust man with a well-creased neck callused by the unrelenting sun, an *O-ring* in the back pocket of his Levi's announcing his weakness for dipping snuff as evidenced when he flashed his small citric smile at the visitors.

"Howdy, Mr. Mackie. Tell me these ain't Matt's kids."

"Yes sir...all the way from New York. Gabe, Willa, say Hi to Crooks. And, this beauty is Summer's sister, Starla."

"Nice to meet ya, Ms. Starla. I mourn the loss of your sweet sister so. Kids, your mama always loved to visit us here at the refuge. There was a stampede to the gate when they saw her, and the peacocks would strut their impressive trains in her honor. And it looks like they know you're kin. Look at 'em...here they come all puffed out and prancing."

"Let's go meet some of our fur-family," said Patrick.

Willa stopped at an empty cage with the door standing open. Inside branches were loaded with seeds, grains, and a mix of blueberries and strawberries, raisins, and cherries. Crooks noticed her pausing, gazing with focus on a bird-less nest. He offered the tale of saving Cupid the Cardinal who fell to the ground from his nest in the live oak tree overhead. The fledgling was feathered so the assumption was the bird was learning to fly but after hours of observation the parents were nowhere in sight. As night began to fall the abandoned bird faced a perilous fate if left on the ground, and since Crooks could not reach the original nest, he gingerly put Cupid in a margarine tub with drainage holes and hung it in the same tree, but on a lower branch. The next morning showed no signs of the cardinal's parents, making it clear Crooks was this bird's lifeline. "I filled a box with shredded paper. Rolled up a hand towel to look like a nest and put the box on top of a heating pad on my kitchen table. I'd made a mash of dry dog food soaked in water and soft fruits and every fifteen to thirty minutes day and night whenever Cupid opened his mouth, I'd feed him from an eyedropper. After he got bigger and could eat solid food, I put him in a cage and opened the door. He'd leave but always return home before nightfall."

"Cool story. Cupid's a lucky bird," responded Willa.

"I was raised by my Granny Violet. She worked nights at a vet's office cleaning cages and during the summer I helped her with chores. She'd carry on a conversation with each one of the animals like they were her flesh and blood. I made a mistake once suggesting we could finish sooner if she didn't chat with each animal. That night took twice as long while she lectured me on our Lord's creatures and heathens. I think she'd be proud that I *learnt* my lesson."

When Gabe spotted the llamas, his legs pumped a path to their pen, and with him making a beeline to these animals, Starla turned to look at Patrick, alarm flooding her expression at the size of animals versus the size of her nephew. After assuring her they were very social by nature and would not pose any danger to Gabe, Starla drew on her Irish Catholic roots by making the sign of the cross. "Look how adorable they are. Ears are perked like they're ballet arms in fifth position...runway-model eyelashes...and that perpetual smile...I want one!"

"These two are Lucille and Desi. How can you not grin back at them? Look at Gabe. He's telling his life story to Desi."

The sun was launching its trek toward closing time just as Willa and Crooks joined the llama-lovefest. Patrick, calling to Gabe to say goodnight to the animals, watched as he covered his ears before ducking in behind Desi creating a euphoric smile to cross his grandfather's face.

"Gabriel, we can still see you. Come on, we gotta get back. GoGo will be mad if we're late for dinner."

"But, Big Pop, Desi and I aren't through talking. Just a few more minutes, please. Then we can ride real fast, so we won't be late."

Crooks walked the gang to the entrance inviting Willa to come back to meet Cupid and insisting Gabe resume his chat with Desi before long. He closed the gate, waving as they raced off on the ATVs.

Secluded in his room, Matt dialed Tina's extension at Seasons LXX and was directed straight to voicemail. He was about to hang up when she picked up the phone apologizing for not recognizing the number until she saw the Texas caller identification. There was an artificial pitch in his voice as he filled her in on Victor and his impending arrest, how Willa and Gabe were adjusting to the new surroundings and singing Starla's praises for the comfort and support she showed him on their trip south. "Matt, that's wonderful news about Victor. Does that mean we'll be seeing your handsome face around here again soon?"

"So, you miss me?"

"Why would you ask that? Of course, I do. You're the brother I never had. What's the matter? You seem, I don't know...wounded."

"I am. My grief is like wearing a soaking wet wool blanket. I don't know why I'm here and Summer is dead. I can't comprehend what is beyond comprehension. It feels like being trapped in a deep tank, treading water, waiting for help, but no one comes."

"It was a horrible accident, Matt. Your guilt is probably tied to not being able to remember that day. Summer would want you to grow your life bigger than your guilt...for your children."

"You're right as usual. Thanks. Send me a bill."

"For you, this will be happy hour pricing. I'm assuming you'd like to catch up on our business."

Matt and Tina turned their attention to the daily sales reports including food, beverage, and cost of goods numbers for each entity. Fixed monthly expenses such as cleaning crews, credit card fees, and salaries were broken down into daily numbers also. Food and beverage sales percentages outpaced expenses, the bottom-line reflecting Seasons LXX was either making money daily or worst case, breaking even, and outperforming last year's numbers with the addition of the online orders and delivery. Taking it one step further Tina added, "I've installed a new system. A daily customer count comparing how much money was generated during that time frame. Actually, it was Bradley's idea—it's how theaters track profitability numbers."

"Bradley Anderson? Biological Bradley? You know how I feel about the guy. How'd that happen?"

"Now don't go ballistic. His MS has forced him to pull out of the Broadway show. The first time he showed up at Seasons he was looking for you. He wanted to apologize for being a jerk and hoped you would forgive him. He's a different person. We've gotten close and I've finally found someone who needs me as much as I need him. Matt, I hope you can find it in your heart to be happy for me."

Matt's pulse quickened with her every word as he struggled to rationalize why he was experiencing the squalls of possessiveness at his lifelong friend's announcement. It was as though another tire was tossed on the fire, fueling the flames of another loss.

"Matt...are you there?"

"Yes, I'm just trying to digest this bombshell, Tina," he said in a quavering voice sounding as brittle as a torrent of ice pellets hammering a metal roof.

"I know the history between you two and it's sudden, but I think Bradley is who I've been looking for all my life."

"History is correct. Summer witnessed his true nature. No telling what Willa might have suffered if he hadn't been selfish enough to dump both of them for his career. I think this is a huge mistake, Tina."

"I'm sad you feel that way. We've always been honest with each other and although I disagree with your assessment, I respect your opinion. I hope you'll do the same for me."

"I think you're asking too much from me."

29

I've Got Texas in My Heart

CONNER FASTENED HIS seatbelt on the passenger side of the Suburban driven by the lieutenant while Axl and Field Major Garver occupied the backseat. She maneuvered the automobile to the ramp for the North Exit of the airport connecting to Interstate 35 for the trip to Lake Texoma. With many years under his belt, Sheriff Boyle could count on one hand the number of female officers he had worked with. Texas Ranger Trisha Minton looked like a stock photo of a pixie-sized dream-girl except she had a high rank, a badge, and was armed. Her eyes were hidden behind the smoke polarized lenses of her black Magnum Blue Line sunglasses sporting an American flag on each earpiece.

Without taking her eyes off the road she addressed Conner's staring, "Is there a question you'd like to ask, Sheriff Boyle?"

"I'm sorry. Yes. I'm curious to why you chose this profession. The only thing I know about the Texas Rangers is from watching *Walker, Texas Ranger* with Chuck Norris."

"Norris is actually one of the honorary Rangers along with John Wayne, Will Rogers, and President George H. W. Bush. I was one girl among five brothers. When I was born my mom was so excited thinking sequins and beauty pageants, but my daily uniform consisted of jeans and boots. Our property had woods, water,

249

wildlife, and horses. I learned to hunt, fish, and ride before I could walk and even set a barrel racing record of 13.4 seconds at one of the national rodeo events."

"In Dallas?"

"No, we lived on the outskirts of Malakoff, Texas, in western Henderson County. It's the third town in Texas tied to Russia. In the late 1800s when the town applied for a post office the officials in Washington suggested the name after a Russian fortification where the battle of Malakoff took place during the Crimean War."

"Cool, but why not follow the professional rodeo circuit?" asked Conner.

"I gave it some thought but my passion for the Rangers clearly developed from my mom's dad who lived with us until his death. He was a consummate storyteller and a skilled penman—his journals read like novels. His nickname was Coffee and he served with the legendary Ranger Hall of Famer, Clint Peoples. They were alongside the Dallas Police Department including their Homicide and Robbery Bureau, the Secret Service, and FBI when Kennedy was assassinated. Ever hear of Peoples?"

Axl leaned forward in his seat tapping Conner on the shoulder. "I remember that name from when Sheriff McAlister told us about the New York connection to that tragedy—the filmmaker of *A Nightmare on Elm Street*. Everyone assumed Craven chose this street as it was present in small towns across America. He admitted the shooting had a profound impact on him as a young man in 1963 and he chose Elm Street as it was close to the book depository where the president was assassinated. For him, the innocent world ended in that moment."

Trisha offered a portrait of the relentless incorruptible Clint Peoples who spent decades in the field with the Rangers, followed by an appointment as the U.S. Marshal for the Northern District of Texas. "His legacy was steeped in intrigue and filled with high profile politicians. He and Coffee worked on major cases during their time together. One was George Parr, dubbed The Duke of Duval, who was part of the family that controlled a Democratic political machine tied to aiding the senatorial election of Lyndon B. Johnson."

She added the involvement of Billie Sol Estes, the flamboyant swindler with ties to the future President Johnson. Estes circumvented the U.S. Department of Agriculture regulations with fraudulent claims and bragging of nonexistent fertilizer tanks. U.S. Agriculture Extension Agent Henry Marshall, after an extensive investigation, expected a procedural settlement of the allocations against Estes, but instead was offered a bribe in the form of a promotion to a high position in the U.S.D.A. in Washington, which he refused resulting in a beating so brutal that one of his eyes hung out of its socket and he was forced to breathe carbon monoxide from his own truck. "It was originally ruled a suicide. Get this, he was shot five times with a long barrel rifle within a four-inch circle on his left chest. How on earth did that happen? Layers and layers of high-level corruption, that's how—which is how an illegal brothel remained open for sixty years in our beloved state."

"Instead of being discouraged by all these stories you decided to join the fight. It would've taken a lot for me to jump into the fray," said Conner.

Trisha steered the conversation about Coffee as if powered by an unseen wind punctuating each word with avidity and love. Within the pages of his journals he spoke of injustices and how the fight against evil was often a losing battle with tiers of deception living within a haven for it to flourish. "At the top of each page he quoted Psalms 141:10—*Let the wicked fall into their own nets, while I pass by in safety.* When he ran across those who chose to let evil win, he was quick to remind them the world was a dangerous place but not because of those who do evil, but because of those who look on and do nothing."

"Sounds like you have some pretty big boots to fill, Lieutenant," said Axl.

"Ol' Coffee is already smiling down on her as she's the first female Ranger to reach this rank," offered Field Major Garver.

"Congratulations," chimed the deputies.

"Hey, can we see Southfork from here? I used to watch *Dallas* all the time. J.R., Jock, and Miss Ellie…those Ewings were something else," said Axl.

"It's about twenty-five miles north of Dallas in Parker County. On TV it looks like you could see it from anywhere in the State, but it's only about three-hundred acres of everything Texas. The original owners lived in the house but sold it because of the hordes of people trying to catch a glimpse of the stars. The current owners have taken marketing the popularity of the series and the location to another level. We had a family reunion out there a couple of years ago and had our picture taken with Jock Ewing's gray Lincoln Continental—a boat of a car measuring nineteen-feet from tip to tail," said Denny.

Trisha proceeded through Exit 498 toward Sherman and U.S. 82 suggesting since they were about halfway to the destination, it would be a good time to fill them in on the Kurtz family and their situation. Conner methodically walked the Rangers through Victor's file, including his idiosyncrasies, background, outstanding warrants, and the expectations for his surrender, painting him as a wanted felon without a propensity for violence, as far as he knew. "It's odd, I know, but I feel sorry for the guy although I've been told that sympathy shouldn't be wasted on pedophiles. His is such a pathetic story and unfortunately, he chose to compound his actions by his latest escapades. His father, Anthony, and half-brothers, Raymond and Floyd, are in a whole different category all together—dangerous and desperate. Again, according to Victor."

"So, our responsibility is to serve the arrest warrant issued by the State of New York to the father and the two sons, correct?"

"That's the plan. Officers from the Texoma Police Department and the Coast Guard Auxiliary Patrol will meet us at the marina. They've been covertly keeping tabs on the whereabouts of our subjects but were told not to approach them. Axl and I will take custody of Victor and hopefully all will go as planned and peacefully—without cause to double-tap the center mass."

"No kidding. A re-enactment of the gunfight at the OK Corral wouldn't be good," said Axl.

The Suburban carrying the teams of law enforcement and the private prisoner transport van bounced along on the unpaved road, a metal logo sign pointing the way to the Grumpy Point Marina. They pulled in alongside a lone car parked by the fuel dock which was occupied by four police officers in the unmarked cruiser. Conner rolled down his window, identified himself, and asked for a report on the whereabouts of the suspects. Anthony was overhauling the engine of one of the commercial fishing boats at the end of Cedar Mills Pier. Raymond and Floyd Kurtz were off today and occupying barstools at Stan and Ollie's Juke Joint.

"Okay, thanks. Lieutenant Minton, here's the warrant for Anthony's arrest. Take two of the Texoma officers with you to apprehend him. Field Major Garver, here's the other warrant. You and the other two remove the brothers from their seats and meet back here. Use caution as these three might not be in a mood to cooperate. Axl and I will track down Victor. He promised me he would stay put if I'd come and get him."

Rattler, sitting on a stool behind the counter, looked up from loading lottery tickets into the game slots when two officers opened the door to the minimart. "Can I help you?"

"We're from the Erie County Sheriff's Department in Buffalo, New York, and we're looking for Victor Kurtz. I'm the person he called from your manager's office."

"Right, I told him he could hide in a vacant boathouse and slip at the end of Landers Pier but had to be careful. It's close to where the brothers detailed boats. I hope they didn't spot him."

Rattler marked the locations on a marina map, handing it to Axl. On the way out they encountered a handcuffed Anthony in custody, his face coloring from red to purple with indignation, threatening to sue for unlawful arrest and violation of his civil rights, while spewing profanities at his captors as they hauled him to the transport vehicle.

Sheriff Boyle and Axl walked the length of the pier under a sky streaked with thin clouds drifting apart as if opening the curtain on another perfect summer day. Arriving at the end of Landers Pier triggered an acute sense of vigilance as they eyed the surroundings for any sign of Victor. Covered by a canopy and anchored in the slip was a thirty-two-foot Sea Ray Sundancer 320 christened *Fear the Roo*. A custom built-out dock paid homage to the Kangaroos of nearby Austin College in Sherman with captain's chairs, floor mats, and dog bowls all in crimson and gold. The water looked as placid as the surface of a mirror until the vessel gently heaved rhythmically rising and falling as the Coast Guard Auxiliary Patrol arrived to assist.

After tying up, the flotilla commodore and another auxiliarist greeted Conner and Axl sharing what they had gathered from observing the area, albeit from a distance as instructed. "After you notified us of his whereabouts, we spotted a person matching Mr. Kurtz's description moving in and around the boat and dock in the early morning hours. Things were quiet until yesterday evening when a rented pontoon boat dropped anchor off the end of the pier. Looked like a group of fishermen, but we lost visuals after dark. We've had eyes on the boat and dock since sunrise and there's been no sign of anyone."

"How did you know it was a rental?" asked Axl.

"It was as we call it, party boat beige, and we tied the state registration numbers on the bow to the *Lake Fun Rentals*. They offer all sorts of rentals from water toys to luxury yachts. We called them. They verified it was part of their inventory, but it was out of the rental rotation because it was in for routine service and detailing."

"Any description of the fishermen?"

"Afraid not. We were too far away but it did look like there were two for sure, maybe three."

"I don't like the sound of this. Let's glove up and get the canopy off the boat and look around," said Conner. They accessed the foredeck by a walk-through on the port side arriving at the bow finding three forward-facing lounges with "Roo" colored headrests and neatly rolled beach towels on each lounge. Moving through the cockpit galley they opened the refrigerator to find a bottle of milk, pimento cheese, a loaf of bread, and lunch meat. Conner repeatedly called Victor's name garnering no response before venturing below. They discovered one of the twin berths covered with a quilt and an alarm clock with its face cracked under the dinette table. A tote bag with a pair of jeans and two sweatshirts, a red Kansas City Chief's ball cap, and a few boxes of candy hearts.

"The clock could be a sign of a struggle but who knows how long it's been broken," said Axl.

After the area was wrapped in yellow crime scene tape, the forensic team was called to collect and bag the evidence and dust for fingerprints on the Sea Ray and the rental pontoon boat. A vein in Conner's forehead throbbed at the realization that his insistence that Victor stay put until he arrived might have put him in harm's way, asking himself a question that had a painfully obvious answer. "The interrogation of the Kurtz clan should be interesting," snapped Conner.

Sheriff Boyle shook hands with the commodore thanking the Coast Guard Auxiliary for all their help. "Before you take off, I'm dying to know how a Texas school winds up with a kangaroo mascot?"

The commodore spoke up, "I can answer that. I bleed crimson and gold as a graduate of Austin College. It reaches back to the 1850s when upperclassmen used to hold *Kangaroo Kourts* where they would put freshman on trial. After these rituals were abolished by the school, the class of 1932 purchased a three-year-old kangaroo from a California zoo. Pat the 'roo' attended pre-game bonfires and football games on a leash. After two more live mascots died, the school determined that kangaroos were not a good fit for the Texas climate but kept the mascot—now played by a costumed human."

While Conner and Axl were involved with the search for Victor and Lieutenant Minton had placed Anthony inside the transport van, Field Major Garver and his backups spotted Raymond seated on a stool inside the bar. A chain of connected beer tabs counted the number of PBRs the twosome had consumed. Floyd stumbled out of the men's restroom and into the arms of the Lake Texoma officers. Raymond swiveled in his seat, a frisson of panic registering in his bloodshot eyes as he tried to comprehend the consequences of what was happening as handcuffs secured his wrists.

"What in the hell is this about?"

"We have a warrant for the arrest of Raymond and Floyd Kurtz issued by the State of New York in connection with the death of an eight-year-old girl, sexually assaulted and buried inside a concrete block. Ring a bell?"

"It wasn't us...our old man...."

"Floyd, shut up. Ya hear me. They got nuthin' on us."

"We'll let the criminal courts sort that out, fellas. Your chariot waits for the ride back to Buffalo."

255

The bartender interrupted saying, "Wait just a damn minute. Who's goin' to pay their tab?"

Field Major Garver removed Raymond's wallet from his back pocket tossing two one-hundred-dollar bills onto the counter. "That'll cover it."

"Hey, you can't do that... we didn't owe that much you prick."

"You won't miss it where you're going. Now, let's go join Daddy-o."

Anthony, Raymond, and Floyd were read their Miranda Rights and separated from each other as Conner began the interview processes hoping dividing would conquer. He had learned the inuendoes of interviewing and interrogation from Sheriff McAlister who always recommended building a rapport with a prisoner. "So, Anthony, can I get you something to drink before we start?"

"I don't have to talk to you," he barked. "Why am I here?"

"The State of New York has issued a warrant for your arrest in connection with the young girl found inside a concrete block in Buffalo. It seems a DNA sample put you at the scene of the crime."

"That's impossible. Victor was charged with that crime."

"Yes, he was but the jury didn't believe the evidence."

"So, what's that got to do with me? I got nothing to say."

"You're within your rights, but that doesn't mean I can't ask you questions. You a fisherman? I'm told there's some great striper fishing at the end of Landers Pier. Had any luck there?"

Anthony's mouth twisted into a snarl, his voice low and raspy as he spit denials at the questions that Conner continued to ask. "When's the last time you saw your son?"

"Which one?"

"Victor. When's the last time you saw him... alive?"

"Maybe a week ago. He flew the coop as usual."

"We've got officers searching your cabin. What are we going to find, Papa Kurtz?"

Lieutenant Minton and Axl conducted the interview of Raymond while Field Major Garver asked the questions of Floyd. Each one probed the relationship with their father and Victor hoping the amount of alcohol the brothers had consumed would loosen their lips. Separately they were informed of the details of the arrest warrants and the impact their involvement in the death of the little girl would have on their freedom. They both painted themselves as the only normal people in a houseful of weirdos...the father a control freak with a deranged personality; the stepmother would make Norman Bates' mother in the movie *Psycho* look like Alice from *Alice in Wonderland;* and brother, Victor, was a jellyfish—spineless with no brain or heart.

The line of questioning shifted to the last time they saw Victor, to which Raymond responded, "A few days ago," while Floyd slurred, "A couple of weeks ago." Axl threw his arms in the air at the dead-end answers saying, "Just as a side note, Raymond, Floyd is spilling his guts. And we're searching your cabin. Anything you want to tell us?"

"He's a mean drunk. Whatever he's saying is a pack of lies. You can put that in writing."

Axl and Lieutenant Minton left Raymond stewing in his lies, meeting Field Major Garver to compare notes, noting both brothers were throwing the other under the bus as well as distancing themselves from Anthony.

"This family is certainly not Andy, Opie, or Aunt Bee in Mayberry, North Carolina," said the lieutenant.

"No, they're not. Think Conner is doing better with Anthony?"

Sheriff Boyle, after learning the results of the search of the Kurtz cabin, returned to further interrogate Anthony, this time armed with two bombshells sure to cause him extreme distress. He was betting his instincts about this prisoner were correct and would proceed with another line of questions designed to push the right buttons. Anthony jumped as Conner burst into the van, his eyes blazing with conviction and waves of irritation.

"You know, Anthony, I don't have any children, but if I did, I would just die if I had a son like Victor. What a loser and a pedophile to boot. He'd be an instant girlfriend to those animals in prison. I don't blame you for walking out on Sophia and him."

Anthony turned his head away from Conner's evaluation, his posture stiffening as if fending off a surge of hurricane-force sub-zero winds. Sheriff Boyle knew from his own relationship with his father that there was an unbreakable love-bond, a repressed longing to address the divides in any relationship. He was gambling that Anthony would defend Victor from his cruel words.

"You have no right to talk about my son like that. We've had our differences, but he's my flesh and blood, so back off, Sheriff, and stick your opinions where the sun don't shine."

"Your other two boys are both pointing a finger at you and at each other. What do you have to say about that?"

"If their lips are moving, they're lying. Loyalty was never a strong suit. It's always been a *two-for-me-and-none-for-you* type of brotherly love."

"Neither one admits they had any role in the death of that little girl—it was all your doing."

"That's bullshit."

"How do you suppose Victor's camera got in your cabin? Your youngest son had few things to call his own. I doubt seriously he would voluntarily leave his prized possession behind."

"Victor snapped a picture of me before he left my cabin. I know for a fact he had it with him when he walked out the door."

"I know that's true."

"How would you know?" asked a stunned Anthony.

"Here's the deal. Victor left your cabin with three confessions in his pocket. He called me, so I know the truth about what happened with little eight-year-old Nancy. You see the problem here? We can't find Victor so it's your word against your other two sons. Accidental death versus manslaughter or murder carries different punishments."

Anthony turned a cold eye at his interrogator before his haughtiness fell to the wayside, his voice full of bluster dimming as he weighed his options. "So, what do you want from me?"

"Victor's camera didn't walk back into your cabin by itself. How did it get there?"

Raymond and Floyd were reunited as Lieutenant Minton, Axl, and Field Major Garver informed them of the results of the search of the cabin. Stoic expressions prevailed until questions surfaced about Victor's camera being found behind some clothes on the floor of their closet. Along with being informed that Victor had called Sheriff Boyle about the confessions, they were also notified that the pontoon boat spotted at the end of Landers Pier was the same one in line for detailing before it returned to the rental company. This revelation resulted into which brother would flip on the other faster, both pointing an accusatory finger at the other on the Buffalo case but declining any involvement with Victor's disappearance. As soon as forensics finished the report from his hiding place on the boat and dock, the Kurtz brothers' future dimmed unless their allusive brother was found alive and safe.

30

Waiting on the World to Change

MATT'S EYES TRANSFIXED on the peaked ceiling and exposed wood beams above the bed that he and Summer shared on visits to his parents' home, bittersweet memories filling every nook and cranny of the room. He folded his arms across his chest, his heart feeling as hard as a granite monument, his soul benighted in sorrow as he inventoried the setting. With his temples throbbing, he questioned whether this discomfort was related to his head injuries or a tension-induced pain from stress. Either way some fresh air might alleviate his symptoms.

A faint wind welcomed him when he opened the sliding doors to the private terrace, the slant of light that offered hope in a darkened sky waning, the horizon looking as though someone spilled canned peaches and lemonade as twilight transformed day into night. Matt leaned against the rail struggling to reimagine the romance of his idealistic life before Summer died.

A mother's sixth sense motivated Margo to check on her son to find Sadie asleep on her back in front of his bedroom door, a dog's intuition also strong in sensing human emotion. She yawned and flipped over when Margo knocked, gently opening the door after calling Matt's name produced no response. The tranquility of his introspection was broken by the sound of his mother's voice.

261

When he turned around his once youthful face showed signs of torment as if his hourglass were running out of sand with fine lines like French seams pressed into the corners of his eyes. "Mom, I didn't hear you," an audible stress reflected in his voice.

"I was worried, and dinner is almost ready. Did you speak with Tina?"

His face grew warm, his eyes piercing into hers as if he were residing in an area lying beyond what was visible or known. "Yes, it'll take some time to digest our conversation."

"How's business?"

"Dandy," he said rubbing his temples. "I have to go home."

Man's primal instinct is survival, and although Victor Kurtz could not claim the shrewdness of hardened criminals, he owned enough subsistence to rival British novelist Roald Dahl's character, Mr. Fox, who used his cunningness and trickery to outsmart the farmers who wished to do him and his family harm. He promised Conner he would stay put until he arrived in Texas but became concerned as the brothers frequently stalked the area around where he was hunkered down. After many hours of pondering, Victor master-minded a plan that would set them up to take the fall for his dis-appearance. He knew it was just a matter of time before Raymond and Floyd boarded the *Sea Ray*, so he left his belongings counting on their twisted minds being unable to resist taking the camera in hopes of discovering pornographic photos from their pedophile sibling.

With the Kurtz family secured inside, the prisoner transport van pulled away from the marina—the destination, Buffalo, New York. Before joining the Texas Rangers for the journey back to the airport, Sheriff Boyle and Axl thanked Rattler for his help. "Before you leave, my manager's pretty pissed. His cell phone went miss-ing after Victor was in his office. Here's the number."

"Appreciate that, Rattler. We might be able to find Victor after all, if he's still alive. Your Coast Guard Auxiliary promised to con-tinue the search and let us know if any bodies float to the surface."

"One more thing, Sheriff. Victor asked if he could ride with me to Sherman where my aunt owns a motel. I waited for an hour, but he never showed up."

The ride back to the airport was solemn with Conner and Axl's mission to bring Victor Kurtz back to New York to face the charges against him falling woefully short. Lieutenant Minton offered some consolation as Anthony, Raymond, and Floyd were being transported back to answer for the crimes they committed. The Texas Rangers bid Sheriff Boyle and Axl farewell, the deputies expressing appreciation to them for their professionalism and assistance.

Willa and Starla, huddled together on one of the couches in the den discussing their visit to the refuge and sorting out Willa's confusion about why Cupid the Cardinal always returned to his cage. Starla admitted not being an ornithologist but extracted her knowledge as a lyricist, creating a narrative with each verse contributing a new imagery, idea, symbolism, or underlying meaning to the storytelling. "If I were writing a song and wanted to highlight the differences of being caged or free, Cupid's story would be a good one."

"How would it go?"

"What hit me initially is a caged bird would be fearful of the unknown, his view of life skewed by the bars that kept him captive, but he still sings of freedom hoping someone will hear his trill on a distant hillside."

"And the free bird?" asked Willa.

"He would leap on the back of the wind current, floating downstream until the ride ended, afraid of nothing, and only thinking of catching another trade wind. Cupid lived both scenarios, never feeling trapped, just loved."

"So, he returns to a place that's safe...the only one he knows," said Willa.

"Exactly."

When Matt and Margo arrived, trailed by Sadie, Gabe flew into his dad's arms, wrapping himself around him. Magnolia, who was sleeping on Patrick's feet on the ottoman, looked toward the commotion before resuming her nap.

Gabe, his body in continuous motion, dizzy with excitement with his words rolling off his tongue faster than the speed of sound said, "Daddy, Big Pop probably broke the law racing home after we saw all the animals. I gotta go back 'cause I've got a new friend and his name is Desi and he's a llama and he's got a wife name Lucille."

A mirthless smile exposed his façade of happiness when he tried to speak to the joy radiating from his young son, his words halted in mid-sentence.

Gabe pressed his hand against Matt's forehead. "GoGo, I think Daddy's sick."

Matt lowered Gabe to the floor, kneeling to meet his concerned eyes. "Daddy's just a little tired. Don't worry. A good night's sleep will take care of it. Then we can meet Desi and all the other animals."

Bringing a temporary close to the conversation, Concha announced dinner was ready. The family took their seats at the dining room table, the spinach salads with cubed cheese and orange slices dressed with a citric vinaigrette ready to eat. In the warming oven individual ramekins held the entrée, homemade chicken pot pie.

Over the dessert course of cinnamon applesauce, one-dimensional conversation floated through the stillness sounding as though they were speaking into muted microphones. Before scurrying off with Willa to enjoy their iPads, Gabe announced he was sleeping in Daddy's room tonight because he wanted to be close to Mommy. Matt shrugged his shoulders at the suggestion, knowing an argument would be useless. "All right, buddy, but you have to promise me you won't hog the covers."

"Deal."

Starla helped Concha clear the dishes from the table while Margo remained seated, shifting positions in her chair, her gaze flitting around the room never landing on anything for more than a few seconds as if in a conversation where everyone was talking, and no one was listening. She caught Patrick's eye, her face holding the burden of concern. He mouthed, "Matthew?"

She nodded.

"Matt, we'd have to be blind not to notice how preoccupied you are. We're all ears if you care to share."

"Dad, I have to go home. Tina's in trouble."

"Anything to do with Seasons?"

"Yes and no. Seems she and Bradley Anderson have become an item and I have to save her from making a huge mistake. She thinks he is who she's been looking for her whole life."

"Son, I recognize your concern and your past with him, but Tina has always had a good head on her shoulders. We should be happy for her."

"I can't. She has to know how I feel...how I've always felt about her."

Starla, not wanting to interrupt what appeared to be an intense father and son discussion, motioned for Margo to join her in the kitchen. She had just spoken with Conner who was waiting for his flight to Buffalo. "Victor is either dead or has managed to escape. His father and two brothers are suspects in his disappearance along with their involvement in the crime Victor was on trial for and are being transported to Buffalo to face charges."

"Unbelievable. Just when we thought our family was safe. I'm just sick."

"Me too. I just overheard that Matt has to go home. He still can't fly so I could drive him back, but I don't think it would be smart for Gabe and Willa to go just yet."

"They seem to be settling in here. I'd hate to throw a wrench in the progress and school's starting soon."

"Matt might agree it's best to leave them here. If I'm not being too nosy, what's the urgency to return to Buffalo?"

"He called Tina to check on business. I don't know if you are aware of their relationship, but they were in college together, tried dating once, and decided they were better friends than a couple. They love each other like siblings. Tina told him she had finally found her knight in shining armor. The only catch is she chose Bradley Anderson—Willa's biological father."

"Not Matt's favorite person for sure. What does he expect to accomplish?"

"That's a good question and I don't know the answer, but on the surface, he's acting like Tina is cheating on him."

"His emotional state is far from stable with everything still so raw with the loss of Summer. Life does move forward whether we're ready or not. It's almost like he's looking back to where he's been and not forward to where he's going."

⚬⚬⚬

Conner unlocked the kitchen door to the Mackie household and was greeted by a tail-thumping Dude and an aloof Halle perched in her usual spot atop the refrigerator, scrutinizing the intruder with one eye and offering a slight mew before resuming her nap. He had called the deputy who took over the housesitting in his absence, thanking him for taking care of the animals, and promising a full report on the Kurtz clan at tomorrow morning's briefing. There was a heaviness in his limbs as he climbed the stairs, the unsayable catching in his throat, the inescapable responsibility that he probably caused another man's fatality hanging in his psyche. *Victor Kurtz was a criminal, a fugitive, a felon, the antithesis of morality, but did he deserve to die?* Another thought weighing heavy was having to notify Victor's mother of the news. Sophia was a far cry from Marmee in *Little Women*, but she did give birth to him.

Although exhaustion filled every cell of his body, it proved fruitless to unburden his mind and sleep soundly. Vivid nightmares of the walls folding in on him and the bed stuck inside a falling elevator startled him awake, a cold sweat dampening the sheets, his conscience reeling with what he could have done differently. The digital clock registered 2:32 A.M. and instead of rousing the animals into thinking it was breakfast time, he tried a couple of the techniques offered by his mentor and friend, Sheriff McAlister, to relieve stress—emulate a cat by tensing and releasing muscles of the body, part by part. After working through this exercise resulted in limited relief, he employed the controlled breathing method, *pranayama* with its roots in yoga, as a last-ditch effort, hoping to remember the routine. *Lie down, close your eyes, press the tip of your tongue to the roof of your mouth, slightly open your mouth, and exhale until you reach the bottom of your breath. Close your mouth, inhale through your nose for four counts, then hold your breath for seven counts . . . then what? I give up. Time to splash*

266

cold water on my face and brew a pot of coffee. My day, Dude and Halle's day will begin before sunup.

Conner parked his black Ford Crown Victoria Police Interceptor in his designated spot with daybreak still closed tightly in nightfall. The moon, coffined in clouds, suggested an ominous beginning to the job at hand—first on the agenda was to check on Sheriff McAlister. His thoughts, rambling around in his mind, were jaded as if the world crumbled, he would shrug his shoulders accepting his fate in stride. He rarely viewed himself like the pessimistic donkey in A.A. Milne's classic *Winnie-the-Pooh,* but today patches of gloom haunted each step as he had hoped to bring good news to his former boss about the capture of Victor Kurtz.

Conner would have to wait for a decent hour to call the McAlisters, so until then organizing his paperwork for the briefing later that morning would fill some time. He unlocked the file cabinet beside his desk removing the Kurtz file. The last entry he had made in the progress report was the Texas trip itinerary circled with check marks atop bullseye targets drawn in the margins. Another sample of failed wishful thinking on his part prompting him to move on to another phase of the report. The fingerprint analyses for the Kurtz brothers matched those found on the boat where Victor had been hiding, driving another piece of evidence in the guilty column in the disappearance of their younger brother.

Axl, arriving before any of the other deputies, opened the office door greeting the first early bird with a yawn. "Chief, you must've given up on getting a good night's sleep, too."

"I hoped exhaustion would take the wheel, but after wrestling with the covers all night, I just got up. You might have to pick me up off the floor when this caffeine high winds down though."

"I've got your back. Any progress on when our *convict-train* might arrive?"

"Last report the prisoner transport van carrying the Kurtz clan will be welcomed to our county holding center hopefully by the end of the week with the goal of incarceration at the Wende Correctional Facility where they can join the notoriety of the late *Jimmy 'the Gent' Burke,* our Irish-American gangster who organized the largest cash robbery in our history."

267

"Let's see how long it takes for them to turn on each other in hopes of leniency," said Axl.

"I personally think Anthony holds all the cards. He's guilty of some things, but I suspect he didn't have anything to do with Victor's disappearance."

"Why is that?"

"Father of the year candidate he is not but when baited, his paternal instinct kicked in. I gambled he had some feeling for his youngest son getting his hackles up when I said I wouldn't want a son like Victor."

"It'll be a battle between public defenders and plea deals."

Conner poured another cup of coffee, glancing at the wall clock before dialing the sheriff's phone number. He was about to hang up when an unfamiliar voice answered, "McAlister's residence."

"Sherry?"

"No, may I tell her who's calling?"

"Conner Boyle."

"Just a moment please."

A few minutes went by before Sherry said hello, her voice hoarse and uninflected as if all moments of hope had withered like a Vanda orchid under the scorching sun of the Baja California desert. "Oh Conner, dear boy...I'm glad you called. Warren's in hospice care. He's been asking for you."

31

Father and Son

GABE, SITTING ON the floor in the corner of the bedroom his parents once shared, his body warmed by the smoldering fire bouncing an incandescent inner glow on his face as if sated with lightning bugs. His whisper room, with its door open and all set for a visitor, had traveled to Texas along with a keepsake box tied with string. When opened the sides fell back revealing places to write notes and compartments holding photos and drawings dedicated to remembrances of his mom. Inside was a small wooden cross necklace with plastic beads he had made after Griff died, an embroidered handkerchief doused with her favorite perfume, and a tribute picture he drew labeled *Magical Mommy.* Her face, encircled by a halo, radiated contentment as a smile extended from one ear to the other. She held an elf on the shelf doll with the caption, *where love begins,* and it was signed Gabriel Edward Mackie, 2011. Gabe, absorbed in the legacy of his mother, was reading out loud a poem she wrote and did not hear Matt come into the room.

> *Dear Gabe,*
> *You're my star, my son of wonderment*
> *You're my star, my son of joy*
> *A jewel in your mother's crown who never*
>   *makes me frown.*
> *I love you, my star.*

Matt stood still barely breathing as not to interrupt his son clearly in the throes of reflection and devotion to his mother. His breath caught in his throat when he heard him say, "Mommy, you gotta help me help Daddy. I'm worried because he's sick. Not sick with a cold or anything. He smiles, but his heart hurts."

The anguish in Gabe's words cut deep into his core uncertain if he could comfort him, but profoundly touched by the depth of his convictions. His son's emotional intelligence was on display, like a little old soul who feels the energy in the room when something is wrong and who's curious and certain the answers are to be found, but he hasn't located them yet.

"Son, can Daddy come sit with you?"

Gabe, surprised by his Dad's voice, patted the floor for Matt to join him, showing him one by one the treasures he had collected before saying, "Mommy told me Griff was lonely, so she had to go and take baby Mack with her, so he'd have a playmate. She knew I'd be okay 'cause I had you and Willa."

Matt pinched his lips tightly to keep them from trembling, a painful tightness gathering in his throat as he searched for words that would not hang empty in the air. A turbulence churned in his dark, humid eyes, and questions swirled as he turned to face his son. "Gabe, how did you know the baby's name was Mack?"

"Mommy told me when she got her angel wings."

Matt let go of the suppressed grief that had been racking his body and soul. His tears, the natural bleeding of emotional wounds, broke the dam paving the way to a life without Summer. With his son in his arms, he rocked back and forth fighting the current of exhaustion until he lost strength to hold on any longer. It took the wisdom of his young gifted child to give him a way to silence his mind and let himself heal.

Morning arrived finding Gabe wrapped like a burrito in a blanket with Matt clinging to the edge of the bed still dressed in his clothes from the night before. Yesterday, he was flailing around in a canoe on the high seas, battling gale force winds while the protector of the universe seemingly slumbered. His body ached as though thrown by a bull named Fu Manchu, but a sense of wellness soothed the discomfort. Today, he would still mourn the loss of his wife and unborn son, but as he slipped out of bed, Matt embraced the realization that although the foundation under the house he built with Summer was shattered, he would rebuild it brick by brick for himself and his children. He showered, changed clothes, and opened the bedroom door without Gabe moving. Sadie greeted him with a full helicopter wag of her tail bringing her hips with it performing the shaky-shaky-happy dance. In her mouth she held Gabe's stuffed turtle, Wiz, as if she knew it would bring comfort to her little companion. Matt rubbed her between the ears before going downstairs with Sadie curling back up in front of the bedroom door, using Gabe's cuddly tortoise as a pillow.

The kitchen was quiet except for the gurgling of the coffee percolating, the accord of roasted peanuts and vanilla, Summer's favorite blend, wrapping its sweet earthy aroma around Matt as he waited for the brew light to turn green. Oddly, he found the delicate scent comforting, losing himself in a constellation of joyful recollections, an estrangement from the dull ache of his loss.

Shafts of golden radiance listed through the trees piercing the beauty and stillness of the morning as he joined his mother and sister-in-law on the wraparound deck. They both looked up from the newspaper when he cleared his throat. "Refill anyone?"

"Matthew, yes, please. Thanks for waiting on us," said Margo.

"I've been on the receiving end of this pampering so it's payback time."

With the keenness of a mother's eye, Margo noticed a brightness in her son's demeanor despite darkened circles under his eyes. "How was your sleepover with Gabe?"

"When I walked in, he was sitting on the floor of the bedroom telling Summer he was worried about me 'cause my heart was hurting. Hearing the words of my child begging his dead mother to help me...well you can imagine. The flood began...it was like an exorcism giving me permission to grieve."

"How can an innocent child effortlessly carry such burdens on his shoulders? It's almost like he's having a chat with the ancient sages about universal truths. I'll go on record that he'll be an incredible sculptor if that's what he wants to be. Creative types with that kind of vision see their spirits with crystal clearness," offered Starla.

"Don't gossip about me behind my back," quipped Patrick.

"I thought we hid your delusional hat," said Margo.

"I have a closet full. Good morning. Guess our grands aren't up yet?"

Concha arrived on the porch with a silver tray of *pan dulce* and a carafe of *café de olla,* pan coffee boiled with raw sugar and cinnamon. "We call these treats, the other side of the tortilla. We've got an assortment of pastries, one in a fan shape dipped in chocolate, Mexican croissants called *bigotes,* sweet *empanadas* like your fruit pies, Mexican wedding cookies, and my favorite *conchas*—my namesake—the ones shaped like a seashell topped with yellow and pink sugar paste...sweet just like me!"

"Tell me this is breakfast," said Starla.

"No, *Senorita.* In our tradition, breakfast is the heartiest and most important meal of the day, so I'll be preparing *huevos a la Mexicana,* scrambled eggs in a tomato-based salsa, and Mexican French toast rolls."

"How do you make the rolls?" asked Starla.

"It's simple. Just cut the crusts off white bread and spoon a tablespoon of peanut butter or preserves in the center, roll them up like a cigar, dip in egg-milk, fry them in butter until they're brown, roll in cinnamon sugar and serve."

"Trust me, they're to die for," commented Margo.

Donny, clad in a baker's apron and chef hat, joined the group saying, "My dear wife, I've whisked the eggs one-hundred-thirteen times so they're ready to add your tablespoon of mayonnaise before you start cooking. We might keep that secret ingredient from Gabe. He might think it has to do with rattlesnakes again."

"My man is such a helper," Concha said dryly following him back to the kitchen, leaving the family enjoying the prelude to breakfast.

Matt, his fingers tapping a rhythm on the side of his coffee mug, searched the eyes of his parents, his own taking on a hunted look. Margo and Patrick looked at each other, then back to their son who was visibly experiencing an element of distress. Before they could speak, Matt announced he had something to tell them. Starla rose out of her chair to give the family some privacy, but Matt insisted she stay as this concerned her sister.

One of the most difficult things to do is finding fault in someone's perfection, and it was not his intent to revisit a troubled time in their marriage, but Matt realized hiding behind his own indiscretions did not give him *carte blanche* in judging the actions of others, specifically his parents. His confession detailed the mutual physical attraction between Assistant District Attorney Randall Reid and Summer. "They spent hours on cases, and I hate to admit it, but I acted like a jealous teenager vowing to find my own outlet, although I chickened out. Then Griff died. She shut me out. I understood her guilt and depression, but I couldn't help her. I attended the New York State Restaurant Association's annual meeting in the City. We were all staying at Le Meridien overlooking Central Park. A group of us, both men and women, were having a nightcap in the lounge one night. Evidently my neediness sent a signal to one of my colleagues that I was interested in some extracurricular activity. She was attractive, available, and aggressive. I followed her like a lost pup on the way to her room. She kissed me, opened the door, and fortunately good sense sobered me up and I bolted. Later, I confessed to Summer and she told me, 'So, now we're even.'"

"Matthew, don't beat yourself up. No marriage is perfect. Why did you feel you had to share this with us?" asked Margo.

"Ours got tested and fortunately we escaped without too much damage. I passed judgment on you and Dad and I shouldn't have. I hope you can forgive me."

"We're also to blame for not telling you. Let's all belt out the lyrics to Cher's song, 'If I Could Turn Back Time' and put this puppy to bed," said Patrick.

A quiet small voice asked, "What puppy. I don't see a puppy, Big Pop."

Gabe, rubbing the sleep from his eyes, crawled into his grandfather's lap. "How was it in the land of nod, big guy?"

"I don't know where that is, Big Pop. I just slept in Daddy's bed."

"That's what I meant, Gabe...slumberland."

"Why didn't you just say so…sometimes you talk funny. Can I have one of those treats? The one with the snow on top?"

By the time Gabe devoured several of Concha's Mexican wedding cookies, he and Patrick were covered with powdered sugar. Willa bounced into the kitchen, followed by Richard Parker, poured a glass of orange juice, hollered good morning to the family, settling into the corner of the couch in the living room with her iPad in hand.

After breakfast Margo and Patrick took a brisk walk along the hiking trails while Gabe, armed with drawing paper and colored pencils, took over the dining room table for his latest project. After chatting with her new gal pals earlier in the week, Willa begged Matt to set up a Wattpad account for her. She explained it was a storytelling application that gives young writers an outlet to be creative. "My new friends all have accounts, and they help each other with ideas. I might want to be a writer one day and this will let me post stories and get feedback. Please, Dad, it means a lot to me. And it's free."

"What do we have to do?"

"If you'll set up an under-seventeen account in my name linked to your email address, then I'll fill out the rest of the profile and get started writing. Oh, but I need a laptop to create my masterpieces and for school too."

"Can't you just write your stories in a journal?"

"That's what old folks do…this is how the new generation of authors roll. Wattpad has like over eighty-million monthly users. I could get discovered and be the next J. K. Rowling."

"Those are pretty lofty goals, Willa…but you've got to start somewhere. Let's get our literary prodigy signed up."

"Daddy, thanks, you're the bomb."

"I guess that's a good thing."

With Tina and Bradley at the forefront of Matt's thoughts, he reflected a determination in how he set his jaw forward adopting an apathetic pose as though strategizing ways to overcome any obstacles in his path announcing he would be in his room.

"I'm going to call Tina to apologize and tell her how I feel about her...how I've always felt about her."

"Aren't you just setting yourself up for another heartache?" asked Patrick.

"Maybe."

"Before you do anything, please ask yourself why this is so upsetting to you. If I were in Tina's shoes and you confessed your undying love for me after all these years, I would suspect it has everything to do with Bradley Anderson and I believe if you're honest with yourself, you'll come to the same conclusion...in my opinion of course." offered Margo.

"What I see is someone you are close to moving on with her life and you're not able to do that yet. You're still grieving Summer. You're not losing Tina. She's been in your life since college and she'll always be there. You know that don't you?" said Patrick.

"Losing my wife made me realize how much I care for Tina."

"I know, but you're not being fair if you put her in a position to have to choose either you or Bradley. It's obvious you and Tina have love for each other...but not the head-in-the-clouds type. Matt, be honest with yourself before you commit to something you can't easily undo," pleaded Margo.

Matt disappeared to his room, standing in his conviction that a frank conversation was mandatory, although not certain how much soul-baring he would share with her. He picked up the phone, hanging up several times before finding the courage to let it ring.

"Seasons LXX, the place of dreams and the best food in Erie County," answered a husky male voice with a poetic cadence.

"This is Matthew Mackie. And you are?"

"Matt, I understand you and Tina have had a conversation about me. This is Bradley Anderson and before you say anything, you have my honest to God word that my intentions toward Tina are genuine. I'm a changed man. She's the best thing that has ever come into my life and I would never hurt her."

"Is she there?"

"She's with a vendor. I'll tell her you're on the line."

A few minutes lapsed before Tina answered his call, her customary singsong voice with its rise and fall as if reciting the underpinnings of a classical music composition, mutating into staccato speech, each sound detached and clipped. Matt's apology for overreacting to her Bradley news provoked silence, followed by a thank you as gelid as December in Mongolia. He tried interjecting some levity into the conversation by comparing her tone as frosty as a cast-iron commode to which she responded with a stifled chuckle saying she hoped he didn't get frostbitten. Seeing a slight opening in the bitter-cold air mass, Matt confessed he was unwilling to accept that Bradley had turned over a new leaf and was now a stand-up guy, he was jealous of their happiness as a couple, and afraid he was going to lose her just like he lost Summer.

"Tina, you know I've always loved you and I don't want you to get hurt."

"I wouldn't trade our relationship for the world. We've always made a great team and I know how much you are mourning Summer. You know as well as I do that our love has never been a romantic one."

"Not in the past, but how about now?"

"You can't be serious after all this time, particularly at this moment in our lives."

"Why can't I?"

"You're talking crazy. Bradley has pushed the wrong button for you, and I know you're not in the market for a future with me...."

"It's never too late to start over is it?"

"I can't believe you're putting me in this position, Matthew."

"I'm just trying to be honest with you. Please don't hate me for loving you."

"I've got to go. I'm begging you to dig deep inside and figure out where all of this is coming from. Summer was the love of your life and now she's gone. It's not fair to me to suddenly think we have a future with each other."

"It took her death for me to face my feelings for you. I'm not taking it lightly and I hope you'll think about our conversation."

"Goodbye, Matt."

32

My Mother's Eyes

SHERIFF BOYLE SLEEPWALKED through the rest of the day, a vague restlessness dominating his thoughts after his conversation with Sherry McAlister. Dreading his next chore, he dialed Sophia Kurtz's number, the phone ringing a dozen times before the breathy mother of a fugitive answered. Conner, after identifying himself several times, suspected a donnybrook playing out in the residence of Mrs. Kurtz most likely involving her neighbor Joseph Samples, aka Batman.

He raised his voice decimals above that of a frightened hyena which garnered a remark, "If you're selling something, I'm not buying, so Ta Ta."

"Sophia, please this is Conner Boyle, the Erie County Sheriff. I've got news on your son."

"Are you that cute young one who visited me with that old guy that almost served up my Mr. Bubbles as a cat appetizer?"

"Yes ma'am. As I said, it's about Victor."

"Did you get my money and my little phone back? Where'd you find the scoundrel?"

Conner explained delicately the scenario that played out in Texas, reporting on the arrest of Anthony and the stepbrothers and that they were headed back to New York to face charges in the disappearance of Victor. "Sophia, I'm sorry, but we believe that your son might be dead. He located the trio, securing a confession from them about the crime Victor was accused of—the girl in the concrete—remember that one? He called me and was going to turn himself in, but when I got there he was gone. We suspect foul play, but right now we don't have a body or any clue where he is, if he's still alive."

After a few moments Conner asked, "Mrs. Kurtz, are you there? I hated to have to break this to you and rest assured we will continue the investigation until we run out of leads."

With a constrained silence filtering through the phone lines, Conner was about to hang up when he heard the muttering of consolation uttered from Sophia's gentleman friend followed by resonate honking and a lip-trembling whine akin to wind howling through an open chimney flue.

"By no means was he perfect, but he was all I had," she said her voice wavering with the enunciation of each word. "If he's dead...well, we can't even give him a proper burial...and if he's alive, we...I just hope he's somewhere doin' something that makes him happy. I gotta go now."

The motherly instinct of Sophia surfaced with the news of Victor. Conner hoped that her son had experienced that side of her sometime in his life, again questioning why he had a soft spot for the troubled young man. He imagined the displeasure on McAlister's face if he heard these thoughts.

With the day winding down and the rest of the deputies already gone, Conner headed to the McAlister home. Sherry greeted him with a gentle embrace. "I told Warren you were coming to see him today and that seemed to perk him up a bit. He even ate some ice cream and is sitting up in his recliner which he hadn't done recently."

An empty hospital bed, parallel to the floor-to-ceiling windows, offered a view of the wooden deck and fishing pond dancing with pastel colors stealing a look through the tree branches before marching toward darkness. The hospice nurse introduced herself to Conner, her faint-blue eyes glazed with benevolence. She squeezed his hand before leaving him alone with the sheriff. His friend was more than that to Conner. Although he had a great relationship with his own father, the connection and respect built between him and Warren McAlister bordered on family for both men. "Sheriff Boyle, how do you like my personal ICU? Great to see you. Come sit and let's catch up."

Conner took a step backward with the intensity of his voice, and although he had lost half of his weight, his handshake was steady as though infused with adrenaline. "Are your doctors licensed? By the looks of you they might have misdiagnosed your condition. I'm so happy to see you!"

"I'm having a good day…and you know me I love a captive audience," he said with his usual wittiness on full display.

After Conner filled him in on the Victor Kurtz debacle, Warren shook his head in disbelief but added the best laid plans often come up short. He congratulated him on the apprehension of Anthony and the stepbrothers, noting finally some resolution to the tragic death of the "little girl in concrete" was now undeniable with the genuine criminals being brought to justice. The conversation turned to Starla Jordan which produced a twinkle in Conner's blue eyes and a dimple-to-dimple grin materializing across his face. After two hours of visiting, the sheriff's voice began to fade as though the thoughts were still there, but the words were out of reach. Sherry, after peeking in on the twosome, recognized her husband was tiring, suggesting they wrap it up for today.

"Honey, I want Conner to have something to remember me by. Would you mind grabbing that little box in the top drawer of my desk?"

Conner promised Warren McAlister would always be a part of his life and he was still trying to fill those big shoes left by him in the Sheriff's Office. A smile with a genuine build lit up the retired sheriff's face as he opened the box, handing his successor his badge. "I wore this proudly for thirty years and had to surrender it, but they reissued it with this retired ribbon, and I'd be honored for you to have it. You've been like a son to me and I am so proud you are following in my footsteps. Erie County is lucky to have such a fine officer and human being. Hold what Theodore Roosevelt said close to you, *Far and away the best prize life has to offer is working hard at work worth doing.*"

Conner ducked his head to his chest trying to wrestle with the emotions of the moment. When he looked up there was an inner glow in the sheriff's moist eyes which he met with the realization that his friend might be saying goodbye. Sherry motioned to Conner that it was time to leave. "I'll be back soon with another full report on our favorite perps, Warren...and thank you for...trusting me with your badge."

"I'm not going anywhere."

Conner left the McAlister's house with his heart on his sleeve, overly optimistic as Warren, other than his physical appearance, acted like his old self, but at the other end of the spectrum he was cognizant of the gravity of his condition. The phone was ringing as he opened the door to his temporary home. "Mackie residence."

"How's my handsome defender of right and wrong?"

"You're timing is superb, Ms. Jordan."

"You sound like you're choking with emotion. What's wrong?"

"I just came from Sheriff McAlister's home. He's in hospice care now."

"I know how much he means to you."

"He's terminal but I'm still hoping for a miracle. He's just such a good man. Anyway, what's up with you? Enjoying your Texas stay?"

Starla highlighted the most recent adventures of the Mackie clan especially his buddy Gabe's escapades insisting Sky Island should be on his bucket list and since his folks were in Texas already, it might be doable. She reported on the presence of Bradley Anderson in Tina's life and Matt's reaction to the news, lifting his spirits when she indicated they might be returning to Buffalo soon.

"I'll drop by Seasons in the next few days to see if I can shed some light on the brewing romance. It's understandable that Matt would have strong opinions on the new development."

"We'd appreciate your input."

"On to us...I'm assuming you haven't found a burly cowboy to replace me yet...or have you?"

"You first...any runway models knocking down your door?"

"Yes, scores of them but I told them I'm taken."

"That sounds like a commitment, Conner Boyle."

"It does doesn't it? I miss you, Starla. We've got some unfinished business."

"Are we in a courtship, Sheriff?"

"From where I stand, sit, or lie down, yes, Ms. Jordan...although it would work better if we were in the same state and zip code."

"That's a medley of promise, fairy tales, and magic bullets all welded together in a chorus of a cloud nine song."

"You should be a songwriter...oh yeah, you are and evidently a good one. I can't wait to see you."

"I promise it will be an eventful reunion, Sheriff."

Conner woke the next morning after a restful night's sleep light-headed with glee at the possibility of a couple-type relationship blooming with Starla. It was as though their hearts were old friends, and with unflinching sureness, he carted his buoyant mood into the office. Axl was in the break room making coffee when he arrived noticing the happiness sign hanging around Conner's neck. "You win the lottery?" he asked.

"Matched all five numbers plus the Powerball."

"All these years and I didn't know you were a gambler."

"Only when the odds are right."

Settling into their routine, each prepared for the morning staff meeting as the deputies filed in one-by-one depositing lunch bags in the break room and pouring a beverage of choice before sinking into their chairs. The first item on the agenda was Conner sharing the details of his visit with Sheriff McAlister, the good vibes of the day interrupted with the ringing of the phone. Conner recognized the caller identification. The one-sided conversation lasted several minutes as everyone looked from one to the other for any signs pointing to the gist of the call.

"Yes, of course. It would be my privilege. Thank you for letting me know, Father Mallery. My best to dear Sherry." Conner hung up the phone, his posture slouching, eyes downcast. The silence, making more noise than a blast of dynamite, was excruciating as Conner tried to gather his composure. When he looked up, the woebegone expression on his face confirmed the suffocating blanket of sorrow wrapping a cold fist over his heart. "It's Warren. He passed last night."

"Conner, I know you were encouraged by your visit with him yesterday. We thought my brother with bone cancer had defied the odds when he did the same thing. It's called rallying—sometimes it lasts moments and other times it's days. The sheriff waited for you to visit so he could say goodbye," said Axl.

The news of Sheriff McAlister's death traveled through all the Erie County law enforcement departments and tributes were in the planning stages in conjunction with his widow to honor their beloved colleague.

As long-time parishioners of the colonial-style All Saints Roman Catholic Church in downtown Buffalo, Bishop Sanderson of the Catholic Diocese presided over the hour-long High Mass for Warren Alexander McAlister. The organist, playing the 1923 Wurlitzer, began the ceremony with the chords of "Ave Maria" and concluded by accompanying the choir with the expressive lyrics of "On Eagles Wings."

The Sheriff's Association organized the funeral procession that would escort his body to his final resting place, the one-hundred-ninety-one-acre Holy Cross Cemetery in Lakawanna, New York. Uniformed motorcycle officers led the hearse followed by scores of mourners for the short drive south from Buffalo where he would be buried beside his daughter, Lily, in the Glorious Mystery of Rosary section.

It was standing-room-only around the burial plot. The chanter from a bagpipe spilled into the air serenading the deceased with the lingering timbres of "Going Home."

Conner, with the badge that Sheriff McAlister had given him pinned to his lapel, touched it before he fulfilled his promise to his mentor. Father Mallery told him that Warren asked for him to recite his favorite prayer at the gravesite.

God, our father, Your power brings us to birth, Your providence guides our lives, and by Your command, we return to dust. Lord, those who die still live in Your presence, their lives change, but do not end ... In company with Christ, who died and now lives, may they

282

rejoice in Your kingdom, where all our tears are wiped away, unite us together again in one family to sing Your praise, forever and ever. Amen."

Before leaving the cemetery, Conner paid his respects to the final resting places of his grandparents, and after locating the plots for Colleen and Dillion Sullivan, did the same for Starla's parents.

With fatigue sinking into his bones after the long and emotional day burying his friend, Conner stopped by Seasons LXX for a drink and dinner before going home. His purpose was two fold, his stomach growling and his promise to Starla that he would check in to see for himself about the Tina and Bradley romance. He sat down at the bar, ordered a frozen margarita, and the answer to his inquiry appeared in a uniform, mixing cocktails. Bradley glanced his way at the same time Tina saw Conner.

"Sheriff Boyle, we haven't seen you in a blue moon. Welcome back."

"Thanks, Tina. I've been swamped catching criminals."

"Hope one of them was that creepy guy who was stalking Willa."

"We thought we had him dead to rights. He's either on the run again or could be in a watery grave."

"How did Matt take the news?"

"Disappointed for sure, but I think he feels safer in Texas."

"You remember Bradley?"

"Yes, has Broadway come to Buffalo?"

"No, my MS took a turn in the wrong direction, so I had to withdraw from the show."

"So, you're a bartender now?"

"Tina has been showing me the ropes and I'm enjoying my job. We make a good team," he said with a wink thrown her way.

"We do indeed. Brad has been a godsend since Matt left. I've got some paperwork to finish but enjoy a complimentary dinner on us," she said pecking Bradley's cheek.

Conner sipped his drink watching Bradley closely while he waited on other customers. He was a natural, a people person, laughing and joking with everyone he greeted. Conner did not let

283

the opportunity slip by when asked if he wanted another drink. "Brad, I'm a good judge of character and I suspect there's more to this relationship than boss and employee. Am I right?"

"Seriously, with all due respect, Sheriff, how is our private life any of your concern? I don't think it's illegal to be in love is it?"

"Fair enough. Sometimes it's difficult for me to turn off my inquisitive nature. Oh, by the way, the investigation into Summer Mackie's death is still ongoing. Let's keep in touch." Conner left Seasons LXX with the answers Matt didn't want to hear but it did appear the couple were seriously happy.

An overwhelming crush of loss followed him through the door of the Mackie's home. Sheriff McAlister's death was still at the center of his thoughts, and having visited his grandparent's gravesite earlier, they were on his mind as well. His grandfather had been a Navy man and he recalled a phrase he used a lot, *dead reckoning,* which in nautical terms means calculating a ship's path using distance and direction traveled rather than instruments or astronomical observation. Papa Boyle also used it to express the loss of his beloved Dianne, his wife of sixty-years. He'd say, "When a person whom you assumed would always be a part of your landscape, like a lighthouse that you passed every day, suddenly goes dark, it leaves you with one less landmark to navigate by." Warren McAlister was Conner's beacon fire.

33

Catch a Falling Star

THE WELL-BEING OF his children was at the top of Matt's priorities. Gabe possessed the ease of adaption, but Willa remained a concern. She left Buffalo arriving at Sky Island with a chip on her shoulder the size of a boulder causing everyone to walk on eggshells in her presence. However, since settling into the flow of her new environment, her Sissy Spacek's *Carrie* persona had thankfully evolved most of the time into that of a Disney princess. Matt, still uneasy about the whereabouts of Victor Kurtz, decided to enroll them in school in Green Tree instead of returning to Buffalo, much to the delight of his parents.

Mother and son drove to the school administration building to fill out the necessary paperwork for both children. Willa would be an upperclassman at Ross Junior High while Gabe would attend second grade at Shaw Elementary. Margo proposed that since Matt was staying in the area, he might be interested in consulting with the renovation team working on the restaurant and bar areas of The Murphy Hotel. "I've tooted your horn many times when I was helping with the project. They could use your expertise evaluating the different designs under consideration."

"That'd be great...will give me some purpose in life."

Margo's hands tensed into a white-fingered grip on the steering wheel before she spoke. "Matthew, I don't like the sound of that. Your purpose in life is clear. You've got a daughter and son."

"I meant beyond parenting, Mom. With Summer gone and now Tina…my mind's numb like it's floating from one random thing to another. My eyes don't see color anymore, just a dull gray."

"Along with everything else, don't forget you've not healed from your brain injury and although I'm not a physician, that has to be factored into what you're experiencing. Son, I don't know what transpired between you and Tina, but it's too soon to write off a fifteen-year partnership with someone you've always considered a sister."

"Let's change the subject, please."

Matt waited in the car while Margo picked up the books for her next book club meeting plus Starla's copy. Blustery gusts of wind had whisked away the morning clouds leaving a clean slate like a teacher's chalkboard at the end of the school day. His arm rested on the open passenger side window, the warmth of the sun hypnotic as a single wave crashing and receding toward the sea. He was startled into consciousness by a woman's voice calling his name.

"Matt, I didn't mean to interrupt your meditation."

"Aria, nice to see you again. Meditation might be too deep. One of my buddies used to accuse me of woolgathering when I got in a stupor. Guess that's where I was."

"How's my favorite sculpting *wunderkind* these days?"

"Gabe is terribly busy being Gabe. Mom and I just registered he and Willa in school here, so he'll probably be at your doorstep more than you want."

"My door is always open to him. Is this a permanent move?"

"We'll see, but for now I've committed to at least a year. Mom is trying to get me involved with the renovation at The Murphy Hotel."

"Great news. If you're working in Green Tree maybe our paths will cross more often."

"I'd like that."

"Me too. Now, I best get on with my errands before my next class. Come by the studio anytime."

Margo arrived just as Aria was leaving exchanging pleasantries before getting back in the car. "She's a lovely girl don't you think?"

"Yes, she is...reign in your matchmaking impulses," Matt said waving his finger back and forth in her direction.

"Don't accuse me of something that a busybody might do," she said lobbing a guiltless smirk at her son while shifting the car into reverse. The next stop on the agenda was to retrieve the rest of her belongings from her suite at The Murphy, a two fold plan designed to entice Matt into considering assisting with the renovation project. When Margo entered the hotel lobby, her presence was a welcome sight to management and the construction workers as they made a beeline to greet her as if Farrah Fawcett had strolled in. Matt looked around while she entertained her *fans,* the soaring ceiling with hand-carved wooden beams supported by decorative corbels and accented with wall sconces blinking understated vibes between the arched windows grabbed his eye.

The restaurant and pub in different stages of completion appealed to Matt's inventiveness sparking an interest that surprised him. Already in place in the bar was a curved polished maple countertop with built-in cabinets lining the wall behind. The ornate ceiling in copper and brown-leaf mosaic tiles held the vintage look of a structure built in 1928. Matt moved closer to inspect a framed poster of a cyclist on the adjacent wall. He took a step back when his mission was interrupted by the scent of buttered popcorn. When he turned around, he was met by a teenage boy with a crew-cut who said, "Who are you?"

"Hi, I'm Matt. Margo Mackie's son. She was working on the renovations here."

"She back?"

"Not officially. No. And you are?"

"Trevor. My dad's the foreman. I work at the movie theater until school starts."

"That explains the popcorn."

"You wondering about that poster? Like everybody. We've got the Prada store sitting in the middle of nowhere, an old metal desk on top of Hancock Hill, and this poster—visitors must think we're a weird bunch."

"I've heard about the desk and the Prada store up the highway from Marfa, but what's up with the poster? It doesn't look like it belongs in a bar in West Texas. I would expect cowboys riding horses or cattle ranches not a train, motorcycle, and a biker."

They both turned around upon hearing, "There you are, Matt. Hi, Trevor. Haven't seen you lately. Looks like the renovations are progressing right along. Is your dad here today?" asked Margo.

"He's having lunch on the patio."

"Great. Matt, let's grab a bite to eat and I'd like you to meet Cody. He'll fill you in on the poster."

When the foreman saw Margo open the door to the courtyard, he rose from his seat, wrapping her in a bear hug, a continuation of the lovefest she had developed with everyone at the hotel. The casual conversation between Margo and Cody turned to the possibility of Matt assisting with the renovation project with mother touting the people skills of her only child and his creative visions tied to the success of his Buffalo business, Seasons LXX. As Margo praised his skills, he flipped a half-shrug and a grin her way, the quintessence of her words caressing his blistered inner self as though wrapping him in a warm bath towel. A flush crept across Matt's cheeks, "Mom, I appreciate your opinion of my skills, but you're making me sound like the second coming of Gordon Ramsay."

"A simple thank you is all that's necessary, Matthew. I'll admit my evaluation of you might be a bit biased, but the giver of compliments is the one who shares how the actions of the receiver of those compliments has influenced his or her lives."

"I trust Margo's instincts even if she is your mother. I'd love to have you on board with the project."

"First, I have to know about the poster in the bar. Is it a holdover or new?"

Cody recited the tale of the poster indicating it had been on a wall in the lobby for years and they moved it to the bar as a focal point hoping it would foster discussion and it had lived up to its expectations being featured in the local papers and picked up by the Associated Press. The poster celebrates the sporting achievement of Belgian cyclist Leon Vanderstuyft, who cycled a world record one-hundred-twenty-five kilometers and eight-hundred-fifteen meters in an hour behind a motorcycle in 1928—the same year this rail and ranch hotel began welcoming guests. "I can only guess the poster might echo the same type of grit involved in building this luxury property. At any rate, it has a home inside our barroom."

"Good stuff. And, yes, I'd be honored to come on board for the rest of the refurbishments. Are you planning to offer locally brewed beers? They've been a big hit at Seasons LXX especially with visitors from other states—they take home a taste of home brews from our Buffalonians."

"Good idea. I'm a big sports junky. Y'all have the reputation of being bitter sports fans. True?"

Margo, bobbing her head in agreement, offered she could attest to that fact. "Three things sum it up, *47 wide-right, Music City Miracle,* and *no goal.* It was 1991. Patrick was still with the Bills as a kicking coach. We missed a forty-seven-yard field goal to win Super Bowl XXV in Tampa. You remember don't you, Matt?"

"I was fourteen, jumping up and down on the sideline, ready to celebrate, but the Giants hoisted the Lombardi trophy instead. The only positive thing I took from that game was Whitney Houston in her patriotic outfit belting out our national anthem. With the Gulf War raging, it was a perfect tribute to our country. It still brings chills."

"Then, in a wild-card playoff game with the Tennessee Titans in Nashville in 2000...sixteen-seconds left on the clock—we're up sixteen to fifteen...on the kickoff their tight end throws a lateral pass, the receiver runs seventy-five yards for the winning touchdown. And we lost the NHL Stanley Cup on an illegal goal. Bitter—yes, I'd say so."

"That was the year the Dallas Stars won right?" asked Cody.

"Brett Hull's goal in triple overtime in game six is still a bone of contention with our hockey fans," said Margo.

"Guess it's obvious we watched our share of athletic events in our family. Back to the task at hand, when I scoped out the restaurant, I thought of a couple of things that might add to the design."

"Like?" inquired Cody.

"You've already got two unique dining options, this casual

outdoor courtyard and the classic style Rio Grande Room, but how about adding a touch of the Big Apple with chef's tables offering a view of the open kitchen?"

"You were right, Margo. Matt's already brought a lot to the table and he's not even hired...yet."

"I can start after Willa and Gabe start school."

Margo left The Murphy Hotel with delight in her step at the successful outing matching Matt with the on-going project as his attitude took on a more positive tone at the opportunity given to him. This would be a good match for all involved. Arriving back at Sky Island found Patrick and Donny in his office but no one else in sight. She peeked her head in asking where the kids and Starla were. "Gabe and Starla are playing Minecraft on the deck by the pool and the last I saw Willa she was sprinting upstairs. I gave her my MacBook Air laptop which produced a squeal and animated grin from our granddaughter. I haven't seen her since."

"You're grinning like a Cheshire cat. Things must have gone as planned with your mission today."

"As resistant as Matt was to the idea, he warmed up and accepted the consulting position. Luckily, Cody was there, and we had lunch. I think he's excited about this. Great to see him with a positive vibe for a change."

The timing of a dinner invitation from Conner's sister, Riley, was welcomed as a chance for him to visit with family, assured that the youthful enthusiasm of Aaron, Barry, Claire, and Daryl would provide a diversion from the doldrums that stalked his every move. It would also be an opportunity to share the more sanguine news about his budding relationship. Riley watched closely as he spoke about Starla, the animation in his voice matching the joy unfolding like a tulip pressed to open by Spring's sunshine. Eager to know more about his mystery woman prompted a flurry of questions about how and when they met, where she was from, what she did for a living...with the final inquiry posed by his oldest nephew, Aaron, who asked, "Uncle Cool, it's about time we got an Aunt Cool. When's the wedding?"

Claire and Daryl's gaze swept from one to the other as they bounced around the room chanting, "We'll be the flower girls and wear beautiful pink dresses and drop rose petals as we walk down the aisle. Mom, when can we go shopping...this will be so fun and...?"

Riley telegraphed a warning to her brood as Conner's cheeks reddened, a hangdog expression making its way across his face. "It's okay, sis. That's a fair question. I don't know the answer, but I'll testify she would without a doubt be a perfect candidate for Aunt Cool. I can't wait for you to meet her." Although Conner's misery at burying his mentor and friend weighed heavy on his heart, her brother's demeanor screamed ecstasy as though he might break out in song with Beyonce's hit "Love on Top."

Riley insisted on inviting Starla to meet the family, but after explaining that she was in Texas and he did not know when she would be back in New York, he promised to keep her up to date. After dessert Conner called it a night returning to the fur-baby-only Mackie household maintaining the nightly ritual of calling Starla to say goodnight. She again expressed how touched she was by his thoughtfulness when visiting her parent's gravesites after Sheriff McAlister's service. "We'll make a date when you're back in town to take some fresh flowers." Between a full stomach and his low energy level, sleep would come early that evening.

The Erie County Sheriff's Department, with responsibility for the entire county, was humming with distress calls as though lawlessness woke up this morning to pattering rain wreaking havoc on the residents of Western New York. Conner arrived in the middle of the clamor of phones ringing, his deputies grabbing hats and rain gear as they dispatched to answer the disturbances.

"It looks as though I'm late to the fire drill. Axl, let me grab a cup of coffee and bring me up to speed. I got inside just as the heavens opened up. It was raining so hard, it looked like the animals were beginning to pair up."

Axl detailed the calls received before dawn. "We got a 10-42 burglary in progress at Ted's Hot Dogs on Sheridan in Tonawanda.

Folklore has it that the Greek immigrant bought the original shack for $100. Supposedly, it was held together with forty-coats of paint with the whole place shaking when the trains passed by."

"I hate that. It's such a feel-good story and has killer dogs. What else we got?"

Axl profiled two seemingly related cases as the proximity to each other dictated, one a homicide of a forty-eight-year-old white male two blocks away and the kidnapping of an infant around the corner. A team on the ground interviewed neighbors as to the connection, following up on the information from the person who called the department suggesting the suspect in both crimes could be the same—the homicide victim's estranged wife who was also the grandmother of the infant.

"Talk about a dysfunctional family. Guess there's no word on the whereabouts of the infant's mother either." Picking up his mug, Conner shook his head in disbelief. "Would love to go back to a simpler time when we served eviction notices and family court summonses. Anything else?"

"Our phones lit up with this one. Seems a woman described as *all decked out in peacock mode* was riding a scooter in the parking lot of the Save A Lot on Broadway drinking wine out of a Pringle's can. The store manager detained her by waving a bottle of Boone's Farm Sangria in front of her. She claimed to suffer from inside storms of the spirit and was performing an internal cleansing aided by the spirits of alcohol."

"That's exactly why we have Kendra's Law," said Conner.

"I've heard of that but I'm not sure what it is...must have been enacted before I moved here in 2008."

Conner explained it was established in 1999 granting judges the authority to require a person who meets certain criteria to undergo regular psychiatric treatment when prompted by a series of incidents involving individuals with untreated mental illness who become violent. The law was named after Kendra Webdale who was pushed into the path of an oncoming subway train by a man suffering from schizophrenia who was off his medication. The law allows courts to order certain individuals with mental illness to receive treatment as a condition of living within the community.

"It's court-ordered outpatient treatment for those who have records of not following recommendations."

"A benefit to the community at large, but I'm surprised it has not been challenged as a violation of civil rights."

"It has but the courts have determined that because of the narrowly defined eligibility criteria and numerous due process protections, it is constitutional and is an appropriate use of the states' *parens patriae* and police powers."

"To help those who can't help themselves and to keep the public safe," said Axl.

"Exactly. Please tell me that's all the craziness so far this morning."

"And it's not even nine, yet."

Before tackling the paperwork stacked on his desk, Conner refilled his coffee, consuming a banana to help kick his potassium level to ten percent of his daily requirement. A ringing phone interrupted breakfast. Recognizing the number as the Coast Guard Auxiliary at Lake Texoma, he motioned for Axl to join the conversation. The call was from Commodore Richey. "Sheriff Boyle, a decomposed body surfaced yesterday five miles from Landers Pier. It's a male, small in stature. Age is anyone's guess. Unfortunately, time of death cannot be determined by organ temperatures. Fresh water preserves this method for only a short period of time. He's just been in the water for too long. It's going to take more than DNA alone to identify him...dental records, kinship analysis, fingerprints. We've been checking missing persons reports but so far none match our victim."

"His size would indicate it could be Victor. Where's the body now?"

"Grayson County Coroner/Justice of the Peace, Precinct 1 in Sherman. I've given them your contact information."

"We appreciate your help."

"We'll continue to keep you in the loop if we have any more floaters."

After hanging up, Conner asked Axl to contact the Coroner's Office notifying them they had Victor's fingerprints on file and inquiring if it was possible to recover any from the body. "I'll call the government's national database of dental records. He's been reported missing for over thirty days. Surely he's had his teeth examined sometime in his life."

"Wouldn't it be easier to call his mother?"

"I don't want to alarm her unless it's necessary. Check with the county holding center and have them send us the Kurtz brothers' fingerprints too."

"I don't get how their fingerprints are going to help identify Victor," said Axl.

Conner explained that although an individual's fingerprints are unique and while they elongate as we age, they do not change in pattern or shape. "However, our fingerprints stem from our DNA making familial fingerprints of siblings important as they exhibit similar patterns when classified according to the three primary categories of fingerprint patterns—loops, arches, and whorls."

"How did you become an expert on fingerprints?"

"An excellent teacher. Sheriff McAlister was fascinated with the science behind forensics and he took me along for the ride."

"If I remember our training correctly, the kinship analysis is the genetic profiling aimed at discovering genealogical relationships between individuals based on DNA samples. That should be a no brainer as we have the Kurtz clan in custody," said Axl.

The whirlwind push to gather all the pertinent information on the corpse found in Lake Texoma culminated with deputies working around-the-clock. The report faxed to the Sheriff's Office indicated it was impossible to determine from the corpse if the drowning victim fell, jumped, or was pushed into the water—drowning is drowning. Results from the forensic pathologist they hired determined the victim was conscious when he entered the water as struggling to breathe resulted in pressure trauma to the sinuses and lungs causing hemorrhaging. Also, he utilized what some professionals considered controversial and an inexact tool in determining drowning with the examination of the bone marrow for presence of diatoms, tiny single-cell organisms that scurry around in both fresh and saltwater. Since diatoms have silica in their cell walls, they are resistant to degradation. If a victim's heart were still beating when he entered the water, any diatoms in

the inhaled water would pass through the lungs, enter the blood-
stream, and would be pumped throughout the body, collecting in
the bone marrow. The coroner added,

> *Their presence was determined in our examination.
> The naysayers might conclude because diatoms can
> also be found in the air and soil, some might be on my
> clothing causing cross-contamination. I don't follow
> that line of thinking and neither does our forensics ex-
> pert. Results of the toxicology screening are not avail-
> able at this time.*

"Okay, let's review what we know and what we don't," said
Sheriff Boyle. "The victim was alive when he drowned but we still
don't know who it is. Any news on Victor's dental records?"

"Nothing so far. I'll call them again. What about fingerprints?"

Conner dialed the number listed for the coroner in Sherman
who answered the phone, "Alfred Lane here," in a British plummy
accent as if playing the role of the seventh Duke of Sutherland.

"Coroner Lane, this is Sheriff Boyle from Buffalo calling about
our drowning victim. We got your report this morning. Thank you.
Were you able to get any fingerprints from the corpse?"

"How do you do, Sheriff. When a body is submersed in water
the skin softens making fingerprinting dubious at best. What our
forensic expert recommended to do with this poor bloke is to sur-
gically remove a hand or finger, construct a casing out of silicone
putty which will capture the finger's pattern ridges."

"Got it. We're still waiting for dental records and will forward
them to you as soon as we receive them. If it's not too personal,
your accent is missing a Texas twang."

"Spot on observation, Sheriff. I arrived from across the pond
in the student exchange program at the University of Texas. I met
my sweetness in anatomy class and never went back home."

34

I'll be There for You

TINA LOUISA LAWSON spent many sleepless nights reliving the conversation she and Matt had weeks ago. Their teamwork over the many years had grown into an unstoppable force grounded in mutual trust and loyalty and her relationship with Bradley Anderson threatened the core of the bond between the friends and business partners. She cared deeply for Brad but her obsession with Matt baffled him, sparking a jealous streak that interfered with the couple's romance. Tina explained that Matt had been a staple in her life and whenever she lost her footing, he swooped in to put *Humpty Dumpty* back together again with empathy and reassurance...like a balm covering an open wound soothing the churning waters. "He always knew where to find the missing piece of a puzzle or where I left my gloves or why some guy dumped me...that kind of thing. I've relied on him my whole adult life and it just doesn't seem possible that our relationship is in trouble. I've got to call him."

"Before we can move forward or if we move forward, you need to have a frank talk with yourself and with Matt. The sooner the better, Tina. It's not fair to any of us to have this hanging over our heads," Bradley insisted.

Tina dialed Matt's number which went straight to voicemail. She hoped it was not intentional and that he was just unavailable.

She debated whether to leave a message or wait for him to return her call. At the sound of the beep she said, "Matt, it's Tina. I've been miserable since we last spoke so please hear me out. I confess I was madly in love with you but after all these years and all our time together, I still love you, but I'm not in love with you. If Brad and I don't work out, I'll be fine. If you and I are still alone, we might take a shot at a relationship. But if you ever cared about me please heal and go find someone that makes you smile again. Love is not a sprint to the finish line, it's a marathon requiring patience. Please say we're friends again."

Matt replayed the voicemail from Tina several times, and although her confessional was difficult to listen to, it was clear their connection had been as resilient and heartfelt as the last leaf dangling from a winter-barren tree. She had tossed the ball into his court. He measured his options—let her win by default by deleting the voicemail or wallop a forehand loaded with his thoughts down the line to gauge her return. Matt inhaled deeply before dialing the number for Seasons LXX, not sure what he was going to say but certain a conversation was necessary.

"Tina Lawson, how can I help you?"

With his voice edged with nervousness he said, "How's my best friend, today?"

"Happy you called."

Margo's book club increased in numbers as word spread among her friends of the selection of *Cold Sassy Tree* as this month's choice. Thunder reverberated through the kitchen as the ladies mingled, sipping coffee and sampling Concha's honey-nut Bundt cake before adjourning to the den for the review and discussion of the novel. Starla noted it was her first experience with a book club, thanking her host for encouraging her to join them. "As I've told Margo, I never warmed up to someone telling me what to read, but I now realize if you live your life in a box constantly reading only what you prefer, your view of the world is limited to one perspective. In music it would be like just listening to Buddy Holly and never tasting the operatic genius of Placido Domingo."

Margo introduced her review by saying the novel has a permanent place on her bookshelf as it provoked thoughts of how differently each of us look at life and death, how differently we view and define love, how seemingly undying relationships are tested, and how unconditional love delineated who the characters were and who they became. "To me the book is about a complex man (Grandpa Blakeslee) with an opinionated gruff side and a heart of gold getting a chance to be the young boy he never was and a young boy (Will Tweedy) representing all that was innocent with a view of life and its challenges identifiable with the human spirit growing into a man. As one stepped backward into boyhood, the other stepped forward into manhood. Now let's discuss the cast of characters who lived in Cold Sassy, Georgia."

Following a lively discussion dissecting the novel's strengths and weaknesses, the favorites and the not so favorites, and choosing next month's selection, *The Art of Racing in the Rain* by Garth Stein, the meeting adjourned.

After Matt authorized her Wattpad account, Willa devoted hours of each day secluded in her room pouring thoughts into words, each one distilling the rebellion troubling her acidic heart as though applying a cathartic bandage to her wounds. As she read her creation out loud, the emotional highs and lows zoomed between a sense of pride at her accomplishment, to a flare of joy seeing her words come alive, followed by shame for the selfishness that drove her actions.

Willa clicked the submit button, euphoria swelling in her eyes as she closed the file, bouncing down the stairs. She paused outside her grandfather's open office door after hearing Margo's voice detailing the circumstances of her latest CASA child, eight-year-old Tara. "Her last foster home was a trailer with three bedrooms shared by sixteen other children, including four babies. Her younger brother, Joey, suffers from ADHD and labeled a troublemaker, was sent to a shelter home. They've been separated for two years. When I first met Tara, she looked at me like I was just another adult making promises I couldn't keep. The siblings deserve a good home together. Doable?"

When Margo hung up the phone Willa was still standing in the doorway. "GoGo, that's so sad. Are all cases like this?"

"All foster care homes are not nightmarish, but the ones that are can permanently damage a child in their care. CASA volunteers make a difference. Although sometimes the circumstances surrounding a child's welfare can be heart-wrenching, it is so rewarding to see a young person blossom and look forward to the future. You should come with me on my next visit. It's a warm and fuzzy feeling to see the transformation from hopelessness to hopefulness."

They both turned upon hearing a cacophony of racket pulsating through the air as if the doors of a trendy discotheque opened allowing the reverberations to ping-pong off the kitchen cabinets. Willa and Margo watched from the dining room as Gabe and Patrick giggled through a game of zombie tag. "BigPop, you're the zombie now and I'm the human and I can throw stuff at you to keep from being tagged," Gabe squealed as he took off his sock, hurling it at his grandfather, hitting him in the head. "You gotta freeze while I count to fifteen and then you can try to catch me again." Patrick obeyed the orders striking a pose with Gabe's sock draped over one eye causing those within viewing distance to double over in fits of laughter. Matt arrived amongst the hilarity joining in the fun by being another human in the zombie tag game.

"Children . . . please, Concha's kitchen isn't a sports venue. Can you take your games outside where you've got more room?" suggested Margo flashing a lopsided smile at her husband.

"GoGo's no fun is she, Gabe," Patrick said pointing a playful finger in her direction.

"She's a girl, Big Pop. Girls don't understand boy games like we do," said Gabe.

Matt grabbed Willa's hand to join in the fun. "What about me, Gabe, I'm a girl. Can I join the game?"

"You're my sister. That's different. Come on. You can be it first."

Margo put her hands on her hips in a semi-protest of the unfairness but delighted to be excluded from the game of tag in favor of curling up in her favorite chair to read. Starla emerged from her quarters where she had been holed up composing some new song lyrics, traversing around the zombie players to the main house. She spotted Margo engrossed in her book, gently tapping her on the shoulder as not to startle her. "Starla, how's the writing coming?"

"It was rocking right along until the phone rang. It was Conner. His mom suffered a TIA. She's going to be fine, but he won't rest until he sees for himself. He's planning a trip to Ozona soon. Do you think Matt and the kids are settling in here where they don't need me anymore... and you, too?"

"I'm sorry to hear about Conner's mom but glad she's going to recover. It's so scary, especially if you're a distance away. As to your other question, I think with Matt being involved in the restoration project and the kids enrolled in school, you deserve to resume your normal life, although we would miss you terribly."

"I'm just being a little selfish about missing Conner and wanting to pick up where we left off. He's a pretty special guy."

"You're one of the most selfless individuals I've ever met. Think about this. Ozona is about two-and-a-half hours from here. Conner could fly into Midland. We could pick him up and bring him here for a short visit. Since your car is here, the two of you could visit his parents and then head back to Buffalo together. Plus, can you imagine how excited Gabe would be to see his buddy again."

Starla's skin tingled at the thought of seeing Conner, a dreamy smile broadening across her face, her eyes shimmering as though harboring sunbeams.

"I can see from your expression that you like this idea. Go call him."

As had been the custom, the group gathered in the evening on the deck overlooking the pool for a recap of the day's activities and a beverage of choice, while Gabe and Willa helped Donny feed the horses in the stables. Margo explained Starla would be joining them after she spoke with Conner, holding off sharing any details of what they had discussed earlier. Concha busied herself in the kitchen preparing the evening meal, the first course consisting of baked cheesy grit cakes topped with fresh crab and shrimp coconut bisque. Patrick and Margo noticed their son's expression had lost some rigidity his mood elevated as if the emptiness in his heart found another place to dwell. They anticipated a conversation explaining the transformation, presuming it had something to do with Tina. Adding to the moment, Starla swept into the area floating on a cloud of enthusiasm, her face bowled over with good cheer as she stopped by the bar to pour a glass of wine.

"I must say the mood this evening on the patio is infectious. Matt and Starla both look as though each holds a big-pocket-pair in Texas Hold'em. Aces versus Kings. It's time to lay down your cards. Fess up. What's going on?" asked Patrick.

"Ladies first," said Matt.

Starla, after outlining the crux of her initial conversation with Conner and his mother's health scare, cited Margo's suggestions, reporting that Conner was arranging to visit Sky Island and drive her back to Buffalo after visiting his parents in Ozona prompting a hindered reaction from Matt.

"You don't look like you're in favor of this, son."

Matt cleared his throat, weighing his words before commenting. "I'm sorry. Of course, that's what Starla should do. She's been our rock since Summer died and part of me thought she would always be there to prop us up."

"Matt, I'd never leave unless I felt you and the kids were in good hands here. And, if you'll let me, since I plan on staying in Buffalo, I could stay in your house and take care of Dude and Halle. Also, if it would help, I'd be glad to pack up Summer's clothes and personal items and either put them in storage until you can go through them or donate some to the women's shelter sponsored by the hospital. Whatever you're comfortable with."

"Yes, I would feel better if you were in the house and if you're up to it, taking care of her things would be a great help. Her clothes can be donated to the shelter. Her jewelry, I've already placed in the safe."

"Settled. Now, what's your news?"

"I've got my best friend back. Tina and I had a long discussion about us, our relationship both personally and professionally, and the future. Bottom line, we both want the same thing. For the business to continue to thrive and for each of us to have someone or something that makes us smile. For her right now, that's Bradley and I promised I would refrain from knocking his head off if he hurts her."

35

At Last

CONNER INFORMED THE deputies of his plans to visit Texas
the following week appointing Axl as acting sheriff in his absence
and assigning the officer who stayed at the Mackie home on the
previous occasion to again take over the household. With airline
reservations secured and the office responsibilities taken care of,
he grabbed his coat from the break room, his exit delayed by
answering the phone when he recognized the caller as Coroner
Lane in Sherman. He advised Conner that the body in his care
was not Victor Kurtz as the dental records did not match and after
scouring the database of missing persons, they were no closer to
an identification now than they were weeks ago. "We'll shelve the
poor chap until all avenues are exhausted in identifying him and
finding a next of kin. If we fail, we'll offer him to the state ana-
tomical board for research. If rejected by them, his remains will
be cremated and buried in a mass grave along with hundreds of
unclaimed bodies."

The pitch in Conner's voice dropped an octave as disappointment rose like cream floating on the top of whole milk. "Thank
you for your help. It's hard to believe someone doesn't miss this
young man."

"Unfortunately, we see this type of thing way too often. It's impossible not to be benumbed by reality in my line of work. Take care, Sheriff."

Added to Conner's list before departing for Texas was notifying Sophia Kurtz of the Coroner's findings. He put his coat on the back of the chair before dialing her number. Her reaction was a mixed bag...relief that the body was not her son and anguish at not knowing if he was dead in a ditch on the side of the road or alive and in hiding.

The arrangements for Conner's visit moved swiftly as Margo and Patrick were to pick him up in Midland for the drive to Sky Island. Starla, after consulting with Concha on where Conner should stay, agreed he would occupy one of the four bedrooms in the party barn. She opened the door to one room furnished with a contemporary style king size platform bed with s-shaped black and white leather curvatures and behind another door, in the center of the room, sat a custom designed round queen platform bed surrounded by a black walnut shelf with a gas log fireplace adjacent to the centerpiece. Either option would suit Conner, but knowing he was arriving soon triggered her stomach to quiver, scrambling her underground circuits, and causing spontaneous joy. Starla visualized the two of them propped up in the round bed sharing a glass of bubbly, enjoying the ambiance of a crackling fire and each other. She scurried to add fresh linens to the bed and towels to the bathroom. Satisfied with the arrangements, she dimmed the ceiling lights and shut the door, returning to the kitchen to help Concha who was preparing a Texas feast for their guest.

With Gabe and Willa in school in Green Tree, Matt started consulting at The Murphy until time to pick up the children at the conclusion of their after-school activities. Willa, aka Buffy, now cast-free, alongside Holly, Dolly, and Yo-Yo, the rest of her N.K.I.T. troupe, were in rehearsals for drill team tryouts while Gabe participated in a recreational flag football league, except on weekends when he spent hours learning the art of sculpture from Aria Kirkman. Conner's visit was cloaked in secrecy—the plan being for him to be chilling in the den when they tumbled in from school.

Patrick in his role as the lookout notified everyone to take their places as Matt had just pulled into the driveway. The car doors flew open with Gabe hopscotching through the front door on his way to the kitchen for a snack. "Hi, Aunt Starla. Can you help me. I need fuel. Maybe a juice box and string cheese, please."

Patrick, Margo, and Conner gawked at each other in disbelief while Starla stood flabbergasted by Gabe's opaque behavior. She was headed to the kitchen when Gabe burst back into the den a jolt of excitement driving every step as he realized what he had missed. He jumped into Conner's lap firing questions in rapid succession leaving scant time for the answers, the last one concerning the fountain. "You just thank the gods for the water and then throw a quarter in it and make a wish. Did you already do that?"

"No, Gabe, I didn't."

"Well, let's go. I'll show you how it's done. Aunt Starla, you can come too." And, with that the time dominance of the sheriff from Buffalo, New York, began. Willa excused herself after dinner to finish her world history assignment of reading the chapters dedicated to one of the major world regions, Africa. Being a school night bedtime arrived far too early for Gabe's taste, but with Conner offering to tuck him in and read a story, he reluctantly trooped upstairs. The rest of the adults retreated to the porch for Patrick's specialty after-dinner cocktail, a Stop-Watch...Dewar's Scotch and Kahlua over ice with a splash of club soda while a panorama of linear colors striping the horizon in hues of crimson and azure played the lead in the divine masterpiece. Conner joined them just in time to witness the majesty of the evening announcing Gabe exhausted all his stall-cards and finally gave up. Patrick handed him a nightcap and he settled in beside Starla on the loveseat. "Does anyone know what he meant when he said his wish had come true?"

Matt nodded remembering Gabe's secret when he tossed one of his quarters in the fountain. "I don't mean to embarrass either of you, but he whispered that he needed an uncle to go with his aunt."

"Our man-child does have his own agenda," said Starla.

"It appears he was born with an extra-perception-gene," responded Conner. "I'm up for serendipity deciding the outcome. How about you, Ms. Jordan?"

"Definitely worth a shot, Sheriff Boyle. It does appear that my nephew might have the inside track on this one."

"Let me tell you the latest in the Victor Kurtz case. I was informed right before I left Buffalo that the body found in Lake Texoma was not him. It's disappointing not to know the identity of the young man and at the same time we were hoping to be able to close out Victor's case if it was him."

"So, now what?" asked Patrick.

"We've run out of leads, but the case will remain active. He'll still be part of the national database of missing persons. Who knows, we might catch a break. And on a positive note, Papa Kurtz and the brothers are in holding cells in Buffalo. Last I heard they were flipping the guilt card around, making plea deals to receive the least amount of punishment in the 'little girl in concrete' case."

"Let me ask your opinion, Conner. Is Willa still in harm's way from Victor?" asked Matt.

"It's hard to say for certain since we don't know where he is, but my gut tells me that since he got the family confession, he's moved on—if he's still alive that is."

With the evening winding down, Starla and Conner walked arm-in-arm to the party barn, the surge of passion boiling over into an exaggerated awareness of each other's needs. He closed the door pinning her against the wall, tenderly kissing her before pulling away. He reached into his pocket removing the silver coin she had given him inscribed with a message, *Please don't leave me.* "And I didn't," he said, his eyes twinkling as if holding the key to the mysteries of the universe.

"And I didn't leave you, either. I don't know about you, but I've never slept in a round bed before."

"I've never done anything in a round bed."

Starla stroked his cheek noticing a maturity in his face not there when she left for Texas, as if the events of the last few months had taken a toll with the investigation of Summer's death, tracking down Victor, losing his friend and mentor Warren McAlister, and being responsible for the entire sheriff's department.

Shadow puppets generated by the flickering gas logs danced on the adjacent wall as though telling a story of longing while the heat produced by the fireplace failed to match the emotional intimacy of the couple uncovering the subtleties of their relationship. Wrapped in each other's arms, tranquility sailed between them with Conner asking, "Did you ever see the movie *The Graduate* when Anne Bancroft as Mrs. Robinson lit up a cigarette after each tryst with the bumbling Dustin Hoffman?"

"Yes, and I now understand how that slender stick of rolled tobacco that stains your teeth, destroys your breath, and shortens your lifespan became one of the successes of modern advertising. Although I never smoked, the unknown lure has an unexpected appeal. You?"

"I couldn't handle any more appeal than what's in front of me right now."

"Aww...likewise, Sheriff. Did I tell you I'm writing a song about us...?

My Fate, Our Fate
Fate found us this way, tragedy defined us that way,
my heart was heavy, yours was kind,
fate found us this way, gone are our pasts,
our future seems hazy, our present is pure...
fate found us this way....

"Sounds like a chart topper to me. You're not going anywhere tonight, are you?"

"My vacant room won't miss me."

Morning light brought rain pitter-patting on the roof while in the distance thunder rumbled like a train hurtling toward its destination. Starla checked her watch before slipping out of bed, a heightened sense of ease following her steps to the bathroom. Conner's face partially buried under his pillow obstructed his breathing sufficiently enough to wake him just as his bed partner surfaced fully dressed. "Were you going to sneak out without a goodbye?" he asked.

"You were zonked out. I was going to write you a note," she teased.

"What time is it?"

"Six. I think I can skulk back to the pool house undetected if I leave now. Concha and Donny should already be at the main house. Since it's raining Margo and Patrick probably won't be taking their morning walk and Matt and the kids will just be getting up."

He patted the side of the bed. "Come sit for a minute. We're both of legal age. Are you ashamed of our relationship?"

"Never. I just don't want any awkwardness since we're guests in the Mackie's home. See you for coffee in an hour," she said leaving him with a lingering kiss.

The kitchen was humming when Conner arrived with Matt relaying Gabe's maneuvering to stay home from school saying he felt hot and was worried he would be contagious to his classmates. "I knew where he was going so I told him if he were feverish, he should stay home, but would have to remain in bed here as not to pass on his illness to any of us. He'll be down for breakfast in a few minutes."

Patrick, after booking a guided tour of Big Bend National Park, shared the details of the trip planned for Saturday. "A safari-style Jeep Wrangler with shaded seating and open sides will pick us up in Green Tree for an all-day excursion. Margo and I have enough hiking shoes for every size except Gabe, but his sneakers will work fine. The trails on our agenda are not strenuous—comfortable for all ages."

What began as a dove-gray early morning sky influenced by featherlike breezes surrendered to white puffy clouds chasing each other through filtered sunlight. With mild temperatures and a family ready for an adventure, the day promised to be one that would kick any worrisome thoughts to the curb. After a brief stop in Study Butte, pronounced *Stew-dee Bewt,* a small community of two hundred, recognized as the gateway to Big Bend National Park, the jeep exited onto a dirt road for the trip to Santa Elena Canyon with a stop at Gilberto Luna's home—a Jackal which is a wattle and daub structure typically found in the Desert Southwest. "Mr. Luna built his home around 1900 using sandstone and limestone blocks, the roof made from ocotillo branches held up by larger poles. He lived there until his death at one-hundred-nine-years old, reportedly raising fifty-eight children and stepchildren."

"Wow, that musta been crowded in there," said Gabe.

"He scratched out a living farming the dry dusty ground. Can you imagine yourself living in this inhospitable land? Listen to the wind. It's the only sound Gilberto Luna heard every day."

"Until one of those fifty kids started hollering for lunch," observed Gabe.

After hiking the Santa Elena Canyon, one of the most scenic trails in the park and possibly in Texas, the group piled back in the jeep. The next stop—a picnic lunch in the Castolon historical area which was the commercial center of agriculture along the Rio Grande supporting the mining industry in Terlingua and growing cotton for export. The Ross Maxwell Scenic Drive offered a variety of scenery with many stopping places on the way to the Chisos Mountain Basin, the center of the cool mountain highlands. From there they walked to a scenic viewpoint on the Lost Mine Trail, where on a clear day one can see one-hundred miles in all directions. "This oasis has been described as lush and *Switzerland-ish*. When we get to the peak, nearly seven-thousand-feet above sea level, the contrast of landscape will be startling between the lush canyon below and the harsh desert in the distance," explained the guide.

With the tour winding down, the Wrangler carrying the troupe continued through Persimmon Gap and on to Highway 385 following the Comanche War Trail. "That nation of nomadic Indians pulled up settlement, departing the buffalo-hunting grounds on the Great Plains during the Comanche Moon, forging southwardly producing a major thoroughfare a mile wide cutting across the heart of Big Bend. As we travel in our modern-day covered wagon, we're following the original trail."

"I've never heard of a Comanche Moon," said Conner.

"I know this one. You have your Harvest Moon but here it's a Comanche Moon because they raided settlements during this lunar event," spouted Margo.

"I'll venture a wild guess and say my wife the avid reader recalls that from a book."

"Guilty, *Empire of the Southern Moon*...fascinating history of the rise and fall of the most powerful tribe in American history and of pioneer woman Cynthia Parker and her mixed-blood son, Quanah, who became the greatest and last chief of the Comanche Tribe."

"I can beat that, Margo-the-book-nerd. *The Searchers*...1956 western starring John Wayne who spends years looking for his niece, played by Natalie Wood, who was abducted by the Comanches. Great movie," hawked Patrick.

"GoGo, why don't you watch a movie with Big Pop, and he can read a book with you?" asked Gabe.

"See children, that's what married life is about. Compromise and willingness to explore outside our comfort zone. Right, Dear?"

"Of course, I'm married to Margo the mediator," he said lobbing a doting grin her way.

Arriving home after their twelve-hour day, showers rinsing the grit from the park down the drain, a change of clothes, a beverage of choice, a hot meal, and an early bedtime were on the agenda. Willa curled up on the couch with Richard Parker on her lap, Gabe sitting beside her using Magnolia and Sadie as a footstool. A note from Concha left on the kitchen counter welcomed them home from their long day hoping they will enjoy her chicken and dumplings and noting marinated asparagus spears in the refrigerator, and separate trays of her specialty cream cheese and powdered sugar stuffed strawberries dipped in crushed dark chocolate and almonds—one for the adults laced with a dash of Amaretto—the *virgin version* minus the alcohol.

Sunday's dawn hung suspended in the crispness of the autumn air. Out for their early morning walk, Margo and Patrick braved an insistent breeze fueling the fallen orange-red leaves from the Shumard oaks and the pink and violet flowers from the desert willow trees to cavort alongside the path. With Starla and Conner leaving the next day, the Mackies planned one last must-see adventure for the out-of-towners, a short trip to the Indian Lodge in the Davis Mountains State Park for brunch at the Black Bear Restaurant with the remainder of the day slated for relaxation. After returning home Starla packed her suitcase while Margo introduced Conner to the horses encouraging him to take a test ride on one of them. Donny saddled up Queenie and Duchess and the twosome trotted around the corral in tandem.

Matt retreated to his room to check his emails for Tina's weekly reports from Seasons LXX. What he found among the reports and spam was a notification from Wattpad that Willa had posted a story on their site that triggered a parental flag, and after reading the content he understood the reason for the alert. Matthew Mackie, son, widower, and father of two children created a blueprint for dealing with this epiphany. He caught up with the horseback riders as they dismounted suggesting Conner would enjoy riding the ATVs on the trails as he had not seen half of the property. They ended up in a secluded portion of Sky Island Retreat, parking the vehicles near a concrete table with a bench on either side overlooking a vista of rolling terrain dotted with Longhorn cattle.

"Conner, I need to tell you something. I've been experiencing flashes of memory about the day Summer died, but now I remember it clearly. I'm glad you're here so I can tell you in person."

Seated across from one another, Conner leaned forward saying, "I'm all ears."

Matt cleared his throat looking Conner directly in the eye. "Summer, Willa, and I were standing on the ledge waiting for Gabe to return from his potty trip. Bradley Anderson strolled up shouting at us...we shot each other the finger and he left. Then Victor approached us, hands Willa a box of candy hearts. Summer starts arguing with him, waving her arms saying to get away, he reached for her and Willa put her hand on her mother to steady her. I stepped in front of Summer to confront Victor and the shale cliff collapsed. It was my fault, but it was an accident."

"Are you certain that's what happened?" he asked, his expression as absent as a babbling brook in the Mojave desert.

"One-hundred percent. You can't believe what a relief it is for me to finally remember what happened that terrible day. At least that clears the slate from an investigative standpoint. Correct?"

"Yes. The case will be closed. If we ever find Victor, he'll have one less thing to worry about. Willa and Bradley's involvement are also moot points thanks to your recollection."

"I trust you'll keep our conversation under wraps. I would

like to be the one to tell my family when the time is right. You can share with Starla on your way to see your folks though. Just be sure she understands to keep it confidential for now."

"I'll take care of it from the Sheriff's Department standpoint. I'm assuming if necessary, you would swear under oath to this?"

"I would. Thank you, Conner, for your diligence in seeing this through. I'm looking forward to turning the page on the whole ordeal."

—⊶⊷—

The family gathered on the front porch to say goodbye to Conner and Starla with Gabe clinging to Patrick's neck. After rounds of hugs and a few tears, they all waved as the car pulled away from Sky Island Retreat for their trip to Ozona via U.S. 67 North to I-10 East. Glancing to the driver's side, Starla noticed Conner dabbing at the corners of his eyes. His patience and enthusiasm for children, especially Gabe, reflected in the moist sentiment. She reached over squeezing his shoulder before saying, "It's wonderous to behold the connection you two have."

Conner assembled his first memory of Gabe recalling how he held a calmness and maturity beyond his circumstances and age. "He just gets under your skin and won't let go. There he was having spent the night alone in the park not knowing the whereabouts of the rest of his family and he trusted me to make everything all right. I tried, but...."

"Summer's death wasn't something you could fix."

Given Starla's propensity to dive into places of unknown knowledge she filled the hours in the car on their way to visit his parents with the finer points about Aiden and Jane Boyle's new hometown, dubbed "The Biggest Little Town in the World." Ozona, located in Crockett County, was the only town in its three-thousand square miles with three-thousand-five-hundred residents calling it home. "Add two to that total," said Conner. Starla continued the tutorial by saying the area is home to some interesting animals including the fox squirrel, nicknamed limb chickens, as they provided the nitty-gritties for a Texan favorite, squirrel stew, noted as tasting like a cross between rabbit and chicken.

"I'm the adventurous type, but I hope that's not on your folks' menu," said Starla, her nose twitching at the thought of a furry rodent as an entrée. The county also claims to be a birders' paradise with *bouquets* of male-black-chinned hummingbirds who woo their partners by dive bombing one-hundred feet, swooping close to their intended at the end of the dive. "It says here they can fly forward, backward, sideways, and even on their backs...they can hover, take off vertically and are able to pivot around a stationary axis."

"In my next life I think I'd like to come back as one of these birds. Did you use *bouquet* to flower up the description?"

"Clever analogy, but no, that's one of the words used to designate their particular flock. Now, if you're talking the speedy roadrunners, they're called a *marathon* of roadrunners. And, as far as the Grande Turkeys go, when they waltz into town to forage the pecans in the fall, they're called a *posse.*"

Starla continued listing the animal and critter farm of Crockett County with the black-tailed jackrabbits who can run thirty to forty miles per hour and fifteen of them can eat as much as a full-grown cow...there's cattle, spiny lizards, horned toads, brown tarantulas, and Angora goats that produce mohair as one of the county's top ranching products with Texas as one of the primary producers in the world. Conner booked a room at the Hillcrest Inn & Suites before calling his parents to let them know they had arrived. Their establishment, Boyle's Irish Snug, was closed on Mondays until 5:00 P.M. so after checking in and freshening up the duo headed out for a visit.

Aiden and Jane's white brick, three-bedroom home on Avenue C featured two fireplaces and a screened-in-porch perched on an acre of land surrounded by mature pecan trees. Conner's mom opened the door reaching out to grasp her son pressing her palms lightly against his cheeks. Jane's dark blonde hair framed her heart-shaped face, a radiance developing across her alabaster skin at the sight of her son.

"Mom, you look so healthy."

"Your father told you not to worry. You can see he was right. And this must be Starla. Riley has told us all about you. Come in. We're anxious to meet our boy's special lady."

Starla shook Mrs. Boyle's hand commenting that it was obvious where Conner inherited his dimples. Aiden rose from his recliner unfurling his ample frame when they entered the living room, apologizing for the mess as the house was still being renovated. His ruddy complexion, a full head of hair flecked with ginger and silver, and prominent nose paid homage to his Irish ethnicity.

"Dad, Starla and I stopped by The Anchor Bar not too long ago. Remember Jimmy? He asked about you and Mom and said to wish you good luck in your new place," said Conner.

"Yes. We could use someone like him here...honest and personable. Tell him he's got a job waiting if he ever wants to get out of the cold."

After catching up on all the news from Buffalo and dissecting everything Starla, the conversation turned to how an Irish restaurant and pub fared in Texas amongst a group of traditional diners featuring mostly Mexican food. "Our banker said we were loopy as a cross-eyed cowboy, but he loaned us the money anyway," chuckled Aiden. "When we first opened the doors, we literally had hordes of people stop by, curious to understand the name and what we might be serving. Fortunately, we've developed our own following combining our traditional fare with the local favorites."

"You'd think since I am Irish-born, I'd know what a snug is...but I don't have a clue."

Jane explained it dates to the late nineteenth century in Ireland. A snug was a small private room with a frosted glass window set above head height. Those who frequented the snug preferred not to be seen in a public bar, paying a higher price for their alcohol for that perk. "A local police officer could have a quiet pint and a parish priest could enjoy his evening whiskey."

"Ours is in the tradition of the snug atmosphere but we're open to everyone, although we do have the frosted glass windows on the outside of the building. Come by tonight. Family doesn't pay for drinks or dinner," said Aiden.

A sampler plate greeted Conner and Starla featuring Irish potato nachos, homemade tortilla chips with Mexican salsa, Buffalo wings, and black bean queso followed by platters of Guinness-battered fish and chips and Shepherd's pie. They topped off the evening with Bailey's Irish Cream coffee bidding the Boyles goodnight with a promise to see them the next day.

Back at their room Conner shared Matt's confession. Starla gaped in stunned silence while he recounted the conversation before asking if he believed him. "His body language told me he was telling the truth. I asked if he would swear under oath to his recollection and he didn't hesitate."

"I get the impression you're skeptical. Why?"

"Partly because of my law enforcement background...the other I can't put a finger on."

"Why would he lie? He hasn't anything to gain."

"Except taking suspicion away from any involvement by Willa."

"I know you've always felt Willa knew more than she was telling us, but I'm relieved that my niece had nothing to do with the death of my sister."

"Sweet Starla...I understand this provides closure for you and I'm happy about that. You mean too much to me to allow this to drive a wedge between us. Matt did specify that he'd like to be the one to inform the family, but that I could tell you if you promised to keep it a secret."

"I will...I promise. I think a hot shower might be in the cards."

"Mind if I join you?"

"You get the water started and I'll be right in," she said placing a box of *Kings* candy cigarettes on the nightstand, a salute to the ecstasy of the intimacy they now shared as a couple.

After a few days visiting with his parents and seeing his mother in good health and spirits, Starla and Conner left Texas in the rearview mirror embarking on their journey back to Buffalo, their bond solidifying with each bend in the road and mile recorded on the odometer.

36

Lean on Me

AS A CONTAINER IS necessary to transport water, words are used to point to the truth. Often dwelling deep in a person's subconscious when given an avenue to surface, they are the vehicles that steer a direct route to reality. After Wattpad notified Matt about a story his daughter authored and submitted to the format, it was as though he was sitting on a boat staring at the endless horizon where his field of vision defined something impossible to comprehend. Willa's awakening stung like opening his eyes in saltwater.

The Wattpad preview read,

> *A teen's tragic story of a young girl responsible for the death of her little brother. Guilt and depression fueled by anger and hatred for her mother because she blamed her for his death drives the story forward by narrating what she did to get even.*

Angels with Dirty Faces
by Buffy M.

Chapter One, Before

My life was perfect before. Mom and me were besties. We'd dress up and pretend we were at a tea party. She read me stories and we baked cookies. I took dance lessons. Her job at the hospital was to help people and keep them safe.

Chapter Two, My Bad

I loved my little brother Griff. We nicknamed him Boo. He'd always sneak up on us. He was ticklish, loved baseball, chewing gum, and grape hard candy. He died. He was only six. Mom said it was my fault. I was the older sister. I shouldn't have tickled him. He was sucking on a gumball. She said I should have called 911. I should have been more responsible. I was only ten. It's her fault. She left me alone.

Chapter Three, Later

Her big important job was to keep people protected, but she couldn't even do that for her own family. We all went to therapy. They told me I should write down how I felt. That's what I'm doing here, although I don't feel better.

Chapter Four, The Cliff

It was her idea to go to the Gorge that day—a stupid family outing. We just had to see this waterfall...so we looked down from this cliff. That day was so confusing. Someone hollered my name, and this creepy dude with a box of candy hearts came up to us. The rest is blurry, but when I pushed her, she grabbed my hand and my Dad tried to hold on to both of us. I wanted to get even with her 'cause of Griff. She hurt me so bad. I didn't want to live like we had been. I thought she might have a concussion or a broken leg...but she died instead of me.

Chapter Five, Regret

I was selfish. I didn't think about my youngest brother, Gabe, growing up without his mother. When he's older and finds out what I've done I hope he'll forgive me. For now, I'm going to try to be the best older sister in the world. I worry Daddy will toss me on the street if he finds out, but I deserve it. I just hope he'll help me

instead. I'm in a better place now. My grandparents'
home is full of love and support. I've got some new
friends and hope to stay in Texas forever.

With the passing of time rolling into patterns of the status quo of life at Sky Island, several months turned into a year with Matt finishing his involvement with the renovation project at The Murphy. Gabe and Willa, both thriving in their school environment, prompted Matt to rethink his involvement at Seasons LXX, noting that since Tina was handling all the responsibilities, an adjustment in their equal share partnership was necessary. He proposed a three-quarter-one-quarter split which she rejected. Matt listened carefully as her voice broke into a tremulous waver instead of her customary liquified honey tone, his intuition on red alert. When pressed, she offered the excuse that her allergies were acting up and she was having trouble breathing especially at night. Then he asked, "How are things with Bradley?"

Sheriff Boyle remained vigilant in checking missing persons reports and connecting with their forensics team for any pings generated by the cell phone stolen by Victor Kurtz from the manager's office at the minimart at Grumpy Point Marina at Lake Texoma in Texas. With no activity recorded the team deduced either Victor was smart enough to know his whereabouts could be traced and tossed the phone or he had not turned it on. Either way, nothing from the number had been recorded until one afternoon, Conner answered the call he had been waiting for. Dressed in plainclothes he joined the large crowd in The 9th Ward, a basement bar venue inside the Babeville, a renovated church located in the heart of Buffalo's theater district boasting one of downtown's most recognizable steeples, an exterior of Medina sandstone, and a roof of Vermont slate. Conner ordered a beer canvassing the crowd for any sign of Victor while waiting for the featured show to begin.

The lights dimmed as the stars of the *Faux Pas Follies* took the stage to choruses of cheering and wolf whistles. The queens, dressed in hot pink tutus, black leather jackets, pink wigs, and white boots, covered the stage in flamboyant struts before launching into a high-kick routine drawing raucous applause from the crowd. The two-hour show entertained with a variety of acts from Cher, Aretha, and Jennifer Lopez impersonators to the finale, a lanky comedian named Bobo, his mouth covered with a colorful mask and black eyeliner drawing focus to his arctic blue eyes. His exaggerated motions attempting to free his tennis shoe from a wad of gum on the floor, prancing around with his head and legs sticking outside of a Ritz cracker box in rhythm to the music of "Putting on the Ritz" triggered an appreciation of his virtuosity from patrons concluding his segment with a hip-hop pantomime. Conner inched his way closer to the stage as the cast of the *Faux Pas Follies* received ovations with several curtain calls from the standing-room-only crowd. If Victor was a performer in this production, the mime fit his physique and eye color, not to mention an act with no speaking parts covering up his vocal tics. However, when the artist took the stage for one more bow, the masked mime receiving the accolades was an amply endowed woman wearing white gloves.

Conner knocked on the stage manager's door, showing his badge and asking to see the list of cast members. "Which one is the mime?"

"They're sisters, Koko and Kandi Mounds. I can't tell one from the other, but it doesn't matter, they're never together." Conner left the building certain that the cell phone ping originated from the venue, the blue eyes of the pantomime artist were as piercing and cold as Victor's, and he had proven to be a master of disguise... *coincidence or a way to let him know that he was alive? Why would he risk arrest?*

Remembering the sassy relationship between Sophia Kurtz and her boyfriend, Joseph, Conner called to tell her they might enjoy the show he just saw at The 9th Ward. A belly-laugh roared through the phone lines, "What a coincidence that you should call. I must have entered some contest I don't remember, because I just got two tickets in the mail to the *Faux Pas Follies* and we're going tomorrow. Guess there's no news on my boy?"

"Victor is still missing. Enjoy the show, Sophia."

The attraction between Starla Jordan and Conner Boyle developed into a romance rivaling characters Oliver and Jennifer in Eric Segal's *Love Story*. They shared Matt's house and the responsibilities for taking care of Dude and Halle after being pronounced man and wife in a small ceremony at the Blessed Trinity Church. Along with the announcement of their nuptials, family, friends, and colleagues received an invitation to a reception at Seasons LXX. Starla dropped in to finalize the menu and give Tina an update on the number of guests to find her scattering papers around her desk, her gaze bouncing from one place to another as if searching for the one-hundred-thirty-three carat Florentine diamond. "Tina, did I catch you in the middle of something? I can come back."

"No, Starla...come in. What can I help you with?"

"It'll wait. You look a little frazzled. What's up?"

"Well, let me see. Brad, now in remission from his MS, has decided his new career is more important than us. So, he's going to California to narrate audio books and wants me to come with him. I'm just stupid when it comes to men."

"How could he ask you to do something that he knows is impossible...that doesn't make any sense."

"I asked the same question. He said I should get my priorities straight and ask Matt to buy me out and THEN...he says...we can use the money to buy a house in Los Angeles. I beat the pulp out of a bag of limes earlier today...it didn't help."

"Tina, I'm so sorry. Is there anything I can do?" asked Starla.

"I'll be fine. You didn't come here to listen to my sob story. Let's get on a happier subject. How are the newlyweds these days?"

"As blissful as a bubble bath at midnight. From the responses to the reception invitation, it looks as though not one person in Buffalo will be anywhere except at Seasons that night. Conner knows everyone in Erie County, and they'll all be here."

The ladies finalized the arrangements, sharing a caring embrace on Starla's way out, leaving Tina with the challenge of repairing her broken heart.

Mr. and Mrs. Boyle flew from one congratulations to another as the party at Seasons LXX was in full swing. His parents mingled with people they had not seen since they moved to Ozona, while Patrick and Margo navigated through the throngs of well-wishers reconnecting with friends and reliving the glory days of Bills football. Conner's smile could not be contained when he spotted Sherry McAlister escorted by Axl on one arm and the newly appointed Commissioner of Erie County Central Police Services on the other. She beamed when sharing the news that the Sheriff's Association had awarded Sheriff of the Year posthumously to Warren. When Starla joined them, Sherry warmly took her hand commenting that she felt like she already knew her from all the conversations between her husband and Conner. Riley, Conner's sister, with her husband mingled among the guests while Aaron, Barry, Claire, and Daryl were engrossed in games with Gabe and Willa.

Matt claimed the center-of-attention award, apart from the newlyweds, dominated by employees and longtime Seasons LXX customers. Tina, however, was missing-in-action or at least he had not spotted her. Matt excused himself touring the outdoor patio, the billiard and game rooms before running into her coming out of the kitchen. She squeezed her eyes shut as if wishing he would disappear and trying to compose herself. "Tina Lawson, you can't keep your eyes closed forever and when you open them, I'll still be standing here."

She obeyed and what she saw on his face was a grin as wide as a canyon. "Matt...please we have to talk but not now. I guess Starla told you about Brad, so you can save the *didn't-I-warn-you-card*."

He grasped both her hands in his saying, "Tina, no I didn't know and I'm sorry. All I wanted to say was that you are the one who makes me smile."

Matt and Aria Spencer remained close friends, enjoying each other's company and their common interest in Gabe's passion for sculpting. After featuring his haloed angel holding an open hymnal in her studio foyer, his talent, especially for his age, received notoriety from local artists and a feature article in the *Green Tree Sentinel* newspaper. With Matt working on the renovation project, he often shared lunch with her father, the two men developing a close bond. Morris Kirkman recognized that hearing and listening were not the same, a skill he honed through years of his ministry, suspecting Matt harbored more than grief and hunger to return to the life he once had. One such lunch started with casual chitchat, turning intense when Matt asked if he could confide in him. Morris leaned forward in his chair, his elbows on the table, hands steepled in front of him.

Matt used his napkin to wipe away the moisture gathered in the corner of his eyes before speaking. "I told no one, not even my wife, that I got a vasectomy. I used a trip with my college buddies to Prince Edward Island as an alibi to get away. I couldn't stand the pain of losing anything else after we lost Griff. But Summer was twelve-weeks pregnant when she died. I consulted with my urologist and was told that if we had unprotected sex within three months of the procedure, it's possible for sperm to still be present, but we'll never know."

"Matt, I'm so sorry. What a burden to carry along with everything else."

"Summer was the mother of my children. I would have raised him as my own. Thank you for listening. I've been hiding that pain from everyone including myself."

"I appreciate you trusting me to help you. Going forward Philippians 4:8 reminds us to think about what is true, noble, right, pure, admirable and be filled with God's love, joy, peace, and prosperity. Let Him take on your worry so that the burden of it will be lifted."

Living in an area void of rush-hour traffic, most young people learned to drive at an early age and Willa had been hounding Matt to teach her for months since all her gal-pals were skilled behind the wheel although none were old enough to secure their official driver's license. She had been practicing up and down the entrance to Sky Island but this Sunday morning the duo headed out on the road to Marathon, a dusty heat rising from the asphalt and Justin Bieber and Nicki Minaj performing their hit, "Beauty and a Beat," on the radio. After a few miles down the deserted road Matt announced he remembered what happened the day Summer died, causing Willa to slam on the brakes.

"Honey, pull over on the shoulder. We have to talk."

"Daddy, I didn't mean to do it. I mean, I did then, but now I know how wrong it was. I wanted to hurt her as much as she hurt me. And I wanted to die. You weren't supposed to fall, too. Gabe needed you...he didn't need me or Mom. I'm sorry I was so selfish."

"How did you know she was pregnant?"

"I found a gold baby-foot-charm in her drawer."

"How did it make you feel knowing another brother would be part of our family?"

"Like I'd be further down the love list. How can you forgive me...and poor Gabe what's he going to think of me if he ever finds out what I did? What are you going to do, Daddy?"

"I've already told Conner it was my fault, but it was an accident. That gets you, Victor, and Bradley off the hook. And just to let you know, I read your Wattpad story. We were so caught up in our own grief we failed you as parents by not realizing the depth of your pain and I am so sorry for that. I was praying you would tell me the truth today. You've taken responsibility for your actions and that's a step in the right direction."

"But what are you going to do, now?" muttered Willa, her vibrato traveling between soprano and contralto voices.

"Find a way to move on...with my family. What are you going to do, Willa?"

"Find a way for you to forgive me."

"What are you going to do with your life?"

"Do something that would have made Mom proud—maybe be one of those lawyers that gets innocent people out of jail, or help kids with depression, or maybe be a teacher...something that will change people's lives."

Matt reached out for his daughter enveloping her hand in his, strong-arming the pain away from them both, their communication deficit unscrambled in the face of honesty as though they were custodians of one of Walter Mitty's vivid daydreams.

The color gray, a blend of two dominant colors, makes a peaceful presence, an unmatched serenity that turns energy into stillness like a savant that offers guidance and maturity to anyone who seeks it. With everything in the outer world serving as a metaphor for the inner world, Matt said, "Willa, this is our kind of hush…our gray area between right and wrong. Summer and Griff are watching, and we'll make them proud of who we've become."

Gabriel Edward Mackie, born with soulful maturity and an intrinsic sense of empathy, gazed at life through a poetic contemplative lens relishing the plangent sounds of the wind dancing through the trees during a thunderstorm, inhaling the nutty scent of roasted peanuts at the ballpark, and firmly believing that if he stretched his arms high enough, he could touch his dreams. Driven by his keen curiosity, ability to find a silver lining in the darkest cloud, and vision, he spent boundless energy revering nature's rarities like the spidery veins in between rose petals and a heron's powder down feathers.

After the excitement of his favorite aunt marrying his favorite sheriff and the family traveling to the reception at Seasons LXX, Gabe repainted his whisper room a verdant shade of forest green adding a bright yellow commanding sun spreading warmth and accord over his final port of call. *G.E.M.* found a purity, a beauty, and a Zen-like charm discovering what was true and worthy in the simplicity that connected his love of heart with his soul. He clasped his hands under his chin satisfied with the pristine appearance, lowered the shades, turning off the nightlight, tucking into bed the shadows waltzing on the walls. The darkness that once lurked on the windowsill before creeping into every corner of the room was dashed by the morning star lighting the way. A jolt of hopefulness coursed through Gabe's body as all was well in the Mackie household, at least for now.

About the Author

JODEE NEATHERY BECAME a firm believer that dreams do come true with the release of her debut award-winning novel, *Life in a Box* (2017), which asked the question: How much would you sacrifice to hide a secret? A few colorful characters were plucked off her family tree, encasing their world inside fictional events to create her literary novel.

The idea for her latest novel, *A Kind of Hush,* appeared in the middle of the night with the profile of the young boy and the first few sentences scratched out on the ever-present notepad on the nightstand beside her bed. "I didn't know the whole story, but I knew that whatever I wrote next, this lad had to play a major role in the narrative and Gabriel Edward Mackie doesn't disappoint."

JoDee was born in Southern California moving to Midland, Texas, at the age of five—a wonderful place to grow up full of dreamers and doers and the friendliest people on the planet. After graduating from high school, her eyes were on attending a small liberal arts college in Louisiana majoring in dance with aspirations of a Broadway career. Her beloved daddy filed that pipe dream away, suggesting that unless she was aspiring to be a nurse or a teacher, finding a job was a better option. She began her professional career in the banking industry prior to branching into public relations, recruiting executives for TracyLocke Public Relations and Bustin & Company in Dallas and Creamer Dickson Basford in New York City.

Relocating to East Texas offered more opportunity to write, handling public relations for the women's club, writing freelance articles for the newspaper, trade publications, and newsletters. JoDee enjoys a byline, "Back Porch Musings," a light-hearted general view of life for an area newspaper.

Her "dream job" has been chairing and writing minutes and reviews for eighteen years in support of the community book club, Bookers. It was those members that championed her novel writing journey. "They believed in me before I did." Further fueling the fire were comments from two renowned authors following JoDee's reviews of their work:

> **Elizabeth Strout**, Pulitzer Prize winning author of *Olive Kitteridge* wrote, "This is one of the most wonderful things I have seen! I laughed out loud reading it and I will keep it and cherish it forever. What a piece of writing it is."

> **Catherine Ryan Hyde**, the award-winning author of over thirty novels, said of JoDee's review of *Don't Let Me Go,* "This is quite an amazing piece of writing!"

JoDee and her husband live in close proximity to their only daughter, son-in-law, two teenage grandsons, a bird dog, four cats, a donkey and a few head of cattle.

JoDee is available for book signings and appearances. Please contact her at jodee@jodeeneathery.com and visit her website https://www.jodeeneathery.com for updates, more details, and to purchase copies of *Life in a Box* and *A Kind of Hush,* also available on Amazon and select bookstores including Bookish, Malakoff, Texas (https://www.bookishcedarcreek.org).

Follow JoDee on social media at these sites:

facebook.com/JoDeeNeatheryAuthor/

twitter.com/authorihope
pinterest.com/jodeeneathery
instagram.com/neatheryjodee/
tumblr.com

goodreads.com/authorihope/
bookgorilla.com/author/
authors.booksniffer.com
reddit.com

linkedin.com/in/jodee-neathery-94b2b33b/
bookers-online.blogspot.com

Rave reviews for **JoDee Neathery's**
award-winning debut novel, **Life in a Box** …

One of those all too rare literary gems…a roller coaster ride
from first page to last…a novel that will linger in the mind
and memory long after the book itself has been finished.
Unreservedly recommended.

—Midwest Book Review

The author has a very smart way of writing…recommended for
readers who like to live life with the characters
and not just read about them.

—Readers' Favorite

An expressive and dramatic work of literature…
she has a way with words that draws the reader in and won't let go.

—Artisan Books

Reading (the author's book) creates a hunger for more…
sparkling prose…an auspicious debut…
drama touched with tenderness and laughter.

—**Grady Harp**, Hall of Fame, Amazon Top 50 Reviewer

A wonderful introduction to the literary prowess
of JoDee Neathery. There's an understated audacity
to her style of writing which I find quite spellbinding.

—**Amazon UK Reviewer**

This book is a literary masterpiece. There is a large group of precisely
crafted and fascinating characters, some weak, some mean, some
strong, and some vulnerable…all memorable and not stereotypical.

—Goodreads Contributor

Rich, vivid descriptions of the people, places, and things…
bring readers into the story as active participants.

—**Rox Burkey**, Goodreads Author

A Kind of Hush

is available for purchase online at
Amazon.com
www.jodeeneathery.com

or through wholesale distribution by
IngramSpark